Journey of Fate

THE GODLING CHRONICLES

JOURNEY OF FATE

BRIAN D. ANDERSON

4 Horsemen
Publications, Inc.

DEDICATION

In loving memory of my brother, Hunter Vaughn Anderson (December. 16, 1986–March 21, 2018) An old soul with the heart of an angel.

CONTENTS

CHAPTER 1

Heaving a groan, Jayden paused to wipe a sleeve across his sweat-soaked brow. He squinted upward. The sun was at its zenith, meaning there was still a full half day to go. Which in turn meant yet more long hours of mindless, back-breaking tedium to contend with before respite finally came. And what did he have to look forward to as a reward for all this effort? Only an endless succession of exactly the same thing in the dreary routine that was his life.

He absolutely hated this time of year. But then again, he hated everything about farming. *One more season*, he silently promised himself. Just one more year, and then he would definitely leave and join his sisters in Baltria. He had already remained in Sharpstone for far longer than he'd intended. The problem was, his mother was desperate to keep him here. As for his father... he pretended to be on his side, but Jayden could tell that he really didn't want him to leave any more than his mother did. All the same, it was his mother's objections, along with the guilt that only she could induce, that was the main factor in keeping him stuck at home.

"I've already lost your sisters," she had told him only a week prior, her eyes rapidly filling with tears.

"You didn't lose them," he argued. "You can see them whenever you want."

"That's not the point," she shot back. "You're all I have left. Once you are gone…" A sudden rush of sobs had rendered her unable to continue.

Had anyone living in Sharpstone been passing by and witnessed her weeping, they would have imagined their eyes were playing tricks. *Kaylia, the elf-warrior-turned-farmer. A woman with a heart harder than granite.* That was what people said about her.

Jayden didn't like that the villagers considered her in this fashion. He knew his mother to be a kind and gentle person who was generous to a fault. Admittedly, she had a temper, but unless anyone was foolhardy enough to upset or endanger those she cared for, it was usually kept well in check. She claimed not to mind the way others thought about her, though in truth, he thought it hurt her feelings considerably.

"Busybodies, the lot of them," she often remarked, and Jayden could understand why she felt this way. The spring after his sisters left home, his Aunt Dina had convinced her to join the village mothers. This had been an unmitigated disaster. Her direct manner and intolerance for gossip did not go down at all well within the group. After only one meeting, there was scarcely a woman in Sharpstone who did not feel that she had been insulted by his mother in some way. Unsurprisingly, she was never asked to return. On top of that, it had taken his father at least a month, and no small number of gifts, to calm things down.

The field he'd been assigned to plow that day was relatively small compared to most of the others. For once, his usual grueling work schedule had eased off a little, and Jayden thought this only right. As the son of Gewey Stedding, the owner of more farmland than all the rest of the farmers combined and second only to Millet Gristal in wealth, one would think life for him would be easy. But no. Instead, he was regularly assigned twice the amount of work given to all the hired hands. That alone was enough to foster his discontent. Worse still, twice the work also brought with it twice the criticism. The disapproval in his father's eyes whenever he failed to finish his tasks on time was infuriating. There was never a harsh word; his father was not like that. But his stare—that said plenty.

Today, however, was different. He needed to be home and bathed early, as his father was due back from Gath at any time. And not a moment too soon. He had been away for a week, and his mother always became short-tempered when he was gone too long.

The plow horse snorted and stomped.

Jayden regarded the animal with a sour expression. "Why are *you* so eager to work? There'll be plenty more of it to do tomorrow."

And the day after that… and the day after that, he added silently.

He was just about to resume his labor when he heard a familiar and most welcome voice call out his name. Turning, he saw Linis striding up from the narrow road at the edge of the field, a broad smile across his face. Jayden shed his harness and ran up to greet him.

He gave the elf a fond embrace. "I thought you weren't coming until tomorrow."

"Your mother said she needed a hand with the preparations," Linis told him. "Tomorrow is a big day, after all." He shifted over to take a look at the field. "Though from what I'm seeing, you might still be quite busy by then."

Jayden frowned. "You'd think I would be allowed one day off."

Linis gave a laugh and slapped him on the shoulder. "Patience. Your birthday isn't until tomorrow, lad."

"I know. But there are plenty of hands. To be honest, I don't see why I have to do any work at all."

"Well, you should, Jayden. You should be able to understand it better than anyone. Just because your family has gold, that doesn't mean you don't have to pitch in. You know, your father ran this—"

"Please," he said, cutting him short. "I've heard it a thousand times. Gewey Stedding, the strongest man in the village, ran the farm all by himself at fifteen years old. You have no idea how sick I am of hearing how great my father is." He looked from side to side in an exaggerated manner. "Where is he now? Tell me that. I don't see *him* out here sweating away in the hot sun."

Linis cocked his head. "You know good and well what your father does."

"I know he stays away from home while I work the farm. That's what I *do* know."

Linis's tone hardened. "Young man, you had better speak with some respect. Your father has done more for you and for this town than you will ever know."

"Just because he expanded trade, that doesn't make him some kind of hero."

"You have no idea what you are saying. You really don't," Linis shot back.

There was tension in the air for a moment. Then the elf let out a sigh. "Look, I don't want to argue with you. Why don't you come along with me to your house? I'll tell your mother I insisted."

"No. I have to finish this field or I'll never hear the end of it."

Linis chuckled. "Don't take too long. Your mother is making mint lamb, and that is definitely best when eaten hot."

"I won't."

After giving his arm a squeeze, Linus set off at a quick pace in the direction of the house. Jayden watched him go with a thoughtful expression. He could tell that the elf had been holding something back when he spoke about his father. But that was not unusual; he often had the impression there was more to Linis than met the eye. He claimed to have fled to the desert during the war with Angrääl, but Jayden didn't believe him. Nor Dina when she claimed to have been a simple acolyte in the Temple of Gerath. It was the little things they both said and how they looked at each other whenever the war was mentioned.

As far as Jayden knew, his father had been trapped in the north and was forced into hiding when the Reborn King's armies marched south. It was there that he'd met his mother. At least, this was the story they'd told him. He had always thought there was a lot more to it, yet no matter how many times he got them to relate it, the details remained exactly the same.

He looked at the waiting plow horse and muttered a curse. A small field it might be, yet at that moment it appeared to be almost twice as large as it had been only a minute ago. As he donned his harness and urged the animal forward, he considered that even one more year might turn out to be longer than he was willing to wait.

The sun was low in the sky before he finally finished his work. With arms aching and clothes covered in dirt, he unhooked the horse and led it the roughly one mile to the barn. Most of the farm hands were already there, busy putting away their tools or stabling the horses.

"There he is," shouted an older man named Varis. He had been with the family since Jayden was a small child. Though a good-natured fellow, he had a tendency to tease Jayden at every opportunity. "Did you enjoy working the smaller field today?" he asked.

This drew laughter from the others. Jayden, though, was in no mood for his jibes and shot him an irritated look.

"Careful, Varis," said a younger hand, who was stretched out on a pile of hay. "One day, he'll be in charge of us all."

Varis chuckled. "He knows I'm only playing."

"From the look on his face, I'm not so sure of that."

Jayden forced a smile. He was not about to let them get the better of him. "You never know," he remarked. "I may just sell it all and move out west somewhere."

"Sell your father's farm?" Varis laughed. "I doubt that. Your mother would have your hide."

Jayden handed his horse off to one of the grooms. "My mother is an elf, in case you hadn't noticed. And my father is human. I doubt she'll want to stay around here after he's gone."

Varis's humorous expression quickly turned sour. "You shouldn't talk like that."

Jayden regretted his words but refused to show it. "It's the truth. My mother will live for hundreds of years yet. What's the most my father can expect? Eighty, perhaps? Ninety, if he's lucky."

"I thought humans who bonded with elves live longer," remarked another hand.

"No one knows for sure," said Varis. "Not enough time has passed. But if anyone can live as long as an elf, it's Gewey Stedding." He met Jayden's eyes. "And you, lad, should hope to become half the man that he is."

Jayden sniffed. "The only thing I hope to do is leave Sharpstone and this bloody farm far behind me."

Varis sighed. "Well, before you go..." Reaching into his pocket, he pulled out a small box. "Here, take this."

Jayden took the offering and lifted the lid. Inside was a thin gold chain with a small gold medallion attached. His initials were engraved on one side and the words "For your coming of age" on the other. He immediately felt a stab of guilt.

"Some of us won't see you tomorrow," added Varis. "Your mother has given us the day off."

"I... I'm sorry. I didn't mean..."

"It's fine, lad," Varis said with a warm smile. "I know what it's like to be young and filled with dreams of adventure. Even your father ran off with old Lee Starfinder for a time. Of course, he ended up spending the whole time hiding in the mountains. All the same, he did go on an adventure of sorts. And don't worry, you'll get your chance to do so as well one day."

Jayden put the medallion around his neck. "Thank you. But you shouldn't have. I mean... this must have cost you at least a week's pay."

"It wasn't just me, we all pitched in," Varis told him. "It's not every day you turn eighteen years old. Besides, your father pays us well enough."

All the farm hands had stopped what they were doing. Their smiles were bright and friendly.

"Thank you all," Jayden said. "I promise I'll try to be a bit less moody." He followed this up with a good-natured smirk. "At least, I will until I sell the farm and put you all out of a job."

The men laughed, each taking their turn to shake his hand and wish him a happy birthday.

After thanking everyone again, he set off to his house just a half mile to the north. Along the way, his mind wandered to the last time he had asked his father for permission to move to Baltria.

"One more year, son," his father had replied. "By then you will have come of age, and I'll have things around here working well enough that you're not needed."

"You don't need me now," he'd protested. "You already have twice the men you need."

"Yes," he admitted. "But you are my son. I can trust you to watch over things while I'm away. Please be patient. Just one more year and then I won't have to travel nearly as much. You have my word."

His father employed far more people than anyone else in the village, and over the years, his farm had expanded to become the largest of its kind for a hundred miles. He had spent years securing trade deals and opening new markets that had not only made them wealthy but also earned their family a respect that extended as far as Helenia. In truth, should his father ever choose to sell all his holdings, they could live in lavish comfort for the rest of their lives. But that was not Gewey Stedding's way. For reasons Jayden could never fathom, toil and sweat were as precious to him as gold and gems.

"I have a responsibility to the people," his father said when Jayden had suggested he retire, or at least reduce his workload. "You'll understand one day."

Jayden suspected that his mother agreed with him. She always looked concerned when his father prepared to leave home. And if he was even a single day late in returning, she very soon refused to eat or sleep until he did.

Rounding the bend leading to the main house, he could smell the smoke from the hearth. The massive two-story dwelling was a far cry from the old house they had lived in when he was a young boy. These days, Varis lived there with his wife, Molly, and older brother, Daris, who had retired two years ago.

The broad porch and elegant front garden looked out of place in its rustic surroundings. It was as if stylish western culture had been plucked up and dropped into the middle of nowhere: a gleaming white jewel in the midst of a savage wilderness. With its arched windows and tall columns supporting an upper balcony, the house design was more akin to elfish homes found near Althetas.

His mother absolutely loved the place, of course, and spent much of her time on the front porch reading or wandering around the garden. On the other hand, his father would often lament about leaving the old home. His tastes were simple, though he was pleased at least that someone who appreciated its charm was living there. Varis had known the Stedding family long before Jayden was born, even having worked for his grandfather, Harman, on a casual basis as a young man.

He made his way toward a small shed just off to the side of the house. Inside, fresh clothes and a pair of soft shoes had already been laid out for him on a wooden table. Stripping off his work clothes, he grabbed a bucket of water sitting on the floor just by the entrance. The cold water felt good, though he was still looking forward to a proper shower later on. It was one luxury his father was pleased to have, and he'd had three of them installed when the house was being built.

After washing and dressing, Jayden made his way around to the back entrance. Unlike the elaborate front garden, here there were only a few oaks and a spacious lawn of neatly trimmed grass. A dozen or so people were busy setting up pavilions and tables for the next day's festivities. At least half of the village was coming to celebrate his birthday, though tonight the gathering would be restricted to just close friends and family. His sisters had wanted to be there as well, but their studies would not allow it. Instead, they had sent him a pair of masterfully crafted Baltrian boots and some fine leather gloves. Not that he currently had any use for such elegant attire; it had been so long since the last time he wore finery he had all but forgotten how it felt.

Everyone waved as he passed, but was far too busy to do anything more than that. Inside, the kitchen was sweltering. However, this was quickly overlooked as the scent of mint lamb wafted through the air and made his mouth water.

Polly, their cook, was kneading dough at the table opposite the stove. She smiled at him over her shoulder.

"Ah, there you are," she said. "Your mother was about to send someone to fetch you."

"That smells good," he responded. "I hope you've made enough for everybody."

Polly laughed. "I should think so. Though as much as you and your father eat, I could be wrong."

She was a kindly woman who had moved to Sharpstone from Althetas just after the war. Both her son and husband had been killed in battle, as was the case with many of the western newcomers. With their lives in tatters and their homes destroyed, they had journeyed east to rebuild and find peace. Eighteen years had now passed since the Reborn King was defeated, and still, the world was picking up the pieces. A steady flow of new arrivals in Sharpstone had continued throughout, doubling the population from when Jayden was a small boy.

He plucked a cherry tomato from a basket on the shelf. "Is my father here?"

"Not yet," Polly replied. "And I can tell you, if he's late, your mother will skin him alive."

He popped the tomato into his mouth, savoring the sweet taste. Father was almost never late. No matter how far away he traveled, he had a habit of reappearing almost to the very minute of when he was expected.

"Are you staying for dinner?" he asked, trying not to let the juice from the tomato spill down his chin.

Polly shook her head. "No. I need to rest my old bones. Tomorrow is going to be a big day."

"They don't have you working on my birthday, do they?"

"If by *they* you mean your mother, then no. But I'll be lending a hand, anyway. Otherwise, she'll work herself into the ground and miss all the fun." Polly flicked a bit of flour in his direction. "Now you had better go and get ready for supper."

Jayden smiled and exited the kitchen. *Missing all the fun* was probably just what his mother had in mind. It wasn't that she hated the townsfolk. Quite the contrary. She had often remarked how accepting they were of the changes, especially compared with what was happening in other places. About twenty or so elves had settled in Sharpstone, and none were treated with anything but kindness and respect.

He found her in the parlor, curled up in a chair with a small leather-bound book. Her auburn hair was tied into a loose braid, and she was wearing her favorite pair of cotton trousers and a shirt. He could tell from the way she was knitting her brow that she was not really reading.

She looked up as he entered and sat the book down on the table beside her. "Have you seen your father?"

Jayden shook his head. "I thought he would be home by now."

"So did I."

On the rare occasions he had been late, she had not bothered to conceal her irritation. This time, it was different. This time, he could see that she was worried.

She forced a smile. "I'm sure he'll be home soon."

Her mood unsettled Jayden. She was almost never nervous or worried, particularly when it came to his father. Angry and irritated, yes. But never worried.

"Who's coming tonight?" he asked.

"You already saw Linis," she replied. "Dina will be along later with Millet. That's all. I thought we would keep it small."

"You know Polly's planning to help out tomorrow?"

Kaylia groaned. "That woman. The Creator bless her, but she drives me crazy sometimes." She gestured to a seat beside her. "Come. We still have time before they arrive. Talk with me for a while."

Here we go again, thought Jayden. These days, there was only ever one reason his mother wanted to sit and talk. But as much as he wanted to, he could not refuse. Taking a seat, he leaned on his knees with shoulders sagging. "Are we really going to do this again?" he sighed.

"Indulge me."

It was not a request.

"I've told you and Father over and over that I don't want to be a farmer. Why can't you understand?"

She frowned. "There is nothing wrong with farming. Nothing at all. Your father has done very well for this family, and you could too if you would only apply yourself."

"Apply myself?" he scoffed, then quickly reined in his tone before adding, "I work as hard as anyone here."

"Yes. I know that. But there's more to it than just work. You never take the initiative, Jayden. I saw you twice walk by a damaged fence last week. Did you think to repair it? Or did you leave it for someone else to do?"

He blew out a breath. "So I didn't repair a fence. So what?"

"Because one day this farm and everything on it will be yours. I would have thought you'd take pride in it."

"I don't want it. For the last time, I don't want to be a bloody farmer."

She flashed him a warning look. "Don't raise your voice to me, young man. You may be as big as your father, but I can still give you a beating."

He was instantly contrite. "I'm sorry, Mother. I know it upsets you, but I just don't want to be what you want me to be."

"Then tell me, what *do* you want? You say you don't want to be a farmer, but you never say what it is you want to do with your life."

After a long pause, he lowered his eyes and admitted, "I don't know. Not yet. All I know is that it's not farming. And that I won't find it in Sharpstone."

"So you would abandon everything... abandon me?" Despite her hard tone, her eyes were unable to hide the pain his words had caused.

Jayden could not stand to see her so distressed, even though he knew it was her way of manipulating him into staying. After every one of these conversations, he would promise himself that next time, it wouldn't work. But it always did.

"I'm not abandoning you," he protested. "It's just that I want to see what else is out there. I've never been away from home. Gath. That's it."

"And what do you think you'll find? Excitement? Adventure? Let me tell you something about the world, son. It's a cruel and dangerous place, filled with people who care nothing for you or anyone else. Here at home, you have peace and family and friends who love you. Believe me, there are more people than you could count who would give anything for what you have right here."

"But at least you *have* been out there. You had the chance to discover all this for yourself. Anyway, I don't believe the outside world is as bad as all that. I listen to the stories people tell. The way I hear it, it's just a few areas where there's still trouble."

"You mean the stories and nonsense those who fled their homes tell you? The ones who came to escape the danger and settle here? Are those the people you're listening to?"

Jayden was on the verge of shouting. Only with great difficulty did he manage to keep a level tone. "I don't care what you say. And I don't care what Father says either. I'm a man now. I will go where I want."

His mother's face tightened, and she glared at him for a long moment. Then, slowly, her features relaxed. "Yes, you *are* a man now, I suppose. But you are also my child. If you are so determined to leave, I will go with you."

Jayden furrowed his brow. "You *are* joking, right?"

"I have never been more serious. I know this world from one end to the other. If you wish to see it, at least let me show it to you properly."

Of anything she could have said, this was the very last thing he expected to hear. "So you want to watch over me? Is that it?"

"Yes," she admitted. "The perils you'll face will be many. I can show you things that you would never be able to discover on your own."

Before he could reply, she stood up and raised a forestalling hand. "You don't have to answer me straight away. Just consider it... for me."

Jayden had no idea how to react. On one hand, the mere thought of his mother hovering over him as he traveled was unbearable. On the other, she was a full-blooded elf who must have seen many places that only someone of her race would know. That was an enticing prospect.

"I'll think about it," he said finally.

Kaylia smiled down at her son. "Good. Then..."

She staggered back, gripping the arm of the chair for support. Jayden shot from his seat to take hold of her hand.

"What's wrong?" he asked.

Kaylia shook her head. "I... it's nothing. I must have stood up too quickly, that's all. I'll be fine in a moment."

"Please, Mother, sit back down."

She waved a dismissive hand and smiled. "Really. I'm fine. Go change for supper, son." She kissed his cheek.

Jayden hesitated. His mother was almost never ill. In fact, he could only remember it happening twice before. And both times had been when his father was away.

She squeezed his hand. "I said I'm fine. You know I don't sleep well when your father is away. I'm just tired."

"If you're absolutely sure..."

"Yes, yes. Just go."

Reluctantly, he left and went upstairs to his room. Clothes had already been laid out on his bed. On the wall was a map of Baltria that his sisters had sent to him the year they left home. They had been only eleven at the time, but were already more mature than most girls well into their teens.

Lady Bellisia, an elf elder and dear friend of the family from the west, had been the one who finally convinced his parents to let them go.

"They need a proper education," she had said. "You know this is not a suitable place for them to learn how to control their powers."

The *flow* had always been strong in his sisters. Playing around with it, they had accidentally burned down the barn when they were only six years old, an incident that left the townsfolk clearly afraid of them. It was this, as much as anything else, that eventually convinced his parents to allow the move. In Baltria, they would be under the care of the elves and taught the proper way to control their powers. It was rumored that a few of the remaining half-men had gone there as well. His father, on the other hand, had told him that none of these were left alive—though how he would know this was anyone's guess.

Jayden took his shower and dressed. From downstairs, the aroma of the coming meal was now drifting up to fill the entire house, and he could hear the sounds of the table being set. Jayden enjoyed it when Millet came to visit. He was always ready with a story or two about his former lord, Lee Starfinder. To hear them tell it, the two had traveled to virtually every corner of the world at one time or another, and the adventures they had experienced together bordered on the unbelievable.

"I can assure you that every word of it is true," Millet had told him. "Lord Starfinder was quite the hero."

His father didn't seem to enjoy it as much, often looking sad when the subject came up.

Jayden heard a coach approaching just as he reached the bottom of the stairs. Linis was talking to his mother in hushed whispers at the dining table, and her face was wracked with concern, telling him without his needing to ask that his father had not yet arrived.

A moment later, there was a solid rap at the door.

Jayden opened it to find Millet and Dina. Millet was wearing an elegant suit and waistcoat, while Dina was clad in a simple cotton dress.

The old man smiled warmly. "You are the image of your father," he said.

Dina kissed his cheek. "But with his mother's ears."

Dina did not bear the distinctive elfish features, despite the fact that she was also half elf.

"I find that elf ears are quite becoming," Millet remarked. He was bent and looking weary; his age had definitely begun to show over the last few years. "And I would wager that the young ladies of Sharpstone feel the same way."

"Yes," agreed Dina. "And you should know that the village mothers are already talking about a match for you, Jayden."

Seeing him blush, she laughed softly. "Don't worry. They're far too frightened of your mother to come here pestering you. But I'd be careful not to get caught alone. They'll have you over to their houses and be parading daughters and granddaughters in front of you before you can blink."

"It's shameful, if you ask me," remarked Millet. "Treating their offspring like livestock the way they do. Young people should be allowed to choose a match for themselves."

Dina rolled her eyes. "I'm joking and you know it, you old grump."

Millet didn't much care for the Village Mothers. What's more, the feeling was mutual. They had never forgiven him for remaining unmarried, complaining that a man with so much wealth had no business keeping it all to himself. This despite the fact that Millet was indeed very generous and did almost as much as Gewey to keep the townsfolk employed.

Jayden led them to the parlor and poured them each a glass of wine. "I think dinner is almost ready," he announced.

"Is my husband around?" asked Dina.

Jayden nodded. "I think he's helping Mother prepare for tomorrow."

"Ah, yes," remarked Millet. "They're saying that only the festival of Gerath is bigger. Then again, I suppose the son of Gewey Stedding deserves no less." He looked at the door. "Speaking of whom, where is that rascal?"

"He hasn't returned yet."

Dina gave an exaggerated shudder. "I wouldn't want to be in his shoes if he misses your party."

Millet chuckled. "He'll be here. Gewey is as dependable as they come." He looked at Jayden. "Since I have you here, what's this your father tells me about you wanting to move away?"

Jayden suppressed a groan. "I just want to see a bit of the world for a while. That's all."

"I fear you'll be disappointed with what you find, lad," Millet told him. "Since the war ended, there's been nothing but trouble wherever you look; though I suppose Baltria is safe enough. The people there want little to do with the goings on in the west."

"Father tells me things have improved now that the elves have an equal seat on the Council of Nobles."

A sad expression crossed Millet's face. "Improved, yes, though there are still many humans who are not so keen on the idea. You would have thought that the war might have banished all those old hatreds. Unfortunately, for a good number of people, the past is all they can understand. Change comes slowly, even for the best of us. And for some, it's impossible. Even I am not immune. Did I ever tell you how I met your mother?"

Jayden smiled. Millet had told him many times, in fact.

"We were fleeing west... well, your father and Lee were, at any rate. I was trying to catch them up..."

Dina cleared her throat. "I think you're confused. You met her up north, while Gewey and Lee were hiding in the mountains. Remember?"

Millet looked at her for a moment, puzzled. "Oh... yes, that's right." He began laughing. "Lee and I were on so many eventful journeys, I must have got them mixed up."

"But that's my point," said Jayden. "I want to actually *do* something. I want to have my own adventures, so *I* can have stories to tell."

Millet leaned back in his chair and took a sip of wine. "You remind me of Lee. More so than your father, in some ways. Hot-blooded and reckless. Did I ever tell you about the time he and I were captured by pirates? Not while at sea, mind you, but deep within a mountain pass."

"Yes, you've told us," Dina scolded playfully. "Many times."

At that point, Linis entered the room. After kissing Dina, he kneeled in front of Millet and took him by the hand. "It's good to see you, old friend. You're looking well."

Millet huffed. "I look old. And I feel older."

Linis rose and slipped his arm around Dina. "Don't you believe what he says, Jayden. Millet may look old, but he's nowhere near as feeble as he likes to pretend."

"If we don't eat soon, I will be," Millet remarked.

"The table is set and ready for us," Linis told them. "We're just waiting for Gewey."

Kaylia entered the room just as he was speaking. "Not anymore, we're not. He'll just have to have his dinner served cold."

Although his mother tried to conceal it, Jayden could see the worry behind her smile.

The meal was eaten in a festive atmosphere, despite his father's conspicuous absence. When the subject of Jayden's desire to travel came up, Kaylia told everyone about her offer to go with him.

"I think that would be a grand idea," Linis responded with sincere enthusiasm. "Your mother knows the land better than most. She traveled quite a bit in her youth."

"My *youth*?" Kaylia repeated, raising an eyebrow. "I'm still in my youth."

Jayden was not sure precisely how old she was. *Over one hundred*, he thought. Elves, however, lived for as long as five hundred years, so by their reckoning, she was still a young woman. He had no idea how old Linis might be. Dina, he knew to be in her fifties, though her elf blood kept her looking as if she were still in her late twenties.

"Speaking of youth," Millet chipped in, "this young man has an appointment with the mayor once all the celebrating is over."

"I told you no," snapped Kaylia.

"And I told *you* I shall do with it as I please," Millet retorted. Reaching inside his waistcoat, he produced a folded parchment bearing a wax seal. He pushed this across the table to Jayden. "Happy birthday, young man."

Breaking the seal, Jayden's eyes ran over the letter's contents. A look of astonishment quickly formed. "This is too much," he gasped. "I can't possibly accept this."

It was a declaration that, upon Millet's death, Jayden would inherit his Sharpstone estate.

His protest was waved aside. "You have no choice, I'm afraid. My friends already have their own homes, and I would not see the Starfinder Estate go to a stranger. My wealth is to be distributed among friends. The house and land, however... they are yours."

Jayden stood up and rounded the table. "Thank you," he said, leaning down to embrace the old man.

"Now you have something to call your own," he replied. "And maybe one day you'll come to think of it as your home."

"Well, this makes our gift seem drab and dull by comparison," said Linis, smiling.

The elf rose and left the dining room for a few moments. On his return, he was holding a long, ivory-handled sword, sheathed in a leather scabbard with elf lettering etched down its length.

Jayden's eyes lit up as he took the weapon and carefully removed it from its scabbard. The steel sang as it slid effortlessly free. It was perfectly balanced and obviously elf-made. The desire to swish it about was almost overwhelming.

"Gewey told me he's been teaching you how to use a sword, so I thought you should have a proper one to practice with," Linis said. "It's a bit heavier than a typical elf blade. But with your frame, I thought it best."

Kaylia frowned. "Let us hope you never need to use it."

"Always a good idea to have one handy, though," remarked Millet. "Particularly if you plan to take him adventuring."

"This week you can show me what you've learned," said Linis.

Jayden sheathed the blade and gave the elf a firm embrace. "Thank you. I love it."

"Love it somewhere else," said Kaylia. "The dinner table is no place for a sword."

"Agreed," said Dina, giving Linis a sour look.

Jayden ran upstairs and put the sword away in his wardrobe. Tomorrow he would find somewhere to store it properly, he thought.

By the time he returned, his mother, Linis, and Dina were already clearing the table. Millet offered to help, but Jayden quickly took him into the sitting room and gave him a snifter of plum brandy.

When the others joined them shortly afterward, Jayden noticed immediately that his mother was not looking well. He knew she was worried, but there was more to it than that. She looked thoroughly drained of energy. Linis noticed it as well.

"We should not linger," he said. "Tomorrow is a big day, and I am sure you need to rest."

"Nonsense," Kaylia responded. "You cannot leave until midnight when Jayden officially becomes a man."

Bowing to her wishes, they sat and talked for a time. Millet eventually fell asleep in his chair with a brandy glass resting on his plump belly, though Kaylia woke him just before midnight so that he could join them in a round of birthday songs and official congratulations. The guests departed shortly afterward. They could see Kaylia was clearly in no condition to go on, even though she tried to get them to stay longer. When Dina expressed her concern, Kaylia merely dismissed it as fatigue from several days of preparation, not to mention the stress of dealing with the village mothers.

Jayden's concern was growing, but he eventually accepted her explanation. It was true she had been working non-stop for days on end. On top of that, his father's continuing absence was doing nothing to help her state of mind.

That night, he listened for the sound of hoofbeats heralding his father's arrival—something he hadn't done since he was a small boy. None came, however, and eventually he fell asleep.

CHAPTER 2

The following morning, Jayden rose early and quickly got dressed. He could already hear the clamor of people working outside. He hoped his father might have arrived during the night, but the look on his mother's face when he joined her in the parlor for breakfast told him that he hadn't.

"He'll be home very soon now," he said to her.

"Yes, I know he will," she agreed, though her tone was unconvincing. "You just enjoy the day and put it out of your mind."

Linis showed up as they finished eating and he and his mother went out on the porch to talk privately for a time, which only served to fuel Jayden's anxiety even further. Humans and elves could not share the same bond that elves shared with one another—at least, that was what he had heard. And yet strangely, his mother always knew when his father was near. Sometimes it was as if she could actually read his thoughts.

On a whim, he decided to lend a hand outside to keep his mind off these concerns. His offer was soundly rebuffed. He was told in no uncertain terms that they would not have him working on his birthday. Eventually, he returned to his room and flicked through a book Millet had given him about the history of the first Great War. The maps held more interest to him than the text. As he dragged his finger over the page, he imagined himself on horseback, setting out to see the wonders of the world.

Earlier that morning, he had made up his mind to accept his mother's offer. Though having her along wasn't exactly what he'd originally had in mind, there was no denying that she would be able to show him things no one but an elf could. And perhaps along the way he could prove to her that he was able to take care of himself. He had already become quite accomplished with a blade—though as yet had never been involved in an actual sword fight. Furthering his sense of independence, Linis had also taught him a great deal about tracking and living off the land.

The sound of carriages arriving told him that it was time to head back downstairs. Outside, the pavilions were already beginning to fill with guests as tray after tray of food was being set out on a long table. Barrels of wine and cases of brandy were stacked high inside a separate pavilion nearby.

All said, more than two hundred people were anticipated to attend. More wagons bearing extra food and other supplies were still arriving. Even a kitchen as well equipped as theirs could only handle so much.

By early afternoon, the musicians had started to play, and the party was in full swing. Throughout it all, Jayden kept a constant, but so far fruitless, look out for his father. His mother had only made one brief appearance amongst the guests, presumably spending most of the time keeping things running smoothly inside the house.

If there was one thing Jayden was dreading more than anything else, it was the coming speech he'd be expected to make. He had no idea what to say. Though in truth, if he kept it as brief as possible, most of the partygoers would likely be pleased. It would be near the end of the night before he'd be called upon, and by then, full bellies and an over-abundance of wine would be persuading most it was time to head back home to their beds.

He had just joined a group of his friends near the edge of the festivities when he saw Linis approaching. The elf's expression was grave.

"I need you to come with me," he said.

Before he could ask what was wrong, Linis turned and hurried away through the crowd. Jayden's thoughts immediately turned to his mother. Mindless of those he passed who tried to speak to him, he chased after the elf.

"Is it Mother?" he called, as they entered the kitchen through the back door.

"She's unconscious," Linis replied. "Dina is with her in her bedroom."

Fear stabbed through Jayden and he broke into a dead run, shoving Linis aside and very nearly knocking several others completely off their feet while pushing his way through to the stairs. Bursting into his mother's room, he saw Dina sitting on the bed beside her, holding her hand.

"What happened?" he asked, rushing over to the other side of the bed.

"We don't know," Dina said, choking back tears.

He placed his hand over his mother's brow. She wasn't running a fever.

Linis entered a moment later. "Polly found her on the front porch just before she collapsed," he said. "She told me that Kaylia only said two words, 'He's gone.'"

Jayden looked imploringly at the elf. "What's wrong with her?"

"I can't be certain. I can only guess. I've sent for an elf healer who lives in town. She'll be here as soon as possible."

"What do you *think* it is?" Jayden pressed.

Linis drew a breath. "I think something has happened to your father. What that is, I can't say. We'll know more when the healer arrives."

"How could something happening to Father do this to her?" Jayden noticed Linis exchange a furtive glance with Dina. "Tell me, damn it!"

"Your mother and father share a special bond," he explained. "Much like the elves share with one another."

"But I thought humans couldn't do that."

Linis nodded. "With most of them, that's true. But Gewey and Kaylia are ... special. That's all I can tell you. When I tried to make a connection with your mother, I could feel that something had happened. I just couldn't tell what exactly. My skills are not as attuned as those of a healer."

"I know how worried you are, Jayden," added Dina. "But please be patient. I'm sure the healer will be able to help."

He could see the lie in her eyes. She was as worried as Linis. A feeling of total helplessness threatened to overcome him.

For more than an hour, they waited. Polly checked in several times and informed them that she'd told the guests Kaylia had fallen ill and that they should return home. As an extra measure, Linis positioned himself outside the door to prevent the curious and concerned from entering.

At last, the elf healer, an older woman named Lania, arrived and immediately ordered the room cleared.

"I'm staying," Jayden insisted.

"You must allow me to do my work," the healer told him in a tender voice. "I can feel your love for your mother bleeding like an open wound, and that is a distraction to me. I must be able to concentrate."

Dina touched his hand. "Come, Jayden. Linis and I will wait with you."

After tenderly kissing his mother's forehead, he allowed himself to be ushered from the room. Downstairs, the servants were cleaning up and taking down the pavilions. A small stack of notes was sitting on the table near the front door, each one expressing well-wishes for Kaylia's recovery.

"You told me just now that my father and mother are different," he said as the three of them sat near the hearth in the living room. "What did you mean by that?"

Linis lowered his eyes. "That is not for me to say. All I can tell you is that they share a connection like no other."

"But humans can't do that."

There was a long silence. It was clear to Jayden that they were keeping something hidden from him.

"Right now, we need to focus on your mother," said Dina.

"I'm not a child so easily distracted," Jayden snapped back at her. "What aren't you telling me?"

"I know you aren't a child. But we made a promise. There are some things we simply cannot tell you."

"I don't care about any promise you've made. My mother could be dying."

Dina reacted instantly. "Don't say that," she snapped. "Don't you ever say that!"

Under normal circumstances, he would have wilted under Dina's gaze. But her refusal to divulge what she knew was only increasing his anger. This had something to do with his father.

"If you know what is wrong and you don't tell me—" he began.

Linis's sharp voice stopped him at once. "That's enough! Do not dare accuse us of withholding information that might help her. You have no idea what you are saying."

His eyes were blazing. Jayden had never seen him lose his temper like this before. "I'm sorry," he hastily apologized. "It's just that... I'm afraid. What if she doesn't wake up?"

Linis leaned forward. "Your mother has survived more than you could imagine. She'll make it through this as well. Whatever it is."

As he finished speaking, he caught the sound of the door upstairs opening and the elf healer making her way slowly down. All three quickly rose and left the room to meet her. The woman's brow was creased and her skin pale. As she moved down the last few steps, she gripped the rail with both hands for balance.

Jayden was barely able to restrain himself. "Will she be all right?" he asked.

Dina was standing beside Linis, holding tightly to his arm.

"I have never encountered anything like it," the healer said. "The bond she shares with her mate is stretched... stretched so thin that I can barely tell it exists at all. By every natural law I know of, it should be broken beyond repair, yet somehow it still manages to hold."

She met Jayden's eyes. "What manner of man is your father?"

He frowned back at her. "I don't understand."

"What I mean is this: your father... is he a half-man?"

"No. Of course not." Yet even as the words escaped his lips, Jayden could not help but wonder. Was this the secret they were keeping from him?

The woman sighed. "Then I cannot explain what has happened. There is one thing I know for certain—Kaylia will not recover unless the bond is made whole again. In time, it *will* break. And when it does..."

A cold chill seized the pit of Jayden's stomach. "How long?"

"I cannot say. This bond is unique; strong beyond anything I have seen before. But it is not indestructible. Whatever has happened to your father, I am guessing that is the cause."

Jayden felt dizzy. A million different scenarios were flashing through his mind when a hand on his shoulder snapped him back into the moment.

"We need to find him," said Linis.

"He went to Gath," Jayden managed to croak out.

"No," said Linis. "He did not." He turned to the healer. "Is there anything you can tell us that might help us find him?"

"Twin girls," she replied. "Over and over they invaded her thoughts."

"My sisters Maybell and Penelope," said Jayden. "It has to be. But what have they got to do with this?"

The healer shook her head. "I don't know. All I can say is that they are somehow connected to her. Although a bond like this is unusual between a child and a parent, it's not unheard of."

"Is there anything else?" asked Dina. "Anything at all?"

"I'm sorry. I've done all I can."

Jayden did not hesitate. Forgoing courtesy, he pressed his way past the woman and ran headlong up the stairs to his room. As quickly as he could, he began pulling clothes from his wardrobe and placing them on the bed. The final item—the sword that Linis had given to him—he hung from his belt.

"I know where you are going."

He turned to see Linis standing in the doorway.

"Don't try to stop me. I have to get to Gath."

"Your father isn't there. I already told you that."

Jayden slammed the door to his wardrobe, nearly tearing it from its hinges. "Then where the hell is he?"

"He went to Althetas."

"Are you insane? He left less than a week ago and was due back here yesterday. There is no way he could travel so far in such a short time."

"I know it's hard to believe. Nonetheless, I promise you that is where he went."

Jayden squared his shoulders. "I think you had better explain."

Linis nodded. "I agree, but not here. Pack your things, and I'll wait for you downstairs. We can talk on the way."

"On the way to where?"

"My farm. I'm going with you. Take only a few changes of clothes and whatever gold you can carry. I'll pack the rest of what we need for the journey."

Having issued his instructions, he left the room.

Jayden quickly did as he'd been told. With his pack slung over his shoulders, he found Dina talking to Linis at the bottom of the stairs. She was looking deeply concerned, though she tried to conceal this as he approached.

"I'll keep watch over your mother while you're away," she assured him.

"Thank you," he said. "I don't know how long this will take. Don't worry about the farm, though. Varis can handle that well enough."

Dina wiped a stray tear from her eye and then embraced her husband. "Just be careful, Linis. You're not a seeker any longer. You're a farmer now."

Her words astonished Jayden. *A seeker? Linis had been a seeker?*

"I will return as soon as I can," Linis told her. "You shouldn't worry. I haven't gone soft." Reluctantly releasing his wife, he started toward the door.

The night was cool and still. Jayden held his tongue until they had reached the edge of the garden and stepped onto the road. Linis's face was a stone mask as he kept up a brisk pace.

"You were a seeker?" Jayden asked.

"I was," he affirmed. "Before the war."

"Why didn't you say anything?"

"My life before the war is no longer important to me. That was a time of blood and hatred. I fought hard to have the life I live now. I never want to look back on those days."

"But why did you tell me you fled to the desert?"

Linis cast him a quick glance. "There is much you have been told that isn't true. But you need to understand that it was done purely out of love."

"Like what?"

After a long pause, Linis blew out a breath. "What do you know of Darshan?"

Jayden furrowed his brow. "Darshan? Just what everyone else knows, I guess. He descended from heaven during the war and took on human form so he could do battle with the Reborn King."

"What about after the war? Do you know what happened to him then?"

"They say he returned to heaven. Other than that, all I've heard are stories about the battles he fought. Mother and Father don't like talking about the war, so I only know what a few of the farm hands have told me."

Linis fell silent for a short time, all the while looking as if he were debating a weighty matter inside his head. "What if I told you that Darshan did not return to heaven?" he eventually asked. "That instead, he remained here in the mortal world."

Jayden shrugged. "I'd say, so what? From what I've heard, he hasn't done much of anything since. There's still fighting everywhere."

"You are wrong. Darshan has done a great deal. He is constantly doing his best to stop the violence and keep the peace. But not even a god can be in all places at once."

"What does this have to do with Mother? Or anything else, for that matter?"

Linis drew a deep breath. "Because your father is not who you think he is. He and Lee Starfinder did not hide in the mountains during the war. In fact, quite the opposite."

The implication behind these words thudded into Jayden's brain. He grabbed the elf's arm, forcing him to halt. "You can't be saying what I think you're saying."

Linis nodded. "Yes. The man you know as your father... *he* is Darshan."

Jayden coughed out a laugh. "Are you drunk? My father isn't a god. That's just crazy."

Linis pulled himself free and resumed walking. "Where do you think he goes when he leaves here? Gath? Helenia? Since the end of the war, he has traveled the length and breadth of our world and done everything he possibly could to keep the peace. Not only between elf and human, but between warring factions within the races as well."

Try as he might, Jayden could not accept what Linis was telling him. How could his parents have kept such a thing hidden? It seemed impossible.

"But what about Harman Stedding?" he asked. "How can my father be a god if he had a human father himself?"

"From what Millet has told me, he and Lee Starfinder brought Gewey here from Hazrah. They then gave him to your grandfather, who adopted him. I only know a small part of that story, so I'm not sure of the reasons for this. Millet could tell you more."

"Millet knows too?"

Linis nodded. "We traveled together during the war. I first met them when they were fleeing the Dark Knight to Althetas. I fought many battles by Darshan's side."

As difficult as it was for Jayden to believe, Linis certainly gave every appearance of telling the truth. "What about my mother?" he asked.

"She was exiled and sentenced to death for joining with your father. The elves thought him a mere human at the time, and such a union was forbidden." A smile crept up on his lips. "Though that was nothing compared to what happened when they found out he was a god."

Jayden was well aware that elves did not care for the gods. "So that's why their bond is so strong?"

"It is. The tale of Darshan is long and complicated. And I only know what I personally experienced. We spent much of the war separated. But in later years, Millet chronicled much of it."

"I don't know what to think about all of this," Jayden sighed. "It just doesn't seem real."

"I assure you it is."

"But if my father is Darshan, what could have happened to him?"

"That is what I find most troubling of all," Linis admitted. "It would take nothing short of a god to lay him low. And even then, it would take more than one."

He glanced across to look Jayden directly in the eye before continuing. "You see, I believed for a time that your father had lost his powers. After the war, he told everyone that this was the price he had to pay if he wanted to remain in the mortal world. Then, a few years ago, I discovered that he had lied to us. I was angry at first. But on reflection, I understand why he would want it kept secret. All he ever desired was a simple life with your mother. And so I helped him keep up the deception. Only a few people know who your father really is. And even amongst them, only Dina and myself know that he still has his powers."

"So you think it must be the gods who have done something to him?" Jayden asked.

"I don't know for sure, though I can think of no other being strong enough to cause him harm. Whatever the case, we'll find out soon enough. For now, we need to focus on getting to Baltria. If this truly is a scheme of the gods, the road could be far more dangerous than anticipated."

As they continued walking, Jayden thought on what he had been told. A part of him was still finding it almost impossible to accept, even though in his heart he knew that Linis was not lying. That left only two possibilities: either Linis was delusional, or his father was indeed Darshan.

Upon reaching the farm, Linis instructed him to saddle two horses while he gathered what they would need for the journey. Unfortunately, there would not be a boat heading downriver for another two days, so they would have to take the road south to Helenia and catch one there.

After saddling the second horse, Jayden spotted another mount in one of the stables that he recognized instantly—the old mare that his father rode whenever traveling. He rushed over, but from the look of it, the animal hadn't been anywhere in quite a long time. His father's saddle was hanging on a hook, polished and perfectly clean.

"Gewey leaves it here with me whenever he's away," Linis told him as he entered the barn, several bundles slung over his shoulder. On his belt, he now wore a long blade and a dagger. After packing both horses, he handed one of them over to Jayden and then leaped nimbly into the saddle of the other.

"I know you have more questions," he said. "But for now, we need to move quickly. Every minute we delay endangers your mother."

Jayden nodded sharply. More questions? That was a gross understatement. Right at this moment, he felt as if his entire life had been nothing but an illusion. It didn't make sense that his parents would keep such secrets from him. Did they fear he would tell people? Or that he couldn't handle the truth? Didn't they trust him at all?

He would find his father. And heal his mother. But once that was done, they would then have much to answer for.

CHAPTER 3

As they rode south, Jayden could not help but notice that Linis was unusually tense. More than once, he stopped and listened intently for several minutes before moving on. The road was fairly wide and flanked on either side by thick forest, though at times they did manage to catch a glimpse of the Goodbranch River over to their right.

Trade had been steady since the end of the war, which meant they were likely to encounter several travelers heading north. Some of these would stop in Sharpstone to unload their goods, while others had different destinations in mind to conduct their business.

He peppered Linis with questions, and while the elf was forthcoming with information, nothing he said helped Jayden to piece things together.

"It was a difficult time," Linis told him. "The elves were still just as divided as they had ever been since *the split*. We didn't even have knowledge of the desert elves in those days. And the great barrier had only recently fallen."

"It is said that Darshan united the elves and humans."

Linis nodded. "He did, at least to a point. You must understand how things were back then. Humans had no memory of the Great War, whereas the elves were led by those who had fought the battles, and still well remembered the old animosities. The Dark Knight was cunning. He used everyone's fears and hatred to reopen old wounds and sow widespread mistrust. It was human against human, elf against elf. And all the time they were fighting each other, the armies of Angrääl were poised to sweep across the land and destroy us."

"What about you?" Jayden asked. "How did you feel about humans?"

Linis smiled. "I was a foolish idealist. I still am, I suppose. I believed the only way forward was for human and elf to co-exist. In a way, that's how I met your father. I guided him for a time and helped him avoid those who sought to do him harm. Of course, he was barely more than a boy back then. I'm not sure he had even come of age."

This sounded strange to Jayden. "If he was a god, why was he running?" he asked.

"He had yet to fully discover the extent of his powers." Linis paused while he smiled at a memory. "He almost killed me by accident when he was still trying to develop them—blasted a ten-foot-wide hole in the ground right beside me, he did."

Jayden had attempted to use the *flow* himself when he was younger but found he lacked the ability. It made sense to him at the time. Whereas his sisters had obviously inherited the talent from their mother, he'd imagined the human half of him had prevented his use of it. Now, however...

He closed his eyes and tried to still his mind. For a few seconds, he felt nothing. Then, as if from a great distance, he heard a heavy thump, rather like a heartbeat, but infinitely deeper.

"This is not the time," snapped Linis.

Instantly, the sound ceased. He looked over to see Linis frowning. "I felt it. Or at least, I think I did."

"You mustn't try that again," the elf told him. "It's dangerous. Especially for you."

"Why? My sisters use it all the time."

"Your sisters are not you."

Jayden was on the point of asking him why, after so many failed attempts, he was suddenly able to connect with the *flow* when Linis drew his mount up short.

"Someone's approaching," he whispered.

Jayden tensed. The forest was known to harbor bandits, though he wouldn't normally expect them to attack two armed men. At first, he heard nothing. Then, a few seconds later, there was a rustling in the underbrush just ahead. Four men stepped out onto the road, each wearing light leather armor and carrying short blades.

"Stand aside," called Linis. "Seek out easier prey." He punctuated his words by drawing his sword.

A man with shaggy red hair and pale skin strode forward. "Our quarrel is not with you, elf. We've come for the boy."

On hearing this, Jayden immediately unsheathed his sword as well.

"You bear the symbol of Saraf," said Linis.

Jayden looked closely. Indeed, the symbol of the sea god was etched upon the breast of each man's armor.

"Again I say—we only want the boy."

"Who sent you?" Linis demanded.

"We come bearing the authority of heaven itself. Hand him over or die."

Jayden's heart was thudding in his chest. He had never faced this kind of violent threat before. All the same, he refused to cower.

"And *I* say, turn back or prepare to meet the gods personally," Linis retorted. He glanced over at Jayden. "Keep your wits about you, and everything will be fine."

Jayden knew he should be afraid, but could feel only rage growing inside him. "I'm ready," he growled.

With the name of Saraf howling from their lips, all four men charged. Jayden saw Linis's mount rear up wildly just as the elf sprang from the saddle, a vicious snarl on his face. His own mount was a touch less startled by the sudden mayhem, allowing him to free himself easily from the stirrups and land with his feet squarely on the ground. He was quickly on Linis's heels.

The elf ducked low as he met their foes, the blade of the attacker to the left of him cutting through the air just above his head. Jayden had never seen anyone move with such speed and agility. Linis split the armor of the next man with a single slash, carving a deep gash into his chest.

Jayden's attack was far clumsier. Soon, though, he realized that his size and strength were compensating to some degree for his lack of fighting experience. Sparks flew in all directions as steel crashed into steel, with his superiorly crafted blade very quickly shattering that of the first man he faced. The sheer might of the blow drove his enemy back and down onto one knee. Jayden stepped eagerly forward to make good his advantage, but a flashing blade coming in from his right-hand side forced him to rapidly adjust in order to block a series of wild blows. He found himself being driven back several paces.

Linis, meanwhile, was already finishing off his second opponent, taking his head from his shoulders in the blink of an eye.

Regaining his balance, Jayden pressed forward again, remembering what his father had taught him. He saw a small opening and lunged. The tip of his sword got through to puncture his opponent's right shoulder, but it was not a telling strike. The man's armor took most of the damage, and Jayden was forced to lean awkwardly back to avoid the counter strike.

By now, his other foe had discarded his broken blade and had drawn a short dagger. Rather than move in close with this, he raised his arm and let it fly. Linis was too far away to do anything to prevent what was about to happen, and the blade whirled toward Jayden. He thought to move left out of the way, but a strike from the enemy he was still battling with prevented this. Pain surged through him as the dagger buried itself deep into his flesh, just below his collarbone.

Running over, Linis rammed his weapon through the enemy's heart, but the damage was already done. Not that Jayden was about to give in. In fact, for a moment, his injury gave him added fury and impetus. Ducking right, he brought his sword crashing down, cleaving the last man's shoulder. His cry of agony was quickly silenced as Jayden followed up with a spinning sweep that cut halfway through his opponent's skull.

Jerking his blade free, he stumbled back and caught his breath. Though blood was soaking his shirt, the pain from the protruding dagger was surprisingly light.

Linis was at his side in an instant. "Let me see it," he said. There was an edge of panic attached to his voice.

"I'm fine," Jayden assured him. "It doesn't even hurt."

Ignoring this claim, Linis ripped open his shirt. "Sit down," he ordered. "I need to stop the bleeding."

Jayden did as instructed, and within seconds, he was very glad that he had. The pain, as well as the blood flow, increased dramatically the moment Linis pulled the dagger free. This done, Jayden expected him to apply pressure to the wound, but instead, the elf placed his hands directly over it.

"This may feel a bit odd," he warned.

Jayden sucked his teeth as an icy sensation swept over his body, as if he'd been dipped naked into a freezing cold spring. Be that as it may, within seconds, the bleeding had stopped and the torn flesh was weaving itself back together.

He had heard about how the *flow* could be used for healing, but had never experienced it himself or seen it done. For some reason, his mother had been reluctant to use her gifts in his presence, and the few minor injuries he had suffered as a child were always treated with traditional methods. When occasionally a farm hand suffered injuries serious enough to require her attention, he was always sent into another room. He had never been sure why this was. Now, however, he suspected it had something to do with what was happening to her and his father.

"That should be enough," said Linis.

The wound was completely closed. As the elf retrieved his waterskin and began to clean his hands, along with the blood on Jayden's chest, he could see that only a light red circle indicated where the dagger had entered. It still throbbed, but the pain was tolerable.

He glanced over at the bodies strewn across the road. "You think they knew where we are going?"

"It would seem so," said Linis. "And that doesn't bode well for us. These were not trained killers. Priests wearing armor, more likely. Definitely not warriors."

"How could they have known?"

"I'm not sure. They were from the temple of Saraf. At least, that's what they wanted us to believe. I can only assume that the gods must have a hand in whatever is going on, so I'm afraid we'll need to avoid Helenia."

"But that will make the trip twice as long," Jayden protested. Now, more than ever, a feeling of urgency was seeping in.

"We can buy a small boat in Darmon," Linis told him. "That's only half a day further on."

That would mean selling the horses. But at least it would get them to where they needed to be more quickly. Once he had retrieved a fresh shirt from his pack, Jayden set about helping Linis drag the bodies well away from the road. He had never killed before. After hearing quite a lot of stories about the war from former soldiers who worked at the farm, he'd imagined it would unnerve him. But it hadn't. Quite the opposite, in fact. He'd found it ... exhilarating.

"Will you teach me the sword?" he asked once they were remounted.

"Your father has already taught you, has he not?"

"Only the basics."

"In that case, you did rather well. In truth, I am impressed with how composed you have been in the wake of it. Most people become upset after their first kill."

Jayden glanced back at the shrubs where the bodies were hidden. "Some men deserve to die."

Linis cocked his head. "And you believe yourself wise enough to judge which men should live and which should die?"

Jayden huffed. "Those we killed wanted me dead. So, yes. And I'll do the same to anyone else who tries to hurt me or my family."

For a brief moment, Linis regarded him curiously. "I used to think you were much like your father. Now, though, I see something very different about you."

"What do you mean?"

"Gewey agonized over every death he caused during the war. You do not seem to have the same problem."

"Are you saying that I'm heartless?"

Linis laughed. "Certainly not. I know you too well to think that. And in all honesty, I was the same. The first time I took a life, I wasn't bothered. Nor did I feel any regret later on. I did what had to be done, and that was the end of it. Your father, however... his emotions run deeper than those of anyone I have ever known. Perhaps it is simply the price he pays for being a god."

He paused to look directly at Jayden. "If my instincts are correct, this will not be the last time you are forced to kill. It is good that it will not paralyze you with grief."

Jayden nodded. His father *was* a man of deep feelings; that much was common knowledge. Perhaps it was his mother's line that gave him this sense of detachment?

He pictured the moment his blade had ended the life of his foe—the look of horror and fear on the man's face and his wail of pain. Not a flutter of emotion from within. No... that wasn't quite true. He had felt something. Power! Just for an instant, he'd felt a tremendous surge of power.

Was that something he *should* be feeling? He thought to ask Linis, but eventually decided against it. He would keep this to himself. He wasn't sure what it said about him, anyway. Rather than any sense of guilt, he'd felt nothing but excitement.

Did he really want to know what kind of man that made him?

CHAPTER 4

Linis led them away from the main road once they drew near Helenia. It was a wise precaution. Though it was possible that their attackers had come from elsewhere, it was definitely the most likely place.

Jayden spent much of the time as they pressed on asking the elf about the war, hoping to somehow reconcile the truth in his mind. He had always thought of his father as a kind and gentle man. Everyone in Sharpstone loved and respected him. To think he had once wiped out entire armies... Even after hearing Linis tell the stories, he still could not quite picture him doing it.

Upon reaching Darmon, they made straight for a livery stable and sold their mounts. The town was little more than a small collection of buildings—a stopover for weary travelers and a handy place for the watercraft that traveled up and down the Goodbranch to make repairs. Linis had timed things well, and their early morning arrival meant that they would not be forced to stay overnight.

With boats for sale in Darmon being quite plentiful, they had little trouble purchasing a vessel that was just large enough for the two of them, well-constructed and stable for its size. The current would take them most of the way, though they had a set of oars for maneuvering whenever needed.

Linis kept a close eye on everyone they passed, paying particular attention to the banks of the river. The few curious glances they did receive could easily be attributed to Linis being an elf. Of course, he might well be taken for one himself, Jayden realized, at least from appearances. Everyone in Sharpstone knew he was of mixed heritage, but his ears made others unaware of this fact think him full-blooded. Though elves had become a far more common sight in the larger cities of late, they were still seldom seen in small towns and villages. Sharpstone was a rare exception to this. It was the presence of Kaylia and Linis that had played a large part in attracting the small number who had chosen to permanently settle.

Yet even in Sharpstone—accepting as the majority of humans living there now were of the new arrivals—there had been no shortage of trepidation and tension at the beginning. A few of the less tolerant citizens had protested quite aggressively. As it was, his father's standing in the community played a large part in calming things down, and eventually, relationships had normalized as much as could be expected. Which was still far from perfect. Even today, some of the older folk would give Jayden a disapproving stare—at least, when they thought he wasn't looking. And they made a point of avoiding his mother and the other elves entirely.

During their first day on the river, the current was swift and boat traffic light, helping them to make excellent time. They spent the first night at a small inn close to the village of Lomin, where Linis inquired about the local happenings. He'd been hoping to catch wind of anything that might give them a clue as to their attackers, but no one had heard anything unusual.

"Feeling out of place?" Linis asked, as they loaded the boat the following morning.

Jayden realized that he had been frequently touching his right ear. "I forget how different I look sometimes."

"To me, you look as much a human as you do an elf," Linis remarked. "But then, I can see your father clearly in you."

The two of them jumped aboard, and Jayden untied the mooring, then took the position at the front while Linis rowed them farther into the river's center.

After a short silence, Jayden said, "Mother always told me I should be careful whenever encountering elves. That I should avoid them completely if I could."

Linis pulled in the oars, allowing the current to take them. "I wish I could tell you that she was wrong. However, the truth is that elves are much more likely to accept humans than they are half-breeds. Not that this should cause you concern. I am well-known among my people. Should we chance upon any elves, they'll think twice before challenging a seeker."

"I still have a hard time picturing it," Jayden responded, shaking his head. "The stories I've heard about seekers... it just doesn't fit."

Linis chuckled. "Why? Because I'm a farmer? Is that it? There is much about me you don't know."

"Do you miss it?"

Linis leaned in as if someone might overhear him. "Don't tell my wife, but yes... I do. Quite often I look into the forest and feel an urge to disappear into its embrace. I sometimes long for the freedom of the wild and the thrill of not knowing what the next day might bring."

"Dina doesn't know how you feel, I take it?"

"Actually, I think she does. But in truth, these urges are only passing fancies. I've found peace in Sharpstone. Perhaps one day, Dina and I will venture away from our farm. Maybe we'll even cross the sea. But it's not yet time. I have not shed the violence completely."

Jayden frowned. "What do you mean?"

"When you've lived through truly terrible times and witnessed as many vile deeds as I have, it changes you. And not for the better. I can still see the blood and hear the screams. There are times when I can even smell the battlefields." He shook his head. "No. When I once again wander the world, I will bring with me the peace I have found as a farmer."

Jayden leaned his elbow on the edge of the boat. "If I could, I would have left a long time ago. You can't imagine how much I hate farming."

Linis laughed. "This is another of my secrets you must keep. I hate it too. But I love my wife, and she deserves a stable home." Reaching into his pack, he produced two apples and tossed one over. "You have no idea how envious I was when your mother told us she had offered to show you the world."

The mention of his mother instantly darkened Jayden's mood. He'd actually been enjoying the newfound freedom he was experiencing, and that must stop. This was not an adventure. He should not be taking any pleasure whatsoever in the fact that he had left home.

Guilt settled in. "I'm not hungry," he said, tossing the apple back.

Linis could see what he was thinking. "Don't worry," he said. "We'll find a way to heal your mother. Trust me, she has survived dangers that would make a hardened warrior weep."

"But what if we can't find my father? She'll never get better."

"Gewey lives; of that, I am certain. I doubt even the combined power of all heaven could kill him. We'll discover where he is soon enough."

Jayden tried to imagine what he would actually say to his father when they came face to face again. What reasons would be offered for keeping him in the dark all these years?

Whatever else happened between them, the lies would have to stop.

Even with the river speeding them along, it took more than a week to arrive in Baltria. Each evening, when they pulled alongside the bank for sleep or to stretch their legs, Jayden asked Linis to work with him on his fighting techniques.

He found him to be a rather stern taskmaster—far less patient than his father had been. A few times during these sessions, Jayden's inattention and casual behavior had earned him a nasty cut on his arm or hand. Linis healed his wounds immediately, but the lesson was well learned.

"Your father was a good instructor," the elf had remarked. "You'll make a fine swordsman in time."

"If I could only learn to channel the *flow*—"

"Not yet," Linis responded sharply. "Not until I know more about what has happened."

"But what if we're attacked again?" he argued.

Linis eyed him for a long moment. "I understand how you feel. It's just that..."

When he did not continue, Jayden pressed him. "Haven't we had enough secrets?"

Linis nodded. "Very well. The truth is, when I healed you the first time, I sensed something unusual. At first, I wasn't certain what it was. Now I am. Someone has been suppressing your ability to connect with the *flow*. And as far as I can tell, it has been going on for a very long time."

Jayden's jaw dropped in astonishment. "Suppressing my ability? How?"

"There are ways," Linis explained. "Some powerful elves have this ability. However, my guess is that your father is the one responsible."

"You're saying that ... for all these years ... the only reason I haven't been able to connect is because my *father* was preventing it?" Jayden's astonishment turned to anger. Throughout his life, he had believed he simply lacked the gift.

"Yes. And until we know why he chose to do this, I don't want you trying to test your abilities. It could be very dangerous for you, and whoever else happens to be nearby. Remember, your father almost killed me when he was learning to use his powers. Accidentally, of course. Not that this would have been any consolation. Dead is dead, accident or not."

"So you want me to do nothing?" Jayden was finding this hard to accept.

"For the time being, yes. When we reach the temple where your sisters are living, the elf elders who teach there might be able to help you. Until then, please do as I ask."

Only with great reluctance did Jayden agree to this.

The temple they sought was not so much a temple as it was a school and place of meditation for the elves. Controlled by the Order of Amon Dahl, it was located on a small island buried deep in the marshland just west of the city. Linis did not know how to find it himself, which meant they would be forced to enter the city and locate the liaison who lived in the temple of Darshan.

They dragged the boat ashore a few miles north of the city and then prepared to travel the rest of the way on foot.

"I can't believe I'm about to go inside a temple that's dedicated to my father," Jayden said as he slung his pack over his shoulders.

Linis laughed. "Gewey wasn't too happy about it himself when he discovered them being built. It made him very uncomfortable whenever people mentioned it." He gave the rope a tug to make sure their boat was secured in place. "I remember one time he actually ran across some pilgrims on their way to the Temple of the Far Sky; all of them were *his* followers."

"How did he react?"

"He gave them each a gold piece. What else *could* he do? He was in a foul mood for the rest of the day, I can tell you." He paused. "If visiting the temple bothers you, there is a friend who lives in Baltria I intended on seeing. We can have him contact your sisters instead."

"Yes, I think that would be better," Jayden agreed.

Conversation was light until they reached the city gates. Linis was immediately on his guard. Unlike times past, there were just a small number of men on duty, and only larger wagons were being searched for contraband. Baltria had not suffered many of the problems facing most of the other cities and kingdoms. Its citizens had maintained good trade relationships with lands both to the east and west, and it was well known that elves were welcome visitors. Many had even chosen to make it their home.

For all that, following the attack on the road, Linis thought it best to be wary and cover themselves. Each of them donned a hooded cloak just before passing through the main gates.

"No need to hide," said a young guard standing beside the gatehouse. "Elves are always welcome here, you know."

"Forgive my caution," said Linis. "I am unaccustomed to the company of humans."

"Come from out west, I wager."

"Indeed, we have."

"Well, things are not as bad in Baltria," he said, smiling broadly. "We all get along just fine around here."

"It will take a little time before I feel comfortable, I suppose," said Linis. "But thank you."

Once inside the gate, Jayden was immediately stunned by what he saw. It wasn't just the vast expanse of colorful buildings and throngs of people buzzing about, sights that on their own would have captured the imagination of anyone who had spent most of their life on a farm. No. Far more than any of this, it was the single massive object dominating the immense square that seized his attention the most. Standing twenty feet high and watching down over everyone was a statue of Darshan. In one hand, he held a sword, drawn back and ready to strike, and in the other, a scepter that was meant to represent his dominion over heaven.

"Impressive, is it not?" remarked Linis.

Jayden was unsure how to feel. He had seen smaller figures of Darshan, though he'd never really looked at them with any special interest. "It doesn't look anything like Father," he said.

Linis laughed. "That's because no one who saw him can recall what he looked like."

"And how did he manage that?"

"You will have to ask him yourself once we find him."

"He'll be explaining a lot more than just that," Jayden muttered under his breath.

He continued staring at the statue until he felt Linis touch his arm.

"Come. Let us find a room and a hot meal."

After taking one final look, he followed Linis into the heart of Baltria. The musky salt air was just like his sisters had described in their letters. The buildings were mostly either single or two-story structures, many of them quite newly built. Since the war, Baltria had become a very wealthy city; most of the older buildings had been torn down, and the new ones replacing them bore the influence of the western architects, with intricate friezes and spiraling columns. The streets had been newly cobbled, and the broad walkways were clean and lined with beautifully crafted iron lampposts surrounded by stunning displays of delicate flowers.

"It's hard to imagine this place being under siege," Jayden remarked. "To think that my father fought here."

"It was actually Lee Starfinder who saved Baltria, not your father," Linis pointed out. "He snuck in through a smugglers' tunnel and set off a series of explosions."

"Then why do all the stories I've heard say that Darshan broke down the gates and cast out the Dark Knight's armies?"

"You shouldn't listen to most of what you hear when it comes to Darshan. It's a big world, and not even a god can be in all places at once. But he did fight many battles, and saved countless lives by doing so."

"I wonder exactly how many lives he took?"

"More than he wanted. That much I can tell you."

"It's said Darshan destroyed entire armies."

Linis nodded. "It is said."

"So it's true?"

"Your father did what he had to do to win the war. You shouldn't judge him too harshly."

Jayden shrugged. "I guess it's just hard to believe. My father has always been so kind to people. I don't think I've ever heard him raise his voice before. Thinking about him laying waste to a whole army... I just can't imagine it."

"It was a difficult time. Right up until the end, none of us could be sure how the war would turn out. The Reborn King and his armies seemed invincible, and your father had yet to realize his true potential."

"Did you see him actually fight the Dark Knight?"

"No. But I went to the desert where it happened a few years later. The sands there still bear the scars. Nothing but mile after mile of green glass spreads out around a massive crater: a lasting monument to the clash of the two mightiest powers ever to walk the earth." Linis shook his head in wonder. "It was the first time I had even a slight understanding of what your father is truly capable of. It's almost beyond mental grasp. And that is why I am certain he is still alive."

Right there on the spot, Jayden made a silent promise to go see for himself where his father had fought.

They rounded a corner to where Linis knew there would be inns frequented by elves, and quickly procured a room in one called the Harbor's End. The common room was empty at the time, though the innkeeper assured them there would be plenty of entertainment after dark. Once they had stowed away their gear, they went out again, with Linis once more leading the way, this time over to the city's manor district.

Jayden was in awe of how huge and luxurious many of the homes were in this quarter, making even Millet's house look shabby by comparison. The pleasing fragrances wafting on the sea breeze from their lush gardens brought an involuntary smile to his lips. The men and women here were dressed casually for such a wealthy area, he noticed. Nothing at all like the elegant attire he had imagined. The reason for this was easily guessed, though. It was probably to do with the blistering heat and humidity, making cumbersome gowns and formal suits impractical.

They approached a particularly large gate guarded by four rough-looking men. Linis motioned for Jayden to lag behind a bit.

"Can I help you?" growled a guard.

"I am here to see Malstisos," Linis replied. "Is he in?"

"He is," confirmed the guard. "But he is not receiving visitors."

"He will receive me. Please tell him Linis is here."

The guard sniffed. "I don't care if you are the god Gerath himself. My orders are clear. He is not to be disturbed for any reason."

It was evident that the man would not be persuaded. However, Linis refused to be deterred.

"Who is in charge of the household?" he asked.

"What's it to you?"

Jayden noticed the elf's hands were now clenched. He was not accustomed to receiving such disrespect.

"Tell whoever it is that I am here. Do it now, or I can promise you'll be looking for a new employer by sundown."

After an extended moment, the guard looked over his shoulder at one of his comrades. "Go tell Ursil that," he paused to sniff in a vaguely contemptuous manner, "Linis is here."

The man grunted irritably but did as he was told.

Linis and Jayden stepped a short distance away.

"Who is Malstisos?" Jayden asked.

Linis kept his eyes trained on the guards. "A friend. And the fact that he has closed his house to visitors concerns me. It is most unlike him."

"Did he know my father?"

"He did indeed. He fought with us during the war... and suffered much as a result."

"Suffered how?"

"The Reborn King corrupted his spirit while he was attempting to escort Sister Maybell to safety."

"Maybell?"

It was a name he was familiar with, mainly because one of his sisters had been named in honor of the woman. His mother had told him that Maybell was the most courageous woman who had ever lived, though she quickly became far too emotional to say anything much after that. His sister often claimed to know the story as well, but he'd always assumed that was a lie. Now ... he wasn't so sure.

A short time later, the messenger returned, accompanied by an older woman with blonde hair and a round face. She wore a black ankle-length dress, together with a white apron tied at the waist. Her bright blue eyes were friendly, and her smile was welcoming.

"You are Linis?" she asked.

"I am," he affirmed.

The woman appeared greatly relieved upon hearing this. "Then you are a most welcome sight. My lord has been sickly of late, and an old friend might be just the remedy he needs." She waved him over. "Come. Let us remove ourselves from this wretched heat."

Linis bowed and then proceeded through the gate. When Ursil spotted Jayden coming with him, she paused. "And who is this handsome young elf?"

"This is my nephew," Linis said quickly, before Jayden could speak.

"My name is Jayden, my Lady," he told her with a courteous bow.

"And do you know my lord as well?"

"I'm afraid not."

"He's a bit too young to have made his acquaintance," added Linis.

Ursil laughed. "Dear me. I can never tell how old you elves are. For all I know, you could be a hundred and not look a day over twenty. I don't think I'll ever get used to it."

"I just turned eighteen," Jayden informed her.

She smiled. "That's coming of age for a human. Though for an elf, I imagine you're just out of diapers."

Jayden bristled but held his tongue. It was true that for an elf, he would be little more than a child. But in spite of his appearance, he was not an elf. He was...

He was what? He wasn't human. Not even half-human. So what then? A half-man? But half-men were half-human and half-god. The idea that he could not define himself was oddly upsetting.

The path leading to the house was lined with marble statues of elf maidens, each one holding aloft a crystal orb. The well-kept garden beyond was criss-crossed with walkways and benches where one could laze and relax. The building itself had been crafted from a highly polished deep gray stone, with a colonnade spanning the front that served to support a balcony directly overhead. The balustrade of this had been expertly sculpted into intricate flowery vines and was capped with a silver rail.

"He must be very rich," Jayden muttered to himself.

Despite his low voice, Ursil heard him. She barely caught a laugh in her throat. "Lord Malstisos? Rich? No, not at all. This manor is owned by Lord Broin, though he has tried to gift it to my lord many times. He always refuses, though, bless him. Nevertheless, Lord Broin provides enough gold that the home is maintained and the servants are paid."

They ascended a broad staircase that ended at an archway, at the other side of which was a small stone fountain surrounded by wrought-iron benches. The air here was remarkably cooler, even though the sun blazed down from a cloudless sky. Linis stopped by the fountain's edge to dip his finger in the water. Touching this to his tongue, he smiled.

"I thought I smelled havash."

"My lord has it brought from the west," Ursil told him. "Though lately, goods shipped from his homeland are arriving rather more infrequently."

Jayden sniffed the air. Nothing but the overwhelming scent of the flowers wafting in from the garden reached him. He kneeled beside Linis and tasted the water. It was bitter, though not unpleasantly so.

"Amazing stuff, that," said Ursil. "It cools the entire house. Makes it feel like late fall all the year round."

Linis glanced over at Jayden. "Can you feel it?"

"Feel what?"

"The *flow*. Havash draws it in so that it cools the air and revitalizes the spirit."

Jayden shook his head. He could feel nothing and noticed that Ursil was looking confused.

Linis spotted her confusion as well. "Jayden has been raised mostly around humans thus far," he quickly explained.

She cocked an eyebrow. "Is that right? Well, he'll have no trouble finding elves for company in Baltria. The city is thick with them. In fact, there are usually a few that gather in this very spot."

She nodded toward the fountain. "They come to enjoy the havash." Her features darkened. "Sadly, I've had to close the manor to visitors since my lord took ill. He would insist on greeting all who came, even when he lacked the strength. And then there are the times..." Her voice trailed off.

"What has happened?" asked Linis.

"I don't know. He took ill a couple of weeks back. No one knows what is wrong with him. Most days he stays in bed, and some of the things he says... they just don't make any sense at all."

The pain and concern in her voice were clear. Linis placed a comforting hand on her shoulder. "I will try to help him if I can," he promised.

She forced a smile. "You are as kind as my lord described. But I fear it will be to no avail. Many have already tried, and not even the elf healers from across the Abyss have been able to help. You know, the ones who use magic. Or the *flow*, as you call it."

Linis thought for a moment. "Are you familiar with the Temple of Amon Dahl?" he asked.

Ursil's eyes darted around the courtyard. "Yes," she whispered. "That is where many of the healers have come from."

"Good. Now please take me to your lord. Then I would ask that you send word to the Amon Dahl temple that I am here."

She gave him a grateful nod. "It will take a day to reach them, and another for them to respond. I'll have rooms prepared for you."

"That won't be necessary. We already have rooms at an inn."

"Nonsense," the woman said, waving a hand. "I'll not have friends of my lord staying at some dirty old inn."

Linis smiled and bowed. "Thank you. You are very kind."

"Kind? I don't know about that. But I do know my lord would be very unhappy indeed with me if I did not provide you with full hospitality."

"Then I will retrieve our belongings after I've seen Malstisos."

Ursil nodded briskly. "Excellent. Now, if you will follow me."

She led the way into the manor at a brisk pace. Given the lavish design of the exterior and the extravagance of the garden, the interior décor was rather understated. Though the furniture was certainly well crafted and the paintings and tapestries beautiful, everything had a somewhat used look attached to it. Chairs were obviously meant to be sat upon, while the baubles and keepsakes appeared to be much handled. Jayden half expected to see children playing on the rugs.

"Until recently, the house was always filled with visitors," Ursil said.

"What changed things?" asked Linis.

She shrugged. "Many of the elves are going east to live in the desert. Others are heading west to aid their kin with the troubles brewing out there." A sigh slipped out. "You'd think with the war being over, people would be weary of fighting by now."

"Change comes slowly," said Linis.

"Too slowly," she agreed. "And please forgive me for saying this, but the elves are as stubborn as any human alive. My poor lord spends half of his time trying to convince his own people that this world must be shared."

Jayden raised an eyebrow. "I haven't seen any sign of troubles here."

"There isn't. Not with the residents. The elves who choose to live here do so in peace. It's those passing through that are the problem. You can see it in their eyes... the disgust and anger."

"What about the humans?" Jayden asked.

"They can be just as bad, though they mind their manners if they know what's best for them. But some of the worst ones did move east to the smaller villages along the coast recently. Good riddance, if you ask me. Not even Saraf was able to get through to that lot."

Linis cocked his head. "Saraf?"

"You haven't heard about that?" Ursil laughed. "The god of the sea himself appeared. Right on the docks, if you can believe it."

"Did *you* see him?" asked Jayden.

"No. But hundreds did. From what I've heard, there was a bright flash of light and then there he was, hovering above the docks. Started telling the people to set aside their differences and begin building a new world together. Then, as quick as that, he was gone again."

"Interesting," mused Linis.

"Meddlesome, if you ask me," Ursil retorted. "If the gods really wanted to help, they should have never allowed that bloody war to happen in the first place. Now they want to come around and start telling people what to do? Saraf isn't the only one, either. I've heard that other gods have made appearances in the temples out west."

"Do you believe the accounts?"

"Before Saraf came, I'd have said no. But now... yes, I think it's probably true."

Linis wore a look of deep concern. "Has Amon Dahl had anything to say on the matter?"

"Not that I know of. But then, they don't tell me much. All the same, you can bet they are looking into it."

"I'm sure they are."

They were now approaching Malstisos's chamber. The door to this room was slightly ajar, and hushed voices could be heard coming from within. Yet when the three of them stepped inside, only Malstisos could be seen. Wrapped in a wool blanket and with his hair bound in a tight ponytail, he was sitting in a plush chair at the foot of his bed, thumbing through an old leather-bound book.

The moment they entered, his face brightened. "Linis, my old friend."

He began to rise, but his face quickly twisted in pain and he plopped heavily back down.

Linis was at his side in an instant. "You should be in bed," he said.

"Indeed, he should," agreed Ursil.

As Linis helped Malstisos gently back into his bed, Jayden could see how thin and frail he looked—the very picture of an elf of extremely advanced years.

Almost everywhere Jayden looked within the spacious chamber, there were bookshelves, every one of them stuffed to capacity with dauntingly thick tomes. As an extra measure, two large tables had been shoved into a corner, both of which were almost groaning under the weight of yet more books and stacks of loose parchment. Jayden had seen people obsess over books before. Millet had quite an impressive collection, in fact. But this seemed to be just desperate and chaotic.

"I'll be fine," said Malstisos, in a tone that convinced no one.

Linis took his hand and frowned. "You are not well. I can feel it."

The elf waved his free hand dismissively. "It's nothing, I tell you. I'll be up and about and as good as new within a few days." He eyed Ursil. "Though if you were to ask her, I'll probably be dead at any moment."

"If you don't get your rest, you will be," she scolded. Moving to the other side of the bed, she made a fuss over adjusting his blanket.

His eyes shifted over to Jayden. "Is that who I think it is?" he asked.

He stepped forward and bowed. "I am Jayden Stedding."

This confirmation brought a smile to Malstisos's face. He turned to Ursil. "Will you excuse us for a while, please?"

The woman scowled. "Just make sure he stays put," she told Linis.

He nodded. "You have my word on it."

After she had left them, Malstisos waved Jayden to come closer. "Let me look at you. Sweet spirits, you really are the image of your father."

"Thank you," said Jayden.

Linis could not hide his surprise. "You remember Gewey Stedding?"

"I do indeed," he replied. "I remember Darshan quite clearly now. In fact, many memories I had thought lost have returned to me of late, some of which I would have preferred to stay hidden."

"How is that possible?"

Malstisos shrugged. "I cannot say. But I do know I am most pleased to see you. There is much to discuss."

CHAPTER 5

J ayden listened patiently as Malstisos recounted the events of his life since the end of the war. At times he seemed to forget where he was and would often lose track of what he was saying. Jayden could see the sorrow written on Linis's face as he held his friend's hand and forced a smile whenever he became confused.

"But I have talked more than enough," Malstisos said, after more than two hours. "I want to hear about you, young Jayden. Why have you never come to visit Baltria before now?"

"I stay busy with the farm mostly," he replied. "My sisters have written to me about it many times, though. And I had planned to come directly after this year's harvest."

"Your sisters?" He looked confused for a moment. "What are..."

After a moment or two, his eyes lit up. "Ah yes, I remember now. Penelope and May ... bell." Tears suddenly began spilling down his cheeks. "Poor, sweet Maybell. I am so sorry I failed you." He covered his face, weeping into his hands.

"You didn't fail her," Linis told him. "You brought her back safely. You were very brave."

"No... no... I failed her. I surrendered to darkness. I let it beat me, and now she is gone."

He continued sobbing uncontrollably. Linis caught Jayden's eyes and gestured to the door. But before he could reach it, Malstisos called out to him.

"Please. Do not go. Not yet. Forgive me, I sometimes lose my grip on the day. It will pass."

Jayden shot a questioning glance to Linis before replying. "Are you sure?"

"Please," Malstisos begged, wiping his eyes. "My illness affects me in strange ways."

"Do you think that is because of what happened to you on the steppes?" Linis asked him.

He nodded. "Possibly."

"What *did* happen to you there?" asked Jayden.

Malstisos did not reply immediately. Instead, he reached over to pick up a cup from the nightstand. After taking a long drink, he sighed with pleasure. "You know, there was a time when I thought I would never taste wine properly again. It was like ash in my mouth." He sat the cup down. "Do you enjoy wine as well?"

"I do," answered Jayden.

He smiled weakly. "That is good. Always find time for the simple pleasures in life. You never know when the darkness will come for you." He shifted in the bed. "Now, you wanted to know what happened to me."

"It isn't necessary," said Linis. "I can tell him the story. You should rest now."

"Nonsense. I'm feeling much better. Though I am surprised he hasn't heard the tale already. Do you not speak of those days?"

"I only found out that my father is Darshan a short time ago," explained Jayden.

Malstisos raised an eyebrow. "Is that right? So you had no idea that you are the son of the mighty god who saved the world?" Seeing Jayden shake his head, he sighed. "Yes, I suppose that is understandable. Such a burden it must be. But you should be very proud of your father. Without him, we would have all perished. That, however, is another story. Mine, I'm afraid, is not all that interesting. And I was nowhere near as brave as Linis would have you believe."

Malstisos recounted his journey from Hazrah with Maybell, and then how the Vrykol had put the corruption of the Reborn King inside him.

"Much of what happened after that is lost," he said. "Lately, some of it has come back to me, though not enough to tell the full story. All I know for sure is that I was healed just after the death of Theopolou and returned to Althetas."

"And what happened to Maybell?" asked Jayden, fascinated by the tale.

"She sacrificed her life to save your father," Linis chipped in. "A sacrifice she would not have been able to make without the strength of Malstisos. He resisted the evil inside him long enough to deliver her safely."

Malstisos smiled and touched Linis's hand. "You are kind to say this."

"It sounds like bravery to me," remarked Jayden. "But I'm curious. You say you only recently remembered my father?" He looked to Linis. "Maybe this has something to do with what's happened to Mother?"

Linis nodded. "Yes, it might well have."

He explained the situation to Malstisos. "Kaylia has fallen ill. That is what brought us here. Darshan has gone missing, and we have come to search for him."

The old elf thought for a long moment. "This is terrible news indeed. Sadly, I cannot remember anything that might be of help to you. Although some memories returned to me a few weeks ago, I have been in decline for more than a year."

He paused before adding, "But now that I think about it, he *did* come to see me fairly recently."

Linis leaned forward. "Really? You mean he actually revealed his full identity to you?"

Malstisos shook his head. "No. That's the strange thing. At the time I did not recognize him at all. He came posing as a grain merchant, wanting to know about how things stood between the elves and humans here in Baltria." His look of confusion grew. "It *is* odd. I should have known him right away. But I didn't. Why do you suppose that is?"

"It's not your fault," Linis told him. "After the war was over, Darshan removed the memory of any connection between him and Gewey Stedding from people's minds. Only a very few of us who were close to him retained the knowledge."

"Ah, I see. That would explain it then. I knew him, though I would not say we were exceptionally close. Not like you or Lord Starfinder were. How is Lee, by the way?"

"Lee is dead," Linis replied.

"Oh, yes, that's right. I forgot. A pity. He was a good man."

"Yes, he was."

Malstisos's eyes began to droop. "So many of my friends are gone. Those who remain never come to see me."

"I am sorry," said Linis. "Had I known you were ill, I would have come much sooner."

"So many lost." The elf's voice was becoming weak, his eyes distant. "Time. That is the enemy, Jayden. Time. We never have enough time. Save him. Save your father. He will need you to be strong."

"Are you sure you don't know where he is?" Jayden asked.

"The war. He fights the war still."

"The war is over," Linis said quietly.

"The war is never over. Darshan fights..."

Malstisos closed his eyes.

After tenderly touching his friend's brow and with tears welling in his eyes, Linis led the way out of the chamber. Just before reaching the door, Jayden glanced back. Aside from being too thin, Malstisos did not look to be seriously ill. Yet there was something around his eyes, as if the life were being slowly drained away from his spirit, leaving him a hollow shell.

"How long do you think he has left?" he asked once they were in the hallway.

"Without knowing what is wrong with him, I cannot say." Linis wiped his eyes. "He was once a noble elf, strong and proud. It pains me deeply to see what has become of him."

"Do you think he knows anything at all that could help us? Maybe without even being aware of it, I mean."

Linis shrugged. "There's no way to tell. Whatever is happening to him might have opened his memory, but it has also severely clouded his mind. I cannot even say how he was able to recognize you as Gewey's son. As things are, I suspect that he cannot be of much assistance."

After asking one of the servants for Ursil's whereabouts, they were directed to a parlor where they found her sitting at a small desk, poring over a ledger. A look of consternation was carving deep lines across her forehead.

"I have no mind for this sort of thing," she muttered grumpily. "Lord Broin was supposed to send one of his men here weeks ago to sort this out."

"What's wrong?" asked Jayden.

She shoved the ledger away. "I manage the day-to-day operations of this manor, while Lord Malstisos always kept the books, ordered the provisions, and dealt with the merchants. Now I'm having to figure it all out on my own. And it's maddening."

She took notice of Linis's grim expression. "Did he fall asleep?" When Linis nodded, she continued, "He's not always like that, though I must admit his episodes are happening more frequently of late. Goes on and on about the Great War, he does. Do you think you can help him?"

"I'm afraid not. Whatever ails him is beyond my skills."

"I thought so. Thank you for trying, though. How long will you be staying with us?"

"Not long," said Linis. "But I will return."

"That's good. He needs his friends, now more than ever."

Jayden couldn't help but wonder if his father would somehow be able to cure the elf. After all, he was a god. Then again, if he had already been here and seen Malstisos's condition, why hadn't he helped him then? Despite what people thought, were the powers of a god actually more limited than they believed? The stories suggested there was virtually nothing they couldn't do. Healing of all kinds was reputed to be well within their capabilities.

Ursil told them that she had sent word to Amon Dahl and that they should treat the manor as if it were their own home while they waited for a response.

Jayden wanted to spend the time exploring Baltria, but Linis fiercely opposed the notion, warning that it was far too dangerous until they knew more about what was going on and who precisely had sent their attackers. While Linis went off alone to retrieve their belongings from the inn, a disappointed Jayden settled for strolling through the manor, along the way taking an increasing interest in the artwork that was displayed on nearly every wall and in every corner.

Though the house retained its comfortable quality throughout, in the lesser-used portions the décor became far more elegant. Even Millet's house could not compare to the treasures he came across here. One tapestry in particular caught his eye. It was woven in such fine detail that at first he was close to mistaking it for a painting. The effort and skill that had gone into its crafting must have been enormous. But superb as it was, what caught his attention most of all was undoubtedly the subject matter.

It depicted the final battle between Darshan and the Reborn King, flying high above the desert sands while locked in a mortal struggle. With streaks of blue lightning crashing down from the heavens above, vast gusts of fire and wind swirled around the combatants in a mighty tempest.

Jayden focused on the image of his father. It looked very much like him—almost as if the artist responsible had known exactly what he looked like. His father's expression was dire, and his eyes burned with white flames.

"That's my favorite," called a tiny voice from behind.

Jayden turned to see a young girl, no more than eight years old, with sandy hair and wearing a blue and white dress.

He smiled down at her. "It is? Why is that?"

"Because it's Darshan, silly," she replied in a tone that suggested he really should not need to be told this. "He ended the war for us."

"Yes, he did." He looked back at his father's image. "At least, that's what people say."

"Of course he did. Why would you say he didn't?" Her cheeks puffed out and her arms crossed firmly in front of her chest.

Jayden held up his hands. "Calm down. I didn't say that. What I meant was, sometimes people exaggerate a bit."

"Not my mother," she said, stubbornly. "She said that she saw Darshan, and my mother never lies."

"And just who is your mother?"

"She's the cook," the girl replied. "She used to work for King Jacob in Althetas and decided to move us here last year."

"Why was that?"

The girl shrugged. "I don't know. Something about the riots."

"What riots?"

She twisted her tiny face. "Don't you know anything? Humans and elves don't get along out there. Well, some of them don't. Mother says it's just a bunch of thickheaded idiots who don't know what's good for them. They don't like it that elves have been moving into the cities."

"And what about you? How do you feel about it?"

She spread her hands. "It doesn't bother me. They're like you, most of them."

Without thinking, Jayden touched his ear. "Like me?"

"You know... nice."

He pressed his hands to his hips. "And why would you think I'm nice? We've only just met."

"Because Lord Malstisos wouldn't let you into the house if you weren't," she replied flatly. "He doesn't allow mean elves inside."

"And what about mean humans?"

"Those too."

It was then Jacob noticed an ever so slight curve to the girl's ears. She was a half-elf, he realized. A newbreed, as they were being called. It was little wonder that her mother had brought her here. There was no denying that news came slowly to Sharpstone, but even there they'd heard of the widespread hatred being displayed toward newbreeds.

The girl cocked her head and looked him up and down. Her eyes then widened as realization dawned. "Hey, you're like me, aren't you?"

Jayden nodded.

"But you look more like an elf... except for your eyes. Was your father an elf?"

"My mother."

"Maybe that's why," she reasoned.

Jayden at first thought to correct her. His sisters had not inherited the same elven physical characteristics that he had. But the girl seemed pleased with herself, so he decided against it.

"Is your father here?" he asked.

Her expression became sad. "No. He died in a fight just before we moved."

"I'm sorry to hear that."

"It's all right. He's with the Creator now. I'll see him again one day."

"I'm sure you will."

As quickly as her sorrow had come, it vanished again, replaced by a bright smile. "My name's Velly," she said, thrusting out an arm.

He shook her hand and bowed. "Mine is Jayden."

"Are you staying for dinner?" she asked eagerly.

"I am."

"Good. Then you can sit beside me. I'll save you a seat."

Just then, the sound of a woman calling Velly's name echoed from far down the hall.

Her shoulders sagged. "That's my mother. I have to go. She doesn't like it when I wander off too far."

"Well, then, you'd better hurry. I don't want to get you in trouble."

Flashing him a grin, she set off running. "See you at dinner," she called out over her shoulder.

Jayden waited until she had disappeared around a corner before walking on in the opposite direction. He'd always had a way with children. His aunt Dina often teased him about it, saying that it meant he would one day be a good father.

"Don't let the Village Mothers see you," she would say whenever she spotted him displaying this skill. "They'll have you married off in a heartbeat."

While walking along, he noticed a full-length mirror hanging in one of the antechambers. Pausing, he rolled his shoulders and tucked his hair behind his ears. He really did look like an elf, albeit a rather big one. The elves on the steppes were broad-shouldered and squared-jawed. However, it wasn't his appearance that gave him away; it was his blood. Elves could sense their own kind, and they immediately knew that he wasn't full-blooded. Most of them he'd encountered so far didn't seem to care about this, but he knew there were some who would look upon him as nothing but an abomination.

"Who cares what *they* think?" he said to his reflection before setting off again.

He found Linis reading in the garden and told him about the riots that Velly had spoken of.

"Yes. Some people simply cannot accept change," he responded. "Elves are just as guilty of this as humans."

"I wonder why things aren't that way here?" Jayden remarked.

Linis leaned back in his chair. "Baltrians have always been a welcoming people, certainly when compared to the humans of the West. The elves who came were not seeking conflict, so they were able to fit in. Those who are resistant to change are trying to hold on to a world that no longer exists. There is no place for them here."

"Is that why some have gone to the desert?"

"Yes. But I don't think they'll find what they're seeking amongst the dunes."

"What are they hoping to find?"

"A life they can understand." Linis paused for a moment. "You see, my people—I should say, *our* people—are still struggling to find a new place in the world. Before the war, we had our lands to ourselves. No human dared to enter them. Now the borders are open, and we are no longer detached. And we are vastly outnumbered by humans. It's simply too much for some of our kin." He shook his head sadly. "As much as people claim to accept that change is inevitable, in their hearts what they really desire is for things to stay the same."

Jayden's thoughts turned to Velly. In his eyes, her bright smile somehow captured the very essence of what the world was gradually becoming. Yet to think that such a beautiful child could also elicit a hatred that drove some people to near madness was beyond his comprehension.

"Anyway, why are you so concerned about the troubles in the West?" asked Linis.

"The little girl I just met," he replied. "Her father was an elf."

A knowing look came over Linis. "I see. Dina and I have discussed this many times. The newbreeds."

"Aren't you worried what will happen once you have children?"

"What parent is not afraid for their children?"

"Yes, but most children aren't threatened with death from the bigotry of others."

"If only that were true," Linis sighed. "The fact is, new-breeds are only the most recent addition to the world's venom. Some people will always find a reason to hate. Fortunately, they are a minority. In the end, what was strange and new gradually becomes common. People grow accustomed to what is happening around them. It might take generations, but it happens eventually."

He reached over and slapped Jayden on the knee. "Enough of this dark talk. I don't want you worrying over such things."

"I wish I didn't have to," Jayden responded.

That night at dinner, Malstisos was noticeably absent. As she had promised, Velly saved Jayden a seat beside her at the table. Her mother also introduced herself briefly before returning to the kitchen.

Just like they did back home, Jayden noted that the staff ate in the main dining hall. Malstisos was apparently well thought of by all present, and a toast was made to his recovery. It turned out that most of the gathering originated from the West, though a few had been born in Baltria. Jayden tried to learn what he could from them, but they were reluctant to speak.

"We do not talk about violence at the table, young man," scolded a woman with a careworn face and silver hair.

"Forgive me," he said. "I didn't mean to be rude."

Velly peppered him with questions about Sharpstone for most of the meal. Jayden was surprised to find anyone interested in the happenings of what amounted to nothing more than a few thousand villagers, some farms, and a handful of shops. Velly, though, did not tire of it in the least.

After they had finished eating, Velly's mother hurried her off to bed, though not without a great deal of complaining and begging. It wasn't until her parent's voice became raised and stern that she finally obeyed. Soon after she had gone, Ursil informed Linis that her lord was now awake and asking for him. Jayden offered to go as well, but Linis thought it best to go alone.

"Malstisos seems distracted by you," he explained. "In his fragile state of mind, I don't want to put too much on him."

Jayden accepted this as being sensible. Then, just as he was about to return to his room, he was invited to join a few of the maids and groundskeepers in a rear garden for an after-dinner gathering. About a dozen or more were there, sipping plum brandy and wine and chatting about trivial subjects.

"So where are you from, lad?" asked a stout gardener. He spoke with a Baltrian accent and his dark eyes bore the creases of middle age.

"Sharpstone," replied Jayden, accepting a cup of wine from a young man standing close by.

"Is that right? A long way to travel. What brings you to the door of Lord Malstisos?"

"He and Linis are friends," he explained, not wanting to give too much away.

"I see. And you say you're from Sharpstone. I didn't know that elves hailed from there."

"My father is ... human."

The man gave an embarrassed smile. "Forgive me. But you do look like one... an elf, I mean. Not that there's anything wrong with that."

"I'm not offended. People where I'm from don't make an issue of it. So *I* never have."

"Well, you won't have any problems here either. But you should be careful if you leave Baltria. East as well as west. Foul rumors are spreading."

"You and your foul rumors," chirped up a young woman, joining in the conversation. She was sitting on a bench beside a small fishpond. Her flaxen hair was braided down her back, and her blue eyes twinkled in the lamplight. She gave the gardener a disapproving look. "What are you trying to do? Frighten the poor man to death?"

"It's all right, really it is," Jayden assured her. "News comes slowly to our village. And even slower to my farm."

"You're fortunate," she said. "The world seems determined to go insane these days. I envy anyone who can stay out of it."

This remark was met with several nods and murmurs of agreement.

"Bren is right about one thing, though," she continued. "Outside of Baltria, you should be mindful. Particularly of elves moving east. They don't like humans, for sure. But they like your kind even less."

Jayden felt a rush of irritation on hearing the words "your kind." He didn't like being made to feel different, even though he was well aware that some people looked down on him. Not that they would ever dare to speak their opinions out loud. When he was just six years old, he had seen his mother beat a man nearly senseless for calling him a half-breed. This young woman wasn't intending offense, of course. Far from it. The way she had smiled at him suggested something entirely different.

The topic of conversation then changed, and his annoyance was soon forgotten. By midnight, with the wine continuing to flow freely, the gathering was showing no signs of dispersing. Bren, the gardener, began to tell lurid stories of elf plots to kill all the newbreeds, but he was promptly silenced by the young woman. Her name, Jayden had learned by now, was Leanna. She was well-mannered and proper, unlike her more boisterous co-workers, and was not drinking nearly as much.

"Bren means well," she said, offering him a seat on the bench beside her. "He's just paranoid at times. He sees plots and schemes everywhere he looks. He actually believes the temples are becoming corrupt, like in the days of the Reborn King."

Jayden stiffened. "Corrupt in what way?"

"What does it matter?" She gave him a curious look. "Don't tell me you believe that rubbish, too?"

He gave her a reassuring smile. "No. Of course not." Despite there being ample room on the bench, he became aware that she was sitting very close to him. "So tell me about yourself, Leanna. You seem more ... cultured than the others."

She gave him a tiny smile. "How kind of you to notice. I am, in fact, a lady of Althetas. Or to be more accurate, I used to be."

"What happened?" He blurted out the words before thinking. Fortunately, she didn't appear to be bothered by the indelicate question.

"My father disgraced our family during the war," she explained. "He was a spy for the Reborn King. When this was discovered, King Jacob stripped us of our lands and title."

"I... I'm sorry."

She touched his hand. "No need to apologize. I was too young to remember any of it. My mother moved me here to get away from the shame he brought upon us. But she made sure I was taught proper etiquette."

"And what of your father?"

The question just slipped out. Jayden instantly reprimanded himself for continuing to press her on the subject, but Leanna's reaction remained one of calm acceptance. She was clearly a person who had learned to cope with the past. Or at least, had learned how to hide her pain well.

"He was killed by those from another family just before we left the city. They blamed him for the death of their daughter during the siege of Althetas."

"I'm sorry, I shouldn't have asked," said Jayden.

She waved a dismissive hand. "It was a long time ago, and I barely remember him. And if I'm honest, he deserved his fate. I'm happy here in Baltria. I have a good life, filled with friends who love me and whom I love in return. And at least here, I don't have to worry about the troubles between the races."

Yes, thought Jayden. *The races... all three of them.* For the very first time, he was beginning to see himself as being separate from other people. Even though his mother would beat the hide from him for suggesting such a thing, it was true nonetheless. Newbreeds were looked upon by many as a completely separate race—not a part of the accepted norms of society.

They continued talking for a time, and then Linis appeared in the garden. Despite his smile, Jayden could see the sorrow behind his eyes. This told him that Malstisos's condition had not improved.

"Another newbreed?" asked Bren drunkenly, though there was only humor in his tone.

Linis laughed. "Dear fellow, I'm as much an elf as they come. A former seeker, in fact."

"Is that right?" the gardener responded. "Then join with us and tell us tales of your adventures. We have been telling our own stories for so long, my ears are tired of hearing them."

Linis glanced over to where Jayden was sitting close to Leanna and shot him a sly grin. His eyes then returned to Bren. "I would be pleased," he said, spreading his hands. "But first, where is my wine? How can I tell tales with no wine?"

A full cup was quickly produced for him. After taking a long sip, Linis immediately began recounting his adventures, most of which centered on times before the war and were familiar to Jayden. In short order, the entire gathering was listening with keen interest, and a few minutes into the telling, Jayden became aware of Leanna taking hold of his hand. When he looked over at her, she met his uncertain gaze with a flirtatious smile.

Even though he had never before lacked confidence around women, this time he felt himself blushing. She might be only a few years his senior, but she was definitely not one of the country girls he was used to speaking with. This was a real lady, one with poise and grace. At that moment, he felt very much the country bumpkin.

After a while, a few of the staff politely excused themselves, saying that they needed to rise early for work. As for Jayden, he was by no means tired. He had thought about offering to take Leanna on a stroll through the manor, but imagined this might be considered a little too forward, given it was their first meeting.

What would Mother tell me to do? he wondered. She had always been the one to advise him on the ways of women. And from the way she'd described his father during their courtship, she was the right one to do so. But then again, given what he had recently learned, how much of what she'd told him of this was actually true?

"Would you care to have lunch with me tomorrow?" he finally asked, after screwing up the courage.

She sighed. "I'm afraid I will be at the market for most of the day."

He felt the sting of disappointment.

"But you could join me," she added quickly. "That is, if you are permitted."

He glanced over to Linis, who right at that moment was draining the last drops from his cup. The elf would want him to remain in the manor. That much was certain. But one look at Leanna's smile and his decision was made. He was, after all, his own man now.

"I would be honored to go with you," he told her.

"Honored, you say?" She tittered a light laugh. "I can assure you that shopping is not something you're likely to enjoy."

"In your company, I'm sure it will be wonderful."

"Such a sweet thing you are. A true gentleman."

She began to rise. Jayden was on his feet in an instant. "You're not leaving, are you?"

"It is late and the day will be long," she answered. "Though I suspect it will feel shorter with you to keep me company."

Reluctantly, he released her hand and bowed as formally as he could manage. "Until tomorrow, then."

She curtsied with elegance and precision. "I rise at dawn and leave by the servant's door in the kitchen shortly after." After flashing him another smile, she glided from the garden.

Jayden watched her all the way until she had vanished from sight, then plopped back down on the bench. So full was his mind, he didn't notice that Linis had joined him until he felt a touch on his shoulder.

"A fetching young girl," the elf remarked. "It's a pity we will not be here long."

"Once I find Father and know that Mother is fully recovered, I intend to come back."

"After just one meeting? She must be even more remarkable than I imagined."

Catching the twitch of a smile on his lips, Jayden replied hotly, "I'm not saying that because of her. I'm not a love-struck child, you know."

"Not like your father then," he said. "He was so awkward and clumsy around your mother in the beginning. It's a miracle they ever bonded. Obviously, he overcame his shyness in the end, though; otherwise, you wouldn't be here."

Jayden frowned. "Do you mind not talking that way about my parents?"

Linis let out a hearty laugh. "Forgive my crudeness. Dina has often warned me against drinking too much wine. She says my tongue becomes far too loose. All the same, it is good to see you have confidence around women. You are a handsome young man, Jayden. Be careful, though. Hearts are fragile things."

"She won't break my heart," he insisted. "I only just met her."

"True. However, yours is not the only heart to consider. I hear that the maidens of Sharpstone are already clamoring for your attention."

"So far, none have met with Mother's approval."

"Have any met with *yours*?"

Jayden shrugged. "They're nice enough, I suppose. But I want ... something more." He turned his head to look directly at Linis. "Something like what you have with Dina. You don't need to know very much about love to see how you feel when you look at her."

Linis leaned back and clasped his hands behind his head. A faraway look crept into his eyes. "Yes, it's true. She is the great love I spent so much of my life searching for. You should have seen her back then. Fierce and determined... defiant of all who would reject her. I think it's safe to say that I loved her from the very first moment we met. Never did I imagine I could be happy as a farmer. Yet with Dina beside me, I could remain within the borders of Sharpstone for the rest of my days and still be contented."

"I wonder if my parents felt the same way?" Jayden asked.

"Of course they did." There was just a hint of chiding in his tone.

"How would I know? The story I've been told of how they met can't be true."

Linis nodded. "I understand how you feel. And it so happens that I know the true tale. If you are not too weary, I will tell it."

By now, only a few people were left in the garden, and even they were easing their way toward the exit. Jayden leaned forward eagerly. "Yes. I want to hear it."

Linis went on to tell him how Kaylia had been captured by bandits, and of how Lee and Gewey had rescued her. "Though he always tells of Lee's courage, your father was very brave as well," he concluded. "Had he not been a god, he would have certainly been slain."

"But the way they describe their bond," said Jayden. "Is that really how it happened?"

"The bond? No, not at all. Actually, Kaylia nearly killed Dina the day your parents first bonded."

Drawing a long breath, he went on to tell of how Kaylia had attacked Dina after discovering the truth about her lineage. "Had your father not intervened, Dina most certainly would have died," he stated. "It was in that moment that your parents' spirits bonded of their own accord. It was quite remarkable, really. They completed the bond sometime later, but the entire story would take far too long to tell in one sitting." He furrowed his brow on noticing the despondent look covering Jayden's face. "That is the truth of what happened. Is it not what you expected?"

"Sounds like it was all an accident to me." Jayden shook his head, as if trying to remove a distressing thought. "And Mother... You're telling me that she tried to kill Dina because she's a newbreed?"

Linis placed a hand on his shoulder. "Your mother acted rashly toward Dina. Do not read something into it that isn't there. She bears no malice toward newbreeds. And even when she did, her heart was quickly changed. As for the bond, nothing like that happens by accident. It is all by the Creator's design. It was *She* who brought your parents together. Just as *She* brought you here now. And if you doubt the strength of their love, do you remember the story of Darshan's unorem?"

Jayden thought for a moment. "Once, when I was a child. Darshan's great love. But I forget where I heard it, though I do remember that no one knew his love's name."

"Her name is Kaylia. And I too have heard the tale. But not from a bard... from those who were actually there. And it's all true. Every word of it."

Jayden looked at him incredulously. The story told of a love so strong that it shattered the gates of hell and cast down the power of the first god, Melek.

"Never doubt for a moment that your parents are intended to be together," Linis continued. "Or that you are meant to be here." He pushed himself to his feet. "Now, I really must go and sleep off some of this wine."

"Thank you," Jayden told him. He felt somehow better... as if at least some of the lies surrounding him had been dispersed. "I think I'll sit here for a while longer."

Linis gave him a fatherly smile before exiting the garden.

The others had departed a few moments earlier, leaving Jayden now completely alone. He looked skyward. Only a few stars were peeking out from behind the clouds, and the air was thick. It was entirely too warm for his taste—something he had not noticed in the least while in Leanna's company. For a moment, he questioned whether he should go ahead with their meeting in the morning. There was no doubt in his mind that he had not felt the same rush of attraction that Linis had described earlier. But had *she*? And if she had, would becoming close to a woman when you were intent on leaving very soon be cruel?

"You're being stupid," he scolded himself. She was only after some company, nothing more. As far as the flirtation went, he had known several girls who flirted without any deep meaning behind it. Besides, he had to stay focused on finding his father and saving his mother. This was no time to be clouding his mind with silly notions.

As he made his way to his room, a wave of anxiety struck him. Here he was, far away in Baltria, without any knowledge of his mother's condition. He had to know that she was still managing to keep whatever plague was ailing her at bay.

After dwelling on this for a few moments, he decided that while he was out with Leanna in the city, he would find a place where he could send a fauna bird. The reply could be delivered to Malstisos's house. Though, of course, by the time it arrived, he might no longer be there.

It was only a few hours before dawn. He tried to calm himself, but his anxiety persisted.

While lying in his bed, more than an hour passed before sleep finally came.

CHAPTER 6

On waking, Jayden's mouth felt as if it had been stuffed full of cotton. He knew he had not drunk too much wine the night before, yet there was a thudding in his head that came with each beat of his heart. Of course, he was not accustomed to such late nights. Life on a farm demanded that you go to bed early or suffer the consequences.

The dim glow through the window assured him that he had not overslept. Even so, for a brief spell, he gave serious thought to simply closing his eyes and forgetting about his outing with Leanna. A moment later, the memory of her holding his hand entered his mind, and this idea was soon dismissed.

Struggling up into a seated position, he rubbed the back of his neck. He'd said that he would join her, and he would. Even if he did feel—and probably look—like death. Tossing back the blanket, he slid from the bed and stumbled blindly into the shower. The initial shock of bitterly cold water before it warmed up drew a loud yelp, but it was effective in reviving him.

With a towel wrapped around his waist, he made his way back into the bedchamber. There, to his surprise, he found Linis sitting at a small table, picking at a plate of fruit. A steaming bowl of porridge awaited Jayden.

"You had better hurry, or Leanna will be disappointed," Linis told him.

He cocked his head. "I thought you wouldn't want me leaving the manor."

"I don't. But you are a man. I cannot force you to do as I say."

He must have overheard their conversation, Jayden realized. While rummaging around for a decent shirt and trousers, he asked, "If you're not trying to stop me, why did you come?"

"To reprimand you," he stated flatly. "You *are* a man now, so act like one. You were going to sneak out and wander the city without telling me where you were going to be. I'm not your father, Jayden. I'm your companion on this journey, and you must keep me informed. What if I had needed you? What if the people who tried to abduct you on the road attacked the manor? How would I even begin looking for you?"

The anger in Linis's eyes was genuine. Jayden was unsure how to react. He had always thought of the elf as an uncle. An older, advisory figure in his life, not a comrade. But he was right. He *was* behaving like a child.

"I'm sorry. I should have told you," he said.

Linis's anger was diminished only slightly by the apology. "You have to change your way of thinking," he responded. "The world is dangerous, particularly for you. That makes it even more dangerous for me. And I have no intention of my wife becoming a widow." He pointed to the corner where Jayden's sword and dagger lay. "Do not forget to arm yourself."

With each scolding word, Jayden felt increasingly foolish. "Won't that draw attention to me?" he asked.

"It might. But better that than being caught unprepared. As it is, I've observed several people walking the streets armed, so it shouldn't attract too much notice." The elf's features then softened somewhat. "I don't mean to be harsh. And I do understand this is all new to you. But like your father had to do before you, you must grow up fast."

"I understand," Jayden said. "And if you want, I will tell Leanna that I can't go with her."

Linis sighed. "No. You should go. If I expect you to behave as a man, I must be willing to treat you as one. You should be safe enough in the markets. And it's a good opportunity to learn of local rumors and gossip. Keep your eyes and ears open for anything unusual."

Jayden began putting on his clothes. "What will you do?"

"I'll stay with Malstisos. I don't think I can help him, but while I'm here, I must at least try. And if by chance his mind does become clearer, he might yet be able to tell me something about what has happened." He nodded to the bowl of porridge. "You should eat now. You don't want to be late."

After finishing his breakfast, Jayden fastened the sword and dagger to his belt, and they exited the room together. Once in the corridor, Linis regarded him for a long moment, a curiously tender expression on his face.

"I wish your father could see you now," he said. "You look every bit the noble warrior."

Jayden laughed. "I'm anything but that."

"Actually, you are much more. If people knew that the son of Darshan walked among them, it would cause quite a stir." He wagged his finger, grinning. "So don't you go telling that lovely young girl just to impress her."

"As if she'd believe me, even if I did."

Linis nodded, chuckling. "A valid point. And now, one final thing before you go: enjoy yourself today. It may be your last chance to have fun for a while."

"I will," he promised, before hurrying away.

He found Leanna waiting for him just outside the kitchen. Her face brightened the moment she saw him.

"I was afraid you wouldn't come," she said. Her eyes drifted to his weapons. "Are you expecting trouble?"

He held out the crook of his arm. "No, but a gentleman must be prepared to protect his lady."

"I see." She took his arm with a slight bow of her head. "Then let us hope that will not be required."

They exited the manor and walked with casual strides in the direction of the market district. Leanna asked him several questions about his home and life as a farmer, listening with far more interest than he displayed in the telling.

"It sounds like a wonderful place," she said.

He huffed a laugh. "Wonderful? Life in Sharpstone is as dull as dead grass. Nothing ever happens there."

"Excitement is overrated," she said. "We have plenty of it here. And frankly, I could do without it."

It wasn't long before Jayden felt large beads of sweat forming on his cheeks. Even the dawn hours here were hot; too late, he realized that his clothes were ill-suited for the occasion. Equally as uncomfortable was the smell of mud and fish that now seemed to cling to everything, growing ever stronger and more oppressive the nearer they drew to the markets.

The shops were already open, and the streets crowded, when they finally arrived. Jayden tried to compare it to the market in Sharpstone with only limited success. Everything here was far larger and grander. As for the variety of goods available, it seemed almost infinite in scope.

Leanna stopped at a vegetable vendor to examine a basket of ripe tomatoes. He, meanwhile, felt a touch of disappointment that he was not able to see the city wharfs from where they were currently standing. Since the war, the docks here were reputed to have surpassed even those of Althetas, supposedly holding up to five hundred ships at any given time—though he assumed this to be a bit of an exaggeration. He watched as Leanna bartered with the vendor for a time, eventually talking him down to almost half the initial asking price before giving him instructions for delivery.

"You would make a fine merchant," he commented approvingly after the deal was concluded.

Leanna cast the vendor a sour look. "He tries the same thing with me every week. And every week I end up paying the same price. I think I would go mad engaging in such stupidity on a daily basis."

"My father hates it, too," he said.

"Tell me about him... your father."

"Not much to tell," he said with a shrug. "He inherited the farm from my grandfather. He spends most of his time out of town, trading."

"And will you take over the farm one day?"

"He wants me to. But I don't think I will."

"That's a pity."

Jayden gave her a sideways look. "Why do you say that?"

"Land should be passed down. I've always felt that heritage and history are important."

It occurred to him that she had lost everything her family possessed. "I won't sell it," he told her. "But I don't want to be a farmer, either."

"So you'll have someone else care for it in your stead? Is that the plan?"

"Probably. There's time for me to decide. I have two sisters. They might want to run things."

Even as he spoke, he knew this was a ludicrous statement. The farm would always be as much theirs as it was his, but they would never want to live there again. They hated farming, possibly even more than he did. Even when they were very young, they'd never seemed particularly attached to their home. This had dismayed their father to no end. Their mother said it was their elf blood calling for them to wander.

Of course, when Jayden mentioned to her that he too would like to wander, the subject was quickly changed.

Leanna nodded. "Where are your sisters now?"

"Back home," he lied.

She gave him a strange look, but did not press the matter.

Jayden quickly turned the subject to Leanna's life in Baltria, though this was interrupted as they reached a textile merchant. As she busily examined the bolts of cloth on display, he noticed a pendant slip out from inside her bodice. At first, he couldn't tell what it was. Then it twirled on its chain and he spotted the symbol of Saraf etched on one side. Seeing what he was looking at, she smiled and tucked it back inside her clothing.

"My mother gave it to me for good luck," she said.

"Are you a..." He was unsure how to put it.

"A believer?" she said it for him. "My mother was. But then, many who live near the Abyss are. Does it bother you?"

Jayden smiled. "No. Not at all. Gerath is the patron god of my village. We have many devout followers there."

"What about you?"

He shrugged. "I was never one for religion."

"Not even the elf faith?"

"No. But don't tell my mother that. As far as she knows, I pray to the Creator every morning."

Leanna laughed. "Your secret is safe with me. I am surprised, though. The people who come here from the small villages tend to be strong in their faith. Elves in particular."

"Well, nobody's perfect."

"So true."

They continued shopping until the early afternoon. Leanna still had a few purchases left to make, but suggested that they stop to eat before moving on. They found a small café with a covered veranda and ordered a light meal of baked fish and greens. It was spicier than what Jayden was accustomed to, causing heavy beads of sweat to re-emerge.

"I'm sorry," Leanna said, grinning playfully. "I should have warned you. Chaldari Bluefish can be rather off-putting for some people."

He dabbed his face with a napkin. "It's good. Just a bit hot." He took a drink of water. "In a way, it reminds me of my mother's cooking. Of course, that's why my father hired a cook."

Leanna covered her mouth to suppress a laugh. "What a terrible thing to say."

Jayden laughed as well. "Don't get me wrong. I quite like most of her cooking. It's Father who has the problem. It's way too spicy for him. He even tried taking over for a while." He exaggerated a shudder. "Let's just say that didn't work out for anyone."

"And I don't suppose you took any interest in learning yourself?"

"I did, actually. I'm pretty good as well. Not good enough to work in a manor. But I can make a decent meal."

"If you hate farming so much, why not become a cook?"

Jayden shrugged. "No time. Besides, to get really good I'd have to go away to school. My parents wouldn't have allowed that."

"I see. Determined to keep you at home, are they?"

Jayden rolled his eyes. "You'd imagine I was made from glass. Either that, or once I'd left home, I would never come back again." He sighed. "I just want to see the world for a while, you know? I've been working the farm since I was old enough to walk. I don't think a little bit of freedom is too much to ask. Do you?"

She gave him an understanding smile. "I'm sure they just love you and worry over your safety."

"They do," he agreed. "And I think I understand their reasons. But I'm of age now. It's time they stopped trying to make my decisions for me."

"My mother used to be very much the same," she said, reaching over the table to touch his hand. "She wouldn't even allow me to go to the market alone. I've come to realize that she simply wanted to keep me safe. And even though you and I both know that's impossible, I imagine that parents simply can't help themselves." She looked into his eyes, a tiny smile on her lips. "But we grow up. And look around you. It seems to me that you *are* seeing the world."

He nodded. "Yes, I suppose I am."

He longed to tell her his true reasons for coming to Baltria; that this was not some grand adventure, or even something as mundane as accompanying Linis on a visit to see an old friend. He was not seeing the world; he was searching it. And the consequences of failure were as severe as one could imagine. They had been attacked once already, and that was unlikely to be their last such encounter.

Knowing this, he held his tongue.

They finished their meal and started back to the market so Leanna could finish her shopping. Along the way, they encountered a few small groups of elves, all of whom took particular notice of Jayden while passing. Not sensing his presence, they would immediately know him to be a new-breed. Though most regarded him impassively, Jayden could see clear disapproval on the faces of some. Leanna noticed it as well.

"I used to think them a mysterious and beautiful people," she remarked. "Sadly, I now realize that they're no better than we are."

He was about to tell her that such behavior didn't bother him when, from the corner of his eye, he caught a flash of movement. Before he could do anything to stop it, a thin figure ran past them, snatching Leanna's coin purse from her grip on the way and then darting off into the crowd.

Clutching a hand to her chest, she winced with pain. "That was everything I had," she gasped to Jayden. "Everything."

He scanned the market. After a moment, he saw the thief pushing his way toward a nearby alley. "Wait right here," he told her.

Without hanging around for a reply, he set off at full tilt after his man.

He reached the entrance to the alley just as the thief was jumping over a row of crates at the far end. His quarry was fast, but Jayden was faster. Still, the sword on his belt was making running awkward, taking away some of his advantage.

Upon reaching the end of the alley, he could see that the thief was now zig-zagging his way along the busy avenue heading east. *Keep your eyes on him*, thought Jayden. Once over the crates, he did his best not to smash into passers-by while continuing the pursuit. He might be faster, but the thief was nimble and obviously knew the city well.

He followed his quarry around the next corner and down another alley that ended in a much quieter residential street. Jayden called for the man to stop. As expected, his words went unheeded.

Gradually, he was closing the gap. Three more streets and two more alleys sent them racing down an empty avenue near the eastern wall. Jayden grinned triumphantly. His quarry was about to box himself in. This was confirmed when the thief entered yet another long alley that came to an abrupt end at the rear of a tall brick building. The man yanked on the door leading inside, but it was locked. He spun to face Jayden, breathing hard and his eyes wide.

Jayden slid to a halt, a hand resting on his sword. He, too, was breathing quite heavily, though he was in much better shape than the other man. The thief was older than he'd first thought—well into his forties, if the lines around his eyes were any guide.

"Just give me back the purse and you can go," he said. He didn't want to get mixed up with the city guard, not when he and Linis were doing their best to remain unnoticed.

Snarling viciously, the man reached to his belt and drew a small dagger.

Jayden could barely conceal his surprise. "Are you a fool?" he demanded. The ringing of steel echoed through the alley as he freed his sword from its sheath. "Don't make me kill you."

"I don't think you'll be killing me, boy," he spat back, deftly twirling the blade in his palm.

The alley was plenty wide enough to swing his weapon. Not that it mattered. Jayden remembered the lessons his mother and Linis had taught him about fighting with a dagger. Short, quick, and close. That was how it would come.

He knew he should just back down and leave. But something was growing inside him. It was that same feeling he'd had when they were being attacked on the road. It was rage; a hot fury that penetrated his very spirit. And it felt good.

"Come on then," he snarled. "Let's settle this."

The thief chuckled. "Young and stupid. Just as we hoped."

The confident look in the man's eyes took him aback. Even a skilled knife fighter should be wary of a man wielding a sword. Then the man's words struck him.

Just as we hoped.

The pain in the back of his neck felt as if someone had pierced him with a red-hot needle. He spun around to see a figure in yellow robes with a hood pulled up standing a few feet away. Raising a hand to where he had been struck, he felt a metal object protruding. Before he could even start to pull it free, the strength in his limbs vanished, and he crumpled helplessly to the ground.

"We should just kill him and be done with it," the thief said.

Jayden could feel consciousness leaving him.

"No, we were told to bring him to the temple," the robed figure replied in a feminine voice. "We must be sure."

"And the girl?"

"Leave her to me."

Leanna! A knot of fear for her safety formed in the pit of his stomach. He tried desperately to move, but found that he was now completely paralyzed. Gradually, his eyes closed and the dull thud of his heartbeat began pulsing in his ears. An instant later he had the sensation of being raised up, although oddly, he was not able to feel even the slightest touch of anyone's hands. The only thing he was still aware of was the loud scraping of his boots on the cobblestones as he was dragged along. That, and the grunts of the man hauling him.

Never before had he felt so utterly helpless—or stupid. They had laid a trap, and he'd fallen straight into it. This was the thought that continued to mock him until he could no longer hold on to consciousness.

Linis paced anxiously around the courtyard, sitting for brief periods and then popping up again, unable to remain still for more than a few seconds at a time. The sun was almost gone, and still there was no sign of Jayden. Though he had sent one of the servants out to look for him some time ago, he was keenly aware that in a city the size of Baltria, the odds of her finding him were slim.

Once again, he chastised himself for allowing the boy to go out alone. Not that there was anything to be done about it now. And the truth was, Jayden was quite capable of taking care of himself. Even if their enemies were aware of his presence, so long as he remained in public areas, nothing dangerous was likely to happen. Security in the markets was quite good. Any type of commotion, particularly one involving violence, would quickly attract the attention of the patrols.

The gate opened and the servant he was waiting for entered. Upon seeing Linis, she spread her hands and shook her head.

"I didn't see him, and the market is closing now," she said. "Many of the shops are open until quite late, though. He could have been in one of those."

He wanted to scold her for not checking this out. But that was ludicrous. It would take all night to check even a small portion of the shops in Baltria.

He forced a smile. "Thank you for trying."

She bowed her head. "My pleasure. It was nice to get out of the manor for a while. As for the young man, I wouldn't worry yourself too much. Baltria is a safe city... as cities go. He'll be along soon enough."

"I'm sure you're right," Linis replied, as convincingly as he could manage.

He continued waiting where he was for a time longer, his fears growing with each passing minute. Eventually, it was too much to bear. He was on the very point of setting off to conduct his own search of the city when he heard footsteps coming from the house. He looked across to see Leanna walking toward him. There was a concerned look on her face that sent his nerves on edge.

"Have you seen Jayden?" she asked.

Linis was astonished at her question. "Isn't he with you?" he demanded, his tone harsher than he intended.

Rapidly, she explained what had happened at the market. "When he didn't return, I thought he might have come back here. Perhaps he couldn't find me again, and this would have been a sensible place to meet up."

"Did you inform the city guard?" His heart was now pounding.

A frightened look came over her. "No. I mean... I tried to find him. And I wanted to check here first. I... I'm sorry."

Linis took a long breath. He needed to keep his wits. "Wait here," he instructed.

Racing inside the manor, he quickly retrieved his sword and dagger from his room and returned to the courtyard. Leanna was waiting, wringing her hands.

"Show me where you last saw him," Linis instructed her.

She gave a sharp nod and then led him from the courtyard toward the market district.

By now, the street lamps were lit and the passers-by were mostly those returning home from a hard day's work. Linis took note of the fact that the city guard's patrols were quite numerous—at least one every two or three corners. It seemed that Baltria was determined to keep its citizens safe from the same sort of violence that was plaguing the West.

The market was completely closed when they reached the spot where the thief had taken her purse. Leanna pointed to a nearby alley.

"Jayden chased the man down there," she explained.

Linis hurried across the square and down the alley. On reaching the end and scanning the area beyond, it soon became clear that the city was far too big for him to have any hope of figuring out their path. A thief would have been twisting and turning in all directions. There was no telling where they might have ended up. He stopped and inquired with a few of the city guards, but none had heard anything that might be of help.

When he returned, Leanna was in tears. "Do you think he's all right?" she sobbed.

Ignoring the question, he asked her, "Where is the temple of Saraf?"

"The temple? Why would you go there?"

"Just tell me where it is," he demanded.

Pulling herself together, Leanna directed him to the temple district. "It's the one nearest to the sea. You can't miss it. But I still don't understand. Why would Jayden go there?"

"I don't think he went of his own accord," he told her. "I think he was taken."

Her expression was incredulous. "You mean by someone from the temple? Why would they do that?"

In truth, Linis wasn't at all certain that this was how things had happened. Just because it was Saraf's followers who had attacked them on the road, it didn't necessarily mean the order as a whole was after them. But right now, it was the only explanation he could think of.

"You should return to the manor," he told Leanna.

"No. It's my fault he's missing. I want to help."

"You can help by waiting at the manor," Linis insisted. "You should be there in case he returns."

Grudgingly, she agreed to do as instructed.

Linis waited until she was around the next corner before starting out toward the temple district. With each step he took, the sinking feeling in his stomach was growing. Jayden might be young and impulsive, but he was not irresponsible. He would not have been lured away by drink and song. And he certainly would not have abandoned Leanna. No. Something bad had happened to him; Linis was sure of it.

The temple district had been rebuilt in a different part of the city shortly after the war ended. The old temples had been badly damaged and vandalized, so it was decided that a completely fresh start would be more advantageous than trying to restore the old buildings.

The new district was quite different. The streets were clean, and lamps lit the broad avenues and paved walkways. The marble façades were highly polished, and so too were the ubiquitous statues, the precious metals from which they were created gleaming in the lamplight. It was a far cry from the days of the Dark Knight. Worship of the gods had seen a major resurgence, and with new worshipers came new wealth. According to Gewey, it was the same in most other cities. From east to west, north to south, temples were being restored and countless new ones being built.

The men and women strolling along the promenade were all dressed in their best finery, many of them stopping occasionally in front of a temple to gaze at the artistry and beauty of its construction. A few monks and priests were about as well, huddled together in small groups and trying to look mysterious by talking in hushed tones. Linis knew differently. His keen hearing told him that there was nothing mystical or secret about their discussions. Mostly, they spoke of common events while sneaking a flask from hand to hand.

He could see the temple of Saraf just a short distance ahead, exactly where Leanna had said it would be. But a few buildings before reaching it, he suddenly stopped short. Before his astonished eyes was something he never thought to see within the walls of a human city. The building was crafted from the finest red marble, with gold veins weaving intricate patterns throughout. Proud columns spanned the front, each one of them helping to support a huge frieze that bore the ancient elf symbols depicting the gates of heaven.

It was a temple dedicated to the Creator Herself. An elf temple.

Linis had to consciously prevent himself from walking closer. It was a truly magnificent sight, more so than any he had seen. Most elf temples had been withered away by time. Either that, or they were small structures hidden well away from human eyes.

"A sight to behold, is it not?"

Linis turned to see a young elf girl standing to his right. She was clad in a human-style dress, though her hair was tied and woven in a series of braids of the elven fashion.

"Yes, it truly is," he agreed.

"My father helped build it," she stated proudly.

"He is to be congratulated."

"Did you come to worship?" she asked.

Linis smiled. "No. I'm afraid not." He noticed a slightly disappointed look on her face. "Though I would very much like to see the rest of it when I have the time."

Her expression brightened. "The doors are always unlocked," she informed him. "Not like the human temples. You can go inside anytime you wish. I can show you now, if you like."

"As tempting as it is, I have business."

Her disappointed look returned. "So few of us take time to come here. It makes me wonder why we bothered to build it in the first place."

"Don't be ridiculous. Such a place is sorely needed."

She shrugged. "Perhaps. But I see our kind entering the temples of the ten gods far more frequently than they visit here."

The ten gods.

Linis almost laughed. Darshan... he was the tenth. A thought then occurred. "Are you familiar with all the temples?" he asked.

"Somewhat. My father does work on most of them. I help from time to time when he needs me."

"What about the temple of Saraf?"

She looked as if she had just tasted something foul. "A strange lot. Since Saraf's appearance, they've become a touch fanatical. Not in a dangerous way, I suppose. But they do wander the streets preaching to everyone that the end of time is coming unless we change our lives and follow Saraf's teachings."

Linis frowned at her. "Not dangerous? That is exactly how danger takes root. Tell me, is anyone allowed entry to their temple?"

"Why would you want to go there?"

"I have my reasons."

The girl shrugged. "I think they would probably let you in. But be prepared for a sermon."

"Is there a way in that is... lesser known?"

She shook her head. "You don't want to be doing that. Breaking into a temple is a serious crime. Besides, the rear entrances are just as well guarded as those in the front."

"I see."

He considered what he should do. Incapacitating the guards was an option, though not a very good one. If he was wrong and Jayden wasn't being held there, he could easily find himself in a whole mountain of trouble. And given the urgency of what they needed to accomplish, being locked up in a prison cell was the last thing he needed.

The girl must have seen something untoward in his expression. "Has something bad happened to you?" she asked.

Linis smiled. "No. Nothing you need concern yourself about. I will just knock on the door, I suppose." He bowed to the girl. "I promise to visit your temple as soon as I can."

She bowed in return. "Lady Zarhari is the high priestess. When you arrive there, say that Feyla, daughter of Prustanis, sends her greetings. That should at least get you an audience. She is a decent enough woman."

"Thank you," Linis said. "I am in your debt."

He had heard the name Prustanis before. If it was the same person he was thinking of, he had been a significant part of the rebellion that had sought to kill Gewey and Kaylia. The elf must have had a change of heart. Or at the least, come to accept the ways of the new world.

Linis resumed walking until reaching the steps of Saraf's temple. Feyla watched him for a time, then walked slowly away with eyes downcast. If what she had told him about her father's creation was true, then it was a great pity. Elves should regularly visit such places lest they forget their history and culture. The Creator Herself needed no worship. But elf temples had typically been places of reflection and learning. It was hard to imagine his kin frequenting the temples of the gods instead.

Just a low wrought-iron fence clearly meant for decoration and not security surrounded the grounds of the temple he now faced. Four guards talking quietly amongst themselves were standing just inside. On seeing Linis approaching, a young man with a red sash stepped forward.

"Are you intent on entering?" he asked. His tone was stern, though not threatening.

Linis nodded. "I am."

"Very well. It is rather late for prayers, but someone should still be up and about."

With no more said, the guard waved him through.

Linis was amazed at how easily they let him pass. Then again, he often found it difficult to understand the new way of things. While moving through the grounds, he recalled a conversation he'd had with Gewey upon his return from a trip to Althetas.

"Ten men with hate in their hearts can feel like a thousand when they scream loud enough," he'd said. "A stranger would think the west was in the midst of civil war, when in reality it's only a handful of the ignorant causing problems."

"You can't expect things to change quite so rapidly," Linis had told him. "People are stubborn. Those of us who fought together have a different perspective. Most didn't fight; most only witnessed the carnage. They didn't form the bonds as we did."

"Or fall in love with elves," Gewey added, forcing a smile. "It's just that I had hoped things would be better. There are times when I look in the eyes of someone and see the hatred they carry, and it makes me wonder..."

"Wonder what?"

"If the Dark Knight wasn't right all along."

"Are you mad?"

Gewey laughed. "Don't misunderstand me. His solution was wrong. All the same, he could see the weakness in humans. He could see their flaws clearly."

"Yes, and he sought to slaughter them for it. The elves too." He placed a hand on Gewey's shoulder. "You may be a god, but you still think like a human. You see the goings-on of the world from the perspective of a single short lifetime. Things *are* getting better. And as the generations come and go, the world for which you have laid the foundation will become the one you are hoping for."

As he neared the temple entrance, he could still see Gewey's face in his mind—eyes doubtful, wracked with guilt and disappointment. He tested the door. As he'd expected, it was locked. He banged three times, each blow hard enough to ensure that it was clearly heard. Almost immediately there was a sharp clack of metal and the door swung slowly open, its massive weight moving soundlessly on well-oiled hinges.

A young man in a long wool nightshirt and close-cropped red hair poked his head out. "Yes. Can I help you?"

"I was hoping to speak with Lady Zarhari."

The man frowned. "It is late, and the high priestess has retired for the evening. You are free to try again in the morning." He began to shut the door, but Linis's hand shot out to stop it.

"Please. It's urgent. Could you tell her a friend of Feyla, daughter of Prustanis, is calling?"

He clearly recognized the name. After a moment, he let out a sigh. "Come on, then. I'll tell her you're here, though I doubt she'll see you."

Linis stepped through the door and into a massive gallery supported by three rows of columns. In the very center of this was a fountain of pure gold, with a prominent statue of Saraf sitting at its hub. Along the walls, he could see carved reliefs depicting various ocean creatures and monstrous storms, while at the far end stood a ceremonial altar. This was covered in offerings of fruits, silks, and a hodgepodge of trinkets left by the faithful in the hope of gaining the god's favor.

He followed the man to the far right end, where a broad archway led through to a series of halls and chambers, each of them boasting a variety of masterful artwork. The refreshing smell of salt air was everywhere, giving visitors the impression of being beside a churning sea, its spray bearing the primal yet pleasing perfume of Saraf's domain.

There were still a few people about, though they had all shed their robes in favor of nightshirts similar to the one worn by his guide. Linis took careful note that those he passed appeared somewhat uneasy, eyeing him with a hint of trepidation. Of course, it could be due to nothing more than the sight of an armed elf walking their halls in the middle of the night.

On the other hand...

He was taken to an antechamber and told to wait there in one of the available chairs. Once seated, he allowed the *flow* to course through him in order to enhance his hearing. As suspected, most of the voices he was able to make out were speaking of his unusual arrival, together with a few complaints as to the lateness of the hour.

It was not often that he used the *flow* these days. When he and Dina first arrived in Sharpstone, Kaylia had given him instruction on how to increase his abilities. But it began to feel rather pointless after a year or so. He rarely hunted, and his fight on the road to Baltria had been the first time since the war that he had drawn blood. There was an uncomfortable truth to face: calling himself a seeker was no longer accurate. He was a farmer. How many times would he need to remind himself of this before his heart finally accepted it? Once, he had been feared and respected by countless elves. Now he was just another member of the community trudging his way through life. He shook his head, scolding himself yet again.

You have been around humans too much, he thought. *Childish pride and the need for fame is not worthy of...*

Not worthy of a seeker. That's what he'd been about to think.

He grunted sourly. Why did this feeling continue to plague him? He was happy. And in Sharpstone he had friends, peace, and most important of all, the woman he loved. He did not miss the conflict and danger. Nor did he miss constantly evading death at the hands of his foes. He could say those things and feel totally secure in his own honesty.

Then what was it? What was wrong with him?

A door opened and a woman in a long blue cotton robe and silk slippers stepped out. At once, he was on his feet as a sense of the familiar washed over him. She was an elf. The high priestess of Saraf—an elf! Her dark hair and copper complexion reminded him of Kaylia, as did her confident strides and intense gaze.

"You are surprised?" she asked, her face expressionless and her posture rigid.

"Indeed," he admitted. "Please forgive me." He bowed. "My name is Linis."

She raised an eyebrow. "Truly? The seeker? Then I am surprised as well. And most pleased to meet an elf of such renown. Your exploits are well known."

He smiled. "That was a long time ago. I live a simple life now."

"Is that so? No more chasing around the wilderness? How sad." She turned to the door. "Come. Join me for a drink, and you can state your business."

Without thinking, he simply followed, transfixed by her fluid, confident movements. They made their way down a short corridor, then turned into a comfortable parlor where a set of chairs and a plush sofa had been placed in front of a welcoming fire. An elegant desk stood at the far end of the room, along with several bookcases and cabinets that were unmistakably elf-made. After offering him a seat, she poured them both a cup of wine.

Her expression softened as she sat down across from him. "Now, what is it I can do for you? Jerrod tells me you know Feyla."

Linis had almost forgotten the urgency of his visit. It now came back to him with a rush. "Not exactly," he said. "I just happened to meet her shortly before coming here. She suggested that I use her name to gain an audience."

She took a small sip of wine. "That being the case, I take it your need is great. Seekers are not known for subterfuge."

Linis realized that he had no idea how to broach the subject. He took a long drink, then placed his cup on the side table. "A dear friend of mine is missing."

"That is indeed urgent. But why come here? Why not report the matter to the city guard?"

He thought for several moments, choosing his words carefully before speaking. "I have reason to believe it may have been followers of Saraf who are responsible. I was hoping you could help me divine the truth."

Lady Zarhari cocked her head. "Why would my people do anything to your friend?"

"So you have heard nothing of it?"

She laughed softly. "Of course not. We are not brigands. All the same, I am curious as to why you would think otherwise."

Linis hesitated, but something in her eyes made him want to tell her the truth. "While on the road, we were set upon by men claiming to be followers of Saraf."

She breathed a heavy sigh. "Sadly, you are not the first person to make this claim. Nor are we the only temple suffering from such outrageous lies. There are those who do not like seeing the restoration of the temples, and they will do anything to discredit us. However, until now I have not heard reports of anything so disturbing as abduction. I am sorry, but I fear you have been deceived."

Linis rubbed his chin. The men they encountered had not been false. Of that, he was sure. Even if *this* temple had no hand in the matter, their attackers had still been followers of Saraf.

"I can see you doubt me," she added. "Why don't you tell me more about what happened? Perhaps I can help you figure out this puzzle... and find your friend."

"I wish I could. But there are things I am not free to discuss."

"Then I do not see how I can be of help."

A strange sensation came over Linis. It was as if something was tugging ever so gently yet insistently at his spirit. He wanted to tell her... tell her everything. Only by the slightest of margins did he manage to hold firm.

"Can I ask you a question, my lady?" he eventually said.

She smiled. "Allow me to guess. You want to know how an elf became a High Priestess of Saraf. Is that correct?"

Linis averted his eyes, embarrassed for asking so personal a question. "Yes. Obviously, you do not have to answer if—"

"I do not mind at all," she cut in. "My ascension to this position was quite recent, actually. As to my reasons for being here, they are not complicated. I truly believe in Saraf and his aspirations for this world. Though I still believe in the Creator, there is nothing in our teachings that forbids me from serving the gods. There is a practical aspect as well. Sadly, the Creator does not let Her will be known to us. The gods do."

"Were you amongst those who witnessed Saraf's appearance at the docks?" Linis asked.

"I was there, yes."

He was having trouble understanding her choices. She was correct in saying that there was nothing strictly forbidding her from serving Saraf. And he supposed it was unavoidable that some elves would choose to worship alongside their human neighbors. He had seen some humans abandon the gods in favor of elf beliefs, so why should it not work both ways? All the same, it did not feel right to him.

He finished his wine and rose to his feet. "I'm afraid I have wasted your time, my lady."

"Not at all," she replied. She stood and glided over to the door. "But before you go, there is something I would like you to see."

"I'm sorry, my lady. I must be going. My friend needs me."

She gave him a disappointed frown. "Can you not spare me one minute? It would mean a great deal to me if you could see the reason why I am here. I can tell that you disapprove."

"No, not at all," he replied.

Lady Zarhari smiled warmly. "It's all right. I understand. I can imagine it being difficult for one like you to bear witness to the changing of the world. A seeker is an elf in its purest form. That is what my father always told me when I was a child."

Linis was a little shocked. Was she right? Was he harboring suppressed feelings of resentment? He didn't want to believe this, but there was something in her voice... something compelling that made her words seem honest and good.

As he followed her from the room, he realized that he felt a sense of comfort every time he looked at her. "Where are you from?" he asked.

"The village of Bylanta," she replied.

"I have been there many times. Though not in years."

"Yes. I remember seeing you there when I was a young woman. You and your seekers dealt with a band of human thieves who had raided one of our grain stores."

Linis recalled the event clearly. Shamefully so. The humans were on the brink of starvation and had come across the store by sheer chance. "I regret what happened that day," he admitted.

"Do you? Why is that?"

"They meant us no harm. We had recovered what they had stolen, and yet still we..." His voice trailed off.

"You killed them all. I know. And now you wish you hadn't."

"They were defenseless. But things were different in those days. Just being a human on elf lands was enough to warrant death."

She gave him a sympathetic smile over her shoulder. "It wasn't your fault. As you say, times were different. So, I am sure, were you. The way I remember it, you were considered a hero. We were close to starvation ourselves that winter. Every sack of grain made a difference."

Linis sighed. "I try not to remember what I was like back then. My mind was closed and my heart filled with hatred."

"You should not think like that," she told him. "You did what you thought was right. And at the time, it was. The humans you killed would have no doubt done the same to you, given the chance. Don't forget, the hatred was felt on both sides."

"And still is," he said. "Yet here we both are, among them, and unharmed. Could this have happened back then? At the time, I felt no guilt at all, only that I had acted rightly. Instead of mercy, I distributed what I thought to be justice."

"But is there not virtue in justice?"

"Yes. But now I realize there is more virtue in mercy. It's hard to imagine someone wise enough to dispense both measures." He paused. "You are a high priestess who is required to enforce the laws of your temple. Do you not find such responsibility daunting?"

Lowering her head slightly, she let out a soft sigh. "I do. At times it is difficult to know what is right and wrong. Not even the guidelines of temple law are enough to deal with every situation. All I can do is trust that, when I act, I do so with righteousness of intent."

Linis nodded. "I acted in such a way, too. Though knowing that does little to salve the regret I feel for lacking the wisdom I have learned since the war."

"And what wisdom is that precisely?"

For a moment, he pictured the faces of those he had fought alongside, humans and elves alike, struggling for a common goal. "I learned that despite our differences, we must all co-exist in this world. Our isolation bred ignorance. And ignorance, in turn, breeds hatred. The humans are neither evil nor weak. Nor are they completely good and kind. In that, we share a bond. We breathe the same air, are sustained by the same food, and all live the short lives of mortal beings." He paused. "Let me ask you something. Before the war, am I right in assuming you would have killed a human without remorse?"

Zarhari nodded. "As would anyone in my village."

"If you had run across a human child, what would you have done? Would you have killed it as well?"

She stopped abruptly and spun around to face him, her face twisted in a look of revulsion. "Of course not. I am not a beast. How could you even suggest it?"

Linis held up his hands. "Please. Do not misunderstand me. I was not expecting you to say yes. But the truth lies within the question. You would have spared a human child. Yet if you were to see that same child years later, you would have killed without hesitation. Why? Would it not be the same person? What could years add that should condemn someone to death?"

"A child has not yet learned to hate and kill," she pointed out.

"Precisely."

He recalled sparing Dina's mother, with the baby who would one day grow into the woman he loved wrapped in her arms. "I realized that the humans I hated and feared were no different from us. They are the children of the Creator, as is every being, mortal or immortal. It was our failing that corrupted this purity. We spent hundreds of years fighting their hate with more hate. And what did it get us? It wasn't until we were forced to set those feelings aside that the light of truth finally shone upon us."

She eyed him briefly, then continued walking. "It's not that I disagree with you. But there is still hatred in the world, is there not?"

"We are two flawed races, doing our best to shed centuries of mistrust. Though this is not happening quickly, it will come about eventually."

"And what of the newbreeds?"

"What of them?"

"Do you not fear for the elves?"

"No more than I fear for the humans. They are the product of love. How could that be a bad thing?"

She cast a glance over her shoulder. "Do you know any?"

"I am wed to a newbreed," he replied evenly.

"I suppose that should shock me," she said. "But after hearing your words, it doesn't. I would suspect that your wife may be among the very eldest of her kind. Those I have met are mere children. Tell me, did she take on the characteristics of a human or an elf?"

"She is human in appearance," he explained. "She is in her fifties, yet she looks like a human female in her early twenties."

"I see. And do you find her attractive?"

"Very much so, both in body and spirit. In her, I see what is best in both races."

On hearing this, Zarhari was quiet for a time, her head remaining slightly bowed as they continued winding their way through several long corridors and down two flights of stairs. On nearing a thick oaken door, she stopped to face him.

"Please leave your weapons here," she said.

Linis hesitated. "Where are you taking me?"

"To the temple prison. There are no weapons permitted." She cracked a smile. "There are some rules even *I* must follow."

Linis removed his sword and dagger and placed them on the floor beside the entrance. He drew in the *flow*. He could hear movement on the other side of the door, but nothing definable.

"Why would you have a prison here?" he asked.

"We are the largest temple outside of Althetas," Zarhari explained. "Believe me, I wish it were otherwise. The temple of the Creator has a prison as well. To the best of my knowledge, all but the temple of Darshan have one."

"How many people are you holding?"

"Three, at present." She produced a heavy iron key from the pocket of her robe. "Our temple has no death penalty, and we do not believe in permanent captivity. So those who find themselves here only have a short stay. We have a monastery in the Eastlands where they can live out their sentences while reflecting on their crimes."

The lock opened with a deep clunk, allowing the door to swing wide on tired hinges. Linis knew that each temple, though similar to the others in its basic nature, had specific beliefs and laws unique to the gods it worshiped. Though not a student of this, he was aware of Saraf's aversion to captivity. Because of this, his followers believed people should be free, regardless of their crimes. They did not lock people away in tiny cells for long periods, so having a monastery such as she had described made sense.

The interior beyond was as stark as one might expect, though not moldy and dank like the other prisons he had seen. The walls were lined on either side with iron-plated doors, each with a tiny barred window and a narrow slot through which food could be passed. At the rear stood a narrow archway, the light from a flame flickering within.

After closing and locking the door, Zarhari pointed to the archway.

"Please," she said, waiting until Linis complied before following him.

The hairs on the back of his neck started to prickle. He felt oddly exposed and was keenly aware that Zarhari was drawing in a significant amount of the *flow*. Of course, there could be many reasons for that. He was doing the same, and surely she sensed it. Her abilities were clearly far beyond his own.

Past the archway stood a tall, broad-shouldered man clad in a leather tunic and dirty cotton trousers. The light from a single torch nearby barely illuminated his scarred and pitted features. Linis could just make out another figure sprawled and chained against the wall behind him.

"What is this?" he demanded.

The man stepped to his left, and Linis instantly recognized Jayden. He was unconscious and bore several dark bruises on his face. His shirt had been ripped open, revealing a chest that was covered in blood.

Linis felt a sudden surge in the *flow*. Before he could react to this, a blast of hot air slammed into his back, lifting him from his feet and flinging him into the wall just beside Jayden. Badly stunned, he slid to the floor. The man stepped farther away, his expression a stone mask. Zarhari, however, now had vicious intent written on her face. Twin balls of flame hovered just above her outreached hands.

"Make one move and I'll roast your friend," she snarled.

Linis's head was swimming from the impact. It also felt as if several of his ribs were cracked, possibly even broken. "What have you done to him?" he groaned.

Her top lip curled. "Nothing from which he cannot recover. Just a few questions. And now we have some for you as well."

Though his brain was scrambled, Linis rapidly tried to assess the situation. He could most likely defend himself against the flames for a short while. His skills in the *flow* might not be a match for Zarhari's, but he could possibly keep himself unharmed long enough to reach her. On the other hand, if she carried out her threat to loose an attack on Jayden, there would be little he could do to prevent it—not in time.

"Why are you doing this?" he demanded.

She sniffed with contempt. "You serve Darshan and protect his offspring, and you dare to ask this?"

"Jayden has done you no harm," Linis responded, his eyes darting around the room. There was nothing he could use for a weapon.

"Perhaps not. But he will in time." She flicked a hand. "Enough talk. You will allow Varn to confine you, or I will end the boy's life here and now."

The flames intensified, punctuating the threat. Linis struggled to his feet, the pain in his ribs biting almost as spitefully as the knowledge that he had walked directly into a trap. One that he had known full well might exist. How could he have been so foolish as to let this happen?

Varn took a cautious step forward. Linis glared at him for a moment before lowering his head and nodding his surrender.

He was pressed against the wall where a second set of shackles hung from chains. These were used to fasten his hands.

Satisfied that he was secure, Zarhari banished the flames and released her hold on the *flow*. "I do regret that this is necessary," she said. "It truly pains me to see you in this predicament. Unfortunately, it cannot be helped."

Linis spat on the ground. "Ask your questions and be done with it."

"Do not hate me, seeker," she said, a strange kindness in her tone. "Hate the one who has forced us to this course. Hate Darshan, the deceiver."

Fear pierced Linis like a blade. "What does Darshan have to do with this?"

"Not a particularly talented liar," she remarked with mild amusement. "That should make what we have to do much easier."

"Should I begin, my lady?" Varn asked, lisping as spittle dripped from his bottom lip.

She held up a hand. "I don't think your services will be needed for a while, Varn. You may return to your quarters for now."

Bowing awkwardly, the man lumbered out. Linis tried to see the extent of Jayden's injuries. At a glance, they didn't look serious.

Zarhari noticed what he was doing. "As I told you, his wounds are not life-threatening," she assured him. "For now, he sleeps courtesy of some jawa's tea. I was surprised it affected him so dramatically. His mother is an elf, is she not?"

"He's half human."

She crossed over to Jayden and lifted his chin. "No, he is not," she declared after a brief examination. "There is nothing human about him."

"Whatever it is you think you know—"

"You mean that he is the son of Darshan?" she said, cutting Linis short. "Do not bother with feeble denials. Saraf himself has told us who this boy is... and what he will do one day if allowed to continue. But now that Darshan is gone, there is hope."

A second stab of fear pierced him, this one even more severe than before. "What do you mean, *gone*?"

Zarhari gave him a sideways smile. "I mean, he is now no longer able to continue spreading his lies." Stepping away from Jayden, she stood in front of Linis. "And it is this matter that we need to speak about. I need to know what you have learned. More importantly, who else is involved."

Linis frowned. "What are you talking about? Involved in what?"

Her anger surfaced for a moment. But it was brief, and she quickly regained her calm bearing. "It is no accident that you have come to Baltria looking for Darshan. Someone must have told you. Who was it? Ayliazarah? Dantenos?" She flicked her hand at Jayden. "This one would not tell us."

"Are you mad? You think we speak with the gods?"

"You deny it?"

"Of course I do. Whatever you have been told, it is a lie. I came to Baltria seeking the aid of an old friend. Jayden's mother is ill, and we hoped he could help to save her."

"Ah, yes. The legendary Kaylia, wife of Darshan."

Hearing her speak Kaylia's name sent a chill racing down Linis's spine. How much more did she know of their quest? And why would she think the gods might have led him to this temple?

"You know," Zarhari continued. "I almost didn't believe it when I was told that Darshan had joined with an elf. The gods tend to take on human forms. Kaylia must be fair beyond imagining to have attracted so powerful a being to her bedchamber."

Just as she finished speaking, Jayden stirred but did not open his eyes. Zarhari looked upon him with clear revulsion.

"And *this* is the result of their union—a demon come to destroy us all."

Linis shook his head emphatically. "No! You are wrong. Jayden is nothing more than a simple farmer. You have no reason to hold him... or me."

Turning her back, she took a long breath. "You will not be here for long, I assure you. As you already know, we do not believe in captivity. Unfortunately for you, not all temples are as disinclined to the idea."

Linis was about to respond to this when the sound of bells and laughter filled the room. Tiny pinpricks of light appeared and began dancing around in the air as if caught on a playful spring breeze. He recognized what it was at once: the *flow of the spirit*. Somehow, Zarhari had learned how to harness it.

"You will not force me to surrender my will," he told her.

She turned to face him again, her expression sorrowful. "You are strong, seeker. But even you are not *that* strong. You will tell me what I want to know. Unlike the son of Darshan, this is a power you cannot resist. Just know that it pains me deeply to this power against you. You were noble and strong... once. A true hero of the elves."

Linis glared furiously. She was right. Of all the aspects of the *flow*, this was by far the most potent. The Reborn King had used it to enslave the spirits of his followers. With it, he had very nearly conquered the entire world. Gewey had made use of its power as well, but only with great caution and hesitance.

The lights moved in to surround him, popping and sizzling as the laughter intensified. Linis could feel a wave of peace saturating his spirit, imploring him to relax and accept what was happening. Bit by bit he could feel his will failing. He wanted to obey—to please. Yes. She was right... right about everything.

"Leave him alone," croaked a weak voice.

Jayden? Linis tried to turn his head in the boy's direction to see if he was awake, but his eyes were totally captured by the lights.

"I said, leave him alone!" This time, Jayden's voice roared. It was a command that demanded obedience.

The laughter instantly diminished, and the lights dimmed.

"So you *do* have some of your mother in you," Zarhari remarked. "I knew I should have given you more of that tea."

Linis struggled to tear his focus away from the fading lights. His will was gradually returning.

"I've already told you that I don't know where my father is," Jayden said, his voice now back to a normal level. It was as if the previous roar of authority had never happened.

"And I told you that I do not doubt your word," she replied. "I am truly sorry for what has to be done. But you are far too dangerous to be permitted to live among us." She glanced over to Linis and shook her head. "You cannot imagine how my heart is aching."

"Then let us go in peace," Jayden implored. "Or at least allow Linis to go free. I'm the one you want."

"If I could, I would," she said. "He was once an elf of great respect and worth. Now, he serves Darshan. For that, he must pay the price."

Jayden leaned forward as far as his chains would allow. "I don't understand. What has my father done that is so terrible? Did he not defeat the Reborn King and save the elves?"

"It is not what he did during the war," she said. "It is what he did after the fighting ceased that we cannot allow."

"What did he do? You keep hinting that he's done some terrible thing, yet you won't tell me what it is."

She stepped forward and placed her hand on his cheek. "You truly have no idea, do you? They never told you anything. Not even who you really are."

Jayden recoiled at her touch. "I know who I am."

"And who is that?"

"I am Jayden Stedding, son of Gewey Stedding. Nothing more. Whatever else you think I am, you are wrong. Even if my father is who you say, I've never known him as Darshan."

"He's telling you the truth," Linis added, though he was still recovering from the lights, and his voice could barely rise above a whisper. "You have no quarrel with him. Let him go home. I'm the one who knew—I've known since the war. If anyone is guilty, it is I."

She raised an eyebrow. "I am impressed by your strength, seeker. Even the briefest contact with the *flow of the spirit* should have broken your will." She flicked her wrist. "Little matter. Soon, the son of Darshan will not be here to interfere."

Only then, as her final few words sank in, did Linis realize that it was Jayden who had broken her hold on the *flow*. But how? Without any form of training, it seemed unlikely to have been a calculated act. It must have been purely from instinct.

"If you are going to kill me, then just get it over with," Jayden told her.

She shook her head. "I have never personally drawn blood. Nor do I intend to start now. Vern will be along shortly to deal with you." Backing away, she crossed over to the door. "Then, seeker," she said ominously before passing through, "we will be able to continue our conversation unhindered."

No matter how much Linis tried to draw in the *flow*, he found that he could not hold it for more than a few seconds before waves of euphoria broke his concentration. Looking across, he saw Jayden was struggling against his shackles, though to no effect.

"How did you find me?" Jayden asked as soon as they were alone.

Linis shut his eyes, trying to force away Zarhari's influence. After a few seconds, he replied, "I took a gamble. Seeing that it was Saraf's followers who attacked us, I thought they might bring you here."

"And you just walked straight in through the front door?"

Linis gave him an embarrassed look. "I know. And to think I accused you of recklessness. She was very convincing, though."

He could see the displeased look on Jayden's face. In that moment, the boy looked older, and in some ways harder—almost like a soldier who had seen too many battles. Why did Zarhari fear him so? It could not be merely his heritage.

Half-men had been around for thousands of years. Why was Jayden different?

"I think I can get free," he told Linis, as he persisted with his struggle. "But it will take some time."

"I doubt we have much of that to spare," he responded. "I'm sorry for this. I should have been with you."

"It's not your fault. Besides, we're not dead yet."

Not yet, Linis thought. But they soon would be. His stupidity had doomed them both. How had his mind become so addled? There was a time when it would have been impossible to lure him into such an obvious trap. His mind turned to Dina. His dear wife would never know what had become of him.

Jayden's voice brought him back into the moment. "What was she doing to you?" he asked.

"She was using the *flow of the spirit* to break my will."

"It was terrible. I could see it swarming around you like angry bees."

"How did you make it stop?"

"I don't know. I just shouted out, and it was like I frightened them away."

The sound of alarmed voices from outside snatched their attention. This was followed by fearful shouts and the clanging of steel. Only a few moments later, the door flew open and Zarhari came running in. Her eyes were wide as she slid to a halt just in front of Jayden.

"Curse you for making me do this," she said, her voice quavering. She raised her hands, pointing them at his bare chest.

"No!" shouted Linis. "Please!"

Tears were pouring down her cheeks. "I have no choice. They have come for him. I cannot allow him to be taken." A fist-sized ball of fire appeared just above her palms. "Please, Saraf, forgive me."

Linis thrashed wildly against the chains, but they held fast. The flame shot forth, striking Jayden with a sharp pop. He cried out as the fire ate into his flesh.

"Zarhari!" called a voice from outside.

Ignoring this, she launched another, much more powerful attack at her helpless victim. This time, though, before it could reach its target, a rush of air shoved the blazing ball aside and sent it crashing into the wall just off to Jayden's left. The flames exploded, peppering his face and chest with tiny flares. Zarhari spun, eyes wide.

"Enough!" cried a female voice. "Don't make me hurt you."

"Witch!" she shouted back. "You dare to enter this holy place?"

A second blast of air rushed through the door, sending Zarhari flying hard against the wall. Linis could hear the elf snarling with fury as she countered with a fireball. It was to no avail. This was merely pushed aside and puffed out of existence. A streak of lightning then flashed, hitting her in the left shoulder. She slid to the floor, badly dazed. Another bolt struck her, this time centrally in the chest, leaving a coin-sized burn mark in her robes.

"Bring them," said the voice. "Hurry, before she regains her wits."

Two men clad in leather armor entered, black scarves covering their faces. One of them searched Zarhari until he found a ring of keys. Linis and Jayden were quickly unshackled.

Linis waved off the man. "I can stand. Help Jayden."

The boy was covered in burns and trembling violently. Only with his arm around the man's shoulder for assistance was he able to hobble from the room. They passed several bodies of dead monks along the way, but other than that, the halls were empty. Whoever the female voice belonged to, she was already gone.

Outside, a dozen armed men were waiting. The temple guards, looking battered and furious, had been overcome and were tied up alongside the gate. Beyond this, a carriage with darkened windows awaited. No sooner had Linis and Jayden been bundled inside than the driver snapped the reins and they were speeding away.

Linis could see the silhouette of a woman sitting directly across from them.

"My friend is hurt," he said. "Can you help him?"

Jayden was shivering and groaning from the pain of his burns. "I... I'll be fine," he whispered. He lifted his head to gaze at the woman. "Who are you?"

"Do you not recognize me?" She leaned forward, allowing a thin ray of light from the gap in the shade covering the window to reveal her features.

"Maybell?" he gasped.

Linis looked at her in equal astonishment. Though barely in her teens, she had the bearing and voice of a grown woman. He could feel the *flow* raging through her as she stretched out and placed a hand on her brother's leg. Jayden gasped softly, then gradually closed his eyes.

"I will heal him when we get back to the temple," she told Linis. "But I fear it will take the combined strength of both me and my sister to fully undo Zarhari's damage to you."

"Damage?"

"The inexperienced should never use the *flow of the spirit*," she said angrily. "They have no control. I'm surprised she did not harm you more than she did."

"Jayden stopped her," he explained.

"Is that right? It's lucky for you he did; otherwise, you would have been permanently cut off from the *flow*. And the Creator only knows what that would have done to your mind."

"How did you know where to find us?" Linis asked.

She placed a hand on his leg, as she had done with Jayden. A rush of warmth instantly passed through him. "Questions can wait," she said. "Rest for now."

Linis tried to remain conscious, but resistance was useless. Within seconds, he was pulled down into a deep and peaceful slumber.

CHAPTER 7

Jayden heard soft whispers hissing like the wind through tall reeds. He tried to concentrate on the words being spoken, but they blended together in an incoherent cacophony of sound that echoed as if coming from within a great cavern.

He opened his eyes. With only a single flickering candle placed on a table beside him, there was nowhere near enough of the dim light to see clearly. What little he could make out were the shadows of furnishings within the small chamber and a half-open door. This was from where the whispers were coming.

"Is anyone there?" he called out.

Movement in the corner of the room caught his attention. "You're awake already?"

He instantly recognized Maybell's voice. He touched his face and chest. No pain; the burns had been healed. "Where am I?" he asked. "Where's Penelope?"

"You're in the temple of Amon Dahl. And our sister is resting. Tending to Linis has drained us both. I was sleeping myself until a few minutes ago."

Jayden sat up. "How did you find us?"

"That, dear brother, is a matter we will discuss once we are all together."

Maybell rose and crossed over to the opposite corner. A moment later, a lantern revealed what had been hidden in darkness.

Jayden could not believe what he was seeing. The spindly little girl he had known was no more. Before him, though in years only fourteen, stood a grown woman. She had the auburn curls and dark complexion of their mother, but her face and eyes were definitely from their father. She was wearing a long cotton nightgown, and her hair was tied into a loose ponytail.

"By the gods, you've grown," he said.

She took a seat on the edge of the bed. "As have you. It seems being strong in the *flow* causes maturity to take an early hold. At least, that is what we think."

He continued to gaze at her. She still looked like his sister: the features and smile were the same. Yet there was something else. As if she had aged not only on the outside but in her spirit as well. "Thank you for healing me," he said. "I didn't know you could do that."

Her laugh was barely audible. "Why would you? You've been kept away from us for so long. These days, we hardly know one another."

"I wanted to come. It was Mother who stopped me. She wouldn't allow it."

"I know. She was protecting you... and us."

"She's ill," he said. "And Father is missing."

"We know that too. Much is happening that will seem confusing to you. But don't worry, I promise you will be told everything very soon."

Hearing the fatigue in her voice, he slid over to make room. "Come. Lie down beside me. Like when you were a child during a thunderstorm. Remember?"

She gave him a fragile smile. "How could I forget? Penelope used to tease me so much about it." She snuggled in next to him.

Jayden wrapped an arm around her shoulders. He had often wondered what his reaction would be upon seeing his sisters again, and Maybell in particular. He had always been closer to her than he had been to Penelope. He had expected a joyous rush of emotion, but that was not how their reunion was turning out. Instead, it felt oddly comforting to have her with him again. It was rather like the blanket that now covered them... warm and familiar.

"Penelope was jealous, I think," Jayden said. "Though she would never admit it, she wanted to be the one that you ran to when you were afraid."

"I used to think you didn't like it when I came to you." Her voice was becoming drowsy.

"I pretended to be irritated. But to be honest, it made me proud that you came to me instead of Father."

"Father scared me. You didn't."

Jayden was surprised to hear this. Their father was many things, but intimidating had never been one of them. He was about to ask Maybell what she meant, but could already hear the deep steady breathing of slumber. She must have been utterly exhausted, he realized. This was hardly surprising. From what he understood, healing was physically demanding, and his burns had been quite severe. Then there was also whatever the two of them had done to help poor Linis.

He recalled the nights Maybell used to come running into his room, her hair in a wild tangle and her tiny hands trembling as she leaped into his bed and curled up beside him.

"It's just lightning," he would tell her. "It won't hurt you."

"I know," she said.

"If you know, what are you doing in here?"

"I can't sleep," she replied unconvincingly. "Penelope snores."

And just like now, she would be asleep before he could say another word.

The day the two of them departed for Baltria, he had found her hiding in the barn beneath a pile of hay. Up until that moment, she had not given any sign whatsoever that she was afraid of leaving. But right at that moment, as he pulled the hay aside, she'd looked terrified. Jayden had sat with her in silence for more than twenty minutes, allowing her to lay her head on his shoulder while she softly cried. Then, as if the last of her sorrow had spilled out along with the final tear, she suddenly jumped up and ran back into the house without saying a word.

That was the last time it had been just the two of them. Since then they had corresponded frequently, though her letters were always distant in tone and without any of the emotional content he expected. Penelope had hardly written to him at all. She wrote almost exclusively to their mother or Dina.

As Jayden felt himself on the edge of sleep, an image of his mother lying in her bed snuck into his mind, threatening to snatch him fully awake again. She was still alive. That much was certain, although how he knew this was a mystery. With a rush of awareness, he also knew that he was the only one who could do anything to help her. Something—or someone—was guiding him, urging him on. Was it the gods? Or was it all in his mind?

He focused on his breathing, shutting out all else. There was nothing to do now apart from wait, and hope that the answers he needed could be found here. But then, as sleep closed in once more, he thought he could hear a faraway voice calling to him and telling him differently.

You must leave, it insisted.

Of course, dreams at the edge of sleep were often strange and misleading. He doubted that he would even remember this one in the morning.

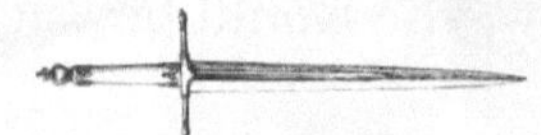

Light poured in through an open window, and with it came the scent of honeysuckle and lilac. Jayden knew straight away that Maybell was gone. He smiled. Even as a girl she was always back in her own bed before he woke, pretending she had not come running in to him afraid of the storm. For some reason, he found it reassuring that this had not changed.

He sat up and stretched, his joints cracking in protest and his neck a little bit stiff from the too-soft pillow. The room was exactly how he expected it to be, relatively plain yet still cozy. The furnishings were obviously imported from the East—well-built pieces made from the hardwoods of the region that, although inexpensive when compared with those crafted in the west, were indisputably sturdier and longer lasting. His clothes had been folded neatly on the foot of the bed, along with the sword Linis had given him. These must have been retrieved on their way out of the temple, he realized.

Sliding from the bed, he reached for his clothes. Though they were torn and riddled with burn holes, he had nothing else to wear. He caught a powerful whiff of his body odor while pulling the shirt over his head. A shower or a bath would have been nice. He had just put on his trousers when there came a soft knock at the door.

A young man bearing a tray of porridge and fruits entered. He looked at Jayden with a puzzled expression.

"Would you not like something less ragged to wear, my lord?" he asked, placing the food on a nearby table.

"Please, call me Jayden. And yes, I would dearly like something else. But this is all I have."

The man chuckled. "This must be your first time with us. My apologies. I assumed that being the brother of Lady Penelope and Lady Maybell, you would have been here before."

He crossed to the far corner of the room and touched a small indentation. With a soft clunk, a hidden door opened outward.

"Many of our rooms are like this," he explained, smiling at Jayden's surprise. "Should the temple ever find itself under siege, we have made sure there are places to hide. You'll learn to detect them after you've been here for a while."

Looking inside, to Jayden's great pleasure, he could see both a shower and a well-stocked wardrobe. "You fear attack?" he asked.

"It's always a possibility. I think that the siege of Valshara was what prompted this measure. Many of the Amon Dahl who died then were caught without a way to escape."

Jayden had not heard of this particular story, but decided not to ask for a telling. After nodding a courteous thank you to the departing servant, he began removing his old clothing once again. The water in the shower was not exactly hot, though warm enough to be soothing. And he was pleased to find a set of fresh clothing in the wardrobe that fit him nicely.

The porridge was cold by the time he returned to the bedroom. Not that it mattered; he was famished. In fact, it wasn't until taking the first mouthful that he realized to what extent. Once finished, he leaned back in his chair and took a long, cleansing breath.

"Feeling better now?"

The unexpected voice made Jayden start. A broadly smiling Linis was standing in the doorway, a glass of what looked like some sort of juice in his hand.

"I feel fine. What about you?"

Linis moved inside to join him and took a long drink. "Never better, thanks to your sisters."

"What was wrong with you?"

The elf's eyes grew dark. "Zarhari used the *flow of the spirit* on me. And clumsily, to be sure. Had you not intervened,

I fear I would have ended up much like Malstisos: weak and sick."

"To be honest, I have no idea how I managed it."

"You have your father in you, my lad. It took him time to learn his powers as well. But it will come."

"Maybe. But do I want it to?"

Linis laughed. "Your father asked the very same thing."

"Too bad he's not here to teach me... or to tell me the truth." Something about being compared to his father bothered Jayden.

"I wish I knew why he and Kaylia chose to keep things from you," Linis said. "All I know for sure is that they only acted out of love."

"Knowing that doesn't help."

"It should. You've lived a good life until now, surrounded by people who love you. I know this is a confusing time, but please remember one thing. Of all the people in this world that you should have reason to hold ill will against, your father is not one of them."

Jayden sighed. "The thing is, I'm not confused. I know what the stakes are, and I know what I need to do. I guess I should be afraid, but I'm not. Instead, I'm..."

He lowered his eyes, shaking his head.

"You're what?" Linis pressed.

"Angry. Not just at my parents. At everything. It's like I have this rage building inside me that I can't control."

"It is said that the emotions of the gods are a tempest—that they feel everything tenfold. This is true of your father. Perhaps *that* is what you are feeling now?"

Jayden shrugged. "You may be right. I just hope I can get it under control before I do something stupid."

"You mean like running off alone after a thief in a crowded city when there are people who are trying to kill you, perhaps?"

This brought a smile to his face. "Yes. Like that, I suppose."

Linis pushed back his chair. "Come. Your sisters are anxious to see you."

Jayden rose and followed him from the room. "Have you spoken to Penelope and Maybell yet?" he asked.

"Only briefly. They wanted you to be present before any serious talk took place."

They set off through a series of broad corridors and chambers. The people they passed along the way, roughly an equal mixture of elf and human, took little interest in them. Their dress was casual and represented styles from nearly every part of the world. Many were engrossed in reading some tome or scroll, while others gathered in small groups to engage in intense conversation. Jayden already knew from Maybell's letters that many kinds of learning took place here, not just the study of the *flow* and its mysteries. Countless scholarly works that had been transcribed, both elf and human, had been brought to the temple for safe storage. In one of her letters, she'd told him how people from every corner of the world came to study and conduct research. She even described experiments based on texts found in the libraries of Angrääl concerning machines and powders of enormous destructive power. He hoped to see some of them while he was here.

The interior was clean and well maintained, though the décor was sparse and leaned much in favor of function over fashion. The few paintings and tapestries depicted scenes of the natural world—no gods or heroes like those one would likely see in a temple dedicated to one of the gods.

They finally arrived at a narrow wooden door with a series of interwoven brass rings fastened upon it. Linis knocked, and a moment later Penelope opened it to greet them. Completely ignoring Linis, she pushed her way past him and threw her arms around her brother.

Jayden was a little taken aback. He had never known Penelope to be overly affectionate. Her raven hair was tied back, and her delicate features, like those of her sister, looked far more mature than they should have.

"I am so happy you are here," she told him. "When we heard what had happened, I feared we wouldn't reach you in time."

Jayden returned the embrace. "It's good to see you, too."

She took a step back, regarding him with approval. "You are quite the man, aren't you? I imagine every maiden in Sharpstone is battering down our door."

"Not as many as you think," he smiled, touching his ear. "Something about elves just doesn't sit right with some people."

Penelope sniffed. "I bet they'd soon change their tune if they knew you were the son of a god."

"So you know about that?"

"Of course, silly." She took hold of his hand. "I've known since before we came here. To be honest, I think I've always known."

Before Jayden could respond, she tugged at his hand and led him through the door into a small parlor. Several chairs and an elegant sofa had been arranged to form a semicircle in front of a brightly lit hearth. Maybell was standing in the far corner beside an open cabinet. She was in conversation with a tall and rather thin elf woman wearing a sleek blue dress cut in an unfamiliar style. Each of them held a glass of wine.

Though twins, Penelope and Maybell looked very different. So too were their personalities. Maybell had always been the emotional one, plainly displaying each feeling regardless of the situation or who was present. By contrast, Penelope was reserved and practical in her thinking.

Maybell smiled warmly on seeing Jayden enter, but the elf woman's eyes shot wide and her hand flew to her mouth as she gasped a breath.

Maybell looked at her curiously. "Is something wrong?"

She quickly regained her composure. "No. Nothing. Your brother reminds me of someone I know from my homeland, that's all." She gestured to the chairs. "Please. We should begin."

Turning to the cabinet, Maybell took the wine bottle and poured another glass. "I think you'll need this," she said, passing it to Jayden and then settling into the chair nearest the fire.

While taking his seat, he was uncomfortably aware that the elf woman was still staring at him. Only when everyone was ready to begin, did she finally look away.

"You are Linis?" she asked.

He bowed his head. "I am. And judging from your accent, you are from across the Abyss."

"I am Sayia," she told him, nodding her affirmation. "Maybell speaks highly of you. I have also heard of you through my friend, Aaliyah."

Jayden had met Aaliyah once when he was ten years old. He remembered feeling ill at ease around her, not enjoying in the least the way she constantly scrutinized him.

"I haven't seen her in years," said Linis. "Is she well?"

"She's home at present, aiding in the assimilation of the newcomers."

Linis chuckled. "And how is that going?"

Sayia flicked her wrist absently. "I wouldn't know. Well enough, is my guess. The elves who have chosen to venture to my homeland do so out of sincere curiosity and a desire to know their kin. Unlike those who choose solitude, they accept the change that's taking place in the world."

Her eyes shifted back to Jayden. "And you. What have you to say?"

A hint of irritation flashed through him. "About what? I came to get answers, not answer questions."

She raised an eyebrow. "Indeed, you are as I suspected."

"And what is that supposed to mean?"

"Filled with conflict and fury. I can see it in your eyes. It was good that you were not taught to use your power, I think."

Jayden shot her a hard look, then turned to his sisters. "Mother is sick and Father is missing. That's why I'm here."

They lowered their heads in unison.

"We know," said Penelope. "We felt it through our bond."

He was somehow not surprised to hear this. "Is there anything you can do?"

Her eyes suddenly burned and she clenched her fists. "If there were, don't you think we would have already done it?"

Maybell reached over to touch her sister's hand. "Calm down. Jayden has no idea what's really happening. There's no need to be angry with him."

Penelope nodded. "Yes, you're right. I'm sorry, Brother. But you cannot know what it feels like to hear Mother's voice calling out in terror every time I close my eyes."

The bond. Jayden was well aware of the bond. There were times when even he thought he felt one between himself and his parents, though he could never be sure.

"Do you know where Father is?" he asked.

Maybell shook her head. "He has vanished completely. We've been trying to reach out to him, but it's like he's disappeared from the world."

"Could he have been killed?"

Sayia laughed. "Darshan? Killed? By whom?"

Rising up, she retrieved the bottle from the cabinet and placed it on the end table. "I can see that this will take some time to explain." She looked at the sisters. "I thought you told me he knows who your father is."

"I do know," Jayden said, frowning. "And I will thank you to speak to me directly."

Maybell gave him a stern look. "Sayia is here to help. Please show some respect."

"I give respect to those who earn it," he shot back.

It was Linis who stepped in to act as the peacemaker. "Perhaps it would be best if we started over," he suggested.

After a short silence, during which he received assenting nods from everyone, Linis continued.

"So far, Jayden and I have been attacked on the road, abducted, and imprisoned while facing torture and death. All this, and yet still we have no idea as to the reason why. I, for one, am growing weary of wandering around in the dark. We know that the gods are somehow involved, but that is all."

"My apologies, seeker," said Sayia. "I know this must be confusing. As to why you were attacked, it is because the gods seek the death of Darshan's son. Or to be more accurate, some of them do. They cannot act directly, so they send their followers to do their work for them."

Jayden shook his head. "I still don't understand why they would want to kill me."

"Because of what you might become," Penelope said. "It's the same reason you were kept ignorant all these years."

"What I might become?"

"If I may," Sayia cut in.

She waited for Maybell and Penelope to nod their approval. "Before you were born, your father was shown a vision, Jayden. It was a choice he had to make. And fortunately for the world, he chose wisely. You see, for all of your father's power, the Reborn King nearly won their battle. The *Sword of Truth* gave him such immeasurable strength, not even the might of the gods could prevent his rise. It was only through supreme self-sacrifice that Darshan survived. Had your father's heart not been pure and his love sincere, all who breathe free air would now be living under the yoke of evil. The elves would be no more, and heaven would be lost."

"I've heard this before," Jayden said. "What does it have to do with me?"

"Everything. In his vision, Darshan witnessed the fall of the world. But it was not the Reborn King who had brought it about, it was you."

Jayden stiffened. "Me? Are you insane? How would I destroy the world?"

"It is important for you to understand that you and your sisters are not simply half god and half elf. You are immeasurably more than that. The blood that flows through your veins is in part touched by the Creator herself. That alone makes you powerful enough to threaten the gods. The damage you could do is beyond reason."

"If this is true, why single me out? My sisters share the same bloodline. Why am *I* so dangerous?"

"It's because you're the first born," Maybell told him. "Conceived when our parents' love was at its fiercest... on the very night of their bonding. We can never be as powerful as you."

"But they are still far more powerful than even Aaliyah," added Sayia. "Your sisters were also considered a threat to peace at one time. However, it was determined that rather than suppress their abilities, they should be trained to harness them."

"So why not train me as well?" Jayden demanded. "What's the difference?"

"Because Father would not have been able to stop you," Penelope said flatly. "Not without killing you. And that was something he knew he could never do."

The intensity, already simmering inside Jayden, now made him shoot up from his seat.

"Stop me? Stop me from doing what? Destroying the world? That makes no sense. I would never do such a thing." He looked at Maybell. "Tell them. I..."

It was only then he realized that everyone in the room was leaning away with startled expressions. At first, he didn't understand why. Then he felt it. The entire room was trembling. An intense heat was racing through his veins. The *flow*. This was the *flow* ... and it was glorious.

"Be calm," said Sayia. "You wouldn't want to accidentally hurt anyone."

But Jayden did not want it to stop. He allowed the sensation to fill him completely. It was as if the world around him had suddenly become transparent. He could see the smallest detail of every object. Each sound was like music he had never heard before. This was what they had been keeping from him? He felt a cold sensation on his arm and saw that Maybell was standing beside him, a look of deep concern on her face.

"Please," she whispered. "Let it go." Her voice, rather than coming from her lips, was from somewhere deep within his mind.

A flash of anger struck him. But this was rapidly overcome by the kindness and love in her tone. She understood what he was feeling. He had never felt so vulnerable, yet he knew he was perfectly safe. Slowly, he allowed the *flow* to subside.

Linis started laughing softly. "At least you didn't nearly kill me by mistake like your father did."

Maybell looked at him with irritation. "This is no laughing matter. The *flow* is dangerous for Jayden. He has no idea how to control it."

"Neither did Gewey in the beginning," Linis pointed out.

As the *flow* left Jayden completely, he felt a stab of guilt for having frightened everyone. Sayia was trying to mask it, but the slight twitch at the corner of her mouth gave her away. After retaking his seat, he took a long breath.

"I guess you'll have to teach me," he told Maybell.

"I'm afraid there might not be enough time," Sayia pointed out. "Your presence is known, and it will not take long before we are discovered."

"I would very much like to know how they found out about Jayden's heritage," said Linis. "Only a handful of people know that Gewey Stedding is really Darshan, and none of them would have betrayed him."

"The gods knew," Sayia said. "And now that Darshan is gone, he is no longer able to conceal this place with his power. They will come... and soon."

"The gods?" Jayden repeated. "What do they want with me?"

"They fear you. They fear what you are capable of becoming. And they will stop at nothing to destroy you."

"I'm not a threat to the gods. How could I be?"

"But you are. As your sisters have been trying to tell you, you are special. You were conceived at the height of the bond formed between your parents. As powerful as Penelope and Maybell may be, you have the potential to be far stronger—strong enough to challenge heaven one day. The gods fear another Dark Knight arising. That is why they're trying to kill you."

"Then why haven't they? Why send humans and elves?"

"From what little we know, all is not well in heaven. There are still gods who are loyal to your father. It's our guess that they have taken measures to prevent any form of direct interference. So, those gods who wish you dead have instead sent their followers to commit the deed. And with your father nowhere to be found, there's nothing to stop them."

"Do you have any idea what has happened to Gewey?" Linis asked.

Sayia shook her head. "We only know that there has been treachery. Fortunately, even the combined power of heaven could not have destroyed Darshan. That being so, we assume they must have trapped him or incapacitated him in some way."

"Why would they do this?" asked Linis. "Gewey saved heaven and freed the gods. Why would they turn on him now?"

"Not all of them have. We know Ayliazarah is still loyal to Darshan. And we think the same is true with Posix and

Dantenos. But the others possibly stand against him. Saraf is his chief rival. That much is clear."

Jayden furrowed his brow. "What has he done?"

"We are not entirely sure. Most of what we've learned comes came our agents living in the temples. The information is incomplete; we only became aware of it a week ago. And it was only thanks to your sisters that we knew something was seriously wrong."

"One thing we do know is that Father has spent years traveling," Penelope added. "He's desperate to quell the violence that has spread since the war ended."

Jayden took a deep breath. His father—Gewey Stedding—a god. In fact, a god more powerful than any other. Much as he tried to picture him this way, he could still only see him in human form, a kindly smile splayed across his face. "What was he doing to stop the fighting?" he asked.

"We don't know," replied Penelope. "He came here a few times, but always refused to speak of exactly how he hoped to make things better. Just that he was working to that end."

Jayden felt a stab of jealousy that only his sisters had been allowed to know the truth of what their father was.

Sayia spoke again. "All we know for certain is that the other gods are involved somehow. That they have moved against you is both unexpected and deeply troubling. It means they do not fear Darshan's wrath. And if they do not fear him, then finding him will not be easy."

"I didn't think it would be," Jayden retorted. "But I did hope you might know something that could help me."

She shrugged. "We know little. We suspect much."

"Then how about telling me what you suspect?" he snapped back. He was becoming ever more uncomfortable with the curious way she kept looking at him. This, combined with her haughty attitude, was quickly stirring his anger.

"It doesn't matter," Maybell said a bit too quickly.

He could see the anxiety in his sister's expression. "You think it has to do with me, don't you? All of it. That I'm the sole reason the gods have done something to Father."

"Not entirely," said Sayia. "Though you are clearly a large part of it. Especially if they are trying to stop you from realizing the vision your father had."

Jayden groaned. "That again? You can't really believe it."

"Father did," said Maybell. "He never said so, but I think he was trying to bring peace to the world before you discovered your power. It pained him deeply to keep it from you. He hated the lies."

Jayden was incredulous. "Am I understanding this right? You think he was afraid that if there wasn't peace, I would become another Reborn King?"

"Perhaps. He knew you to have a kind heart. But hearts can be twisted. Even yours."

This struck him hard. That Maybell, of all people, believed he could do what they were suggesting, sent a chill to the pit of his stomach. He almost wished he had never learned the truth.

She saw the pain in his expression. "I'm sorry," she added. "I didn't mean to hurt you."

There was an extended silence. Jayden cast his gaze down to the stone tiles. "So what do we do?" he asked.

It was Penelope who spoke first. "The last thing I saw through our bond with Father was the desert. But I don't know if that was where he went. Only that it was in his thoughts."

Sayia was gripping a silver locket hanging from a thin chain around her neck. "Yes," she stated. "That is where we should start. I will come with you, Jayden. I can give you instruction along the way."

Maybell looked at her curiously. "I thought you said you would stay here and protect the temple."

"Things have changed," she replied, her eyes still fixed on Jayden.

"And what about Mother?" he asked. "Someone must protect her."

"Your sisters will be given that task," she told him. "Linis will accompany them."

Maybell opened her mouth to object, but Penelope spoke first.

"She's right. We should be the ones to look after Mother."

Linis frowned. "I do not like the idea of abandoning you."

"I'll be fine. Help my sisters and Mother. They need you more than I do."

"He will be well guarded, seeker," Sayia assured. "And now I think we need to consider evacuating the temple. If our location is discovered, they might think to come."

Both Maybell and Penelope nodded.

Maybell stood. "I'll tell the others to prepare," she said, before exiting the room.

"Where will we start?" Jayden asked Sayia as soon as his sister was gone. "The desert is enormous. We can't just start wandering around and hope we find the right place."

"There are several towns on the desert's edge," she told him. "We'll need to supply at one of these before entering, and there's a good chance we'll be able to find out from someone there where the elves are currently residing."

Jayden moaned inwardly. Just getting there would take them several weeks. And from what his mother had said on the few occasions she had spoken of the desert elves, they lived mostly near the mountains located to the far north. That meant traversing the entire breadth of the sands.

"It won't take as long as you might think," Sayia said. "And it will give me some time to train you."

"What about when you get there?" asked Linis. "Desert elves may not feel hatred toward newbreeds, but they are not alone."

Sayia shrugged. "A necessary risk. As I understand it, those seeking a new life in the dunes follow the customs of their desert kin. We can only hope I have heard correctly."

Linis grimaced. "That is not especially encouraging. But I suppose you're right. It is a risk you must take."

"There is one other thing," Penelope chipped in. "Father once told me about creatures that live beyond the mountains. He said that he had a special connection with them. Should the elves not be able to help, you might try to find them."

Jayden raised an eyebrow. "Creatures? What kind of creatures?"

"He didn't say. Only that they were peaceful."

He had heard stories of great reptilian beasts wandering about inside the bowels of the mountains. There was no pass between the peaks, only a labyrinth of tunnels going through. No one who dared to enter these tunnels ever came back—at least, that was the rumor.

"Is there a safe way through to the other side?" he asked.

"If there is, Father didn't say. The elves might know of one, though."

Jayden then noticed tears in Penelope's eyes. "What is it?"

"You've only just arrived," she said. "And here we are already making plans to be apart again. We've waited for so long to see you, and now..."

He touched her arm. "You're right. I've been waiting a long time too. We can wait a day before leaving."

His words brought a smile to Penelope's face. "Yes. We can afford an extra day, don't you think, Sayia?"

The elf began to protest, but Jayden cut her short. "We *will* afford a day for family." His voice was firm and resolute. "There is nothing more to say about it."

Sayia breathed a heavy sigh. "Very well. I can see there is no point in debating the matter." Rising to her feet, she turned to Linis. "I would ask you to accompany me to the supply room. You will know better than I what we need to bring. You can help me map out a route. And perhaps offer some advice."

"I would be pleased to."

They left the room together.

Now alone with his sister, Jayden regarded her for a long moment before speaking. "I still don't see why I was kept ignorant of my heritage," he began. "If they had only sent me here, I could have learned how to control this... whatever it is."

Penelope nodded. "I understand. But let me ask you this. Remember what it felt like when you were angry, and the *flow* swelled inside you?"

"Yes. It was like I could feel everything around me all at once. It was wonderful."

"Well, that was but a tiny taste of what you can do," she continued. "Everything Sayia said was true. I didn't believe it until just now. Then I felt how much of the *flow* you were able to draw in ... even without any training."

"Whatever I'm capable of, you know me," he objected. "You know I would never hurt anyone. I'm not dangerous."

"The men you killed on the road to Baltria," she said. "How did that feel?"

Jayden scowled. "That's not fair. They were trying to kill us. I only did what I had to do."

"I know. And I'm glad you did. But I have learned much in my time here. There are some of us who are meant to heal, while others are intended to build. Some, like Mother, have free spirits. And then there are those like Father who carry the weight of the world on their shoulders. They feel its suffering as their own."

She reached out and took his hand. "Every mortal, great or small, has a destiny: a thing they are meant to do. Those who discover what this is and follow its call are counted among the lucky ones. They live lives of purpose and fulfillment. Maybell and I have learned to recognize this in people by using the *flow of the spirit*."

"And you can see this in me?" Jayden asked.

Penelope nodded slowly. "I... *we* can. But you are unlike other people. We see many things in you: a builder, a father, and also a healer. Yet there is one destiny that dominates them all."

For a second, her grip on his hand tightened. "You, brother, are a conqueror."

Jayden was astonished. Pulling away, he huffed a sardonic laugh. "I think you're seeing something that's not there, Penelope. I can't even conquer a field of hay. Sure, I've had a bit of a temper lately. But Mother is ill, Father is missing, and people are trying to kill me. Who wouldn't be angry?"

"I agree with you," she said. "It's control that you need. Soon you'll learn that the *flow* allows you to feel things with an intensity you have never before experienced. Without guidance, this can be dangerous even for an elf. For you, considering who our father is, it is much more. Pay attention to what Sayia teaches you. She may not possess our power, but she knows more than almost anyone alive about the *flow* and its potential." She gave him a playful poke, lightening the mood. "You wouldn't want to hurt someone by accident."

Jayden knew she was right. He *had* felt things more keenly of late. And if he was honest with himself, his temper had always been on the edge of being out of control. It was only his father's calming influence and his mother's warnings that kept him from exploding at times.

"I will take care," he said, smiling. "I promise."

Penelope slapped both hands on her knees. "Good. Now enough of dark talk. We only have a short time together, and I want to know everything that has happened back home. Do you have a special girl in your life? Surely you must."

He shook his head. "No. Mother chases them away. Though I think that's more to avoid the Village Mothers than not liking the girls."

This remark produced a round of cheerful laughter. For the next hour, Jayden recounted the latest happenings in Sharpstone. Even though none of these could ever be considered exciting, his sister hung on every word. Food was brought to them after a time, and they continued catching up until it was well into the afternoon.

Penelope then led him from the room for a tour of the temple, pointing out several paintings and statues of their father, none of which resembled him in the slightest. Maybell eventually joined them, having spread the word that the temple was to be evacuated.

"No one is very happy about it," she told them.

"Neither am I," said Penelope. "All the same, it *is* necessary. If we were to be attacked, there are no knights here to defend us."

Jayden had heard of the famed knights of Amon Dahl. They were reputed to be the fiercest of all human warriors—their courage unwavering and their loyalty beyond question.

"Why are none here?" he asked.

"Until now, there's been no reason to have them," Maybell replied. "They're needed in the west. Our enemies might not know where this place is, but it's better to be safe."

They stepped out into a spacious courtyard, where a small pond filled with multicolored fish bubbled and rippled from some deep underground spring. With each moment that passed, Jayden felt ever more pained that their reunion would be so brief. He could see that both his sisters felt the same way.

"Will you come to stay with us for a spell when this is over and done?" asked Maybell.

"I hope to," he replied. "Though Mother and Father will surely have something to say about it."

"I think they may change their minds when this is settled," said Penelope. "Things will be different. I doubt they'll expect you to stay on the farm any longer."

They were joined for dinner in Jayden's quarters by Linis and Sayia. Linis seemed to be in good spirits. Sayia, on the other hand, continued to keep her eyes on Jayden, her expression one of deep concern. After they finished eating, there was only a short time for further talk before Sayia insisted that they all needed to rest.

Jayden was growing to dislike the woman. "I don't need to be told when to go to bed, thank you," he snapped.

Penelope quickly spoke up. "She's right. I'm still tired from healing Linis, and I'm sure Maybell is, too."

Further helping to calm his irritation, Maybell gave him a heartfelt embrace. "We'll be leaving the temple together," she said. "So even after we're on our way, we'll still have a bit more time."

Once everyone had left, Jayden took a while to ready his things before slipping into bed. Sleep was elusive. His mind was racing as he tried to get a grip on all the incredible events that had unfolded since leaving home. He had come here for answers. And though he had succeeded in finding them, they had only left him with even more questions.

None of this mattered, he eventually told himself. Saving his mother had to be his primary concern. Everything he had so far discovered suggested that this was not going to be easy. Powerful forces were moving against them. And for this, there was only one person to blame.

His father.

Darshan.

CHAPTER 8

The loud clattering of steel jerked Jayden from his slumber. For a moment, he thought it was nothing more than the echoes of his own dreams startling him awake, but the muffled shouts from outside his room quickly told him otherwise.

Throwing back the blanket, he hurried over to where his clothes lay and began frantically dressing. The door flew open just as he was reaching for his sword. Two men in ragged chain mail tunics and bearing small hand axes rushed in. Pulling his blade free, he took a step back.

"Here's one," said the man on his right. "Looks about the right age." He fixed his eyes on Jayden. "Put it down, boy. Come with us and you'll be spared."

"Leave now or *you* won't be," he spat back.

Snarling, the pair moved farther apart, weapons gripped menacingly. Jayden could feel his heart thudding. He was not afraid, even though he knew he should be. These two were seasoned fighters; he was a mere novice. Instinctively, he reached out for the *flow* and felt a surge of disappointment. Rather than the raging torrent he had been hoping for, only a small trickle of power seeped in. It was enough to heighten his senses and make him keenly aware that his enemy was ready to pounce, but a long way short of the power he had previously experienced.

The man to his right leaped forward, axe sweeping low. Jayden twisted aside to avoid having his knees crushed, only to find himself directly in the path of the second foe. He jumped farther to one side, stumbling several paces and swinging his sword in a series of frenzied strikes. It was not enough to keep them at bay. The man to his left lunged, smashing the flat of his blade into Jayden's chest. The impact slammed him into the far wall, leaving him gasping for breath.

"Give it up, boy," the foe nearest ordered. "Stop now before we end up having to drag you out of here."

This only enraged Jayden further. Pushing all the pain aside, he shifted left and slashed at the man's midsection. As this attacker was forced back, the other one moved in. But Jayden had counted on this. Pivoting to face this new threat, he raised his sword to just above shoulder level. The man lifted his axe to parry the anticipated downward swing, only realizing too late that the move was merely a diversion. Jayden kicked out with all his strength, the hardened heel of his boot smashing into his opponent's knee. A sharp snap was immediately followed by an ear-splitting wail of pain. The intruder slumped against the wall, his injured leg bent into an unnatural position.

His comrade's face twisted in fury as he renewed the attack. Jayden was only just able to avoid a succession of fevered blows unleashed upon him. He made an attempt to counter, but his more experienced opponent easily avoided his strikes.

With his foe once again pressing relentlessly forward, Jayden felt something bump against his hip while backing away. This was followed by the clinking of glass. He grinned inwardly, remembering what old Varis had told him when he was a young boy. *Fight dirty if it means your life.* At the time, his mother had not approved. She would now, he wagered. He stabbed out awkwardly twice, feigning desperation by allowing his eyes to dart toward the door. His opponent let out a malevolent chuckle, sensing that the fight was all but over.

In one rapid motion, Jayden reached over to the table and seized hold of the crystal decanter filled with plum brandy. Before his foe could react, he heaved it at the man's chest. The delicate crystal shattered into a thousand tiny shards as it struck the chain mail tunic, sending both glass splinters and splashes of burning spirit flying up into the intruder's eyes. He staggered blindly back, wiping at his face with one hand, with his blade held up defensively with the other. Jayden merely shifted a little to the right before plunging his blade into the man's ribs. The chain mail offered only a small amount of resistance before giving way, allowing the steel to sink deep. His defeated foe gave a gasp and a gurgle and then sank to his knees, his life rapidly draining away.

Yanking his sword free, Jayden quickly turned to the still-groaning attacker with the shattered knee. Rage filled him as he loomed over the helpless man, his now bloodied blade raised threateningly.

"Who sent you?"

Fear penetrated the pain splayed across his face. "I was hired by Lady Leanna."

Jayden's eyes popped wide, a sense of betrayal immediately hitting him like a blow to the stomach.

"Leanna?" he repeated, almost as if hoping he had misheard the name. Though he knew that he hadn't. A memory of the pendant with Saraf's symbol he had spotted her wearing at the market flashed through his mind.

The man nodded. "She's with the temple of Saraf. She sent us to capture someone named Jayden."

There was no time to dwell on her treachery. "How many are you?" he demanded.

"Twenty. But the temple will send more." He shifted, clutching at his injured leg. "That's all I know. Please ... spare me."

The clamor of steel drifted in from the hallway. Jayden's thoughts turned instantly to Maybell and Penelope. "Pray to whatever god you serve that my sisters are not hurt," he told the man. "If they have been, I swear I'll come back and gut you like a trout."

The *flow* was coming through more easily now, lending strength to his muscles. He could barely contain his rage as he moved over to the door to peer outside. Several temple members ran by along the hall, some of them bearing weapons.

Maybell and Penelope's quarters were to the left and down a short way. He exited the room at a quick walk. There was some comfort in knowing that his sisters would be able to defend themselves with the *flow*, but he only had the wounded soldier's word for it about the number of men that were attacking.

He grabbed a young girl who was running by. "Have you seen Maybell or Penelope?"

The girl shook her head as she gulped for air, her panicked breath at first disallowing speech. Jayden waited until she had calmed enough to reply.

"There are a dozen men outside their chambers," she finally managed to gasp. "But they haven't tried to enter."

"What about Linis, the elf who came here with me?"

"I haven't seen him. He might be defending the inner sanctuary with the others. There's a passage leading there from the temple. That's where everyone is going."

Jayden released the girl and steadied his nerves, picturing the approach to his sisters' quarters in his mind. He would need to fight his way through a large number of armed men alone. The prospect should have terrified him. But it didn't.

The hand gripping his weapon was rock steady. With the *flow* increasing in intensity and filling his limbs with ever more power, any idea of failure was lost to him. He would hack his way through, and no one would stop him. Had the situation not been so dire, he would have found it almost enjoyable.

As he drew close to the corner leading to Maybell and Penelope's rooms, he could hear the gruff voices of his enemy. The few words he could make out over the surrounding clamor suggested that they were unsure what to do next.

"They've already killed five of us," came one voice. "You go in there if you want to. I'm not. They're not paying me anywhere near enough to get myself roasted alive."

"Take it easy, lad," said a second, more commanding voice. "We don't need to be charging in. He'll be along soon to sort things out. We just need to keep them from getting away. That's all."

Jayden peeked around the wall. Eight men, their backs to him at the moment. If he moved in quickly...

At that instant, a hand seized his shoulder, pulling him back with enormous strength. The power in the steely fingers caused pain to shoot down his arm.

After regaining his balance, he raised his sword. Before him stood a tall figure clad in a dark gray cloak, the hood pulled over its head, obscuring any features. In its right hand was a short blade. Though the face was hidden, Jayden could feel eyes bearing down on him.

"I hoped you would come here," a thin male voice said. "You have saved me quite a bit of trouble."

Fury coursed through Jayden's veins. Without thinking, he lunged with the tip of his blade. It should have found its mark, but the figure moved to one side with speed the likes of which Jayden had never before witnessed.

The newcomer gave a soft laugh. "That will do you no good. No good at all. So please be sensible. Do not make me fetch those brutish men. They will not take the same care that I will to ensure you are unharmed."

A cold chill caused the hair on the back of Jayden's neck to prickle. Something was not right about this man. It wasn't just the incredible speed with which he moved. That could mean he was possibly an elf of significant skill. No, it was more than that. It was as if he radiated some fell power that was wrapped around him like an invisible mist.

"What *are* you?" Jayden demanded, taking a step back. In his present position, there was nothing between him and the empty hallway. He could run if he chose to, though he doubted he could outpace this thing before him. Not that it mattered. He would never abandon his sisters.

"My lord!" called a voice.

One of the soldiers must have heard them and was coming to investigate.

"You and the other men stay where you are," the figure commanded. "Young Jayden and I are just having a little chat."

"But ... my lord. Our orders are—"

"Your orders are to obey me," he snapped back.

With a concerned frown, the soldier nodded and then moved away to rejoin his comrades.

"I will ask you only once, son of Darshan," the hooded man continued. "Will you come with me willingly?"

Jayden shook his head. "I'm not going anywhere with you." He could feel the *flow* coursing through him, fueling his muscles. "And if you think those pathetic excuses for soldiers can stop me..."

"Actually, I am sure that they could. Remember, you are as yet untrained. Even with the power you now hold, their numbers would be enough to overcome you. That is, presuming I allowed it to happen... which I will not."

Jayden considered his options. There were none that might save him that didn't involve abandoning his sisters. Even as this became obvious, the enemy moved closer, though his movements were so fluid it was as if his feet were not touching the floor.

A blur of motion shot past the left side of Jayden's head, missing it only by a small fraction. An instant later, the man in front of him clutched at his chest. Jayden could see the handle of a dagger protruding from his cloak just above the heart.

"Run!" Linis's voice called from behind.

Jayden knew he could not do that. But there was another way he might seize advantage of the situation. He swung his blade in a rapid downward arc. Astonishingly, it found only empty air. Though this hooded opponent had to be severely injured, he was still able to lean quickly back, so avoiding the fatal strike.

Linis stepped past, his short sword flying in a flurry of blows that drove the man back and shredded large sections of his cloak. Several of these strikes, Jayden felt sure, must have found flesh as well. Yet the man's arm reached into the folds of his garment and the glimmer of steel appeared. How could he still be standing? Even if he were wearing armor, some of Linis's thrusts were certain to have made it through.

"I said *run!*" the elf roared, blocking a counter that was so fast it could scarcely be seen.

"My sisters," Jayden protested.

Three soldiers, having heard the melee, came running around the corner.

Drawing a second dagger with his left hand and ducking low, Linis squirmed forward and then rapidly up again to force himself inside the hooded man's reach. Even as he was still rising, he plunged the weapon into his opponent's gullet. The man stumbled back, yet was still able to inflict a small wound to Linis's right arm before the elf could move away.

"Your sisters are not here," he told Jayden, blood already pouring from a three-inch gash. He spun, grabbing Jayden's arm and propelling him along.

With the sinews of his legs invigorated by the *flow*, Jayden was well aware he was moving far more rapidly than normal. Even so, Linis was soon far ahead of him. He could also hear footfalls behind him drawing ever closer.

He raced through a series of large chambers and broad hallways, barely able to keep Linis in sight. No one should have been able to keep up with them, yet he could still hear his pursuer closing in. It could only be the cloaked man, he thought. Men in full armor could never run this fast. But after the wounds the man had suffered, how could it be? He had no right to still be alive.

Along the way, Jayden was forced to step around several bodies, mainly those of temple residents but one or two of the invading soldiers as well. Smoldering furniture also littered his path, and many of the walls he passed were badly scorched. He spotted Linis approaching a pair of large double doors at the far end of the main dining hall. Just outside of these were standing two unfamiliar elf men, together with Sayia. Even from a distance, he could see her eyes burning as she spread her arms wide.

Jayden reached the doorway a few seconds after Linis had passed through. He glanced back to see that the cloaked man was indeed uncomfortably close behind him. This was obviously the moment Sayia had been waiting for. She let loose a blast of icy air that struck his pursuer in the lower torso, instantly halting his advance. A second blast then lifted him completely up, hurling him back more than thirty feet.

Gasping for breath, Jayden pulled up. "Where are my sisters?" he asked.

Sayia's face was twisted into a vicious snarl. "They're safe for now. Get inside."

The man was already rising, sword in hand, and poised to charge once again. "You cannot kill me, witch." His voice thundered with incredible volume. "Saraf will not be denied."

Sayia gave the two elf men a slight bow, then turned to Jayden. "I told you to get inside." This time, there was more than an edge of impatience in her tone.

The elves stepped forward, their hands outstretched, tiny balls of flame flashing into existence above them. Sayia grabbed Jayden's arm and pulled him roughly through the door. He tried to resist, but even with his *flow*-enhanced strength, she was still able to overpower him.

On the other side was an oval courtyard. Statues of the gods had been placed around the outer edge, while in the very center, he saw a great silver sword at least six feet long, whose blade looked as if some time in the past it had been buried into the stone tiles a few inches shy of the hilt. Linis was standing with four other men near a narrow archway.

The door behind them boomed shut, and Jayden heard a loud rush of fire.

"You're just leaving them?" he asked Sayia in a shocked voice.

"They will buy us the time we need," she said, her face expressionless and her voice cold.

"Come on," urged Linis. "We must move quickly. They won't be able to hold that Vrykol for very long."

Jayden looked at him in astonishment. "Vrykol? It can't have been." He had heard of them—creatures of pure evil created by the Reborn King during the war. But they were all supposed to have been destroyed along with their master.

"No time for questions," Linis barked.

"I'm not going anywhere until I know where my sisters are."

He received a firm nudge from Sayia. "They've already left the temple. Now hurry. I do not want my kin's sacrifice to be for naught."

Finally yielding, he followed Linis through the archway and down a long corridor. After several more twists and turns, they came to a small storage room, at the far corner of which was an open trapdoor. Linis was already ushering the four men with him down. While he did so, Sayia stretched out her hands and closed her eyes. The room immediately began to tremble.

Several large chunks of the ceiling broke loose in front of the doorway just as Linis followed the other four down. For a moment, Jayden was transfixed. He could feel the *flow* raging into the elf woman, its tremendous power bending to her will. It felt different this time—like a steady pulse rather than a swirling tempest. Another great lump of stone crashed to the floor, shocking him back into the moment. The entire room would soon collapse.

Sayia shoved him toward the opening. He nearly fell as his foot slipped from the iron ladder fixed to the shaft wall. Though she was no longer using the *flow*, the woman had already done enough for the room above to continue crumbling. A shower of small stones and debris followed them down.

Once at the bottom, they were forced to duck low as they passed along a narrow passage. The light quickly faded, and Jayden soon found himself reaching out into utter darkness. Nonetheless, they kept moving at a steady pace for almost half an hour. He stumbled a few times at points where the passage twisted and dipped, but Sayia was there to reach out and prevent him from falling.

At last, the pitch of the floor began to slope gradually upward, allowing a tiny amount of light to filter down from ahead. This revealed a roughly hewn staircase, at the top of which was stood a man bearing a stout axe. Directly behind this sentry, an open door led them out onto the surrounding marshland, where Maybell and Penelope, along with more than twenty others, were nervously waiting. His sisters immediately ran over and threw their arms around him.

"We were so afraid you'd been captured," said Maybell, tears spilling down her cheeks.

"How did you two get out?" Jayden asked. "I thought the soldiers had you trapped."

"Our room has a passage leading to the far side of the temple," Penelope explained. Though she was not crying, she was visibly shaken. "We tried to get to you, but there were too many."

"We can discuss what happened once we're away from here," Sayia cut in. "I've sealed off the exit, but it won't take them long to begin searching outside the temple."

At first, her words went unheeded. The twenty or so men and women standing around in small groups were mostly still in their nightclothes. Only a few of them bore arms, and all appeared to be in a state of stunned disbelief.

"Please," said Sayia, raising her voice for everyone to hear. "I know you're afraid. But we have to start moving immediately."

"Where can we go?" asked an older woman, clutching desperately to a small bundle. "Those men came from Baltria."

"I have a ship docked to the west," Sayia replied. "You'll be safe there. But I need you to be strong. If they come for us, more will die."

She turned to Linis. "Do you know where Loroni Rock is?"

He nodded.

"Lead them there. I will join you before you arrive."

"Where are you going?" asked Penelope.

"I have business to attend before I can leave," she answered, clearly unwilling to say any more than that. She hurried away before any objections could be raised, vanishing into the thick of the marsh.

Linis took stock of their situation. Under normal circumstances, Loroni Rock was only a day and a half's walk away, though with so many people in tow and some well into the latter years of their lives, it was sure to take longer. Gathering them all together, he had them form a single line.

"Follow exactly in my steps and your footing will be sure," he announced. "Do not wander. These marshes can be dangerous."

Jayden and Maybell went to the rear, while Penelope stayed with Linis.

Though the light of the full moon illuminated the way well enough even for human eyes, the line still moved painfully slowly. For Linis, who had traveled this area many times in his days as a seeker, it was no challenge to find the best way through. In their favor, the trees here bore *nan* vines that could be cut open and the fresh water inside drunk without fear of illness. Food, however, was another matter. Hunting would be impractical, and unless several more of these people had foraging skills, he alone could not provide enough for everyone. But empty bellies could wait.

"What business did Sayia have?" he asked Penelope after they had walked for close to an hour.

"I don't know for sure," she replied. "But I suspect she's going to see to the one who sent those men."

Linis furrowed his brow. "Is she mad? She's going alone into Baltria?"

"Right now, I think she might well be mad. Beneath that practical exterior, Sayia is quite a passionate woman. She reminds me of Mother, actually." She gave him a weak smile. "You shouldn't worry. Only Maybell and I are her match in raw power. And Jayden, of course."

"Perhaps," said Linis. "But it's not elves and soldiers I worry about."

After a while longer, they took a brief respite on a patch of solid ground large enough for the group to spread out on the mossy turf. During the break, Maybell and Penelope walked from person to person, offering words of comfort and hope. Many wept into their arms, lamenting the loss of their home or the death of someone close.

Jayden plopped himself down beside Linis. "Now that we're safe," he began, "you can tell me what the hell that thing we fought was. Nothing could take the kind of wounds you inflicted, yet still it kept coming."

Linis stared down, absently rubbing a bit of moss between his fingers. "It was a Vrykol," he said. "I've already told you that. Though I have no idea how it came to be there."

Jayden huffed a dubious laugh. "They're all dead. They died with the Reborn King."

"Yes. That is true. They could not survive without the power of their maker to sustain them. And yet, it *was* a Vrykol we faced in the temple. But this one was different from those I have fought before. It was somehow... Better, I suppose is the best way to put it."

"You actually fought against the Vrykol?"

Linis grinned. "There is much I have done that you do not know of. Even before the war, I had many adventures."

"Tell me all you know about these monsters," Jayden pressed.

"There isn't that much to tell. As you know, the Reborn King joined the cursed souls of the First Born to the dead bodies of mortals to create something that was foul and wholly evil. But he was not the first to do this. That's what the stories tell us. Long ago, the gods created the Vrykol to do their bidding. These were hunted down by the elves until only two of them remained."

"Do you think that thing was one of those two?"

"No. The survivors were a brother and sister. One was killed during the war. As for the other... she is enjoying a well-earned peace. The one we encountered must be something new."

"So it was made by the gods? Is that right?"

"It seems likely. It has the same *feel* as the other Vrykol I faced. Its speed and strength were similar too. Yet it was less corrupt in spirit."

Jayden leaned back on his elbows. He had heard some of the stories before, but only of those Vrykol that had fought in the war. As Linis had explained, they were pure evil, molded from the bodies of the dead and suffused with the power of the Reborn King. Beyond that, he had no knowledge.

"Can they be killed?" he asked.

"Yes, but only by taking their heads or if they're consumed in fire. No simple task. And gathered in numbers, they're able to suppress the *flow*. If the gods have enough of them to do their bidding, I fear that we would be out-matched, even should you learn to use your abilities."

Jayden noticed a look of deep concern in the elf's eyes. "You're worried about Dina?"

Linis shrugged. "I *always* worry about her when we're not together. I'm sending danger to my own doorstep: the kind I thought never to see again. What I'm unable to shake is the fact that your father could not resist whatever force was set against him. It is clear that the gods are moving with intent. But they could not do so without first dealing with Gewey." He rubbed his arms. "The strength that would take to accomplish is beyond my comprehension."

"Is he really so powerful?"

"Your father is the son of Garath and the Creator herself. Her fire burns within him; within you and your sisters as well. None can match him."

"The Reborn King almost did," Jayden pointed out.

"Yes. But only with the stolen power of many gods. And your father was cut off from heaven at the time. Had the door been open, and he'd been able to draw from its strength, he could have easily cast him down."

"How do you know that?"

"Gewey and I have spoken often of the past since the war ended. He told me much."

"He told *me* nothing."

The anger Jayden was feeling had become a constant companion. None of this would be happening if he had been told everything from the beginning. And now, having been sheltered all his life, he was unprepared to face the dangers of the real world.

He glanced over to Maybell, who was talking quietly with a young elf girl, stroking her hair with a consoling smile. Penelope was a short distance away, tending to a minor scrape on an older man's arm. They were younger than he, and yet in many ways, far older.

"Don't dwell on things beyond your control," Linis told him. "Gewey fought his way through the gates of hell. Whatever trickery the gods have loosed, it will not be able to contain him forever."

Jayden gave a heavy sigh. "I hope you're right."

Lady Zarhari leaned back in her chair, the cup of wine on the table beside her untouched. She had not anticipated the Vrykol's involvement in this matter. It was unsettling. Unfortunately, she had been left with no choice but to accept the situation.

Lady Leanna, who sat over by the window flipping through a book of sketches, looked up. "Why are you so nervous?"

"How could I not be? Have you any idea what could happen should this go afoul? If we fail, the wrath of Darshan will descend upon us like a storm."

"I already told you, Darshan is no longer a threat."

"How can you know this?"

Leanna closed the book and stretched her arms above her head. "Your lack of faith causes me to grow weary. It is not befitting the station bestowed upon you. Please try to be a bit more positive. Soon, Jayden will be back in our hands and this ordeal will be over."

Zarhari did not like this woman. Her little slights were a constant source of irritation. Why Saraf would favor her was baffling. Yet the words that had been passed on were quite clear: Lady Leanna was his emissary and must be obeyed.

"I do not lack faith," she responded. "But the power the boy possesses should not be underestimated. I felt it first-hand. You did not."

"He is untrained and ignorant," she countered. "Nothing but a farm boy."

"As was his father. And look what *he* became."

Leanna groaned with exasperation. "Jayden is *not* Darshan. What's more, the gods who oppose us are power-less to intervene."

"Don't be a fool. They are far from powerless. And though Jayden may yet have to discover his power, that can change very quickly. He has the elf from across the Abyss to aid him, not to mention his sisters."

Leanna stood, tucking the sketchbook under her arm. "You are young for an elf, am I right? Less than two hun-dred years?"

"I am of age," Zarhari replied. "But yes. I am considered to be in late youth by my people."

"Then you were not around during the Great War."

"What does that have to do with anything?" Her dislike for the woman was increasing by the second.

Leanna placed the book down on the table beside Zarhari and took a seat opposite. "Let me tell you a story," she said. She drew a long breath before beginning, as if summoning the memory. "When I was a little girl, my mother took me on a journey to see the Oracle of Manisalia. Well, in truth, Mother was the one who wanted to see her. But I was per-mitted to go along. Unfortunately, an early winter prevented us from getting to our destination, and we sought shelter in the manor of a minor lord named Gromich. He was originally from Hazrah but had chosen to leave the turmoil of the city." A distant smile eased its way up from the corners of her mouth. "A sweet man. He didn't give a second thought to offering us aid. Both of his sons had gone to Angrääl to serve the Reborn King, so I think it was as much to do with loneliness as anything else. Regardless, we were grateful and did our best to help where we could.

"Mother was an accomplished cook, and I, though young, was old enough to help keep things tidy. Not that Lord Gromich wanted me to work. He objected every time he caught me dusting and would instead take me away to his library to read me stories. He believed that a young lady should spend her time in learning, not fiddling around some old house that was already as clean as he cared for it to be.

"I loved listening to him; he had this rich baritone that made each tale come alive. It was a special treat when the books had drawings. Though I've never had a talent for art myself, I do love it so. Lord Gromich noticed, of course, and showed me his collection of sketches and drawings. Most were from Hazrah—images of the people and mountains, things of that sort. But there was a special book I loved most of all. The skill was far superior, and the pictures of a fantastical nature. I spent hours just gazing at them. When the snows melted, Mother decided to forgo the trip to the oracle and return home to Althetas. I wanted to stay. I'd enjoyed far more freedom to do as I pleased than I did back home, though I would not have admitted this to Mother. I never saw Lord Gromich again, but he did give me something to remember him by."

She nodded toward the book she had placed on the table. "It's quite old. From the days of the Great War."

Zarhari rubbed the bridge of her nose. "Please tell me there is a point to this."

Leanna laughed. "You are impatient for an elf. Of course, there is a point. And when you understand, your fears will be laid to rest. All is unfolding as it should."

"I have no fears. I am simply being cautious. We need Jayden to be returned to us. Should the Vrykol fail—"

"It won't matter a whit," she said, cutting her short. "Jayden's fate is sealed."

Zarhari cocked her head. "How can you know this?"

"There is a favorite picture of mine," she replied, nudging the book a little closer. "I've always been drawn to it. I think you'll like it too."

"I do not care to look at pictures, thank you."

"Humor me." Her smile broadened. "There's a page marker."

Zarhari rolled her eyes in resignation. "Very well."

Placing the book in her lap, she flicked through the pages until coming to a thin strip of red silk. The scene was of a battle: two massive armies clashing on a field of yellow grass. The banners they carried were unfamiliar. One depicted a bull inside a silver star, and the second, a red flame on a white background. In the very center of the sketch was a pair of warriors on horseback, both of them with swords held high and poised to strike the other down. The detail was truly magnificent, almost to the level of elf artisans. Whoever had drawn this was definitely a master.

"It's very nice," said Zarhari. "However, I still do not see the point you are making."

"It depicts the Battle of Maiden Pass. Have you heard of it?"

"I have indeed. It was what allowed the remains of our forces to escape annihilation at the end of the war. The humans were turned back at the cost of many elf lives."

"That is one version, yes. And possibly the correct one. This particular sketch was procured at great cost by Lord Gromich from the Temple of the Far Sky. Human hands created it, so it's possible some of the details were altered.

Nonetheless, the heart of the story is the same. As we tell it, there was a man who took pity on the elves and fought to save them when all others were bent on their total destruction. No one knows his name. It really doesn't matter."

"*None* of this matters," Zarhari responded, trying not to let her irritation bleed into her tone.

Leanna pointed to the book. "Keep looking. You'll see it, eventually."

She returned her attention to the picture. Nothing. Just a battle. Then, as she was about to look away again, she noticed something curious. It was one of the two commanders. She held the book closer.

"Turn the page," said Leanna, spotting her reaction. "Then you will be sure."

Zarhari did as instructed. The next picture was of the same two men, this time on foot with swords clashing. Her eyes went wide. "That's not possible," she whispered. "A coincidence. Nothing more."

"You think so? There's another marker. It has a title."

After staring at the picture for several more seconds, she turned the pages until she found a second piece of red silk. Her mouth opened, but her voice was completely gone.

"I had the same reaction," Leanna told her. "As you can see, there is no question."

Zarhari closed the book and looked up at Leanna. "Do you know what this means?"

"Yes. It means we cannot fail. We are already victorious."

Holding the book tightly to her breast, Zarhari stood and crossed over to the window. "I am not so sure that is what it tells us."

"How could you still doubt? Do you not believe your own eyes?"

"I can believe what I saw well enough. All the same, we cannot know what it means."

Leanna let out a derisive laugh. "Perhaps *you* cannot. But I know what it means to me. It means Darshan is gone forever. We have won."

"I would not be so sure about that," came a voice from the doorway.

Both women glanced across to see the figure of an elf woman standing there. Clad in black and with a long knife in her right hand, she moved toward them with deadly intent in her eyes.

"Sayia!" gasped Zarhari.

"You were expecting someone else?" she mocked. "The Vrykol, perhaps? Or the men you sent to slaughter the innocents at the temple?"

"They were not innocent," Leanna snapped. "They earned their fate."

Sayia switched her attention to glare at the human. "I think I do not care to hear your voice any longer."

Her movements became nothing but a blur as she spanned the gap separating them and let fly her blade; the steel sliced across the tender flesh of Leanna's exposed throat in one clean strike. The woman's eyes shot wide. With fresh blood spurting in time with her every heartbeat, she clutched desperately at the fatal wound in a futile attempt to stem the flow. Inevitably, it was over quickly. After gurgling out her final breath, she slumped back in the chair.

Zarhari stared with horrified eyes at the blood-soaked corpse. "Please. Stay your wrath. You do not understand what is happening."

Sayia sniffed. "I understand that you have betrayed your own people. It matters not whether it was you or this pitiful wretch who sent those beasts to the temple. You did nothing to prevent it."

Still clinging to the book, Zarhari pressed her back to the window. "I am in the right. Can't you see that? Darshan would have damned the world to darkness. He had to be stopped."

"Perhaps. Perhaps not. I did not come here to debate."

"So you're nothing but an assassin? Is that what the elves have become?"

Sayia sheathed her blade. "When I first came here from my homeland, I did not understand vengeance. I could not fathom the need for retribution. But at the time, I had never lost anyone I loved to betrayal. This has now changed. You and your kind changed it."

"If you think I would want elf blood spilled—"

"You think elf lives are all that matter?" Sayia's voice ripped through the air, the ground trembling as the *flow* penetrated every fiber of her body and spirit. "The men you sent... they..." Tears welled in her eyes. "There was a young boy I knew named Kaleb. Not a child of particular talent, perhaps, but he was blessed with an extraordinarily kind soul. Something I doubt you could ever understand. He gave willingly when he had barely anything for himself. And when he had nothing left, he still offered compassion and comfort to anyone who needed it. He was the first human to touch my heart. This young boy could see my loneliness. He saw how isolated I felt in this new place and found the words to give me strength. For him, it was nothing. A simple part of his nature. His parents had died, so he too knew what it meant to be alone."

By now, her tears were falling freely. "I planned to take him to my home so he could see the splendor of my land. I wanted to show him that he need never be alone again. But he died before that could happen—a sword rammed through his gullet. Killed by the men you sent to the temple. He died alone and afraid; the only voices he could hear were the terrified screams of his friends. Yes. I well understand the meaning of vengeance now. *You* taught it to me."

Zarhari's eyes darted around the room, seeking an escape route. "I swear I had nothing to do with that," she protested. "I would never order the death of children. Never!"

"Maybe not. But you knew it would happen. And you did nothing to stop it."

"Please! Spare me. There are things you do not know. Things only I can tell you."

"Of that, I am sure. But even if I were inclined to spare you, the soldiers you sent are due to return soon. And as much as I would like to watch them die as well, I have not the time."

Zarhari held out the book. "Look at this. Please. You *must* look."

Sayia sneered. "You think to bargain with me?"

A blast of air slammed into Zarhari, causing the book to tumble from her grasp. In retaliation, her arms shot out to send a series of tiny fireballs racing toward Sayia. These were easily deflected and sent harmlessly to the floor. Letting out a feral cry of fear and fury, she released another blast that had the floor beneath Sayia's feet erupting. Yet again, the assault failed. Leaping sharply to her left, Sayia used the *flow* of the air to hurl the resulting debris at her foe. Several large pieces of this thudded into Zarhari's chest and legs, pummeling her to the floor.

"You cannot match me," Sayia told her.

Pressing herself up on her hands, Zarhari glared spitefully back. "You think not?"

Bells and laughter filled the room. Sayia could feel the *flow of the spirit* pressing in, trying to subdue her will.

"Impressive," she remarked. "In time, you might have become truly powerful."

Terror splayed across Zarhari's face on realizing that her attack was ineffective. The look was still there when another blast of air lifted her to her feet and slammed her flat against the far wall. Sayia walked casually toward her, stopping a few feet away.

"You have lost," Zarhari spat at her. "Whatever you do to me, know that you have lost."

The bells and laughter returned, this time at the beckoning of Sayia. "That may be true," she admitted. "But you will never be able to relish my defeat."

The *flow of the spirit* descended upon Zarhari. At first, it was like a gentle rain; then its power increased. Though the blast of air was no longer holding her, she could not move. The *flow of the spirit* had saturated her completely, crumbling her will and laying her mind bare. She opened her mouth to scream, but could manage only a soft whimper.

Sayia stepped in close to meet her eyes. "No. You will not be aware of my defeat, should it happen. You will not be aware of anything. I leave you hollow. A spirit trapped in flesh."

She watched impassively as the *flow* twisted and snaked its way deep inside her enemy, severing all ties to the living world. She knew that Kaleb would not have wanted it this way. His soul was too gentle; his heart too loving. For all that, she was certain her actions were just. And if they were not, then let the Creator be her judge.

She glanced down at the book Zarhari had been holding. What could it contain that she had thought might be enough to buy her a reprieve? Picking it up, Sayia cast a final glance at the now vacant-eyed woman. Even though she knew she should be feeling at least a certain amount of guilt for what she had done, in reality, there was nothing but righteous satisfaction. Zarhari would spend her remaining years as a tortured shell until age finally caught up with her. That, or until someone showed her mercy by ending her existence with steel.

As she exited the room, she could hear the boots of the returning soldiers stomping their way closer. She could feel the Vrykol among them. The rage returned. Now, though, was not the time. She had never before faced a foe such as this creature, and could not risk any more than she already had. There was too much left to do. Jayden had to be instructed; that was vital. Though Maybell and Penelope were certainly able to serve this purpose equally well, they were needed in Sharpstone. Should their mother be killed because they were not there to protect her, there was no telling what such a catastrophe would do to Jayden. The wrath buried inside the boy might well be unleashed in a colossal fit of uncontrollable rage. That would spell disaster for everyone.

Once outside the temple, she checked to see that the two guards she had incapacitated were not permanently injured. They had done nothing to warrant death. As it was, both were already starting to rouse.

The fact that she felt no guilt—not a hint of it—continued to play on her mind. What did this say about her? Aaliyah would think her callous and cruel. Then again, Aaliyah had bonded with an elf of deep emotion and passion. This had changed her. She had always been a woman of conviction and sincerity, though never what would be considered soft-hearted.

A long sigh slipped from Sayia's mouth. Had she truly become hard and unfeeling?

After thinking on this for a short time, it did not feel as though she had. Nonetheless, something inside had definitely changed. Or possibly been awakened? Seeing the tiny form of Kaleb curled in the corner, his life's blood pooled on the floor around him, had stirred a rage that she had not known possible.

And it was far from spent.

CHAPTER 9

The salt air carried on the morning wind, forcing back the stench of the marsh. Jayden marched on, his boots caked with slimy mud and every inch of exposed flesh covered in bug bites that threatened to drive him mad with their incessant itching.

Sayia had rejoined them the morning after her abrupt departure. In her arms, she'd been carrying a large leather book that she packed away immediately. Since then, her attention once again had been focused almost entirely on him. There was a curiously stoic look in her eyes. She had gone seeking revenge. The question was, had she found it? It seemed odd that an elf from across the Abyss would do such a thing. Jayden had met several from there and found them to be ill at ease with the passionate nature of the humans and elves from his own land. Vengeance unquestionably demanded a great deal of passion and anger.

His mother had always discouraged acts of retribution, even when it was warranted. Yet she was not beyond handing out a little of her own on occasion. Not that it was ever anything overly severe. If a woman in the village were to pay his father too much "special attention," she might find herself tripped in the street and consequently covered in mud—all by accident, naturally. That was about the limit of things. Beyond this, he had never seen her be truly violent or spiteful to anyone. *Spirited* was what his father called her. All the same, knowing that she had fought in the war, Jayden could not help but wonder what she might have done back then. How many had she killed? Had she enjoyed it? And if so, did she now feel any regret or guilt?

The marshes were behind them and the ground had become dry, though the large patches of yellow sand made walking no easier than before. Most of the others were looking bone weary from the trek, and the growling of empty stomachs had become a constant companion. Sayia assured them that there was hot stew and good wine waiting for them when they arrived. She had been in contact with her vessel, and the landing craft would be there to greet them.

That she could communicate over distance by using the *flow* was nothing short of astonishing to Jayden.

"Once you've learned more, you'll be able to do the same," she had told him.

"How far can you be from your ship and still reach them?" he asked.

She shrugged. "I don't possess the talent of Aaliyah. But many miles, nonetheless."

This made him excited for their journey together to begin. The power he'd felt as the *flow* entered his body still lingered in his memory. It had given him a strength unlike anything he had thought possible. The potential was enormous. It would give him all the power he needed to protect those he loved. *Is this,* he wondered, *why my father did the things he did?* With all his vast power, maybe he felt responsible for keeping the entire world from harm? Of the possibilities Jayden could think of, this to his mind seemed to be the most likely explanation.

Glancing to his left, he noticed Maybell gazing at him, her expression sorrowful. He moved over to walk beside her.

"Are you all right?"

She took his hand. "It's not long enough. You've only just arrived."

Jayden smiled. "I know. But we'll have as much time as we want once this is over."

"I'd like to travel," she told him. "Just the three of us. I want to see as much of the world as I can."

He gave her hand a reassuring squeeze. "We will. Though I think there will be four of us, if Mother has her way."

"She will get better, won't she?" she asked, eyes downcast. "I need to hear it."

At that moment, she appeared to him as the little girl he'd known before she left for Baltria. "Of course she will. I'll find Father, and he'll make her better."

"Promise me you won't get yourself killed. That you won't do anything foolish."

He gave her a roguish grin. "Me? Who's more careful than I am?"

She did not return the smile. "I'm serious, Jayden. This isn't a game. The gods want you dead. The *gods*!"

"There's nothing I can do about that. Anyway, maybe you're worrying too much. If it were within their power to just come down from heaven and kill me, I think they would have done it by now."

He could see his words were not helping. "Listen to me, Maybell. I promise you I'll be as careful as I can. I *will* find Father, and I will *not* get myself killed. If you've ever believed anything, believe that."

This seemed to have an effect. Her lips formed a tiny smile. "I believe you. But you should be sure to say that to Penelope as well."

Jayden raised an eyebrow. "I will if you want me to."

He had not noticed Penelope behaving as if she were too worried. At least not as much as Maybell. Most of the time, she'd appeared to be her usual pragmatic and somewhat distant self.

"Don't let her fool you," Maybell said, as if reading his thoughts. "She might act tough, but I know she's about a hair's breadth away from abandoning everything and going with you."

Jayden looked over his shoulder to where his other sister was walking beside Linis and Sayia. In a strange way, knowing that she cared more than she let on made him feel good. Not that he doubted her love. It was just that she rarely expressed it openly.

"I'll speak with her," he promised.

The piercing cry of the seagulls was suddenly unwelcome. The excitement to begin his journey he'd felt only minutes before was now drained away. In the short time he'd spent with Maybell and Penelope, a realization had dawned. A piece of him had been missing. He now had a sense of belonging that he'd never felt in Sharpstone. He would keep his promise; he would survive. And together they would see the world, just like Maybell had said.

It was well past midday when the sound of the breakers at last reached the party. This visibly lifted their spirits as the danger of pursuit faded and the prospect of a hot meal grew.

Loroni Rock towered high above the dunes that concealed the shore. A swirling mixture of red and black granite, it stood more than a hundred feet tall, its winding form looking as if a great hand had reached down and twisted it up from the depths of the earth. It was believed to have been used in the distant past as a lighthouse for some ancient city, though any evidence of this had long since deteriorated. Other rumors suggested that it was the earthly home of Saraf. Many of his followers had indeed once come here to cast offerings into the sea in order to gain his favor, though this practice had been abandoned in recent years. Elves were known to wander the forests nearby, and most humans still felt uneasy in the wild when they were around. Worship these days was largely confined to within the temples.

A lone figure crested a dune ahead of them and raised a hand. Sayia returned the gesture.

She then turned to Jayden. "You and your sisters can have a few hours to say farewell. It will take time to transport everyone aboard."

"What do you mean?" he demanded. "We're all getting on your ship, aren't we?"

"Maybell and Penelope will be. You and I will not."

Jayden squared his shoulders. "When did you decide this?" He'd assumed they would be together on the ship, at least for a short time.

"Does it matter?" she asked.

"Yes, it matters a lot," he snapped back. "You aren't the leader here. You don't get to make all the decisions."

"I have no intention of doing so. In this case, however, if the Vrykol follows us, we will need it to believe that you are aboard the ship."

Jayden sniffed. "Yes. Because only a fool wouldn't be."

Whenever he had raised his tone to the elf woman, she'd appeared utterly unmoved. Now, though, he thought he saw an ever so slight twitch mar her expression.

"Foolish or not, that is our course," she replied. "And I suggest that in the future, you learn to listen to the council of those older and more experienced than yourself."

"You'll need a few more supplies for your journey," Linis hastily interjected. "If your ship can spare them, I can give you a list of what you might need."

Sayia nodded. "Thank you. You are most kind."

She led Linis away, leaving Jayden still fuming.

"She doesn't mean to be difficult," said Maybell.

"I can't believe I'm going to spend weeks traveling with that woman," he responded. "How can you stand her? She's infuriating."

Maybell laughed. "She's really a nice person, I promise. And she's a fine teacher. I'm sure you'll find a way to get along."

He stared after Sayia as she and Linis spoke with a member of the ship's crew. "It's not just what she says, it's the way she looks at me all the time. I know she's hiding something."

"If she is, then I'm sure there's a good reason." Maybell took his hand. "Come. We don't have much time left."

They found a spot between two dunes where they could sit and talk away from the others. People were already being loaded into the landing craft and transported across to the ship, which was anchored a few hundred yards away from the rock. Penelope joined them shortly afterward, holding a small tin flask. Within moments, the air filled with the aroma of plum brandy.

"Aren't you a little young for that?" Jayden teased, snatching the flask away and taking a small sip.

"Mother says elf children mature faster," she said, feigning offense. "She let me drink wine when I was only six."

Maybell pushed her sister playfully. "Liar! Mother caught you stealing a drink from the bottle."

Jayden laughed. "I remember that. She made you drink the whole cup at once."

Penelope's mouth twisted as if she had just tasted something foul. "I couldn't bring myself to drink wine again until about a year ago. Even then I watered it down."

"She knew just how to make us sorry for misbehaving," said Maybell.

"What would you know about that?" Jayden asked. "I can't recall you getting in trouble. Not even one time."

"Little Miss Perfect was too scared to act up," added Penelope.

"That's not true!" Maybell objected. "I can't help it if I was better at getting away with things than you two."

They talked and laughed for more than two hours, reminiscing over the days back in Sharpstone—happy days before the world and its problems had intruded into their lives. Throughout, Jayden kept glancing over to the gathering of people preparing to board the ship, his heart aching each time the landing boat ferrying them reduced their number.

When he spotted Linis and Sayia approaching, Sayia with a pack across her back and Linis carrying another, he knew it was time.

Maybell burst into tears. "It's too quick," she sobbed. "We're not ready yet."

He wrapped his arms around her. "It's all right. We'll see one another again soon, I promise."

Penelope joined the embrace. "Of course we will," she added.

It was heartbreaking for Jayden to release his sisters. He glanced up at Sayia, standing over them. Her expression was a stone mask.

As if in response to an unspoken command, the three of them rose to their feet as one. Jayden stepped back, allowing Penelope and Maybell to say their farewells to the elf woman. It was during this parting embrace that, for the very first time, he saw a hint of emotion on Sayia's face. Not that he thought her devoid of feeling. But seeing even this small display made him feel a little more at ease about traveling with her. She was hiding something, of that he was sure. Thus far, trust in her had been a commodity that was difficult to find.

"I don't want you to worry," Linis told him. "I'll take good care of your sisters—and your mother. You just concentrate on finding your father."

Jayden held out his hand. "I will."

With a laugh, Linis brushed his offered hand aside, electing instead to give him a firm hug. "You take care of yourself, Master Stedding. And find your way safely home."

As he drew back, Jayden noticed him flash Sayia a peculiar look. It was gone in an instant.

Teary-eyed and gripping each other's hand, Penelope and Maybell hesitated for a painfully long moment before finally following Linis down to the waiting landing craft. Maybell looked back just once. After that, she needed the support of her sister to continue the rest of the way.

"Come," said Sayia. "We cannot delay. The Vrykol is still hunting us."

Jayden cocked his head. If they'd been followed, he would have bet anything on Linis being aware of it. "Are you sure about that?"

"He's tracked us the entire way," she replied. "Hopefully, he'll think we have all boarded the ship and turn back. But if he finds us here, we'll be forced to fight. And until you are trained, this creature is not an opponent you are ready to face—even with my help."

"But won't it just follow those on the ship?"

"Possibly. If we're lucky."

"And you sent them, anyway?" His anger began to swell.

"The Vrykol is after you. Not your sisters. And even were that not the case, they are more than a match for it." She tossed Jayden the pack that Linis had left on the ground nearby. "No time for questions. I need you to trust me."

Such was his fury, Jayden barely heard her last few words. Tossing the pack back down, he ran as fast as he could toward the beach. It was pointless; the small boat was already well on its way to the ship. He spun around and returned to where Sayia was waiting. He longed to strike her and was only just able to resist the urge.

"The Vrykol will be here soon," she reminded him. "We need to be far enough away so that he cannot sense your presence." Without waiting for a reply, she set off at a quick jog.

Jayden waited nearly a minute for his temper to cool before chasing after her. She was moving swiftly, and it took no small effort to catch up.

"Do not use the *flow* until I tell you that it's safe," she warned once he was within earshot.

Use the *flow*? It wasn't as if he was able to do so on command, anyway. He wanted to say something back to her... something cutting. He shook away these thoughts. He mustn't let his suspicion and dislike for the woman cloud his mind. If the Vrykol really were after them, then she was right to want to escape. He might be young and brash, but he sure as hell wasn't stupid. If one as powerful as Sayia feared the creature, he should do so as well.

Quickening their pace, they plunged headlong into the forest. Sayia proved to be quite adept at winding between the trees and brush, though naturally, nowhere near as accomplished as Linis. Or himself, for that matter. Most of his childhood had been spent tramping around in the wild with either his parents or Linis. The seeker had often praised his ability to read the signs that would guide him to the best path. He even considered taking the lead, if for no other reason than to irritate Sayia. But as he had no idea where they were going, the notion was quickly dismissed.

After more than five miles, Sayia halted, her expression dark and her body tense. She closed her eyes for several seconds.

"Is it following us?" Jayden asked.

"Quiet," she snapped.

All he could hear was the rustle of the wind through the high branches and the chirping of the birds. He sniffed the air. The salty aroma of the sea was now gone, replaced by the musky smell of pine and earth. A deer was grazing somewhere off to their right, and a family of gophers scurried about beneath a pile of leaves and twigs a few yards behind them.

"No one is here," he stated, keeping his tone at a defiantly normal level.

"I said be quiet."

"I've spent my entire life in the woods," Jayden boasted, continuing to disregard her order. "There's no one here but us."

"You should listen to your elf guide, boy," a voice called. "She is clearly wiser than you."

Rapidly shedding his pack, Jayden reached for his blade. It sounded like the Vrykol he had fought within the temple. He tried to determine the voice's location, but it was as if it surrounded them.

"Show yourself," he demanded.

Sayia had also let her pack drop, though her two long knives remained in their sheaths. "Stay close to me," she said.

"You didn't think I would be fooled by that little trick, did you?" the voice continued.

This time, Jayden thought it came from a particularly thick patch of the forest a few yards ahead. "What do you want?" he responded.

The Vrykol, clearly addressing Sayia, continued as if he had not spoken. "I have no interest in the females. Nor does my master. They are inconsequential. Give me the boy, and you can go your way in peace."

Angry at being spoken about as if not there, a low growl slipped from Jayden's mouth. "Come out and I'll send *you* on your way," he challenged.

A mocking chuckle sounded. "He is fierce, is he not? Surely you know that he cannot be allowed to live. You know what he will become."

"Yes, I do," replied Sayia. "But you obviously do not. If you did, you would leave here and return to the hell from which you were spawned."

"Hell? Is that where you think I come from?"

Jayden caught a movement from the corner of his right eye. A figure clad in a light tunic and travel-worn trousers stepped out from behind a young birch tree. Far from having a demonic aspect, the Vrykol looked like a young human in his early thirties, with brown shoulder-length hair and dark eyes. Tall, though not quite as tall as Jayden, he was of slender to average build. To all appearances, he was nothing more striking than a typical villager. A blade hung at his side, along with a pair of throwing knives. Glancing only momentarily at Jayden, he smiled at Sayia.

"Do I look like I was spawned from hell? If indeed there is such a place."

Jayden started to take a step forward, but Sayia caught his arm and positioned herself in front of him. "I will give you one chance to leave," she stated.

The Vrykol laughed. "Or you will do what? Kill me? I am not one of the foul beasts you've heard tales of; the one you knew as the Reborn King is not my master. I was created by the god Saraf. You are no match for me, elf. As for the boy, he is completely untrained. I will have him. You can either give him to me willingly, or I will kill you and take him, anyway. It seems a simple choice to me."

"Yes, it does," she agreed.

Jayden felt the *flow* entering her body. He tried urging it to enter his own as well, but for some reason, it would not.

"You see?" said the Vrykol. "You're alone in this fight, elf. The son of Darshan is no more help to you than any other human might be."

"I think you underestimate the talents of humans," Sayia retorted.

"Perhaps. But I do not think that is the case here."

After a long pause, the Vrykol let out an exaggerated sigh. "Stubborn, I see. That, at least, you have in common with humans."

So fast was it that Jayden did not even see the Vrykol's arm move. The blade seemed to materialize in its hand. In response, Sayia let loose a ball of fire, but by the time it arrived, the creature had already shifted several yards to one side. To his astonishment, the elf woman then turned and shoved him hard to the ground. His sword slipped from his grasp as he fell.

Scrambling to his feet, he saw that Sayia had now drawn her weapons and was slashing furiously at their foe. She was almost as fast as Linis he thought. Even so, the Vrykol was faster, his parries effortless and his movements graceful.

The creature countered with a barrage of precise thrusts, two of which found flesh—one on Sayia's left arm, the other higher up on the same shoulder. Though the wounds forced her to give ground, she was undeterred and quickly renewed her attack, all the time attempting to place herself between Jayden and her opponent. In an attempt for outright victory, she delivered a sweeping strike aimed at taking its head. With time to spare, the beast ducked below this and then landed a fist to her jaw. Even before she fell, two more rapid thrusts opened wounds in her right forearm and left thigh.

The Vrykol loomed over her, a vicious grin stretched across his face.

Horrified, Jayden reached for his sword and charged, a feral scream rushing out as he advanced. But rage alone was never going to be enough to vanquish this foe. The Vrykol simply stepped over Sayia and slapped the flat of his blade hard across the side of Jayden's head. Had it been the edge, it would have surely removed the top half of his skull. Even so, the impact was enough to severely daze him. He staggered forward and dropped to one knee.

The Vrykol returned his attention to Sayia, his sword raised for a killing stroke. Kicking desperately at the ground to move away, she sent a gust of wind to delay his approach.

This was followed up by a ball of energy that caused the earth beneath her enemy's feet to shake and heave.

Neither was sufficient to delay the creature for more than a moment. Moving smartly away from Sayia's assault, he shifted into position to cut off her retreat. Watching this, Jayden felt a wave of desperation. There was nothing he could do to stop what was about to happen.

Then, as if in response to his rising panic, a voice called out from deep within his mind.

The power of heaven is within you.

Time immediately slowed to a crawl. He could feel it. The *flow*. Only this time, it was immeasurably stronger than before. The pain from the Vrykol's blow was banished, and the sword in his hand suddenly felt as if it had no weight at all.

Though Sayia was no more than a heartbeat or two away from death, from Jayden's new perspective, it was as if he had all the time in the world to save her. Movements that until seconds ago were a blur to his eyes now appeared virtually suspended, as if time itself no longer existed. A fire raged within his spirit. This was more than the *flow*; this was a power unlike anything he had ever imagined. The words he had heard kept repeating in his thoughts: *The power of heaven is within you.*

Was this what he was now feeling? The power of heaven? It seemed impossible. Yet there could be no other explanation. The world around him had all but halted. What else but heaven itself could accomplish such a thing?

His eyes fell upon the Vrykol, its blade threatening to end Sayia's life. Emotions instantly raged. *Fury... Hatred... A Need to Destroy.* In an instant, he felt them all tear through him as never before.

Rising to his feet, he ran headlong at the Vrykol. Only then did the passage of time resume. His rage was all-encompassing as he swung his steel at the beast's neck. The Vrykol looked up in wide-eyed astonishment, but for only the briefest of moments. Jayden's steel found its mark, the flesh and bone of his victim no barrier whatsoever to the strength he had unleashed.

Even after its head had rolled from its shoulders, the body of the Vrykol remained standing. Jayden regarded it with a sinister smile before kicking it contemptuously to the ground.

Sayia was still on her back, staring up at him with an unreadable expression. In his eyes, she now seemed tiny… insignificant. No more important than a pet or pack animal. The world around him had changed as well. It wasn't a place in which he dwelt any longer. It was his. A possession. A thing with which he could do as he pleased.

He closed his eyes. He no longer felt human. Nor did he feel the elf blood that ran through his veins. But if he was neither of these, then what was he? The answer quickly came. He was quite simply … more. Everything was now clear. He knew what he had to do. It was all so simple, so very obvious. He realized that he was laughing.

No. This is not the way.

The voice felt like claws raking at his mind. His anger returned tenfold upon realizing that the power was leaving him. A furious scream escaped, though he could not be certain if it actually passed his lips or if it was contained within the torrent of his spirit. Frantically he tried to hold on to whatever power remained, but it was like trying to wrap his hands around a gust of wind.

A great weight crashed in. It was gone. The power of heaven had completely deserted him, as if it had never been there at all. He was only vaguely aware of dropping to his knees. The pain in his head from where he had been struck returned. He toppled over onto his side, unable to move as darkness began closing in around him. He could not fight against it. As strong as he had been only moments ago, he was now equally weak.

He thought he felt a pair of hands touch his brow, but the sensation was fleeting. Only seconds later, the darkness became total, and the last vestiges of consciousness disappeared.

CHAPTER 10

Once settled into his blanket in a dry corner of the cargo hold, Linis ran a hand over the cover of the book Sayia had passed onto him. Her instructions had been not to open it until they were at least two days away. *An odd request*, he thought. She had said simply that it contained sketches dating back to the Great War and was an interesting piece of history. However, the dire expression on her face as she handed it over suggested that it contained something of great importance.

"Do not show this to Penelope and Maybell until their mother is safe," she had instructed. "I cannot have them chasing after us."

"If there's something I need to know—"

"If there were, you have my word, I would tell you. For now, I can only beg your trust. Please do as I ask."

They had been at sea for two days and were due to arrive at the port of Zinia by the morning. From there, they would purchase mounts and head northwest until reaching the Goodbranch. A roundabout way to go home to be sure, but it ensured that any pursuers would have great difficulty in following. The rest of the temple residents were to be then transported on to Althetas, where King Jacob would give them sanctuary.

While reaching over and turning up the lantern, a mild sense of dread came over him. Yet again, he recalled the troubling way in which Sayia had looked at the book before handing it over. This alone had made the temptation to view it prematurely hard to resist. But seeing as how there had been no ill intent in Sayia's voice, and the fact that both Penelope and Maybell seemed to trust her, he had waited for the instructed time. Now all would be revealed.

He opened it to the first page. *Visions of Life and Death,* by Nor Byrathisen.

Linis had never cared for human art. The themes were too common and the perspectives narrow. Not that he had ever been particularly enthusiastic about elf art, either—with the exception of that created by the elves of the steppes.

The first few sketches were of various animals and flora found mostly in the west. He guessed this was likely where the artist had originated from. Then his eye was drawn to the top of a red ribbon poking invitingly out midway through the book. It had to be there for a reason. With curiosity now peaking, rather than wait until reaching it page by page, he took a deep breath and jumped ahead. He was immediately struck by what he saw. Reaching over, he brightened the lantern.

For the next twenty minutes, he could do nothing but stare in shocked disbelief. Several more pages had been marked out, each one of them further verifying his suspicions. But it was impossible. Even though it was here before his very eyes, he still could not force himself to truly believe what he was seeing.

Hearing footsteps approaching, he quickly closed the book and shoved it under his blanket.

Penelope moved with careful steps, hopping over the packs and blankets of the passengers, most of whom were currently on deck or in the galley.

"Is that the book Sayia gave you?" she asked. When Linis didn't reply, she laughed and took a seat beside him. "I saw her give it to you. There's no need to hide it. I won't pester you about it."

He gave what he hoped was a casual smile. "It's nothing important... nothing you need be concerned over."

Penelope shrugged. "Whatever you say."

"Where is your sister?"

"With the navigator again. Maybell's determined to learn how she controls the flow of wind and water." She rolled her eyes. "As if she could learn all that in a matter of a few days. I told her not to bother, but she doesn't listen."

"She was always stubborn," Linis remarked.

To him, they were still the small children who had left Sharpstone years ago. Though they had grown in body, their personalities had remained exactly the same. Dina had always thought Penelope to be far too detached for one so young. Linis, however, saw through her façade. She was deeply emotional, but unlike Maybell, was afraid to let it show.

"Are you excited to see home again?" he asked.

Penelope lowered her head. "To be honest, I don't know how to feel about it. What with Mother being ill and Father missing, it doesn't really feel like I'm going home at all."

"Your mother is strong," he assured her. "She'll make it through this."

"The funny thing is, it's not Mother or even Father I'm worried about. I know I should be. But I'm not."

Linis sat up and leaned his back against the ship's hull. "What is it, then?"

"It's Jayden. I fear what will become of him. What if the vision Father had is true? Could it have been more than a warning? What if it really was an image of the future?"

Linis smiled warmly. "Jayden has a good heart. You have to trust in that, as I do. He is not capable of evil and has no desire to rule and conquer."

"Maybe that was true before. But what about now? Back home, he had no knowledge of his power. There, he was just the son of a farmer. Now, suddenly, he has discovered that he's the son of the mighty Darshan."

"He is still Jayden. I've known him all his life. Only your parents know him better. He will not become what your father's vision foretold. I'm confident of that."

"I pray you're right."

Linis could see there was more on her mind. He reached out and placed a hand on her arm. "You can speak freely with me, Penelope. I may not be as wise as my wife. But perhaps talking might help."

She sighed. "It's just something Sayia said shortly before you arrived in Baltria. About how troubles in the world would make it easy for someone strong—like Jayden—to make themselves an all-powerful king or emperor. We've already seen the start of it in the West. Rebellious nobles have tried to dethrone King Jacob three times because of his relationship with the elves. The last attempt was nearly successful."

"And you think your brother would attempt such a thing?"

"Like you say, he has a good heart. What if he thinks that to save the world, he must first rule it? Isn't that what originally motivated the Reborn King? He wasn't evil in the beginning, either."

"His rise was born from anger," Linis pointed out. "He felt betrayed by those close to him. Jayden is—"

"He feels the same way," she said, cutting him short. "He feels betrayed by our parents for having lied to him. Haven't you noticed how angry he gets?"

"All young men get angry. It's part of being young. I was no different myself. As far as feeling betrayed, I agree that he isn't happy about what they did. All the same, I think he understands. He loves Gewey and Kaylia very much. He will learn to forgive them."

"Will he? Are you sure? Are you willing to risk the fate of the world on it?"

Linis could see the pain in her eyes and hear it in her tone. "I am. I have seen all manner of evil in this world. I have witnessed the very worst in both human and elf. Jayden is not like that, and never will be." He paused to look Penelope directly in the eye. "You cannot compare him to the Reborn King. That man was raised to serve the gods in a world corrupted by their influence. He was taught there is only one path to salvation, and he learned his lessons well. Jayden was not brought up with such a narrow vision of the world. Despite being sheltered in Sharpstone, he is well aware of the realities of life. He has no false beliefs to cling to. The foulness of the world will not shatter him as it did the Reborn King."

Penelope forced a weak smile. "I want to believe that—more than anything. I know I don't show it, but I love my brother very much. I could never stand against him."

"It's a choice you will never need to make," Linis assured her.

He could see in her face that she meant every word. Should he be wrong, and Jayden did in fact one day seek to accomplish what the Reborn King could not, it would be much worse. Her love would not allow her to oppose him. Rather than that, she would possibly stand *with* him.

His mind turned back to the sketches hiding beneath his blanket.

"If you're going to keep hovering over that book, you're going to make me too curious to leave it alone," Penelope told him.

Linis realized that he had subconsciously placed his hand on the blanket directly above the book. "I'll show you what it is soon," he said. "Just not now."

Her smile widened. "I'm sure it's some dread secret Sayia thinks should be hidden from us. Ever the mysterious elf, she is. It took her a year before she even told us that she knew Aaliyah. Of course, we already knew; Aaliyah had sent us word that Sayia was coming. Yet when she sat us down to tell us, it was as if she were revealing the very secrets of heaven."

That might well be what the book contained, Linis considered. The secrets of heaven. The implications of what he had seen in its pages were like a cyclone whirling through his mind, jumbling all his thoughts. It had to be a forgery. Yes. But telling himself this did not make him believe it. And if it *was* real, then the future was already fixed—made irreversible by the past.

He felt a hand push on his leg.

"*I'm* supposed to be the broody one," Penelope teased. "Remember?"

Linis chuckled, trying to disguise his worry. "This is true. At least, that's what you like people to think." He pushed himself to his feet. "Come. I am hungry. Join me."

Penelope rose and took his arm. "I hope they don't serve any more of that dreadful stew."

"Dreadful? I thought you liked elf cooking."

"I like my mother's cooking," she corrected. "And I like elf candy." She gave him a lopsided grin. "You don't happen to have any, do you?"

"Sadly, none with me. But I think there's a jar in a cupboard in Sharpstone that will please you very much. Though I think you might have to fight your sister for it."

They both burst into laughter.

In spite of this merriment, Linis's thoughts lingered on the book. He almost stopped to retrieve it. Of course, that would only further heighten Penelope's curiosity. Besides, the time was not right. If what he had seen was true, then there was nothing that could be done about it, anyway. So there was no need to burden her further.

All the same, bearing this knowledge alone was proving unexpectedly difficult. He wanted another pair of eyes to point out something he had missed—something that would disprove his calculations. Both Maybell and Penelope had studied the history of The Great War extensively. Perhaps they would be able to see through it and lift the growing weight pressing down on him.

Deep in the recesses of his mind, he knew this hope was futile. He knew the histories well enough, too. It was true. All of it. And he was helpless to change it.

CHAPTER 11

When consciousness returned, Jayden's head was throbbing wildly. He attempted to move, but it was as if all his strength had been completely drained away. The chirping of crickets filtered through the pounding. It was this sound, and the coolness of the air, that told him it was well into the night.

Peeling open his eyes, he tried to call out, but no sound came. Not even his voice would obey his commands. What had happened? He concentrated on the events of the day. At first, he could recall only the fight between Sayia and the Vrykol. Then, little by little, the fog surrounding his memory lifted.

"Lie still."

He heard Sayia rummaging through her pack. He wanted to ask about her injuries, but was still unable to speak. Surely she was in pain. Yet without the skills of healing, there was nothing he could do to help her. There was also the not inconsequential fact that the only time he seemed able to use the *flow* was when he was enraged.

He lay there motionless and mute for several minutes until he felt a hand gently touch his brow. A cold chill shot through him, sending a wave of welcome relief to his paralyzed limbs.

"I..." he started to croak.

"Don't try to move yet," she told him. "I can restore only a small portion of your strength for now."

"Are you all right?" he asked. "What about your wounds?" At least he could talk, even if his dry mouth and swollen tongue were making each word an enormous effort.

"I will heal," she replied. "You needn't concern yourself."

He saw her silhouette moving against the moonlight a few feet away. She was limping severely. "How bad is it?" he asked.

"I said I'm fine. Self-healing is difficult, but I will manage."

"What happened to me?" Ignoring Sayia's order for him to remain still, he struggled onto his side and propped himself up on one elbow. Even this slight movement made him a touch dizzy, and for a moment his vision blurred.

"You're as stubborn as your sisters told me," she scolded.

Despite there being only dim moonlight, he could see the dark stain of blood seeping through the bandages on her shoulder, arms, and legs. "Can you still travel?" he asked.

"I'll be slowed for a few days, that's all. Fortunately, I brought with me salve made by the desert elves as a precaution. That will aid in the healing."

Jayden cast his eyes around for the dead Vrykol, but Sayia had apparently moved it. "Do you think more of those things will come?"

"There's no way to know. But we should assume they will." She locked eyes with him. "Now, I want you to tell me how you did it."

He shifted up a bit. "Did what?"

"How did you kill that creature?"

"You were there. You saw for yourself what happened."

She leaned in closer, as if attempting to peer inside him. "I saw ... something. Though I cannot tell you what it was. One moment you were standing a few yards away; then there was a blinding flash of light. The next thing I saw was you lying on your back beside the decapitated body of the Vrykol. No amount of the *flow* could have enabled you to do that. So, I ask again, how did you do it?"

Jayden paused to consider what he had experienced. *The power of heaven.* Yes. That was it. The feeling was like a distant memory, but it was still there. It had been bliss. Pure bliss.

"I heard a voice in my head," he began, unsure how to describe the experience. "Then it was like time had stopped. After that, I don't know. But you're right. It wasn't like the *flow*. It was something different."

Sayia narrowed her eyes. "What did the voice say to you?"

He hesitated before replying. Though his sisters trusted this woman, he did not. And as for revealing that he was able to channel some mysterious force even more powerful than the *flow*... no. That was a secret he would keep for now. "I can't remember," he said. "It was just a voice."

"Was it male, female, neither? Surely you can recall something about it."

"No. Nothing. It all happened so fast. I just remember that you were on the ground and I had to stop the Vrykol from killing you. The next thing I knew, I was lying here."

He could see that she doubted him. Nonetheless, after a few seconds, she shrugged and reached for her pack.

"I suppose it will have to remain a mystery... for the time being," she said. "At least the Vrykol will not trouble us for a while. Whatever it was that happened to you, for *that* I am grateful."

Jayden was indignant. A sharp response saying that she should be grateful to *him* for saving her life rose up. Only the invading memory of something his mother used to say prevented it from actually coming out. He could almost hear her reprimanding him.

We do things because they are right. Not for praise or gratitude.

Sure, he thought. Even so, the woman could still show a bit of appreciation.

He could feel the small portion of strength her healing had given to him rapidly fading. Sayia must have noticed this, too.

"We have a few hours until dawn," she said. "You should sleep while you can."

He was loath to follow any suggestion that she might give. All the same, she was right. The power he'd used had completely drained him. His body was spent.

Rolling onto his back, he shut his eyes. *The power of heaven.* These four words continued to resonate in his mind, along with an image of the Vrykol and Sayia both frozen in time like two fleshy statues. What did it mean? Sayia clearly wasn't able to tell him.

Father would be certain to know, he finally decided. There was going to be much for them to discuss. And this time, he would not accept anything other than the truth. The full truth.

*****

The following morning, he was awakened by the tempting aroma of fried bacon. At first, he imagined he was still dreaming. Then, as a shaft of sunlight found its way through the trees and struck his face, he realized he was not. He pushed himself up into a seated position. Resting on the ground beside him was a plate of bacon and three slices of bread. Sayia was sitting cross-legged nearby, her back against a pine sapling and an empty plate by her feet.

Jayden looked around but could see no fire. "How did you cook this?" he asked.

"The *flow* is not only for warfare and violence," she explained. "It has many practical uses as well."

To him, the idea of cooking bacon with the *flow* seemed somehow comical. And in a vague way, a misuse of its power. Not that such misgivings diminished his hunger. The rumbling in his stomach quickly overcame all other considerations, and he quickly devoured the offering.

Sayia was now moving about more easily, her limp less pronounced than the previous night. His own strength was still low, but at least he was able to stand up. After a few minutes of stretching and gentle exercise to get the blood flowing, he felt reasonably confident he could manage a decent pace—though for how long was uncertain.

After gathering their belongings, they set out at what would have been no more than a leisurely stroll had they both been fully fit. Even so, they covered a fair amount of ground before fatigue eventually forced Jayden to halt. Sayia looked displeased when he insisted they stop for a break, but had little choice other than to accept the situation.

"Tonight, we begin your training," she told him while changing her bandages and spreading a thick blue salve over the wounds.

The prospect was exciting. "What will you teach me?"

"To hide."

"Hide?"

Sayia winced as she tightened the bandage around her leg. "Yes. We're likely to run across elves that will not be accepting of what you are. To a human, you might appear to be a full-blooded elf, albeit one with a thicker build than most. An elf, however, will know the difference right away."

This was puzzling to Jayden. "Linis's wife is a newbreed too, and the elves in Sharpstone can't sense what she is. Why would they know what I am?"

"Your elf features will give you away," she replied. "The desert elves do not use the *flow*, but you do not resemble one of them. So that means those hostile to newbreeds will naturally assume you're half-human."

"Other than chopping off the tips of my ears, what can I do about it?"

"You will see. The *flow* can do remarkable things."

"So you've taught this skill to others?"

"No, but your sister Maybell has. And I was a witness." She shouldered her pack. "At the time, I didn't agree with the practice. I felt no one should be forced to hide who they are. Now, though, I can see that it has its uses."

Hearing these words assuaged some of his dislike. In her place, he would have probably reacted similarly. Hiding what you were was wrong. However, as he was discovering of late, being faced with the realities of the world often led a person to places they never imagined they would go. Back home, if he had been offered a way to be perceived as anything other than what he actually was, he would have been furious. As would his mother and father. But here, far from the life he knew, survival meant that pride and integrity had to suffer.

They set off again and continued until the sunlight was nearly spent, pausing briefly only twice for a meal and to rest tired muscles. Sayia stayed in the lead, all the time listening out for any sounds of pursuit and making sure they did not run into anything—or anyone—unexpected. A few of the well-beaten paths they crossed might have seemed out of place so deep in the wilderness, but it was well-known that this was an area frequented by elves traveling east—the kind of elves they certainly did not have any wish to encounter.

By the time they found a decent place to camp for the night, the muscles in Jayden's legs felt as if they were on fire. Sayia looked to be in no better condition, although she was doing her best to mask the discomfort.

After a quick meal of jerky and a small portion of bread and cheese, Sayia built a fire. She then told Jayden to sit on one side while she took a seat directly opposite.

"To conceal your heritage, you will use the *flow of the spirit*," she said. "This is not a thing I would prefer you to learn first, but our situation dictates it. I am afraid we must teach you to fly before you have learned to walk."

"Exactly what *is* the *flow of the spirit*?" Jayden asked, frowning.

She smiled. "A good question. Unfortunately, as I am not entirely sure what the *flow* really is in any of its forms, I do not have a good answer for you."

"Linis described it to me as being the energy of the world. What do you think of that?"

"I suppose that is one way to see it. I tend to think of it more as drawing power directly from the Creator. Each of the *flow*'s aspects possesses its own unique qualities. The most powerful of these is the spirit."

"But wouldn't fire or earth or even water be stronger? What can the spirit do? It can't stop an army."

Sayia laughed softly. "You sound like Penelope. She, too, did not grasp the power of spirit. Not until she saw it for herself." She folded her hands in her lap. "The strength of an army is not forged in steel. It is the will of those who fight that gives it power. The will of those who lead. Take that away and you crush it without a single blow being struck."

"And the *flow of the spirit* can do this?"

"How do you think the Reborn King was able to command such blind obedience from his followers?"

Jayden thought on this for a moment. "My father. He has this power as well?"

"He does," she affirmed.

"Then why not use it to force people into peace? If saving lives is the point, wouldn't it make more sense to just change the way everyone thinks?"

She shook her head. "That isn't peace; that is slavery. And what of the generations to follow? Do you continue to alter the minds of the children and grandchildren until the end of time? No. The change must come willingly from within the people."

Jayden sniffed. "I guess you've never been to a farming town. People don't change. Not really. They like things to stay the same. It makes them feel safe." Even as the words escaped his lips, he knew that he had heard them from someone else. Millet, perhaps? Whenever the old man had consumed a bit too much wine, his mood often became dark and cynical.

"And yet here you sit before me," she pointed out. "In your village, are you not known to be the son of an elf and a human?"

"My family is rich compared to the rest," he countered. "We employ half of Sharpstone. And most of the other half owe us something. They don't accept me. They tolerate me."

"Tolerance is a start," she said. "It is a foundation from which understanding can be built."

"But how is tolerance based on the fear of my father's wealth and influence any different from using the *flow of the spirit*?"

"Because they still have a choice. They can choose to risk the wrath of your father. Should he alter their minds with the *flow*, the choice is taken away."

Jayden considered this. In truth, it would not be his father that Sharpstone needed to fear. It was his mother. More than once, in his early youth, she had lashed out at someone for making a derogatory comment about him or his sisters. It didn't take long before it was well understood that such behavior would provoke swift retribution. Jayden felt certain she would never become seriously violent. Regardless of this, elves were still feared, and the people of Sharpstone were far less convinced of his mother's restraint. As for his father, he would shrug such nonsense off as ignorant banter.

Sayia breathed a heavy sigh. "You make me wary of teaching you this power. Unlocking the mysteries of the spirit is a tremendous responsibility. The damage you can do should you decide to abuse it is incalculable."

A flash of irritation shot through him. "I thought you were showing me how to conceal my heritage, not alter minds."

"I am showing you how to manipulate the *flow of the spirit* so as to alter the perceptions of others. Were you an elf child, I would not be as concerned. As it is, you are the son of a god. You are also young. Perhaps too young to use your gifts wisely."

Once again, his anger flared. "You don't know me. I don't care what that damned prophecy says. I'm *not* going to try to rule the bloody world."

"It was a vision, not a prophecy. Or to be more accurate, a warning. At least, that's how I interpret it... a warning that should not go unheeded." She regarded him closely. "Look at yourself, Jayden. Even now, the rage is boiling in your veins."

"You act like being angry is some strange thing."

"For you, anger is dangerous. Perhaps not now. But one day, when you've learned to use your powers, it could be."

He wondered if this was what his parents thought about him, too. Still, this woman was infuriating in a way that seemed to bring out the worst in him. "Either teach me or don't," he snapped. "I'm tired of all your lectures and accusations."

After a long moment of thought, she nodded. "Indeed. I have no choice, do I? Events will unfold as they must. Right now, seeing that you are safely delivered has to be my priority."

"Then why don't we get started?"

Although his gruff tone might have disguised it, Jayden was caught off guard by her apparent concession. There was also something about her tone and the way she gazed at him that he found unsettling.

Sayia's eyes lingered on him for a moment longer. She then closed them and folded her hands in her lap. "Let us begin by breathing," she said. "Slow, steady breaths."

He shut his eyes and did as instructed. For more than ten minutes, this continued without pause. Soon, he became restless.

"You're not concentrating," Sayia scolded. "Focus."

"On what?"

"The rhythm of your heart and the sound of the air as it enters your lungs. You must shut out everything else."

Unwilling to appear an impatient youth, Jayden suppressed his irritation and set about fully focusing his mind. After several minutes of this, he was finally able to do as instructed, successfully blocking out all but the steady rhythm of his heartbeat and breathing. He had seen Linis do this a number of times while they were on hunting excursions. On a few occasions, he had even tried to imitate the elf, but youthful restlessness soon had him distracted.

He was on the verge of giving up when a rush of warm air passed over him, and for the briefest of moments, he felt himself become completely weightless. His eyes shot open. Sayia was nowhere to be seen. Scrambling to his feet, he searched for his sword. He knew full well that he had placed it alongside his pack. That too was no longer there.

Jayden's heart pounded loudly in his ears. The campsite had not changed. The fire still crackled brightly, and all the rest of their gear was exactly where they had placed it. Even the surrounding trees and shrubs appeared the same.

"There is nothing to fear, son of Darshan."

The voice was deep, and commanding, and came from all directions.

"What's going on?" he demanded. "Who are you?"

A single coin-sized point of light flickered into existence a few feet in front of him, followed quickly by a second light a short distance farther away. Gradually, these expanded to take on human forms. The one nearest to Jayden was clearly male, though its facial features were undefined. The other remained only loosely human in shape, without any distinguishing characteristics whatsoever.

"I am impressed that you were able to reach this place," the man said. "Only a few mortal souls have ever seen it. Of course, I should have known you would come, eventually."

The figure was tall: a full head taller than himself. As the light radiating from him began to dim, Jayden could make out silver hair and piercing green eyes. His aspect, though still clearly male, bore an almost feminine beauty. He was dressed simply in an open-neck blue shirt and black trousers, and a silver horn hung from his belt.

With the man's gaze remaining fixed on him, Jayden felt a surge of panic. The penetrating eyes seemed to peer into his very essence. He wanted to run and hide himself away. But try as he might, his legs would not move and he could not look away.

"Enough," called another voice that came from the second figure. This one was soft and definitely feminine. "You will abide by our agreement, Saraf."

The man looked over his shoulder, his expression twisted into a deep scowl. "I have no intention of breaking our agreement, sister. I was only trying to prevent him from fleeing."

"You were trying to frighten him," she countered, her tone hardening.

The man shrugged. "I never agreed to be gentle."

"Saraf?" Jayden's voice was barely a whisper. His thoughts instantly turned to Sayia.

"The elf woman is unharmed," Saraf assured him, reading his thoughts. "Her spirit is merely delayed so that we can have this opportunity to speak."

With a great effort, Jayden forced his nerves to calm. He would not cower to this ... thing. This god who supposedly wanted him dead. "Where am I?" he demanded.

"Exactly where you were before," Saraf replied. "At least your body is. As for the rest of you—that is another matter. If my dear sister would allow it, I could show you. The trouble is, she fears it might be more than your mind could handle."

"So it's the spirit realm."

Saraf raised an eyebrow. "Very good. Your father has told you more than I would have thought."

"My father told me nothing. It was my mother."

"Oh, yes. The elf who fancies herself a goddess," he sneered.

"Do not speak ill of my mother."

Saraf chuckled. "Such courage to speak thusly to a god. Then again, I suppose you are practically one of us."

Jayden could hear the sarcasm bleeding into his tone. His anger flared. "I'm nothing like you. And would I never want to be."

"Oh, but you are. In fact, I am surprised your father has not explained to you just how powerful you really are. You could have even rivaled the Reborn King had your true nature been revealed to you sooner. Alas, Darshan chose to keep you blind ... and mortal. Such a waste."

"What have you done to my father?" he demanded.

Saraf flicked his wrist, causing a wooden chair to appear on either side of the fire. "Please, sit. We need to talk."

Jayden stood firm. "Tell me where he is. Then we can talk."

Saraf sat anyway. Leaning casually back, he said, "All you need to know is that your father is beyond your reach. But seeing as how your mother's life is at stake, you would be wise to listen to what I have to say."

Reluctantly, knowing that he had no real choice in the matter, Jayden complied. He had heard tales of people falling to their knees and weeping at the mere sight of a god; all he wanted to do was lash out. The awe and wonder he would have expected to feel were totally absent.

"If you have hurt either one of them," he growled in his most threatening tone.

Saraf laughed boisterously, slapping his thigh several times in amusement. "What will you do? Kill me? I am afraid not even Darshan himself could have done that. And though you have potential, Jayden, your threats are empty. You would do best to save them."

His anger was close to full-blown rage. "Say what you've come to say and be done with it."

"I can see the hatred inside you," Saraf remarked. "It festers like an open wound. Not that I blame you. You have been denied your destiny for no other reason than fear. Even one such as I would find myself embittered over this blatant deception. You are undeserving of this."

His expression softened, becoming kind and almost fatherly. "I can help you. I can undo what has been done. Through me, you can become what you were always meant to be."

Jayden sniffed. "So you would make me a god? Is that it?"

"You *are* a god already. At least in part. But you are tainted by the blood of mortal beings. I can cleanse you and make you whole. Through me, death and disease will never touch you."

"And what must I do to receive this generous offer? Bow, scrape, and pray to you?"

Saraf frowned. "Do not mock me, boy. Should you reject me, you will not achieve victory. In the end, you will die... as will your mother. Your spirit will dwell here, in this place, for all eternity. Heaven will be denied you. And I can promise, the gentle forest you see now will be replaced by a never-ending landscape of fire and dust."

"Saraf!" called the second figure. "I am warning you. Threaten him once more and I will end this immediately."

He cast her a sideways glance. "You are right, of course. My apologies, dear sister."

He smiled over at Jayden. "Ayliazarah can be quite protective at times. Particularly in matters involving Darshan. It was all we could do to keep her from revealing herself to you before now. The one wise thing your father ever did was to forbid our interaction with you and your sisters. A policy that, until now, I would have upheld."

"So why have you broken it? So far, you have only tried to kill me. Why come to me now?"

"Because I realize that my initial reaction was incorrect. I should have been more diplomatic. Darshan's actions are not your fault."

"What exactly has my father done that is so terrible? How is trying to spread peace a reason to kill him?"

"First of all, we have not killed your father."

"That's only because you can't," Jayden snapped back.

"That may be the case. I can't truthfully say one way or the other. To be sure, he is extremely powerful. And in the history of time itself, only Melek has ever killed a god."

The name was unfamiliar, though Jayden thought he saw a flash of anger on Saraf's face while speaking of Melek's accomplishment. But it was gone in an instant.

"Whatever the case," he continued. "Darshan is now incapable of doing any further damage. The two races will be allowed to find their own destiny without his interference. They will stand or fall untouched by divine influence. Unfortunately, we were unable to convince your father to leave the world alone and join us where he belongs. Where *you* belong."

Jayden stiffened. "What are you saying?"

"I am saying that you will soon be faced with a choice. One for which the consequences are dire indeed—for both you and for those you love." He looked over at Ayliazarah, who gave a nod of consent. "I take it you have never seen the vision your father had during the war against Angrääl?"

"No. I have heard about it, though. It supposedly shows me conquering the world."

"That is one interpretation, yes. But looked at another way, it could just as easily suggest that you will save it."

He waved his arm in a sweeping circle. All light instantly faded. Jayden leaped up, fists clenched.

"Do not fear," Saraf told him. "I only mean to show you the reason why you have been kept ignorant for your entire life."

A flash behind Jayden had him spinning around. The forest was no longer there. In its place was a barren landscape riddled with mountains of rubble and lit by thousands of raging infernos. Splitting this scene down the center was a shattered road, its bricks broken and large portions scattered about. In the road were three figures, two of them kneeling with heads downcast. Between them stood a towering warrior clad in black armor and wearing a gold circlet on his brow.

At first, Jayden did not understand the significance. Then, as he looked more closely, he saw that the armored warrior bore his own likeness. It was older and hardened by battle, but there was no mistaking whom it was meant to depict. Instinctively, he knew those kneeling beside him were his mother and father. They were weeping, begging him to stop. Pleading for him to lay down his sword and come home.

"Darshan believed that you would not be able to resist the temptation of power and conquest," Saraf went on. "And he knew he could not bring himself to stop you."

Jayden could feel the heat radiating from the fires. The stench of ash and decay filled his nostrils. "Where are my sisters in all this?" he asked.

"Not everything has been revealed. Perhaps they are dead. Or perhaps they are not a part of it. There is no way of knowing. What I can tell you is that the vision you see is not what it appears. Where Darshan saw only doom and destruction, I can see hope. You, Jayden, have it in your power to prevent any of this from happening."

The cries of those who had perished drifted on the wind, their pain stabbing at Jayden's heart. He finally understood why he had been kept ignorant. Though he was seeing only a small portion of it, this vision was depicting the entire world. All lands were to suffer the same fate.

His legs became weak, forcing him down onto one knee. "None of this will happen," he cried out. "I have no desire to conquer. I don't want power, I swear it. All I want is for my father to come home and my mother to get well. If this is the price I would pay for leaving my home, then you have my word that I will stay on the farm and never leave."

He felt a hand on his shoulder. Saraf was standing beside him, gazing down with a sad smile.

"It's true. You are so much like your father. You feel as mortals do. You experience their pain in a way the gods cannot. It is for this reason that you must listen to me now."

Jayden allowed the god to lift him to his feet. "What must I do?"

"Nothing that you will not do eventually, anyway. All I want is for you to join us. Return with me to heaven and leave this mortal world behind."

"Leave? How?"

Saraf took a long breath. "That is the hardest part, I'm afraid. Though you possess the blood of a god, you are not fully divine. The part of you that is mortal must perish."

Jayden stepped away. "You're saying I have to die?"

"It is only mortal death," he explained, his tone kind and soothing. "A fleeting moment of fear and pain. But followed by life everlasting."

"What about my mother and my father? What will become of them?"

"They will live on," he assured.

"I told you to speak no lies!" Ayliazarah's voice roared with almost physical force.

Suddenly, she was standing beside Saraf, her form clear. The *flowing* white dress she wore accentuated her ice-blue eyes. Her flaxen hair fell loosely to her shoulders, and her ivory complexion was flawless. Jayden had never beheld such beauty. For a brief moment, all else ceased to be. He was utterly enthralled.

"They will not live on, as you say, Saraf." Her voice was like steel, yet still musical to Jayden's ears. "They will be consigned to oblivion."

"You do not know that," he shot back.

The goddess's final few words shattered Jayden's entrancement, bringing him sharply back into the moment. "Oblivion?" he repeated.

Ayliazarah's stare never left Saraf. "My brother would have you believe that if you do not agree to his terms, what you have seen is a certainty. But there is something he did not tell you—that it was this same argument that drove Darshan into action to begin with. Your father hoped to spare you your fate by bringing peace to the world before you discovered your true nature and learned of your power."

"You dare to blame me?" Saraf shouted.

"Who else is there?" she responded. Though the air was still, her hair whipped wildly, as if caught in a stiff wind. "Was it not you who warned Darshan of the dangers? Was it not you who begged him to leave the mortal world? Was it not you who told him that only peace could help his son escape his fate? A fate that no one is sure is real."

"I did not tell him to masquerade as one of us. I did not tell him to attempt to alter the fate of the world. We are not the Creator. Destiny lies in *Her* hands, and *Hers* alone. He had no right to take matters so far." He turned to face Jayden. "Do not be deceived. There is only one way for you. Though it is true I do not know what will become of Darshan or your mother, neither does my sister."

"Can you at least tell me where he is?"

"I have already told you what you need to know," Saraf replied. "If you choose to continue in your defiance, more than the fate of your parents will be in peril."

Jayden looked at Ayliazarah. "And what do *you* want from me?"

"Unlike my brother, I trust Darshan," she told him. "It was he who saved us. And it was he whom the Creator chose to be the instrument of *Her* will. Though I admit I did not condone his direct interference with mortals, his connection to their world is as strong as his connection to the Creator. What my brother and those who have sided with him have done is wrong. I would have you oppose him. I would have you save your father."

"But where is he? I can't save him if I don't know how to find him."

"Only Saraf knows that," she replied, casting her brother a furious look. "And I cannot force him to say. All I and those who still stand by Darshan can do is to prevent Saraf from harming you directly. You must be the one to find the answers."

"Can you at least tell me if I am heading in the right direction?"

"I can only say that you should trust your instincts. Your heart will guide you rightly."

Saraf huffed. "And *I* will tell you this. Should you somehow discover where your father is, you will not like what you see. All attempts to free him will fail. What's more, you will certainly doom yourself and all those you care for."

Jayden knew what his choice must be without thinking. "I cannot abandon my father," he stated.

The god's face contorted into a vicious snarl. "Fool. Then so be it."

Ayliazarah smiled. "A fool he may be. Even so, I believe he will succeed. And when he does and Darshan returns, I am sure he will be quite eager to see you ... brother."

Jayden could see the sudden fear jump into the god's eyes. It drew a stifled laugh.

"I shall enjoy watching you suffer," Saraf growled. "But not before all those around you curse your name."

With this final threat, his form began shimmering like ripples on a pond, eventually fading away to nothing. Ayliazarah remained, her face etched in sorrow.

"I do not want you to think that my brother is evil," she said. "He truly believes that what he is doing is right."

"And you? What do you believe?"

"Only that Darshan needs your help. Your father saved us all, and for that he has my loyalty. And his love for the world has earned my trust. You *must* find him. For the sake of us all."

"Surely there is something you can tell me that will help."

"Sadly, no. Saraf was very careful to conceal his actions from us. Not even his allies know the details of what he has done. However, you are definitely going in the right direction."

"How can you know that?" he asked.

"Because Saraf is moving to stop you. By creating the Vrykol, he has violated a long-held agreement never to do so again. From here to the desert, your path is beset with peril. Seeing as the way west is clear, I can only presume he prefers you go that way."

"What can he do to stop us?"

"Nothing directly. Ever since the death of Gerath, the balance of power in heaven is even. Four of us support Darshan, four oppose him."

"Death of Gerath?"

Ayliazarah waved a dismissive hand. "That doesn't matter. What is important is that this even balance prevents Saraf from harming you directly. While it exists, the most he can do is to send his followers to attack you. If you are clever, you'll be able to avoid them."

Jayden suddenly regretted not having Linis with him. If anyone could avoid detection, it was the old elf. Of course, having him here was not possible. That would leave his sisters alone in an unfamiliar wilderness. Anyhow, he was quite adept in the woods himself. Though nowhere near as skilled as Linis, he was better than most elves at navigating the forests.

"Sayia intends to help me mask my human side," he said. "That should help."

The goddess laughed. "Human side? You have no human blood within you, child. Your father is not mortal. He only chooses to appear as such, as do I at this moment. When heaven was opened, his human form became a product of his will. He can appear as anything he desires."

"The power of heaven," he muttered. "Is that what I felt?"

"Yes. It is the love and splendor of the Creator herself. But be warned: you must never deliberately seek it. In your moment of need, you were able to hear my voice and reach across the divide. But you are only able to wield this mightiest of all powers for a few seconds. Any longer would annihilate your mortal blood entirely."

"What would happen?"

"Your father was already powerful when heaven was opened to him. That's why he is able to remain. But you are not. Your mortal blood binds you to this realm. Lose it, and you will ascend. Once that happens, there is no way to know when you will be able to find a way back. A thousand years might have passed, and all you know and love will be dust. And your father will be lost."

Her form began to shimmer in the same way Saraf's had. "I am running out of time. Quickly, touch my hand."

Jayden extended his arm, then drew back as tiny flecks of blue light began to dance around Ayliazarah's celestial flesh.

"Please hurry," she urged.

Taking a deep breath, Jayden stepped forward once again and did as instructed.

The instant their hands touched, it felt as if his blood had become molten rock. Searing pain raced around his entire body, paralyzing his limbs. He crumpled to the ground.

"What have you done to me?" he asked through gritted teeth.

"The same as you were about to attempt with the elf woman." Her voice sounded distant.

Bit by bit, the pain lessened until he was finally able to prop himself up on his knees. Ayliazarah was gone. Even before he saw Sayia still sitting across from him, he instinctively knew he had left the spirit realm.

The elf was on her feet in an instant. "What happened to you? Are you hurt?"

Jayden took a moment to gather his wits. "I'm fine."

Sayia rounded the fire and placed a hand on his shoulder. "You didn't sound fine when you screamed. I thought you..." Her eyes suddenly widened. "How... how did you do this?"

Brushing her hand away, Jayden forced himself to his feet. Though the pain was now completely gone, he felt renewed fatigue in his muscles. "How did I do what?"

"If I didn't know better, I would believe you to be an elf," she replied. "It should have taken several lessons from me to accomplish this. How did you do it on your own?"

Aside from the fatigue, he felt no different. This must have been what Ayliazarah had done when she touched his hand. She had concealed his nature, allowing only the elf side of his heritage to come through. But it was just a façade. He could not sense Sayia's presence whatsoever.

"I had help," he explained.

He then told her of his experience in the spirit realm. Sayia's face gradually darkened as he recounted the words of Saraf.

"Then he doesn't know," she muttered when he was finished, sounding quite relieved.

"Know what?"

She waved a hand. "Nothing. I was just thinking about your sisters. It doesn't seem like he has any interest in them. For that, I am grateful."

Jayden threw up his hands in exasperation. "That's enough! Whatever it is you're hiding from me, I wish you would just say it and stop treating me like I'm a dolt."

She seemed unmoved by his display of frustration. "If I had information I thought you needed, I would tell you. So whatever I am keeping to myself does not concern you."

"But you keep hinting that there is something behind all this," he countered, unwilling to back down. "What is it?"

"You *know* what is behind it. Unless what you told me was not true, it is the gods who are moving events."

"That's not what I mean, and you know it."

"Do I?" This time there was anger bleeding into her tone. "What is it exactly you think I know? Am I not permitted to have secrets? Must you know everything that is in my mind? Do I not deserve at least some private thoughts? I am here to help you. Should that not be enough?" She planted her fists on her hips. "And what of you? Will you tell me all of your secrets? Or do you not have any? Surely you do."

"I didn't mean to suggest you tell me everything," he said, feeling himself wilt under her gaze. His mother had done the same thing to him when he was young. In truth, she still did. Was it an elf trait to make him feel like a little boy caught up to mischief? Or did all women have this talent? He held up his hands. "I wasn't trying to offend you. It's just that I can't help but feel as if you're hiding things from me."

"Perhaps I am," she admitted. "And perhaps you should trust that I am older and more experienced than you. If you need to know something, I will tell you. Is that clear?"

They locked eyes. After a few seconds, Jayden found himself cracking a smile. Gradually, this became half-stifled laughter. "I really hope you get to meet my mother," he said. "The two of you would get along wonderfully."

Sayia was not amused. "I'm sure I will," she responded. "And now that you have no further need of the *flow of the spirit,* we'll begin with the basics instead."

She turned and took her seat by the fire. Jayden was weary, but the stern expression on her face told him that she would not be refused.

He leaned down and massaged the muscles in his thighs. "What then? Fire?"

"Earth," she replied. "Your father was the son of Gerath. It seems the best place to begin."

As he took his place and resumed his steady breathing, the revelation that Gerath was dead flashed through his mind. He had left this detail out of the story. This caused a tiny smile to form. Now *he* had a secret. Petty as it might be, it felt satisfying to know this, while Sayia remained ignorant. His mother would have scolded him for such childish behavior.

There was a moment of melancholy. He missed his mother so much. Even the scoldings, which were frequent. Whatever obstacles were placed in his path, he would not fail her.

CHAPTER 12

The first lesson was hugely frustrating. When he was calm, he could feel the *flow* entering Sayia, but was not able to draw it into himself. The rhythm of the earth that she had described remained stubbornly absent. Yet exasperating as this was for both of them, and given her previous short attitude, the elf woman remained surprisingly understanding and patient.

"It will come to you in time," she said after several hours of fruitless effort.

"Why can I only feel it when I'm angry?" he asked. His head was pounding and his back ached from sitting cross-legged for so long.

"In a sense, the *flow* is passion," she explained. "Most are taught to feel it from a young age. I was barely three when my lessons began. Your sisters were also very young. Children are emotional beings, so it's easier for them to learn to feel it than it is for an adult. Once you pass your childhood, you learn to control your base instincts. But it is these very instincts that you need."

That she referred to him as an adult was oddly gratifying. His father had told him many times of his own struggles when he was coming of age. Not that Jayden had any such insecurities. Those he had regular contact with had stopped treating him like a child the moment he began working full days in the fields. Most boys after they came of age assumed themselves adult, but he had felt as though he were a man long before his official birthday.

On those occasions when someone would tease him about his youth, he merely found it irritating. Their taunts made no impact whatsoever on his confidence. He knew very well who he was. For as long as he could remember, both his parents had made a point of instilling him with a sense of pride and self-worth. Because of this, some in the village had considered him arrogant, claiming that the Stedding family thought they were better than everyone else. But this was nothing more than petty jealousy, easy to see through, and easier still to ignore.

Over the next few days, Jayden noticed a change come over Sayia. Though she still looked at him in a peculiar way from time to time, she was now starting to smile more often, despite their lessons continuing with very little progress. By the time they reached the banks of the Goodbranch, he had barely managed to accomplish the basic ability of hearing the pulse of the earth. And even then, it was faint.

Upon crossing the river, Sayia allowed him to take the lead, citing his familiarity with the region. This was only partially true. He knew the maps well enough, but they were many miles south of Helenia. Aside from this recent trip to Baltria, he had never actually traveled so far away from home.

They chanced upon a small band of elves just as the flatlands and forest gave way to the grassy hills of the Eastland kingdoms. Jayden was a bit nervous at first, but he soon learned they were not elves journeying to the desert. These had built their homes among the hills and were simple craftsmen and artisans who sold their goods to the nearby towns and villages. They accepted him as a full-blooded elf without question, as they did Sayia's story that they were heading for Dantory to visit kin. They even went so far as to offer them lodging for the night. After weeks of sleeping on hard ground, it was an offer they eagerly accepted.

Jayden found their hosts to be of good humor and free with their hospitality, quite different from the elves in Sharpstone, who tended to keep mostly to themselves and were reluctant to speak to anyone unless approached directly. Rather than taking an interest in the events happening in other lands, these elves seemed to care nothing for the troubles in the west. They considered those escaping to the desert to be most foolish.

"Nothing has changed," said an older woman named Glorsia. They were gathered around a small fire just outside the home of a weaver, where the group habitually gathered each evening to sing and talk. "I was a tailor before the war. And I'm still one now. What should I care that humans are wearing the clothes I make? They don't bother us, and we don't bother them."

"So they give you no trouble at all?" asked Sayia.

"The humans? Not a bit. All a bunch of silliness, if you ask me." She eyed Jayden, who was sitting on the ground near the fire. "And where exactly are you from?"

"I was born across the Abyss," he replied. "But I was raised in a small town along the Goodbranch." It seemed like a good lie. The elves from Sayia's land who crossed over were few. It would explain his accent and unusually large frame.

"Raised?" she laughed. "You can't be a day over twenty."

Jayden smiled. "Eighteen. Even so, humans say I'm of age."

"Humans mature faster," she said. "With such short lives, they have to. As for yourself, don't forget to enjoy your youth, child. The first one hundred years are when you have the most fun."

He suppressed a laugh. "I'll keep that in mind."

The woman clicked her tongue. "You already sound too old, if you ask me."

The first one hundred years. The concept was difficult to fathom. He knew that newbreeds lived longer than humans, though exactly how long was unknown. It was a question he had asked his mother on many occasions when he was a child. She'd only told him that he would definitely live for a very long time, which was more or less what any mother would say to a child who began to think about their own mortality. Dina looked young, and that comforted him. But then his thoughts would turn to his father. At the time, he'd believed him to be human. It would bring him to tears, thinking that he would watch him grow old and die.

"You'll have your father around for a long time," his mother had promised. And it was true; he did not appear to age. A few lines around his eyes was all. Apart from this, he looked very much the same year after year.

Now he knew the truth. It was *he* who would age, and his father would live on forever.

The morning after, they were directed to a lesser-used road that the elves said would be a faster way through the hills. As they walked, Jayden found his mind wandering to events of his childhood when his father would take him to Gath. Those occasions were rare, but he had always enjoyed their times together. Thinking back, he tried to recall anything his father might have said or done while they were away from home that would have given a clue to his true identity. How could someone with so much power resist using it? And why had he chosen such a mundane life? Why a farmer, of all things?

He noticed Sayia looking at him out of the corner of her eye again. "Why do you keep doing that?" he asked.

"Doing what?"

"Staring at me."

"I haven't noticed that I do," she replied.

"All the time. What is it?"

"You remind me of someone. That's all."

"A husband or boyfriend?"

He had considered the possibility that she might be attracted to him. But though she was certainly beautiful, he did not feel the same. When he looked at her, nothing stirred within him.

"I am unmarried," she replied. "And I have no suitor."

"Who, then?"

A touch of annoyance crept into her voice. "My grandfather, if you must know."

Jayden laughed. "Your grandfather? Surely I don't look *that* old."

"My grandfather is a kind and gentle man," she responded, frowning. "And you would do quite well to become as wise and good."

Jayden held up his hands. "I'm sorry. I didn't mean to offend you. I'm sure he's wonderful."

Her expression was peculiar—a mixture of low boiling anger and sorrow. "He raised me from the age of three. He was the one who first taught me how to use the *flow*."

"Really? Where were your parents?"

She hesitated for a long moment. "I would rather not talk about that."

"I'm sorry. I just wanted to know more about you. We still have a long way to go."

Her eyes were now fixed firmly on the road ahead. "You did nothing wrong. It's just that I have trouble speaking of my past. I miss home terribly; my grandfather in particular."

A tear formed in her eye, but she wiped it quickly away before it fell.

"So why did you come here?" he asked. "And why stay for so long if you miss home?"

"I am accomplished in the *flow*, and the elves here were in need of instruction."

"Let me guess. You felt like it was your duty to help them."

"My grandfather did. Not I. He asked me to come. I could not refuse."

"So he sent you away?"

She nodded. "I admit I was hurt by the request. But I now understand his reasons."

"What reasons?"

"It doesn't matter." She glanced up at the late afternoon sky. "I think we will stop early today. I am growing tired."

He frowned. The wounds she had suffered were no longer hindering her, and hadn't done so for many days. Whatever was in that salve, it had worked far better than Jayden would have thought possible. He considered that perhaps he should not have asked about her home, as it seemed to have brought Sayia to a dark place.

They halted an hour before sunset. Typically, they would eat and then begin their daily lesson. This time, however, Sayia unrolled her blanket and lay down without so much as unpacking a morsel. Although feeling guilty for putting her in this state, Jayden was afraid to say anything more. He well understood the pain of missing those you loved. Any further words from him would likely make matters worse.

He had trouble sleeping that night. Usually, a hard day's walk followed by several hours of training left him spent. Without these exertions he was restless, so he decided to practice on his own.

It didn't take long for him to become frustrated. Without guidance, he found the *flow* to be even more elusive; he couldn't hear or feel even the slightest pulse. Unable to concentrate, his thoughts kept drifting back to Sayia. There was something in her expression whenever she stole a glance at him. Though it had bothered him in Baltria, he had taken it for her simply being judgmental. Now he pondered more deeply on the matter. What exactly did she see when she looked at him? Surely it had to be more than merely resembling her grandfather.

On waking the following morning, he found her to be in better spirits. The melancholy of the previous day appeared to have been banished. So much so, she even took to humming a lively tune as they threaded the hills at a rapid pace. He wondered what had changed, but did not dare to ask.

Shortly after their midday meal, they caught sight of a small village to the north.

"We need to resupply soon," Jayden pointed out. Though they still had a few days' worth of food, their water was almost spent.

"Yes," Sayia agreed. "I think I would like to sleep in a bed tonight. And you could very much use a bath."

He raised an arm and sniffed. "Smells fine to me."

"Believe me, it does not."

He caught the hint of a wry grin. Whatever had changed her mood, he hoped it would continue. Sadly, his instincts told him this was a temporary reprieve. There was definitely something still weighing on her mind, and it was unlikely she would be willing to share it with him. It could simply be down to being homesick, of course, yet somehow he felt it went deeper than that.

He wondered if the events in the temple were still causing her distress, especially the death of the young boy Maybell had told him about. Such horrors were far from easy to set aside.

"Are you sure we should risk staying the night here?" he asked as they drew near the village.

"Perhaps not," she replied. "But I do not sense the presence of a Vrykol."

Jayden said no more. The idea of a decent meal and a soft bed was appealing to him as well. And with Sayia's abilities, any foes other than a Vrykol would be easily dealt with.

They rounded the west end to approach from the road.

A small faded sign indicated that they were entering Harvest Hill. Though from first glance he could see it was not a farming town, Jayden counted no fewer than six liveries situated along the main road. More likely a place for horse trading, then. The route they were on cut dead center of the Eastland, and several large cities were within a hundred miles. It was a logical place to trade. There was actually a fair chance that some of the horses bred in Sharpstone might be here.

The buildings were of sturdier construction than he'd expected, the streets were clean, and the people walking about appeared to be in good spirits. In a way, it reminded him of home. A few people took notice of their passing, but no one seemed to care that there were two elves in their midst, leading Jayden to deduce it was probably a common sight.

The aroma of spices and fresh bread lured them to a small inn, where they found the common room to be lively and filled almost to capacity. A young man wearing a stained apron bounded up as they entered, a perplexed look on his face.

"Are you two needing a room?" he asked.

"And a meal," said Sayia.

"Really? Here?"

"Is that a problem?" Jayden asked.

The boy held up his hands. "No problem at all. It's just that the elves who pass through here don't usually care much for human cooking. They prefer the rooms at the Prince and Herald." His smile widened. "But if you want to stay here, you are most welcome. They have enough business."

"It looks like you're not doing too bad yourself," remarked Jayden.

"It's my father's birthday," he explained. "We're not usually this busy." His gaze shifted to the weapons on their belts.

"You'll need to leave those in your room, though. We don't want to scare folks."

Sayia nodded her agreement. "We've been traveling for a long time," she said. "We would very much like to clean up."

An older man standing near the bar called over in their direction. "Matt! Stop standing around. Get on with your work."

The boy rolled his eyes, then gave an embarrassed grin. "That's my father. Sorry. He's been at the wine since early this morning."

Sayia fished out a silver coin from her pouch and handed it over. "I understand. This should be enough to cover our rooms and meals."

"I'm afraid we've only one room left," he responded. "But I'll have a cot and some wash water brought to you right away."

He whistled to another man, slightly older and with sagging shoulders, who meandered unhappily over. Matt issued a few quick instructions, while all the time his father continued calling for him over the noise of the crowd.

Jayden noticed Sayia stiffen uncomfortably. "I'll drop off my things and then wait out here while you clean up," he said.

"Yes, you will," she told him.

They were led through the crowd and down a narrow hall. The room itself was small but tidy. A chest of drawers and a brass washbasin were at the rear, and a single bed sat off to the right.

"I'll be back with some water," the man said.

After placing his pack in the corner, Jayden removed his sword. "I'll be in the common room," he said. On impulse, he flashed an impish grin. "Unless you want me to stay."

A look of utter revulsion appeared on Sayia's face. "Suggest that again and you will be sleeping in the street tonight."

"I was only joking," he protested, backing hastily toward the door.

"Get out!" she shouted.

More than a little taken aback by her volatile reaction, Jayden retreated to the common room. After taking a seat at the bar, he regarded his surroundings more closely. A flutist was playing in the far corner, much to the delight of several patrons who were dancing and singing along with the melody. As for Matt, he was still rushing back and forth, serving drinks and doing his best to ignore his father's constant shouts for him to work faster.

Sayia emerged after half an hour dressed in fresh clothing, her hair damp and pulled into a tight ponytail. She sat beside him without a word.

"I really was only playing around," Jayden told her. "There's no need to be angry."

"Get cleaned up," she said, her eyes focused straight ahead. "I'm hungry."

Heaving a sigh, he returned to their room. A cot had been brought in and shoved into the corner, as far away from the bed as was possible. The remaining water was no longer warm, but he was accustomed to using cold, anyway. In short order, he was washed and clad in a pair of fresh trousers and a shirt.

By the time he returned to the common room, Sayia had moved from the bar to a table, where a plate of steaming vegetables and roast pork awaited him.

"Are you still mad at me?" he asked, plopping down opposite her.

"What you suggested was improper," she said. "Do not do it again."

"I said it was a joke."

"It wasn't funny."

Jayden stuffed some pork in his mouth and shook his head, chuckling softly. He knew it wasn't appropriate. Had his mother heard him speak to a woman in such a way, particularly one he barely knew, she would have boxed his ears. His father would not have liked it either. Then again, his father was about as polite and proper as anyone could ever imagine—never engaging in the coarse humor or crude innuendos common with field hands.

They ate in silence for a time. Finally, Sayia pushed her plate aside and met his eyes.

"I might have overreacted," she admitted. "I am unused to such familiarity."

He smiled. "Your grandfather must have been as stiff as my father." He regretted the words as soon as he'd spoken them.

"My grandfather is a man of good humor. He is anything but stiff."

"I'm sure he is," Jayden quickly said. "I wasn't trying to be insulting."

"You there! Elf." It was the voice of Matt's father. Jayden turned to see him staggering over in their direction. "Sing us an elf song."

This suggestion was met by loud cries and hoots of encouragement. The man leaned both hands against their table. Jayden wanted to cover his nose from the reek of wine on his breath.

"You wouldn't want to hear me sing," he said.

"It's my bloody birthday, and it's my inn," he argued, letting out a loud belch. "And I want to hear a bloody elf song."

Matt rushed over to grab his father's arm. "Go sit down and leave him alone. I'll bring you more wine." He shot Jayden an apologetic look.

The innkeeper yanked his arm free, almost toppling over in the process. "You mind your own business, boy."

"Perhaps you should do as he wants," Sayia suggested in a low whisper.

Jayden gave her a small nod. His mother had taught him many elf melodies, and at her insistence, he was often coerced into performing at festivals and celebrations. In spite of this, he had never much cared to sing in public. This, though, was an extremely awkward situation.

He looked up at the drunken man and smiled. "Of course. It's your birthday, after all."

Cheers erupted from the crowd as he rose and approached the flautist.

"Do you know 'The Maiden of Longshadow'?" he asked.

The man nodded. "It's not really an elf song, though."

"It's close enough," he said.

Quite by chance, "The Maiden of Longshadow" had a melody that was virtually identical to an elf song, "Elinor of the Vale," that his mother used to sing to him as a child. It had remained his favorite tune throughout his life.

He closed his eyes and listened as the flutist played the opening notes. Gradually the crowd hushed.

In winters past I saw her weep,
Tears of joy and sorrows deep,
I was afraid to hear her name,
It called for me to stay.
Through years untold
The bitter cold,
I see the gates of hell,
The loving hand which once held mine,
Sweet Elinor, farewell
For you are lost within the flames
Your essence weak and frail
'Twas I who sent you to the depths,
Elinor of the Vale.

He continued through several verses before nodding to the flutist that he was finished.

The crowd was quick to show their approval. A cacophony of boisterous shouts, stomping of feet, and banging on the tables quickly rose up at the end of his performance. Jayden smiled and nodded his gratitude.

Upon returning to his table, he found that Sayia was no longer there.

"The lass seemed upset," said the drunken innkeeper, who had remained beside the table throughout. "I guess your song wasn't to her taste." He slapped Jayden on the shoulder. "Don't you worry, I liked it just fine, and so did everyone else."

Jayden surveyed the room, but there was no sign of her anywhere. Hastily, he pushed through the crowd, receiving several words of praise along the way. Back in their bedroom, he found a note lying on the bed.

Jayden,

Do not be concerned, I just need to be alone. I will be back before morning.

Sayia

He stroked his chin while wondering what had upset her. It couldn't have been anything he had done. After a few minutes of pondering on this, he decided to return to the common room. There was nothing else to do. Whatever it was that had disturbed her, he would have to wait to find out.

He sat at the bar listening to the music, though at times it was quite difficult to hear over the raucous laughter of the partygoers, especially that coming from the increasingly drunken innkeeper. He thought it astonishing that the man was still capable of standing.

Before long, tiredness began to creep up on him. He was about to return to the bedroom when he spotted two elves sitting at a table not far away from where he was seated. He hadn't seen them come in, but they had clearly noticed him.

Both were clad in hooded robes that were stained with mud and worn from travel. The slight bulge at each of their waists told him they were armed. He suddenly felt exposed and vulnerable. As their eyes met, one rose from his seat and walked over.

"We were wondering if you might care to join us," he said.

Trying hard to appear calm, Jayden stood and gave the elf a respectful bow. "Actually, I was just about to turn in for the night."

"Please," he pressed. "We won't keep you long."

Jayden forced a smile. "Very well, then."

He took a seat opposite the two elves. One poured him a cup of wine—an empty third cup that they'd seemingly had at the ready, with him in mind.

"I am Mavri," said the elf to his left. He was thin, with sandy blond hair and dark eyes. His companion was thicker in build and sported close-cropped bright red hair—unusual for an elf. "This is Havlion."

"I am Jayden." As he spoke, it occurred that using his real name might not be the best idea. Not that there was anything he could do about it now.

"From where do you hail?" Mavri asked.

"Across the Abyss."

He raised an eyebrow. "A long way to come all alone."

"I have a companion."

"Would it happen to be the woman we saw leaving a short while ago?" asked Havlion.

"It is."

"She seemed quite put out."

Jayden nodded. "She can be ... difficult."

Both men laughed.

"For one so young, I imagine all women can be difficult," remarked Havlion. He paused. "You say that your name is Jayden?"

He nodded, but said nothing.

"There are rumors flying about. They say that the followers of Saraf are seeking someone going by that name.

They even say there are fell creatures about, aiding their search. Creatures that should not exist. You wouldn't happen to be *that* Jayden, would you? I only ask because he is said to be traveling with a woman."

Tension gripped him. "No one is looking for me. Certainly not the followers of Saraf."

"Be at ease," said Mavri. "We're only curious. In fact, we could possibly help you."

"In what way?"

The elf smiled. "Before I tell you, there is something I must know." He held out his hand and nodded for Jayden to take it.

He leaned away. "What is it you want?"

"A test," he replied. "You see, we've also heard that Jayden is a newbreed." He shrugged. "Most likely, it is nothing more than a nasty rumor spread to enlist the elves in their search. However, if it did happen to be true, such a being would be a most unwelcome sight. Wouldn't you agree with me?"

Jayden's heart began to pound. "Can't you sense my presence?" he asked.

"Yes. But you did not sense ours, and that makes me wonder. Perhaps you have found a way to ... hide your true nature?"

With a sharp movement, Jayden pushed back his chair. "I didn't come over here to be offended by you," he retorted. "And I have no intention of allowing you to test me."

"I would not attempt to leave," Havlion told him, his hand drifting ominously to the bulge beneath his cloak.

For a moment, Jayden considered his two options. He could try to make a run for it and hope he was fast enough to escape. That did not seem like a good choice. With so many people packed into the room, he would likely be skewered before he got even a couple of yards. That left only the very risky second option. Heaving a sigh, he leaned forward and held out his hand.

Mavri touched the back of it with his fingers. Several seconds passed by, during which his face gave nothing away. Jayden's heart thudded as he awaited Mavri's verdict.

The elf then leaned back in his chair, a smile forming. "You see, Havlion? Rumors. Nothing more. Jayden is as much an elf as we are." His smile grew wider. "And now that we know this, I hope you will accept our help."

"What makes you think I need it?" Jayden asked, doing all he could not to let the flood of relief he was feeling show through.

"Because between here and the desert, there are dozens of men looking for you," he replied. "Not to mention what appears to be Vrykol. Which raises the question: Why are you being hunted? And how can there be Vrykol when the Reborn King is no more?"

Before Jayden could respond, Sayia appeared from amongst the crowd directly behind Havlion. After placing both of her hands on the elf's shoulders, a light wisp of smoke began seeping out from between her fingers. He gasped and winced, clearly in considerable pain.

"As you can see, we can take care of ourselves," Sayia told him. "And if you threaten my friend again, you will be the ones in need of aid." Her eyes were red from tears, but her expression was cold.

Mavri leaped from his chair, but did not reach for his weapons. "We meant him no harm. You must know this."

"Could you have still said the same had he turned out to be a newbreed?" she retorted, venom in her tone.

"We seek only to preserve our race."

"If bigotry and hatred are what dwells in the hearts of elves, then perhaps we are not worthy of being preserved."

"Please," Jayden chipped in, touching her arm. "Let him go. He didn't hurt me."

By now, several patrons were taking notice of the commotion. With a final look of contempt, Sayia released her hold, leaving behind a pair of scorch marks where her hands had been.

"Come," she said. "We need to rest."

As he followed her through the crowd, a voice called out. "Wait!"

He turned to see Mavri running after them.

"I apologize," the elf said.

Sayia sneered. "For what? For being closed-minded?"

His shoulders slumped. "I cannot help the way I feel. But I do regret threatening your friend. I should not have done that. Please, allow me to make restitution."

"There is no need," she said.

"If you are going to the desert, then you should know that you are truly being hunted. I was not exaggerating the danger. Come with us, and I will see that you arrive safely."

Sayia flicked a hand. "We'll be fine on our own."

"There are more than twenty of us," he added. "Plenty enough to ensure that you can travel unmolested."

"It might not be such a bad idea," Jayden remarked. Though he was still angry at the way he had been treated, there were other things to consider. If they really were being sought by a combination of humans, elves, and Vrykol, they could easily find themselves in a situation they couldn't handle alone.

"Where are the rest of your people?" Sayia asked.

"Most of them are camped a few miles north of the village. We came in for supplies and noticed the two of you. We had recently heard other elves speak of a newbreed being hunted by Vrykol, and—"

"And you thought you would see if it was true?"

Mavri nodded. "And I am now truly sorry. But if others like myself have heard this talk as well, you could find yourself faced with a large number of foes. No one will think to look for you among our group. And even if they did, I doubt anyone would be so foolish as to attack us."

Sayia locked eyes with him for a long moment. "Very well," she finally said. "We will join with you in the morning."

Mavri smiled and bowed. "We will wait until you arrive. And hopefully, by journey's end, I will have made you think better of me."

Sayia turned away from him without speaking any further.

Once back in their room, she sat on the bed and waited for Jayden to close the door.

"I am not sure this is wise," she told him. "It is precisely elves like Mavri and his companions that I was hoping to avoid."

He moved over to his cot. "Yes, but if what he said is true, then it's got to be better than getting caught out in the open alone. Besides, they think I'm a full-blooded elf."

"Perhaps. All the same, you should avoid any idle banter. You were raised more as a human than an elf. Your words might yet rouse further suspicion."

A short silence developed. Jayden then leaned his elbows on his knees. "Do you feel like telling me what's really wrong? Why did you run off like that?" He cracked a smile. "My singing isn't *that* bad, is it?"

"You have a lovely voice," she responded. "It was the song that upset me. It brought back memories. My grandfather used to sing it to me when I was a small child." She returned his smile. "It was nothing more than that."

"You really do love him."

"Yes. I miss him terribly."

"I'm sure you'll see him again."

She averted her eyes and took a long, cleansing breath. "I hope so. But you do not need to hear about this. We need rest. Elves travel at speed, and it will take all of your strength to keep up with them."

Jayden dimmed the lantern and took off his boots. While lying on the cot, he wondered if Maybell and Penelope had ever felt as homesick through the years as Sayia did now.

On the few occasions he had been around elves from across the Abyss, they had spoken of their land with great excitement. It must be a wonderful place, he thought. His mind then wandered to his own home and the farm. In a strange kind of way, he did miss it. Seeing the world thus far had not been exactly as he had hoped.

Of course, when he had pictured what it would be like on his adventures away from home, he hadn't imagined that there would be people trying to kill him at every turn.

CHAPTER 13

They arrived at the elves' camp just as dawn was breaking. Mavri greeted them warmly, quickly introducing them to his band of travelers. As he'd said, they numbered just over twenty, evenly split between male and female.

"I have explained who you are," he told them. "You have nothing to fear while you are with us. Those who hunt you will have to kill us all before they can have you."

Sayia gave him a slight nod but said nothing in response.

As expected, travel was swift, but not so much that Jayden could not keep pace. Though it was well known that elves from across the Abyss were particularly strong in the *flow*, Sayia had thought it best to forgo their lessons for a time. If there were any Vrykol about, she had no desire to draw their attention.

Most of the elves in the group were from the West, with just two of their number originating from the steppes. As with the majority of those who had journeyed to the desert, they were choosing a secluded life away from what they considered to be the downfall of their people. Their general feelings toward humans ranged from dislike to outright hatred.

Only a few of the group were young, and it soon turned out that they were there to accompany older relatives rather than having any great personal need to distance themselves from humans. It was true, Jayden reflected, the young were indeed more accepting of new ways. This was what he had heard his mother say time and again when news of the troubles reached their farm.

To his relief, none pressed him about where he was from or why they were being sought, though a few did eye him curiously from time to time. Sayia kept herself close, jumping in to answer the few questions posed before Jayden could speak. Several inquired as to the goings on across the Abyss.

"I had thought about settling there myself," said one of the young women.

"Why didn't you?" Sayia asked.

"My brother," she replied, nodding toward a man a few yards ahead. "Our parents were killed in the war, and we are all that remains of our family. He couldn't bring himself to leave our shores. Nor could he tolerate living among those who slaughtered our people. So eventually he decided to go to the desert. As much as I wanted to see your lands, I could not abandon him."

Those who slaughtered our people. The words struck Jayden. He had never made any allowance for this. It was true that human and elf had fought together, but they had fought against *human* armies. Had the Reborn King led the elves into battle, how would the humans feel? Perhaps *they* would be the ones heading to the desert?

In the evenings, he found them to be of good nature—a contrast to what he'd been expecting. They seemed excited by the prospect of a new life, hopeful that it would be one worth living. Sayia remained aloof throughout, though her attitude had softened somewhat toward Mavri.

"They're afraid," she said to Jayden after the first few days of travel. "It's impossible not to pity them."

Camp had been set up for the night on a low rise. They appeared no different to any other group heading for the desert as the elves gathered for their evening meal, though Jayden knew this would change in an instant should he be discovered.

"I bet they wouldn't seem so pitiable if they knew the truth about me," he offered in reply to her remark.

"No doubt you are right," Sayia agreed. "And when I think about the emotion that drives them, I feel it is best that they remove themselves from the rest of the world. If they did not, they would soon be forced out anyway. Change does not tolerate stagnation; they are mortal foes. And change always proves to be the stronger."

"It makes me wonder what my father intended to do about them."

She shrugged. "Leave them to the desert, is my guess. There they can do no harm. And as the desert elves are far more accepting people, perhaps in time they too will change."

"I don't know. My father is a stubborn man. He might have thought he could be the one to change them."

"Perhaps that is why the gods turned on him," she suggested.

"I think you might be right," he replied, eyes downcast in thought. "What's worse, I'm not totally sure that those who did were wrong."

Sayia placed her hand on his shoulder. "Even if he *was* wrong, he did not deserve betrayal."

Jayden sighed. "No. He didn't."

The days passed uneventfully, with no sign of their pursuers. The few people they did come across were human travelers, and these did their best to avoid the elves. Jayden feared that his companions, being so far away from witnesses, might take this opportunity to lash out at their perceived enemies, but they did not.

"Do you really hate humans that much?" he asked Mavri.

"Yes, even though I know I shouldn't. Your friend is right about me. That's why I am leaving. I have no place among them. Should I stay, I would only give them reason to hate us in return."

"So you admit that humans don't hate elves?"

He suddenly had a faraway look in his eyes. This was clearly a subject that he had dwelt on at length several times before. "They fear us. And they distrust us. But no... most do not hate us." He paused to look over his shoulder. "At home, I thought I was safe. That was before war came to my door and I witnessed the horrors of what humans could unleash. Even after the death of the Reborn King, I soon came to realize that no elf is truly safe, not even among their own kind. The humans will rule this world. They will have dominion over all. Perhaps not today, but someday. It is in their nature. Yes, I hate them. Not for what they did; rather, for what I know they will do."

"I think you're wrong," Jayden said. "Humans are not so very different from us."

Mavri smiled over at him. "You only say that because you have seen them at their best. But you are still young. Mark my words. In time, their true hearts will be revealed."

In a strange kind of way, Jayden agreed with him. Human dominance had been a threat to the elves ever since the end of the first Great War. Though the uneasy truce that followed remained in place, there was never any hope of real relations starting to develop. He had heard Linis speculate that, had the Reborn King not arrived when he did, the elves would have eventually faded away to nothing; at least on this side of the Abyss.

As they neared the border of the desert, the hills flattened and the air became noticeably hot and arid. Mavri was clearly growing ever more agitated with each day that passed.

When Jayden asked him if he was all right, he smiled and replied, "I cannot help but wonder what life will be like in such a harsh land. Back home, I knew how to survive. It's a little unsettling to realize that I'll to learn such things all over again."

"I'm sure it won't take long for you to adapt," said Jayden.

He puffed a laugh. "An easy thing to say at the onset of one's life. Not so easy when you have more days behind you than ahead."

The day before they were due to arrive at the first border town, Jayden noticed a look of concern on Sayia's face.

"What is it?" he asked.

"Vrykol," she said. "At least, I think so. It's still a good distance away and right on the edge of my abilities."

Jayden didn't bother trying to sense the creature himself. They had meditated only a few times since joining up with the party. Nevertheless, it was encouraging that when they had taken time out to do so, the rhythm of the earth had come through to him quite clearly. He had even managed to channel a small amount of the *flow* without being emotional. That was definitely a breakthrough.

"What should we do?" he asked.

"We must hope they pass us by."

"And if they don't?"

"We fight," she said. "And some will die."

For a short time after, he felt a touch heavy-hearted. He had grown quite fond of several of the elves, Mavri in particular, who seemed to go out of his way to be kind and friendly. It was difficult to imagine that beneath their welcoming exteriors lurked hatred and fear.

Sayia approached Mavri to explain the situation. He nodded sharply and then set about spreading the word among the others. Sayia, who normally lagged at the rear, now took the lead. Jayden walked alongside her.

The march was slow compared with the previous days, and the tension was palpable. By midday, Sayia still could not be sure if it was in fact a Vrykol she had sensed.

"I have heard that the desert possesses strange qualities," she explained. "If we were not so close, I would not question it."

It wasn't until the sun was low on the horizon that she finally relaxed. The threatening presence had dissipated.

"There's a small elf settlement nearby that helps newcomers to the desert," Mavri informed them. "We should be safe once we reach there."

Jayden had his doubts. It felt strange to him that they had not run into any resistance at all. By now, he had expected to encounter at least a few of Saraf's devotees. Of course, it was quite possible that some of the god's followers had already seen them but had been simply too afraid to approach a large band of elves. And one Vrykol on its own would be no match for them either. It would take far more than that, even without Sayia's powers.

That night, none of them slept, and conversation came in quiet whispers. By now, the nights had become as cold as the days were hot. Equally dispiriting, the ground was covered with a short, dull brown grass that offered little in the way of comfort. Jayden did not enjoy the cold, and working in the fields had taught him to hate the heat. To his mind, life in the desert did not sound even a tiny bit appealing.

As dawn broke, he spotted several columns of black smoke rising in the far distance. The others, seeing it as well, rushed to gather their belongings.

Mavri approached, grim-faced. "That is where we were heading."

Jayden's stomach knotted. "What are you going to do?"

"There is only one thing we *can* do: hope that we can get there in time to help."

"We should send a scout ahead," Sayia suggested. "Charging in blind could get you all killed."

"And if they're fighting for their lives this very moment?" Mavri challenged. "Though we may die, we will not hesitate to aid them." As if to emphasize his determination, he drew the short sword hanging from his belt.

"Stay close to me," Sayia instructed Jayden.

There was no need for Mavri to tell the others of his intentions. They were all of the same mind. But the smoke was far away. Even at a dead run, it would take hours to reach the settlement. By then, any fighting would probably be over.

As one, they started out, some with blades in hand, others with bows. The pace was incredible. Jayden found himself falling behind in just a matter of minutes. He reached out for the *flow*, and this time it came effortlessly. Strength filled his limbs, allowing him to swiftly join Sayia at the fore. She looked over and gave him a sharp nod of approval.

They made it to the small outpost far sooner than he'd expected. Not that it helped. Even when still a fair distance away, he could see that they were too late.

The camp was just a tight circle of what Jayden thought had once been tents, together with a row of three small wooden buildings. All were now naught but smoldering timbers and ash. Completing the distressing picture, a dozen bodies lay strewn about the ground, their corpses hacked and broken.

The band halted a few yards from the outer edge of the camp, rage written clearly on every one of their faces. Most of the dead were within the circle of tents. A surprise attack. The toppled pots and shattered plates suggested that they had been set upon during their afternoon meal.

"Whoever did this will pay," vowed Mavri in a voice that carried loudly enough for everyone to hear. His knuckles turned white around the handle of his weapon. "Look for tracks."

"No need," Sayia said, turning north of the destruction. "They're coming back."

The elves immediately set about removing their packs and forming a line. Jayden felt the *flow* surge within him as his anticipation increased. He wanted them to come. A glance over to the bodies of the fallen elves brought his anger returning tenfold. The Vrykol had done this because of him. They had slaughtered innocent people who had no part in what was happening. He bared his teeth, the *flow* rising with each breath. *He* would make them pay.

"Do not lose yourself," warned Sayia. "Do as I say and stay close."

Jayden nodded, but his eyes were fixed straight ahead. He could see six figures in tan cloaks approaching, each one of them bearing a savage-looking serrated blade. Behind them came another three dozen men, humans in light armor, with the symbol of Saraf on their breastplate.

"Can you destroy them?" Mavri asked Sayia.

"Alone, no. But I will be able to burn a few before they can span the distance."

A sudden thought occurred to Jayden. "Are there enough Vrykol to stop us from using the *flow*?"

As if in response to this question, three of the creatures broke away from the others and joined hands to form a circle. Together, they began to sway to and fro. Almost at once, Jayden felt his grip on the *flow* fading. He tried to hold on, but in seconds, it was completely gone.

Sayia held out one hand, her brow knitted with concentration. "It would seem to take fewer than I imagined." She unsheathed her long knives and widened her stance. "Those with bows should target only the humans. Arrows will do nothing to stop the Vrykol."

Once within range, the elves loosed a volley of arrows. Four human soldiers fell, but this did nothing to slow their advance. Full of hatred, Jayden felt an almost overwhelming urge to run forth alone and meet their attackers head-on.

The three Vrykol still advancing veered left, away from him and Sayia, and directly toward the archers. With the creatures closing fast, the elves dropped their bows and drew their blades. Jayden set himself to join the fray, but Sayia caught his arm.

"Stay beside me," she ordered.

Ignoring her words, he ripped himself free. The *flow* might have left him, but the confidence and uncontainable defiance it produced still remained. He charged forward.

An almighty clashing of steel tore through the air as blades collided. The humans were still a good distance back, unable to keep up with the Vrykols' furious pace. It made little difference to the sway of the battle. After only a few seconds, three elves had already been cut down.

Roaring with rage, Jayden hacked into the back of an enemy. The Vrykol twisted violently around just as the sword touched its flesh, sweeping its own blade across in a lightning horizontal strike that was intended to take the head of its attacker. So fast was the creature's reaction, Jayden felt a flash of terror on realizing that he almost certainly did not have enough time to duck out of the way.

His mind was still trying to force his body into taking evasive action when a pair of long knives caught the blade only inches from his neck and deflected it harmlessly away. Sayia, her face contorted into a vicious snarl, then shoved him hard back with her shoulder before letting fly a blistering series of strikes at the creature.

His narrow escape from death had drained every trace of Jayden's rage. Stunned into realizing his own limitations when without the *flow*, for a few seconds he simply watched her battle. But then, after seeing the Vrykol's counterattack open a long gash in Sayia's left arm, he quickly recovered his wits.

He knew that the humans would be on them in moments. They needed to deal with the Vrykol quickly, or they would be totally overwhelmed. He stabbed low, sinking the tip of his blade into his enemy's thigh. It had little effect. Undeterred, the Vrykol continued its attack on Sayia, driving her ever back. Twice more Jayden struck, and twice more his blade opened wounds that would have felled a mortal foe. His eyes constantly searched for an opportunity to take the beast's head, but it was well aware of the threat and never allowed its neck to be exposed. Jayden was becoming increasingly desperate. With the two other Vrykol also fully involved in the battle nearby, more elves were falling victim around him.

The humans were now spreading out to encircle the group rather than confront them head-on. Jayden lunged at the Vrykol yet again, just as Sayia was parrying. This time his sword sank deep into the creature's chest, and the scraping of bone vibrated up the hilt. It reacted by twisting hard right, ripping the sword completely from Jayden's grasp. Sayia instantly spotted her opportunity. Diving low, she rolled behind the creature, then popped up again to sweep her weapons in a backhanded crossing pattern. Her aim was true and the blades lethally sharp. The Vrykol's head rolled from its torso.

Seeing this, the remaining two backed away. But by now, they had already slain at least half of the elf party. Those still alive were gathered in a tight group. The humans had them completely surrounded. One charge would end it. Jayden retrieved his sword and took his position beside Sayia.

"So this is it," he remarked with a calmness that even he found astonishing. "I always thought I would be afraid to die."

She glanced over. "We're not dead yet." There was a strange sense of assurance in her voice, despite the desperate state of the situation. They were outnumbered and already decimated.

The small group of surviving elves were equally resolute, staring out at their would-be killers with a defiance that clearly displayed they would fight to the last.

"Surrender," called one of the Vrykol. "We only want the boy."

Mavri stepped forward. Though bleeding from several wounds on his chest and legs, he held himself erect. "Take him if you can," he shouted back.

"Foolish elf. You would lay down your life for a mongrel half-breed?"

"He is no half-breed. And you will take him only when I have drawn my last breath."

The elf's words caused a flood of guilt to rush through Jayden. This must not be allowed to happen. He would not watch these brave people die fighting for a lie. He couldn't do that to them.

He turned to Mavri. "The Vrykol tells the truth. I am a half-breed. I deceived you and your people. You don't need to die for me."

Confusion showed on the elf's face. "But I touched your flesh," he countered. "You are not of human blood."

"What I am doesn't matter," Jayden said. "I can't allow any more of you to die because of me." He turned to the Vrykol. "You will let everyone else go if I come with you?"

"You have my word."

"And what is that worth, demon?" spat Sayia.

"It was not *I* who lied to my own people," said the Vrykol. "The boy must die. We have no interest in the others."

"Even if what you say is true," said Mavri, "you have slaughtered many of our kin. We cannot allow such a deed to go unanswered."

"Your kin died due to their own lack of wisdom. You need not share their fate."

"Please," Jayden cut in. "They'll kill you all."

"And they will kill *you* if we surrender," Mavri pointed out.

He shrugged. "They'll do that either way."

"Step forward," commanded the Vrykol. "It will be swift. I can promise you that."

Sayia moved in front of him. "I will not let you. It cannot end like this."

Jayden tossed his sword to the ground. "It has to. There is no other way." He placed his hands on her shoulders and smiled. "We tried."

She was on the verge of tears. "You drew on the power of heaven before. Surely you can do so again."

"If I could, I would," he told her. "But I don't know how. I have no choice but to surrender."

His defeatist tone galvanized her into action. She shook her head wildly. "No! You mustn't. I will not allow it." Shoving Jayden with all of her strength, she whirled around and charged straight at the enemy.

Taken off guard, he fell flat on his back. Sayia had already covered half the distance by the time he was able to roll onto his knees. The enemy simply waited, weapons at the ready. Jayden was horror-struck. She would be cut down in seconds.

A mighty bellowing roar echoed from out of the desert just as Sayia reached the enemy line. She battled with a furious intensity, but after only a short exchange of strikes, Vrykol steel pierced her stomach. She slumped to her knees. Another roar sounded—deep, menacing, and rapidly drawing closer. The Vrykol withdrew its blade and turned to gaze at where the sounds were coming from.

All eyes were drawn to the horizon as a third roar called out. A dozen hulking figures were racing toward them. As tall as bears up on their hind legs and with thick black fur covering virtually every inch of their bodies, they were running at a truly astonishing speed. The Vrykol and the humans looked utterly perplexed.

"What the hell are those?" asked Jayden.

No one replied. The elves were seemingly just as confused about the creatures as their foes.

The enemy rapidly turned to form a new line of defense, not that it did them a scrap of good. Great clawed hands swiped them aside as if they were nothing more than blades of tall grass. The Vrykol hastily gathered in a small group well away from the initial fray, refusing to join their human allies. The newcomers' savagery and strength were unlike anything Jayden could have imagined. But were they friends? Sayia was looking up at them while clutching at her wound, the pain on her face giving way to terror.

One of the Vrykol glanced over at Jayden, its eyes narrowed with spite. Then, as one, all five of them turned and fled. The remaining humans attempted to flee as well, but their attackers were far too quick, pummeling them to the sand with bone-shattering blows. It was over in less than a couple of minutes.

With the humans slain, the newcomers stood still and silent amongst the carnage they had created, as if waiting for something. They had flat broad features and dark eyes. Jayden could now see that their fur was not matted or dirty, as he'd imagined, but surprisingly well kept, even giving off a light sheen in the heat of the sun.

Sayia was kicking at the ground in an effort to move away. He ran to her side, his eyes never leaving their strange rescuers. Her wound was severe and bleeding badly.

"Run," she said through gritted teeth. "Leave me."

Jayden stripped off his shirt and applied pressure to the wound. "I'm not leaving you."

"The elf is dying," said one of the creatures, its voice deep and guttural.

Both Jayden and Sayia looked up in astonishment.

"How does a Morzhash speak?" said Sayia.

The creature snarled, revealing a row of sharp fangs. "We come to save you, and receive insults in return?"

"She meant no offense," Jayden hurriedly said. "Please, help her if you can."

The giant figure reached into its fur, where a small pouch on a leather strap was concealed. This was tossed to the ground beside Sayia.

"Treat her wound with this. It will seal the flesh."

Inside the pouch, Jayden found a small vial of blue liquid. With the opened vial in one hand, he gently removed his folded-up shirt from Sayia's injury. This immediately produced a renewed heavy flow of blood. A moment later, her eyes fluttered. Desperate, and at a loss for what else to do, he simply emptied the entire contents of the vial directly onto the wound. With a hiss, steam rose up. Sayia let out an ear-splitting scream and her head thrashed about wildly.

Horrified, Jayden looked up. "What have you done to her?" he demanded.

"We have saved her life," the creature replied calmly. "The wound was deep, but the pain will pass."

Sayia's hand reached up to grip Jayden's arm, her nails digging deep into the flesh. Groaning through a clenched jaw, she continued to writhe about. But to Jayden's astonishment and relief, the steam subsided, and it became clear that the bleeding had ceased and the wound was rapidly healing. A few moments later, she went completely limp and unconscious.

Jayden waved over the other elves, who approached warily.

"Who are you?" he asked the creature.

"We are the *yetulu*. You must come with us, son of Darshan."

He tensed. "How do you know me?"

"Darshan?" repeated Mavri, who, along with the other elves, was now within earshot.

"I am sorry I deceived you," Jayden told him. "Yes, it's true. My father is Darshan."

"Then the stories are true," he muttered. "Darshan took one of our kin as his unorem."

Jayden could not tell if the elf was angry or simply in shock. He nodded. "That's why I'm here. To save his unorem's life." Gently placing Sayia's head on the sand, he rose to face the remaining elves. "I am sorry that I lied. But I had no other choice. My mother is dying."

Mavri fixed his gaze on Jayden. After a long silence, he bowed. "Darshan saved the elves. This much we all know. Had it not been for him, the Reborn King would have seen our entire race slaughtered."

He moved closer. "Though I understand your need for secrecy, we still would have aided you had we known who you are. Our hatred for humans and loathing of half-breeds may well be wrong-minded, but it would not have prevented us from offering you our help. And knowing that my kin gave their lives to help Darshan's son eases my mind somewhat. They were honorable deaths."

Jayden was unsure what to say or how to feel. It hadn't occurred to him that, although they despised humans and, like most other elves, did not care for the gods, they would feel differently about Darshan. But it was true. By defeating their greatest foe, his father had saved them all from extinction. Even back home in Sharpstone, most elves had a figurine of Darshan placed somewhere in their house and would often ask for his blessing. Shame and guilt began to run through him.

"Thank you," was all he could manage to say.

"We must go," said the *yetulu*. "Time is short, and the journey is long."

The rumbling voice snapped Jayden back into the moment. "How did you know to come?" he asked, turning to the hulking creature.

"Your father sent us."

He took a rapid step forward. "You know where he is?"

"In a way, yes."

"In a way? What are you saying? Do you know, or don't you?"

The *yetulu* looked to his companions and let out a series of low grunts and grumbles Jayden assumed was some sort of language. After a moment of this strange discussion, three backed away and set off at a run in the direction the Vrykol had fled.

"I have spoken to him. But it will be difficult for you to understand unless you see for yourself."

Sayia stirred. "Jayden," she whispered.

Kneeling, he brushed the hair away from her face. "Don't move. You've lost a lot of blood. But the *yetulu* saved you. You're going to be just fine now."

"Don't leave me," she begged. "I must come with you. You can't..."

The effort was too much. Her voice faded away, and she fell back into unconsciousness.

"We cannot wait for the elf to be well enough to travel," the *yetulu* told him. "My brethren go to clear the way, lest there be more foes ahead. We are strong, but not immortal. Should the gods send more than a handful, we may not be able to protect you."

"What about them?" Jayden asked, nodding to the elves.

"There is a group of their kin already on their way here. They should arrive by nightfall." The creature looked across to Mavri. "Bury your fallen. You will be safe so long as the son of Darshan is not among you."

His words amplified Jayden's guilt. He had been the sole cause of the attack. He alone was the reason why so many of their group had died. *I should have never agreed to travel with them,* he thought, cursing himself.

"You should go now," Mavri told him. "We will care for Sayia."

"I..." Jayden choked on his own words.

"There is no need for regret," the elf continued, as if hearing his thoughts. "All mortal beings die. My kin are with the Creator now. You have done nothing wrong. It is I who am to blame. My own hatreds forced you into a deception. Even one so flawed as I can see that. Go. Save your mother."

Jayden glanced over to the *yetulu*. There was one final question on his mind. "How do I know that my father really sent you?" he asked.

The creature's dark eyes looked directly into his. "Why else would we come? We have exposed our existence to the outside world. Only Darshan could have asked this of us."

It was enough. Jayden switched his attention back to Mavri. "Tell Sayia that I'm sorry, but I couldn't wait."

After gathering his belongings, he cast a final look at the elves. His mother had described elf funeral rites to him; he was well aware that it would be a most sorrowful night. Their fires would be seen for many miles. In a way, he regretted not being able to take part. After all, he was the reason their kin had died.

He approached the *yetulu*. "I'm ready."

Without a word, they set off due east. The elves were already gathering the bodies and had begun erecting a small tent to shield Sayia from the sun. In spite of their quarrels, Jayden now realized how much he would miss her company.

He wondered if he would ever see her again. Something told him yes. She would make sure of it. In her final words before lapsing back into unconsciousness, he had heard enough to know that she genuinely cared a great deal for him. Though why that should be was impossible to guess.

After peeling open her eyes, the chill morning air sent a shiver through Sayia's body. For a moment, all she could think about was the pain in her stomach. At the very least, it should have been sharp and nagging. Incredibly, though, it was little more than a dull throb. Then, with a rush, realization struck her. She shot bolt upright, shouting out Jayden's name.

"He is gone," a voice told her.

Mavri was sitting a few feet away beside a small fire, a plate of bread and fruits on his lap.

"Gone?"

She tried to stand, but what had been a dull pain now protested sharply at her sudden movements. She doubled over, sucking her teeth. Only when the spasm had subsided did she notice that her wounds had been newly dressed and she was wearing fresh clothing.

"You should not move just yet," warned Mavri. "The *yetulu* healed your wounds, but not completely. It will still take time."

"Morzhash! You let them take him?"

"Jayden went willingly," he replied. "He is safe. Seeing that they saved our lives, I do not think their intentions were ill."

"They are animals," she shot back. "Vicious animals. They are more dangerous than you can possibly imagine."

Mavri gave her a curious look. "They did look remarkably bear-like, I admit. And from the way the Vrykol fled, I would say that they are indeed dangerous. But animals... no. You would be dead if not for the *yetulu*. They deserve your gratitude."

Sayia had heard that the Morzhash were long vanished from her land and presumed extinct. It was impossible to imagine how they had suddenly arrived here, as if out of nowhere. What was more, those creatures had been capable of speech; she remembered that clearly. Not that this surprising revelation made any great difference now. Jayden was gone and had been for some time. There was nothing more she could do to aid him.

Around her, the funeral fires were still smoldering. Slowly, she rose to her feet. There was pain, but it was tolerable so long as she made no abrupt movements.

"What will you do?" she asked Mavri.

He shrugged. "Nothing. Those of us still alive will go on as planned. The *yetulu* told us that desert elves will be arriving here any time now. I suppose we will continue our journey with them."

Her pack had been placed on the ground a few feet away. With careful movements, she put it on and then gave the elf a smile. "I wish you good fortune. And thank you for your aid."

"You will never catch them," he said.

"I don't intend to."

"Then where are you going?"

She stared out over the rolling expanse of desert. Her part in this was done. She had failed, and Jayden would now have to face the trials alone. There was only one thing left for her to do.

"I will go to Sharpstone," she said.

Her grandfather had once predicted that she would find her joy across the sea, that this was where she would learn what it was like to feel truly alive. He had been wrong. Thus far, she had found nothing but sorrow and disappointment.

Mavri insisted on giving her a few extra supplies for her journey, after which she bade farewell to the others. Most of the elves were still reeling from both the loss of close friends killed by the Vrykol and then the shattering discovery that the youth who'd been traveling with them was actually the son of the mighty Darshan. This meant that her parting words with them were brief.

Turning west, she started out at a steady pace, the image of her grandfather's smile wandering into her thoughts. That was what she missed the most about him: the way he looked at her whenever she was sad or frustrated. He had only ever been angry with her once—when she had said that humans were untrustworthy beasts. She'd only been in her teens at the time, and the barrier was still separating the two lands.

"Do you know any humans?" he'd asked of her.

"No. But the stories…"

He sniffed, curling his lip. "The stories are false. Humans are no different from us. At least, not at heart. You should not speak ill of people you have never met. You never know, perhaps they think the same way about elves."

"Why would they?" she countered. "We have no war. No hunger. No one wants for anything. Do you really think that humans can boast the same?"

"Have you ever considered the possibility that the elves across the barrier might be different from those living here?" he asked.

She wanted to reply, but the truth was, it had never once crossed her mind. She had always assumed that elves were the same throughout the entire world. She could not imagine any of their kin, no matter where they were living, as warlike. Still, she was not about to allow a lack of thought on her part force her into giving up on the argument.

"Do you know for sure that they are different?" she demanded. "Do you have proof? I mean, it's not like you have been there to see for yourself. No one has. It's impossible."

He scowled. "Young lady, I know things that you cannot possibly imagine."

"I know that you haven't been across the sea. I know you've never met a human. I do know that much."

It had been a childish outburst. And in her heart, she knew that he was right. He did know things. Far more things than she could have imagined possible. It hurt now to recall that she had never apologized for doubting him and for storming off in a huff. She wondered if he even remembered the incident. Yes. Of course he did. He remembered everything.

More than anything, the desire to beg his forgiveness tugged at her heart. For the argument... and for so much more.

CHAPTER 14

The *yetulu* traveled at tremendous speed, and despite their thick fur, did not appear to be bothered in the slightest by the heat. Jayden, on the other hand, was faring far less well. The unrelenting sun was threatening to scorch his exposed arms and face, and by midday he had already drunk most of his water supply. The fact that he needed to take two paces for every giant stride that the *yetulu* took was not helping matters, either.

"You are most unlike your father," remarked one of the *yetulu* named Morda. Though to Jayden, male and female *yetulu* looked identical, Morda, it turned out, was female. "You are weak," she added. "Not like Darshan at all."

"My father is a god," he snapped back between deep gulps of air. "I am mortal."

"That's not what I mean. You do not draw strength from the mother."

It took a moment for Jayden to understand what she meant. "Oh, you mean the *flow*? I've only just begun to learn."

She cast him a sideways glance. "Your father did not teach you? That is strange."

"Yes," he agreed. "It is."

"We can carry you, if you would like," she offered.

He shook his head. "I'll be fine." He would not allow himself to be carried like a weary child on a long outing. That would be too humiliating to bear.

He tried to reach out for the *flow*, but as was often the case when there was no danger or high surge of emotion within him, it was elusive.

"There's an oasis not far ahead," Morda revealed. "You can rest there."

"How far are we going?" he asked, almost afraid to hear the answer.

"Many days," she replied. "But you will arrive much sooner than we. The blood will speed your journey."

"The blood?"

She gave him what he thought to be a smile. "You will see."

Not far turned out to be several miles, and by the time they reached the small oasis, Jayden was on the verge of collapse. It might have been little more than a patch of turf, a few palms, and a small puddle of water, but just then, it was the most welcome sight imaginable. Without a moment's hesitation, he dropped to his knees beside the pool and began slurping down handful after handful of water.

"You cannot continue without strength," remarked a large male named Hrundun.

Jayden did not reply until he had gulped down several more mouthfuls. "I'll manage," he insisted, splashing water over his face and neck.

"Morda has offered to carry you."

He jumped sharply to his feet. "I will *not* be carried."

After letting out a deep grumble that could have meant anything, the *yetulu* strode over to the edge of the oasis where the others were gathered. By now it was late in the afternoon, and Jayden started to wonder when or where they planned to stop. This seemed like a good place to him, but it didn't look as if his escorts intended to halt any time soon.

After filling his waterskin, he took out some jerky and flatbread from his pack. While eating, a thought occurred. Perhaps if he delayed his meal long enough, they would agree to wait until the next day before moving on. He was still trying to draw things out some twenty minutes later when the three *yetulu* who had gone after the Vrykol turned up. He could hear them making their report in a series of guttural growls and hisses.

After a few minutes, Morda approached and stood over him.

"The enemy has fled far," she told him. "Even so, we should be going now. They could return."

"From what I saw, you can handle them easily enough," he remarked through a final mouthful of bread.

She shook her head. "The enemy is strong. They chose not to fight this time, possibly because they did not expect to encounter us. Should they come again, in greater numbers, who can tell the outcome? We might kill them, or perhaps they might kill us. Your father saved us and returned us to our people, and for that, we owe him our lives. But we will not throw them away when escape is possible."

Having finished what she wanted to say, in the blink of an eye, Morda reached down to wrap her thick arms around Jayden. With one effortless movement, she hefted him over her shoulder.

She had him in position almost before he realized what was happening. "Put me down!" he demanded, kicking his legs and pounding furiously at her back.

She paid him not the slightest heed. After only a few seconds, Jayden's struggles ceased. He could feel the immense power holding him in place and knew there was nothing he could do to resist it. Another *yetulu* picked up his pack, and within moments they were speeding across the desert at a pace that made their previous tempo seem like a slow crawl.

It wasn't long before his mood mellowed. Though he was loath to admit it, this was the best way. By nightfall, they had covered more distance than he could have managed in an entire day.

The *yetulu* were tireless, not halting until it was nearly dawn. When Morda at last placed him on the sands between two dunes, she let out a rumbling laugh, her fangs gleaming in the moonlight.

"What's funny?" Jayden asked, a heavy frown on his face.

"You," she replied. "How angry you are that you cannot keep up."

"I don't like being carried."

"Why? I don't mind. You weigh very little." She sat down beside him, her massive girth stirring the sand. "You should accept what you cannot change, son of Darshan. Pride gains you nothing."

The *yetulu* carrying his pack tossed it over beside him. Jayden rummaged around inside for more jerky. His eyes then shifted to Morda.

"You said that my father saved you," he probed.

She seemed quite willing to talk about it. "Yes. We were trapped. Hunted by elves. Darshan brought us home and reunited us with our people."

He was shocked. "The elves hunted you?"

"Yes. They thought us mindless animals. But it was they who were the invaders. They drove us from our homes, pushing us ever back. We fought them, but they were powerful and many. We could never hope to win."

Jayden recalled the fear on Sayia's face when she had first seen the *yetulu*. Realization dawned. "You lived across the Western Abyss at one time, didn't you?"

"Yes. Though it was not our true home. We had been forgotten, cut off from all we knew and forced to survive however we could. Then Darshan came to help us. He brought us back to our rightful place in the mountains." She pointed off to the north. "That is why we were willing to help you."

"How did he get your people all the way there?"

"Darshan is mighty," she explained. "He made a doorway and helped us through. And now, we are whole again. You will understand once you speak with him. He is waiting for you."

Jayden furrowed his brow. "What has happened to him? Why didn't he come himself? My mother is sick, and he needs to come home."

"I do not have the answer to your questions. Though it pains me to hear of your mother; she is a kind and generous woman."

"You know her?"

Morda nodded. "We have met many times. If she were ill, your father would rush to cure her if he could. That he does not is troubling."

Jayden bowed his head for a moment. He had hoped to learn something about his father's fate, but now he was only more confused than ever. Suddenly, being carried did not seem like an embarrassment at all. He needed to know what had happened, and the sooner he could get to wherever they were going, the better. Pride be damned.

He looked up again. "You said I will get there ahead of you. How?"

"I told you. The blood will carry you."

"You mean the Blood of the Sands? I thought they were destroyed during the battle between my father and the Reborn King."

"Darshan remade them."

Jayden shook his head in wonder. It was still so hard to fathom that his father was powerful enough to achieve such an incredible thing. Each tale of Darshan he heard showed him more and more just how little he knew about the man— the god—who had raised him.

"Sleep," said Morda. "We will leave with the sun."

Jayden hadn't realized how tired he was until that moment. He wanted to keep talking, but Morda stood and joined the others, who were gathered in a circle a few yards away. There would be no further discussion. With resignation, he took out a blanket and lay down, using his pack as a pillow. He wondered if his father knew his mother was ill. Surely he did. Their bond would tell him, wouldn't it? If his sisters knew, he had to know of it as well. Something must be keeping him there... wherever *there* was.

The morning came, and this time, he did not protest when Morda picked him up over her shoulder. The ride was quite smooth, actually. The *yetulu* strides, though broad and swift, were remarkably even, reducing any jostling to a minimum.

By the third day, his anxiety was increasing. The dunes stretched on for what looked like an eternity, with only the occasional tiny oasis to offer any respite. As evening drew close, he had already asked Morda numerous times that day how much longer their journey would be. When he asked her yet again, she placed him on the ground with a tad more force than before.

"Our path together ends here," she told him.

For a moment, he thought she was angry. But then she pointed to a distant row of dunes, in front of which stood a twisted rock pillar roughly twelve feet in height.

"She awaits you within," Morda told him.

"Who?"

"The elf," she replied. "She will accompany you for the rest of your journey. Forgive us for not taking you closer, but our hearts cannot forget what her kin did to us. We spoke once, and that is all we are willing to suffer."

From out of a narrow crack in the rock, Jayden saw a figure emerge.

He turned back to Morda. "Thank you for your help," he said. "I will always be grateful to you."

She said nothing in response, making just a small lowering of the head before moving away to join the other *yetulu* waiting for her a few yards away. Jayden watched with a strange sense of affection as the tightly bunched group set off in a northerly direction toward their mountain homeland, their pace markedly slower than before.

He watched after them until they were several minutes away before heading over to the waiting elf. She was older, though it was difficult to say exactly how old. Her skin was surprisingly fair, given the desert climate, and her piercing eyes were fixed firmly on his. She wore a light tan shirt and loose-fitting pants along with a headscarf, presumably to protect her from the blazing sun.

"You are the son of Darshan?" she asked.

"I am Jayden," he replied, giving a curt bow.

"I am Weila, sand master and friend to your father." She scrutinized him for a lengthy moment. "You have his bearing. But I see your mother in you as well."

"How did you know him?"

"It is a long tale. One that I can recount as we travel."

She then led him down a long, stone-hewn stairwell that ended in a narrow corridor.

"Who built this?" asked Jayden.

"No one knows," she replied. "The gods, perhaps. Darshan restored it to its former state to help the people of the desert. But I doubt even he could have built such a thing without aid. The Blood of the Sands is truly vast."

The air at this level was warm, though comfortable when compared to the surface, and not nearly so dry. After about half a mile, they entered a circular chamber with a low domed ceiling. Here, a pair of tunnels directly opposite each other were connected by a four-foot-wide strip of sand. Leaning against the wall, just off to their right, were several flat disks. Weila picked up two of these and lashed them together with a strip of leather from her pocket.

She waved Jayden over to help her carry them to the edge of the sand. "Jump onto the rear and sit down as quickly as possible," she said.

Though confused, he nevertheless did as told. They jumped virtually together, each of them landing atop their own disk just as it made contact with the sand. Instantly, the entire strip burst into life, much like a rapidly flowing river. Such was the force, Jayden was almost thrown off. Only Weila twisting around to catch his shirt collar saved him. The next thing he knew, they were passing into the tunnel ahead at an alarming speed.

"By the gods," he cried out. Having heard stories about the blood of the sands had not prepared him in the least for such an experience. This was exhilarating almost beyond belief.

Weila smiled. "Yes. I have ridden the blood many times, and I still marvel that it can exist."

Much as he was thrilled by the ride, Jayden was eager for information. "Tell me how you knew my father," he said after a few moments.

"I met him here in the desert," she responded. "He was with my son, Pali, when the creatures of the Reborn King took his life. Later, we followed him to aid in the fight against Angrääl."

Many desert elves now lived in the west. Jayden had met a few of them when he was a boy. He'd always found them to be far more pleasant than most other elves, totally lacking in what he felt was their western cousins' haughty and overly formal manner.

"Why did you agree to leave your home?" he asked. "The war was far away."

"Your father's coming was foretold long ago. Even so, we did not believe him in the beginning. But he soon proved himself to be true. Then, after the war, I tried to live in the wetlands. It did not work out; my heart was always calling me back to the sands. I wasn't alone. Many others returned with me." She smiled over her shoulder. "Change is difficult when you grow old."

"It's not so easy when you're young, either."

"No. I don't suppose it is." She twisted to face him more fully. "I had very little recollection of Darshan for a time. Only that I had fought with him. It was when the elves of the west began coming to the desert that he appeared to me and lifted the veil he had placed on the world. He did not want people knowing who he was... or at least, who he was still pretending to be."

"Yes. Linis explained it to me."

"A fine elf. I have not heard his name for some time. How does he fare?"

Jayden proceeded to tell her about Linis's life in Sharpstone. Weila seemed surprised that he had become a farmer.

"However does he quench his thirst for adventure?" she remarked, chuckling softly. "Though I suppose love can accomplish the impossible."

She went on to tell him the details of her time with his father: their first meeting, the death of her son, and the siege of Baltria. As it turned out, he had restored her memory so that she could better aid those coming to live in the desert.

"I understand why they come," she continued. "But it is no easy task to teach people a new way of life. They hope to escape the relentless tide of change by coming to a land that does not feel the touch of time. I pity them. They do not understand that change comes to the dunes as well. Even now, human tribes are venturing forth to live among the sands. True, they are not yet arriving in great numbers, but I feel that will change before long."

Jayden did not feel qualified to remark on this, so he remained silent.

Weila continued, "Darshan explained to me that he restored my memory to help the elves understand the real story behind the war. That humans and elves are really two people with one heart, and that their new world is not something that should be seen as their demise." She gave a sad smile. "Even the gods can be naïve. They come. And I can see all too clearly that for most, their hearts will remain unchanged until the day they die." She took a long breath. "In truth, I think he restored my memory because he feared I would not bear the burden unless I knew we had once been friends."

Jayden frowned. "Why would he think that?"

"Because it was Darshan who gave them the idea of coming here in the first place."

He raised an eyebrow. "You're saying that he actually *told* the elves to leave their home?" Up until now, he had assumed that his father had been trying to find a way to get people to live together, not split them apart.

"He planted the seed," she said. "But only in those he feared would cause problems and might become violent. And he never forced anyone to go against their will. Though how he accomplished all this is unknown to me. Only he can tell you that."

"So, you are really bringing me to him?"

"In a way. I was with him when he ... departed. He gave me instructions should something go wrong."

Jayden sat up straight. "You know what happened to him?"

"No. Not exactly. I only know that he is gone. Where he went and who is behind his disappearance, I cannot say."

"It was Saraf."

Weila cocked her head. "Truly? That would explain his apprehension. He came and told me that you might come. I have never before seen Darshan fearful, but this time I could see it in his eyes. He was afraid."

"Afraid of what?"

"As I said, I am unsure. Hopefully, he will be able to tell you himself."

"You're not making sense. If he's gone, how can he tell me?"

"You will see. Quite soon, in fact. We're nearly there." She rose to a crouched position. "When I say jump, do not hesitate. If you do, you will be lost."

Seeing a bright light rapidly approaching, Jayden mirrored her stance. Then, with a rush, they exited the tunnel and raced through an immense chamber whose walls and ceiling glowed with a strange, pale light. Fear clutched at his chest as he looked ahead and saw exactly what Weila meant by being lost. At the far end of the chamber, the stream of sand they were riding on abruptly spread out, twisting and swirling into a great vortex that seemed to plunge down into the very bowels of the earth. To be sucked in could only mean certain death.

The disks they were on were about to pass alongside a narrow platform.

"Jump now!" shouted Weila once they were within range.

The sand master leaped. But Jayden was a split second late reacting, causing the unbalanced disk to slip sharply to one side. He reached out frantically, his fingertips only just catching the lip of the platform. Weila had made it easily enough, and at first did not notice his peril.

"Help!" he cried out, already feeling himself losing his tenuous hold.

Weila spun around and dove low to stretch out and grab his wrists, one in each hand. With a heavy grunt, she pulled. Jayden could feel the racing sands gripping at his boots, threatening to suck him onward into the vortex. But the elf was amazingly strong. For a few seconds, she merely resisted the pull of the stream. Then, bit by bit, she overcame it and dragged him far enough forward that he could scramble to safety. He rolled onto his back, his heart pounding and his breath coming in quick gasps.

"Are you injured?" she asked.

Jayden waved his hand. "No. I'm fine, thank you."

Weila sat back, hands draped over her knees, a deep frown on her face. Her tone was curt. "Did your father teach you nothing?"

"No. He didn't." He found her irritation fueling his own. "If you want the truth, you've known who my father really is for much longer than I have."

"I see."

He noticed her frown had now become a look of doubt. "What is it?" he demanded.

"If you have come to help Darshan, I thought you would be better prepared."

"He *is* prepared," said a familiar voice.

CHAPTER 15

Awave of elation and utter relief washed over Jayden. Leaping to his feet, he ran headlong toward his father. But then, when he wrapped his arms around him, he knew immediately that something was not right. His father felt ... different. He backed away a few steps. His father's raven hair, strong jaw, and broad shoulders were just as they had always been. Even his kind eyes and warm smile were the same. But there was something about his clothes that was odd. The white shirt and tan trousers shimmered with an unnatural light, and his skin had a sheen to it, as if it were covered in oil.

Darshan turned to Weila. "Thank you for bringing him."

She bowed. "I will leave you alone. When should I return?"

"There's no need. You can go home now."

Weila started toward the far end of the chamber, where Jayden could see a narrow archway leading to an ascending stone staircase. She paused to smile back at him. "I do hope we meet again," she said. Without awaiting a reply, she bounded up the stairs three at a time.

There was silence for a moment. "Are you really my father?" Jayden asked.

"Of course I am," he replied. "Who else would I be?"

"Then why do you look so … strange?"

"This will be hard for you to understand. I am your father, but I am only a small part of him. I am the part of his essence that he left behind."

Jayden's eyes narrowed. "His essence? You mean you're some sort of ghost or spirit?"

He smiled. "You could put it that way, I suppose. I have all his memories and emotions. Yet I only have knowledge of what has happened up until the moment I was created."

"If that is true and you really are my father, then tell me this. What is my favorite food?"

Darshan chuckled. "You tell your mother it is her spiced beef. But you only say that because you're afraid to hurt her feelings. What you really like the most is fish porridge with vanta root and onions… the way Dina makes it."

His mother had first made spiced beef for him when he was a child. And it was true that he had told her it was his favorite. She had been so happy that he liked it, he couldn't bear to tell her that he didn't. Of course, to his chagrin, this meant that she had continued to make it for him at every opportunity. Only his father would know about this.

"It really *is* you," he said.

Darshan spread his hands. "It really is."

"You have to come home. Mother is ill."

"I know. But I cannot leave this place. And even if I were able to, there isn't anything I could do to help her. Only if my true self returns will she be saved."

"Then where did you—he—go?"

He pointed at the mass of churning sands. "Into the vortex."

Jayden turned to look, a deep frown forming. Why would he go in there? A chill ran through him. "Where does it lead?"

"I wish I knew. When I remade it, I used it to bring the *yetulu* home from across the Abyss. But Saraf has altered it somehow. I have no way of knowing what he did."

"So my father... you... went in there to find out what he had done?"

Darshan stepped forward and placed his hand on Jayden's shoulder. "I know it's difficult to comprehend. When I first met my own father, I had a hard time, too."

"You mean Gerath?"

"That's right. He left a part of himself in the Black Oasis. And now I must do for you what he did for me."

The touch of his father's hand felt no different than it always had. It *was* him. And yet, in a way that was hard to describe, it wasn't. "What must I do?" he asked.

"If you are to save your mother, you must follow."

Jayden stepped back. Somehow, he had known in the back of his mind that this was what his father was going to say. Nonetheless, hearing it confirmed caused apprehension to rise sharply within him. "What will happen when I do?"

"I'm not sure. But you shouldn't be afraid. I will protect you. Come with me. I'll show you."

He walked over to the far left wall, near which a small silver box had been placed on the floor. He handed it to Jayden, who raised the lid and saw an egg-sized blood-red jewel inside.

His eyes widened. "What is this?"

Darshan smiled. "What you see of me is merely an image. The power that sustains my existence is within that stone. The moment you touch it, I will become a part of you. I will protect your mortal self through the vortex."

"So what will happen to you?"

"I will cease to be."

Jayden found this to be acutely upsetting. He could accept that the man before him was not really Gewey Stedding—merely a ghost left behind. But ghost or not, it had all of his father's feelings and memories. It somehow felt wrong to allow that being to sacrifice himself, who was in essence still his father.

"It's all right," said Darshan, sensing his apprehension. "This is what I was created to do. I may be only a reflection of your father, but I still love Kaylia in the same way he does. Only you and your sisters do I love more. In fact, so deep is my love that I would stop you from going if I could. But to do that would only leave you vulnerable to my enemies. With me gone, Saraf will not suffer you to live, regardless of what he might have told you."

Jayden could see the pain in his eyes. "Why didn't you tell me who I am a long time ago? And who *you* are?"

"I wanted only to protect you, my son. I was shown a vision long ago—one that I could not allow to come true."

"Yes. I was told of this. But you can't possibly think I would ever do any of the terrible things that vision foretold. I'm not a conqueror."

A sigh slipped from Darshan's mouth. "The Oracle of Manisalia once told your mother that to bring about the end of the world with love and good intent is no better than ending it with fire and fury. You have a kind heart, Jayden, but you are not without failings. No one is. I recognized in you the same weakness that I see in myself." Sorrow and regret filled his eyes. "It has been hard for me to stay out of the way of mortal affairs. In fact, I often failed to do so. I've interfered in things that I should have stayed away from. I was afraid that you would not be able to resist the lure of meddling any more than I have."

"So, what are you saying? That you think I would become like the Reborn King?"

"If you know the history, then you will be aware he was not always evil."

"Then you think I could *become* evil. Is that it?"

Darshan shook his head. "No. I think you would remain good and kind. Nevertheless, in the end, you would realize what I have come to understand... and it would destroy you. You would not be able to live with your deeds, or with the truth of the world."

"So tell me, what is the truth?"

His voice dropped to barely a whisper, almost as if he was speaking to himself. "The elves are right to fear. Humankind *will* eventually dominate. It is in their nature. Though I used to think otherwise, I now know that in time, hatred wins. When I fought in the war, I was certain that if people could just understand one another, peace would be the natural result. But the harder I tried to make this come about, the more distant they became."

Jayden set his shoulders. "No, not everyone is like that. Look at the people of Sharpstone. Look at Dina and Linis."

"You have not seen what I have, son. It's true there are a few who can set aside old notions, but most simply cannot. Tolerance is not acceptance or love. You can tolerate an unpleasant neighbor; yet should that neighbor fall on hard times, you would not shed even the smallest tear at their departure. That is what the world has become. And it gets worse by the day."

"I don't believe that. I know it will take time, but people *will* eventually learn to live together."

His father gave him a warm smile. "That is exactly why I didn't tell you who you are. Because I know you believe with all your heart what you are saying. Your strength and love would not allow you to simply leave the world to run its course. Like me, you would do all you could to help them see reason. And like me, you would fail. In the years since the war ended, I have created nothing but more problems and misery for mankind."

Jayden squared his shoulders. "Believe me, I have no intention of forcing the world to do anything. Whatever mistakes you might have made, I can promise you that I won't be repeating them."

He'd firmly believed that upon meeting with his father once again, he would have many questions to pose that demanded answers. Or at the very least, a long and fierce rebuke for having been kept in ignorance all his life. But now that the time was here, he had nothing to say. No words would change what had to b be done. Seeing his father's image standing in front of him and hearing of his regrets and failures totally extinguished the flames of anger he had carried ever since leaving home. In a way, he now pitied him. All the power of heaven at his disposal, and still he was helpless to change things.

"Whatever happens," said Darshan, "I want you to know that I have always believed in you. I know you will triumph." He moved in close to embrace his son.

Jayden returned the affection fully. There was no question in his mind that his father loved him with all his heart. Even this sliver of spirit left behind was filled with devotion. Releasing his hold, he stepped back to take a last look at his father's face. "Goodbye," he said.

Darshan laughed softly. "This is not really goodbye, son. In a way, I will always be a part of you. My consciousness will fade, but my spirit will dwell inside you forever."

This was a comforting thought. He had always wanted to be close with his father; now he would be. Far closer than any human or elf father and son could possibly be. Still thinking of this, he reached inside the box and lifted the stone. At once, it crumbled to dust in his palm. As it did so, the spirit before him blinked out of existence. A warm sensation rushed through his entire body, and for a moment he could feel the love of his father wrapping itself around him.

After taking a deep breath, he turned to face the vortex. It no longer appeared ominous and threatening. It was simply a door—one through which he would pass. All fear dissipated, replaced by resolve and even a touch of anticipation. The muscles in his legs twitched and tensed.

It was time.

Bursting into a dead run, he planted his foot on the lip of the platform and leaped. Time slowed as he flew through the air. Then his foot touched sand, and he felt the warmth of his father's love intensify, acting as a shield against the power of the vortex.

Having launched himself to within just a few feet of its whirling center, he was quickly taken by its grip and pulled down. But rather than the anticipated darkness, a blinding light at first surrounded him. It felt as though a great weight was pressing in on his chest, and he had the sensation of being shot through the air at an unimaginable velocity. Flashes of red and yellow exploded in front of his eyes like spitting embers from a fire.

Suddenly, all went completely still. The light faded, and total darkness enveloped him. For a few seconds, he had the eerie sensation of floating in mid-air. Then he was falling. Down and down he plunged for more than a minute, wind roaring in his ears. Sooner or later he was bound to reach the bottom of whatever this was. And then, surely, that would be the end of him. He was falling far too fast to survive.

When the impact finally came, though it rattled every bone in his body and forced all trace of breath from his lungs with an almighty whooshing sound, it was still far gentler than anything he could have prayed for. Yes, the initial pain was intense, but he had survived.

Was this the spirit's doing? Surely it had to be.

He lay still for a short time with what he took to be grass pressing against his cheek, trying to recover his breath and clear his jumbled thoughts. Gradually, the raucous clatter of what sounded horribly like battle filtered in: steel clashing on steel, men shouting orders, and great wails of pain.

While cautiously raising his head to investigate, as if to order, light was suddenly restored, allowing him to take in his surroundings. He was lying in a thinly wooded area, and in every direction he looked, men and elves were engaged in fierce combat. There appeared to be no organization to the melee, no battle lines or tight formations, just utter chaos and death. The elves were vastly outnumbered, and many were attempting to flee. Taking quick stock, Jayden spotted a narrow gap in the fighting just off to his right, where the forest thickened. Scrambling to his feet, he ran as hard as he could.

After only a few yards, as if appearing from nowhere, he found a large human in leather armor suddenly blocking his path. Snarling furiously, the man swung the axe clutched in his right hand in a vicious strike at Jayden's skull. He veered sharply left away from the attack, at the same time fumbling to unsheathe his sword. But before the blade was even halfway free, with amazing speed and agility, the warrior spun and smashed the small circular shield he was holding in his other hand directly into the side of Jayden's head, sending him sprawling. With the deadly axe raised to strike at him again, Jayden made a desperate roll to the right, gasping with relief when he saw the descending blade thump harmlessly into the earth a foot or so away. But this was only a momentary reprieve. A heavy boot thudded into his ribs three times, robbing him of breath, and for a moment, any further ability to take evasive action.

Scarcely had he arrived, and it seemed his journey was already coming to a bloody end. His foe stood over him, poised to deliver a life-ending blow. Jayden closed his eyes.

The whistle of an incoming arrow was the first thing to suggest that he might not be about to breathe his last. This was instantly followed by a loud bellow of pain. His eyes flicked open once again to see a red-fletched shaft protruding from the warrior's chest. With both shield and axe now discarded, the man was staggering about and clutching tightly at the missile with both hands. A second later, he sank to his knees.

The sheer urgency of the situation galvanized Jayden back into action. Although still badly winded and pained from the kick, he struggled to his feet and stumbled on.

The clear call of a horn penetrated the confusion. In response, the elves began to give more ground. Jayden could see that they were attempting to pull back into a single mass and break away. He tried to move across to join them, but soon found himself cut off. In contrast to their earlier apparent disorganization, the humans were now forming ranks with great speed and discipline.

Utterly desperate, Jayden ran as fast as his legs could manage toward a small gap that he hoped might yet get him through to the elves. It was not to be. A massive, heavily armored shoulder slammed into him, sending him sliding across the slick grass. Before he could even start to recover, there was a sharp blow to the back of his head.

For a split second, he was aware only of the taste of blood and earth filling his mouth. Then he lost consciousness.

When he came to his senses, the throbbing in his head was at first almost unbearable. He was lying on his side with both hands and feet bound. Nearby were more than a dozen similarly trussed-up elves, many of them severely wounded. About ten human soldiers stood in a group guarding them.

Farther back, he could see several rows of tents pitched just at the edge of the now calm battlefield. Small teams of men were sorting through the bodies, gathering weapons and various valuables. Those corpses already picked clean were being hauled away to where another group of soldiers were digging what Jayden presumed must be a mass grave.

The battle was over, and the elves had lost. And now he was a captive.

But where was he? He hadn't heard any rumors of an elf uprising. He focused on his surroundings, though the blow to his head was making it difficult to focus on any one thing for longer than a few seconds. The banners fluttering atop the tents were like nothing he had seen before. Who or what a red bull's head over a white five-pointed star represented was a complete mystery. This same emblem was also splayed across the breastplates of the soldiers.

"I don't know you," said a male elf lying a few feet away. He had a large gash across his cheek and his blond shoulder-length hair was plastered with dried blood. "What is your clan?"

Jayden was unsure how to answer. He knew the names of a few elf clans from his mother, so he said the first one that came to mind. "Hastriatis."

His answer drew a curious look. "Hastriatis? Then how did you find yourself here? Your people fight in the west."

"I... I'm not sure. Where are we?"

"What do you mean, where are we? Galmaria, of course. Where do you think you are?"

Galmaria? The name was unfamiliar. "I'm lost."

The elf's eyes narrowed. "Lost? Or fleeing? You were not among us before the battle. Explain yourself."

"Fleeing what?"

"Are you addle-brained? Or did the blow to your head rob you of your senses?"

"Quiet over there, or I'll cut your elf throats," shouted one of the guards.

Jayden's mind was reeling. Where the hell was he? Had the vortex sent him somewhere other than where his father had gone? More immediately, how was he going to get out of this mess? From the look of things, the prospect of survival was slim.

By now, the sun was sinking over the horizon, and fires were being lit throughout the camp. The elf captives remained silent and still, awaiting their fate. So far, nothing Jayden had seen or heard gave even a small clue as to where he had ended up. In fact, he began to wonder if he was even in the same world at all. Could he have been transported to some undiscovered land? It seemed unlikely, yet what other explanation could there be? He'd overheard several humans speaking of the battles in which they had recently fought and of the "tide of war" turning in their favor. But there was no war. At least, not of which he was aware. If there were, he would surely have heard about it. News of such a major event would reach even a small town like Sharpstone.

Three men, one with a red plume on his helm and obviously the commander, approached just as night fell. They stood over Jayden, scrutinizing him with spiteful expressions.

"Is this the one?" asked the commander.

"Yes," affirmed one of the others.

Jayden's leg bindings were severed and he was unceremoniously dragged to his feet. So tightly had the bindings been that the blood flow had been cut off, causing his feet to go numb. It took the support of two guards to keep him standing.

"What is your name, elf?" the commander demanded of him.

"Jayden," he replied.

"Bring him."

With that curt order, the man spun on his heels and strode away. Jayden was forced to follow as best he could, which at first meant that the two guards acting as support needed to almost drag him along. His head still ached furiously, but after a few yards, the sensation in his feet began to return and he was better able to walk on his own. Within a minute or so he found himself being bundled inside a round pavilion, where a group of what looked to be senior officers were gathered around a table.

Determined to present as bold a front as possible, Jayden firmed his jaw and pulled himself up to his full height. But then the officer, who from the look of his resplendent silver armor was the most senior man present, came fully into view. All pretense of assurance instantly vanished and his eyes shot open wide.

"Father!" Jayden shouted.

There was no mistake. As impossible as it seemed, there was his father, standing with his palms pressed to the table.

"You hear that?" mocked one of the other officers in the pavilion. "He's crying for his father. Well, it's too late. He can't help you now, elf."

The entire gathering laughed... including his father.

"Lord Zarin," said the commander, who had led him to the pavilion. "This is the prisoner you asked for."

His father stepped around the table and started toward him. As he drew close, the soldier behind Jayden kicked the back of his knees, forcing him down.

"Kneel in the presence of His Lordship."

Jayden was dumbfounded. Lord Zarin? Why would they call him that? Equally confusing was the look in his father's eyes. It was unlike anything he had ever seen before—there was nothing but pure hatred and disgust in his expression. Jayden had seen his father angry on a few occasions, though not very often. Rare was the day when there wasn't a warm smile given to everyone Gewey Stedding encountered. How could a man so well-loved and kind now appear so utterly terrifying?

Lord Zarin tossed a coin onto the ground in front of him. "How did you come by this?" he demanded.

Even his voice was different—hard, forceful, and cold, and filled with the same hate as was displayed in his eyes.

At first, Jayden was speechless. A boot heel to his back, then forced a response. He glanced at the coin and saw that it was a Baltrian copper. "Baltria," he said. "I got it in Baltria."

In the blink of an eye, his father drew a dagger from his belt. Just as quickly, he jerked Jayden's head back by his hair and held the blade to his throat. "Lie to me again, elf, and the last thing you'll see is me smiling as you bleed out."

Jayden could not believe what was happening. "I'm not lying," he protested.

With a threatening growl of impatience, his father thrust his face closer. "This coin bears the image of someone named Byvern, yet we all know that Baltria is ruled by King Ferdinan. I'll give you one more chance."

He pressed the steel until a trickle of blood ran down Jayden's neck. "Now tell me again—where did you get it?"

King Ferdinan? No, that could not be, Jayden told himself. Sweet spirits! This had to be a dream or an illusion. If what had just been revealed was true, that meant...

His mind hastily switched track, searching for an answer to the more immediate question. "I found the coin when I was foraging. I don't know where it came from."

"My lord," called a tall, older man standing a few feet away. "He was also in possession of some coins from Althetas and Helenia. None of these bore their true king's image, either."

"Did you find those as well?" his father pressed.

"Yes, that's the truth," Jayden quickly confirmed. "They were all together in a pouch I chanced upon." Never had he been so afraid. The strength of his father's grip, combined with the malice in his voice, had shaken him to the core.

"My lord," continued the man. "It is possible that someone else was attempting to forge these coins. Since when did elves have any need for human money?"

His father held his gaze for several more seconds before finally removing the blade and shoving him onto his back. "That still does not explain the wrong images. Perhaps the elves were using them for bribes."

"It is possible, my lord. But they know as well as we who rules these kingdoms. If it is a deception, it's a very poor one."

Jayden spotted his pack and sword leaning against a support post. "I was fleeing the battle when I just happened upon the pouch. I swear that's the truth."

His father sniffed contemptuously. "A coward, then. In that case, I'm sure your people will not mourn your death." He looked at the men standing behind Jayden. "Take him back to the others. I want to see them all hanging from the trees come morning."

Jayden was hauled to his feet.

"Wait," he cried. "Please wait."

His father paused. "The coward begs. So what do you have to say, coward?"

Tears fell. "Don't you know me? You must. You have to remember something."

His father's scornful laugh said plainly that he had no idea what Jayden was talking about. "A coward... and an insane one at that. The world will be well rid of the likes of you. But don't worry—soon the rest of your wretched race will be joining you. Though I doubt they'll welcome your company in the afterlife."

He gave a dismissive wave, signifying to the guards that they should take the prisoner away.

The reality of what was happening to him was threatening to break Jayden's mind. The truth, no matter how unavoidable it appeared, still seemed utterly impossible.

Once back among the other prisoners, he was tied up again and thrown to the ground.

"What did the Bull want with you?" asked the elf who had spoken to him previously.

"The Bull?"

"What is wrong with you? Lord Zarin. The Bull of the West."

"How long has the war been going on?" he asked, praying to the Creator that he would not hear the answer he knew would come.

"You really *are* a simple one, aren't you?"

"Please," Jayden begged. "Tell me."

"Four years," he replied. "But from the way our fortunes have turned, I fear it will not go on much longer."

This was all the confirmation Jayden needed. Somehow, the vortex had done more than transport him from the desert. It had taken him—and his father before him—back to the time of the first Great War. This explained why Darshan seemed to have vanished. But it did not explain why he remembered nothing of his past; not even his own son.

His father had called him insane. Perhaps he was. Maybe the vortex had done something to his mind. To both their minds.

"Take heart," said the elf. "All is not lost. The Creator will welcome us home soon."

That the elf was so accepting of death stirred unexpected anger. Jayden had not come this far to give up now. If it turned out he had gone mad, or that this was an illusion, then so be it. Either way, he had no intention of dying. His mother's life depended on him staying alive. Somehow, he would have to make his father remember who he really was. Unfortunately, a plan for how to achieve this was not readily forthcoming. Determination alone—no matter how much he possessed—would not cut his bonds nor get him past the hundreds of armed men. And assuming his father's orders would be followed, he did not have long to think of a way out.

His bonds had been tied well. He might possibly have been able to free himself, but it would take hours, and time was something he did not have. Just beyond where the guards were standing, he could see another soldier, keeping himself intentionally in view of the prisoners, already preparing the nooses.

As the minutes passed, it became depressingly clear that there was nothing he could do. He'd attempted to use the *flow*, but had succeeded in drawing in only a small portion, not nearly enough to give him the strength needed to break free.

The elf beside him decided to speak again. "You never told me what you're doing so far away from your home," he said.

"I don't know," Jayden lied. "I have no memory of anything before a few days ago." It seemed as good a story as any. "I just remember waking up in the forest."

"Were you ill?"

"I don't know. Maybe."

"I have heard of a brain fever robbing an elf of his senses. But to lose your memory completely... still, I suppose it *is* possible."

Jayden could see that he didn't believe his story. Not that it made a great deal of difference. If they did somehow manage to escape, he would deal with the matter then.

It was less than an hour later when a detachment of soldiers began hefting them all to their feet. The soldiers then cut their ankles free and forced them into a ragged line. There was something about the way the elves appeared accepting of their fate, almost to the point of being docile, that Jayden found infuriating. How could they simply march off to their death so calmly? Even if they all simply fled in a rush, a few might manage to escape.

The men carrying the ropes led them far into the forest. Soon, the camp itself was completely out of sight. Why they were going so far was perplexing; they had already passed several rows of trees that would have easily accommodated the number of condemned. Whatever the reason, Jayden's hope was renewed. This would be the perfect opportunity for a mass escape. It would take time for the camp to react and send more men. Sure, some of the elves would be killed, but not all of them. Unfortunately, there was no way to convey his thoughts to the others without arousing suspicion.

A soldier commanded them to halt beside a line of young oaks.

Jayden knew he had to take a risk, or this would be the end. He shifted as close as he dared to the elf with whom he had spoken earlier and whispered, "We should all make a run for it. Now, before it's too late."

"Have faith," the elf replied calmly.

A surge of anger filled him. Have faith? In what? Did he think that the Creator *Herself* was about to descend from heaven and save them? His mother often told him that everything was by *Her* design. An easy thing to say when you were not faced with the hangman's noose. Then again, he knew that she had faced death more times than he ever had, or likely would from the look of things.

Ropes were thrown over the various limbs, and the elves were herded beside the trees in smaller groups. The elf he'd spoken with earlier was standing to his left, an almost imperceptible smile on his lips. Had Jayden's hands been free, he might well have throttled him. He decided there and then, even though it looked like he would have to do it alone, that he would still make a break for it before they put the rope around his neck. His chances of survival would be minimal, but even a tiny chance was better than no chance at all. His eyes searched for a likely path to take.

"Are you scum ready to see that Creator you love so much?" called one of the soldiers.

His taunt drew harsh laughter from the others.

"They can't fight," remarked another. "Let's see if they're any better at dying."

"I hear they piss themselves with fear," said yet another. "I'll bet they even—"

He never finished the sentence. The whistle of the arrow came a moment before it sank into his heart. A perfect shot.

Suddenly, the air was full of deadly missiles as soldier after soldier was struck down.

"Now we run," said the elf.

So strong was Jayden's surprise at this sudden turn that he was at first too stunned to react. But instinct quickly kicked in, and he raced to follow the now fleeing elves into the darkness of the forest. Twice a pursuing soldier came within a few feet of catching him, but each time a well-aimed arrow struck to clear his way. The problem was, with his hands still bound behind his back, he found he wasn't able to run as fast as he normally could. Adding to this problem, the humans behind him were already raising the alarm. In short order, the camp would be aware of the elf attack and come rushing to their comrades' aid. He needed to cut his bonds before then or be in serious jeopardy of recapture.

Keeping the elf ahead of him in sight, he zig-zagged with the rest between the gradually thickening trees and brambles until coming upon a dozen bowmen, all of them still firing rapidly at their pursuers. An elf nearby with a long dagger was cutting the ropes of his kin as they quickly halted and then vanished into the night.

A wave of relief rushed through Jayden once his turn came and his hands were freed. But by then the humans had recovered sufficiently to counter with more than a few arrows of their own, one of which thudded into the leg of the elf who had been in front of him, sending him to his knees. Jayden wrapped an arm around his waist and lifted him back to his feet.

"Leave me," the elf told him. "If you don't, they'll catch you."

Ignoring his protests, Jayden pulled him along as fast as he could manage. He'd expected that other elves, seeing them struggling, would stop to help. But none did. They simply raced past them as if they were invisible.

It soon became obvious that the injured elf was right. They would undoubtedly be caught if they didn't pick up the pace. Even so, Jayden knew he could not leave him behind. And he was sickened that the other elves were willing to do just that. Linis, his mother, or any other elf he had known would never have acted so cravenly. Not that there was time to dwell on this right now.

Glancing over his shoulder, he saw torches flickering in the near distance. The camp was roused and was giving chase. The sound of orders, curses, and swords being drawn penetrated the forest.

"Leave me," the elf repeated. "Our lives are too valuable to waste."

"I agree," said Jayden. "So we have to move faster."

By now, the rest of the elves were completely out of sight. The situation was looking dire. Jayden then spotted a tall birch tree a few yards ahead, and an idea formed. Without warning, he ceased walking and grabbed the shaft of the arrow, removing it quickly from the elf's leg with a sharp tug.

His companion yelped and dropped to one knee. "What the—"

"Can you climb?" Jayden asked him, pointing to the tree.

He seemed to grasp at once what Jayden was thinking and looked up, his face racked with pain. "I can try."

With Jayden pushing from behind, they gradually made their way up. Blood dripped from the elf's wound throughout, most of it landing directly onto Jayden's face and arms.

Only after what felt like an eternity had they climbed high enough to reach the thicker branches that Jayden was sure would not break under their weight. Once there, he stripped off his shirt and bound his companion's leg. The very last thing he needed was for dripping blood to fall on anyone below who was searching for them.

Within the thick of the leaves, he was certain they wouldn't be spotted. And seeing as how their pursuers were without dogs, he was counting on them walking straight by. Linis had taught him this ruse as a boy when they would play hide and seek in the forest during their frequent hunting trips.

"No one ever looks up," Linis had told him. *"Not so long as you're quiet."*

Only minutes after they'd settled into position, the pursuing soldiers were upon them. Jayden held his breath as two of them walked by only a few feet away from the tree. A combination of the cool night air and the fact that he was now bare-chested spread goose pimples over his body.

The humans made it a few more yards before a horn blast halted them. A moment later, shouts from the direction of the camp could be heard calling them back.

"What now?" said one of the men.

"It could be a trap," suggested the other. "The Bull is smart. He's not going to let them lead us away. Come on. We're not going to catch them, anyway."

Jayden barely managed to contain a sigh of relief. He waited until the torches had completely vanished before speaking a word. The elf was looking none too well, most likely due to the loss of blood.

"Can you still walk?" Jayden asked.

He nodded. "I can manage."

Once back on the ground, they set off in the direction the other elves had taken earlier.

"What's your name?" Jayden asked.

"I am Theopolou," he answered. "And since it seems we have managed to evade capture, you can now tell me who you really are and why you lied to me." There was no threat insinuated in his tone. "I felt the *flow* running through you. Only a seeker can hold so much, yet I know every seeker in the Hastriatis clan, and you are not among them."

Jayden was uncertain how to reply. The truth of what had happened to him was still impossible to accept. For all he knew, he had gone insane.

"I can't tell you," he said. "Just be assured I am not an enemy. That will have to do."

"You are not the first elf to run from the war," Theopolou responded. "Even I have considered it from time to time."

"I'm not running. I just can't tell you the truth. I have my reasons."

"We all have our reasons. But if you intend on joining us, you would do well to think of a way to explain yourself. You use the *flow*, yet you did not sense our kin arriving to save us from execution. That on its own is concerning."

"I can't feel our kind like other elves do. I don't know why."

He hoped this lie was somehow convincing. The last thing he needed was for the elves of this era to discover his true nature. He was already facing the dilemma of his father. That alone was making his situation appear hopeless.

Theopolou scrutinized him for a moment. "Perhaps you were ill as a child. Though I know of no illness that would affect you in this way."

Jayden thought it best to change the subject. "Tell me about the one they call the Bull."

His question attracted a curious look. "You know nothing of the Bull of the West? You are indeed a mystery. Still, as we have time before we reach my kin, I will enlighten you."

He drew a deep breath before continuing. "The Bull arrived two years ago. No one amongst us knows where he's from or how he rose to his position. What we do know is that, until he took command of the human forces, we had the war all but won. Despite this, somehow or other, he managed to galvanize the squabbling human rulers and shape their armies into a vast and all but unstoppable force. It is widely believed that he will one day become a king himself. His men are completely loyal, and though we know little of him, most think him to be a half-man. His strength is well beyond that of any human or elf. It is said that to face the Bull in single combat is to stare into the eyes of death itself."

Jayden's mind reeled. It was almost unbelievable to think that his father, one of the kindest and most gentle men he had ever known, was feared and despised by the elves. Of all the tales he had heard about the first Great War, never he had come across anyone called the Bull of the West. Surely such a fearsome warrior would have been well remembered and much spoken of?

A few minutes later, Theopolou staggered, and had to steady himself against a nearby tree.

"You should rest for a moment," Jayden told him.

The elf looked as if he might protest, but a wave of dizziness forced him to kneel. Jayden examined the wound. Though the bleeding had lessened, continual pressure from walking was not allowing it to stop completely. Theopolou needed proper treatment, or he might well bleed to death long before they reached his people.

Jayden weighed his options. "How far away are the others?" he asked.

"We should arrive at their camp by morning."

That was much too long; Theopolou would certainly be too weak to travel well before then. Though not hopeful for success, there was one thing he could try.

"This might feel a bit strange," he said.

Placing his hands over the wound, he shut his eyes. For more than a minute he concentrated, taking long, even breaths while reaching out for the *flow*. Like in the enemy camp, at first only a small amount of it responded. He tried to recall the sensation he'd felt when Sayia had healed him. The *flow* itself had felt different then though in what way exactly was impossible to understand. He tried imagining Theopolou's wound healing itself, but nothing happened. Bit by bit, more of the *flow* seeped into him. He then tried to redirect this into the elf's body, still meeting with no success. He was on the brink of giving up when the words of his mother entered his mind.

"Healing is a way of giving," she had said. *"A good healer is selfless by nature."*

His mother had been talking about the elf healer who had taken up residence in Sharpstone several years prior. The woman would rarely accept payment beyond what was enough to feed and house herself. Some thought her daft. Kaylia, however, brushed aside such talk as ignorance.

With this new insight driving him, Jayden renewed his attempts, on this occasion imagining giving an actual part of himself to Theopolou through the power of the *flow*. This was successful beyond his greatest hope. In an instant, he could feel the healing power entering the elf's leg, wrapping itself around the wounded flesh to do its work. Theopolou gasped. Jayden could practically see the elf's tendons and muscles knitting together and the skin growing anew. It was wondrous. It wasn't until he felt a hand shake him that he opened his eyes again.

"That's enough," Theopolou told him, already looking much healthier and in no small way surprised. "You mustn't drain yourself too much."

Jayden lifted his hands, breaking the contact. A sudden fatigue rushed over him as he dropped back onto his elbows.

Theopolou leaned forward to place a hand on his shoulder. "Are you all right?"

He forced a smile. His head was starting to ache and his body felt as if he had spent a hard day in the field behind the plow. "I'm fine. It's the first time I've tried to do that. I guess I might have overdone it a little."

Theopolou cocked his head. "That was your first time? Amazing. It takes most healers many years to mend such serious wounds. You truly have a gift."

"It was luck," he said. "I remembered something my mother told me. Otherwise, I don't think I could have done it."

"I don't know who your mother is," Theopolou replied, now smiling broadly, "but she must be one of the wisest elves breathing free air if her words enabled you to do this."

Pushing himself to his feet, Jayden shivered slightly. The cold air was biting even more viciously than before. "We should get moving," he said.

"Agreed."

They set off together, Jayden on rather unsteady legs at first.

"I owe you my life," Theopolou said. "Once we arrive, I will stand by you when you are questioned."

"Thank you."

Being questioned did not sound like a good prospect. He would likely need a much better explanation than the simple claim of a loss of memory.

Death at the hands of his own father, or death at the hands of the elves? It did not seem like much of a choice.

The essence of his father had expressed belief in his abilities, though at this moment, Jayden did not share his confidence. This was a situation far beyond his understanding. Nonetheless, he was duty bound to battle on. His mother's life depended on it. As for his father, the thought of him remaining the brutal warlord who was more than happy to kill any elf who happened to cross his path was more than he could bear. He had to make him remember who he really was.

He would find a way to save both of his parents, whatever the cost.

CHAPTER 16

Linis had been deliberating for weeks on how to tell Penelope and Maybell what he had discovered about their brother. He looked again at the drawing of a young man, bent down on one knee and leaning heavily on his sword. The face was unmistakable. And even if it were a lookalike or a coincidence of some kind, the titled scrawled in gold lettering near to the bottom of the page was more than enough to banish any doubts. "Jayden Prays."

The first drawing was of Jayden battling another man, who by all accounts resembled Gewey. But the idea was just too far-fetched. Gewey would never fight his own son. Not for any reason.

"Are you ever going to tell us what's so important inside that damn thing?"

Linis looked up from his place by the fire to where Maybell was sitting nearby. He closed the book and shoved it under his bedroll. "Not yet. I've already told you that I promised not to reveal anything until your mother is safe."

"We'll be in Sharpstone tomorrow," she pointed out.

"And we have no idea of her condition until we arrive."

That said, he had been mightily relieved that both of the girls could still feel the bond with their mother. If nothing else, it at least meant that Kaylia still lived.

"Why are we taking her to Felsafell's old house?" Maybell asked.

"Because only a few people know how to find it. I've told you this a dozen times already."

"So we're just going to carry her there the entire way?"

"If we must."

The house of Felsafell, last of the First Born, was the safest place he could think of. Throughout the ages, countless elves had tried to locate the secluded cabin and failed. It was only if the old hermit wanted you to find him that you were able to do so. Of course, as Linis had learned from Gewey, Felsafell was now mortal and traveling the world with his true love, Basanti, the Oracle of Manisalia. Penelope had pointed out that, seeing as how the First Born no longer actually lived there, it might not be as safe as it once was. And Linis conceded that she might be right. But short of heading north into the mountains, a journey which would take them much longer and be far more difficult, he could think of nowhere better.

The next morning, they set off at a determined pace. The mounts they'd acquired two days prior after leaving the river were of good quality, and by midday, Linis thought they might reach their destination sooner than expected.

Though uneventful, he had remained ever vigilant throughout their journey. The closer they came to Sharpstone, the more anxious he became to arrive. Dina would be worried and likely making everyone around her suffer for it with her dark mood. All the same, he had to admit, it gave him no small measure of satisfaction to know how much she cared. It was the one thing about his new life to which he had never quite grown accustomed. When a seeker, he'd always had kinship with his brothers and sisters. But no one ever gave a thought as to his safety when he was out alone in the wild. After all, he was a *seeker*. He could take care of himself. As it was with Dina, he had seen the same concerned look in Kaylia's eyes whenever Gewey was away. And *he* was a god. Yet, as it turned out, her worry was justified. Even gods face peril sometimes, it seemed.

When they were about five miles away from Sharpstone, Linis sensed a presence—Vrykol. The girls sensed it as well.

"There are three of them," said Penelope. "They're waiting for us about a mile ahead."

Linis could see the fury and hatred in their expressions, and he felt a massive surge of the *flow* entering both.

He drew his blade. "Three, we can handle," he said with as much confidence as he could muster.

"You don't need to handle a thing," Maybell told him. "We'll take care of this."

Linis nodded. He doubted very much that three Vrykol would be capable of stifling their combined power. The only time he had ever felt the *flow* stronger in anyone was in their father. It looked like the hunters were about to become the hunted. Had the situation not been so dire, he might have been amused.

Just as Penelope had stated, a mile farther ahead, he saw three cloaked figures standing in the road, though none of them had weapons drawn. The Vrykol in the middle stepped forward and held up his hand.

"Peace, daughters of Darshan," he said. "We have not come to fight."

"You are right about that," Maybell responded, malice dripping from her every word. "You have come to die."

The Vrykol pushed back his hood, revealing the features of a young, dark-haired human. "We are not your enemy. We serve Ayliazarah, and have been sent to both warn and aid you. Be aware that a dozen of our kind who serve Saraf await you ahead."

Maybell exchanged pensive glances with the other two.

"We cannot trust him," said Linis.

"Your trust is not required," said the Vrykol. "Should you wish it, we will leave. Our mistress has instructed that we do as you command. But know that I am telling you the truth. There are enough of my kind to prevent you from using your powers. And more than enough to kill you all... including your mother."

"If that is so, why have they not killed her already?" Penelope shot back.

"To lure you in," he answered. "They are aware of the connection you share. You would know at once should something befall her, and they did not want you alerted to their presence in Sharpstone until you arrive. Fortunately, Saraf is not the only god capable of creating my kind. As he has sent Vrykol to hinder you, so my mistress has sent us to help."

Linis shook his head. "I still don't see how we can trust them."

After a long silence, Maybell said, "But if they *are* telling the truth and a dozen of those creatures are waiting, that's too many. All this will have been for nothing."

"Not necessarily," the Vrykol told her. "As I said before, we came to aid you, not fight." He opened his cloak and spread his arms wide. His companions did the same. "As you can see, we come to you are unarmed."

"So it seems," agreed Penelope. "But tell me exactly how you intend to be of aid us."

Linis could not believe what he was hearing. "You can't be serious. Why are you even listening to them?"

"I see no other choice," said Maybell, a look of reluctant resignation in her eyes. "If they are willing to help us, we need them."

"And if it's a trap?"

"They needn't have made themselves known to us," she pointed out. "They could have just waited for us to arrive. Why warn us ahead of time?"

The Vrykol spoke again. "Your enemies have withdrawn and are waiting in the forest beyond your farm. Only one of them will remain within the range of your senses. They think you would not be afraid of a single foe. But the moment you step inside your house, he will call on the others. My kind are swift, and carrying an unconscious elf will make your passage much slower. They will surround you long before you can bring your mother to safety."

"So what do you propose?" asked Linis, with undisguised antipathy.

"I suggest that you allow us to retrieve the elf woman for you," he replied flatly. "They will not recognize us as an enemy until we are well away. They are unaware Ayliazarah has created us, so will think we have been sent by Saraf. You can wait for us at the docks along the Goodbranch. If your enemies give chase, we will hold them off long enough for you to escape."

"I don't like this," Linis muttered. "I don't like it at all."

"Neither do I," said Penelope. "But he's right. If they sense us coming, they could have us surrounded long before we could get away. His plan has a far better chance of working. I will scuttle all but one craft at Sharpstone's dock. That should give us the time we need."

Maybell's brow was knitted and her eyes downcast. "My sister is right, Linis. I can see no better alternative."

He pondered for a moment, then looked directly at the Vrykol. "Tell me, beast. How would they perceive *me*?"

"As an elf, nothing more. But the sisters' power is unique. They would know them instantly for who they are."

"Then I will go with you," he said. Before either Maybell or Penelope could object, he added, "They want *you*. Not me.

I have fought their kind many times. Besides, Dina is likely at the house too. I must be sure that she is safe."

The sisters exchanged glances, then nodded their agreement.

"When shall we leave?" Linis asked the Vrykol.

"The daughters of Darshan should leave now," he replied. "We will wait until nightfall."

Linis steeled his wits. *This is madness.* However, regardless of that, Maybell was correct when she said they had little choice in the matter. And if Dina was watching over Kaylia—which she almost certainly was—he must get them both out of from there.

He considered the situation for a moment. It did make sense. If Saraf could create Vrykol to oppose them, then it was reasonable to think that the gods still loyal to Darshan might create others to help. All the same, he could not bring himself to trust them. The memory of what these creatures had done during the war was still fresh in his mind. Pure evil; that was what they were. To think that there might also be good Vrykol was more than he could wrap his head around. He knew Basanti was one; or at least, she had once been. But she was different, at least in his mind. None of this settled his fears and misgivings.

"Try not to attract too much attention to yourselves," he told the sisters, dismounting and handing them the reins of his horse.

Maybell smiled. "It's been years since we were in Sharpstone. I doubt anyone will recognize us. I do wish we could see the farm, though. I miss my old bed. I was really looking forward to a good night's sleep."

"Me too," sighed Penelope. "I suppose it will have to wait until this is over."

"If we are not there at the docks to meet up with you by daybreak, head west to Althetas," Linis instructed.

Both Maybell and Penelope laughed as if to say they had no intention whatsoever of abandoning him ... or their mother. Even to suggest it was an absurdity. They were still smiling as they set off once again along the main road that led into the heart of Sharpstone.

Linis watched them ride away for a few moments, then joined the Vrykol.

Leaving the road, the four of them walked quickly on. After pausing at a nearby shrub to recover the weapons his new companions had hidden, they wound through the forest for about two hours, eventually halting a few miles south of the road leading to the Stedding farm. The Vrykol did not speak a word throughout. Linis kept well behind them, his hand never drifting far from his blade.

While they waited for the sun to go down, he found it somehow odd that the creatures sat and appeared to rest. Did Vrykol *need* to rest? Surely not. They even began making light conversation with one another. In fact, had Linis not been able to feel the vile power coursing through them, he would have taken them for nothing more than simple travelers.

"Tell me," he said while leaning against a tree a few yards away. "Was it painful when the gods created you?"

"Yes," replied the Vrykol who had been their spokesman on the road. He appeared to be their leader. "*Very* painful. But it was our pleasure to serve."

His remark took Linis aback. "You mean you actually volunteered to become ... this?"

"Of course we did. What have I become that would make you speak of me so? I am an instrument of the goddess Ayliazarah. To serve fills me with great pride."

"To become a monster fills you with pride?"

"Perhaps I am a monster. I certainly am when compared to those who came before me, when humans were but servants and the elves their masters. Their mission was to guide and shepherd the world. Mine is to fight for it. I have not yet spilled blood, though I will undoubtedly do so soon. If I have one regret, it is that."

Linis was well aware of the history. Much of the *Book of Souls* had been translated, in no small part thanks to Gewey. It spoke of the gods' efforts to influence the world through their creations, which the elves named Vrykol and hunted them to near extinction. This differed from the elf legends, which described them as ruthless assassins. Only two had survived throughout the ages: Basanti, of course, and her brother, Yanti. And while she had remained pure, her brother was tainted by violence. It had changed him, making him vulnerable to the Reborn King's influence. For Linis, however, it was impossible to forget the foul and vicious beasts he had fought against in the war.

"Do you have names?" he asked.

The creature smiled a very human smile. "Of course we do. I am Berma. My friends are Tylar and Chase."

Even hearing him refer to those of his own kind as friends felt strange. "I must admit that you are not as I expected."

"I am sure. Becoming a Vrykol, as you put it, was not as I expected either."

"How do you mean?"

"Before we were changed, we were but simple monks. When the goddess came to tell us what had happened and why she needed our help, I admit I was more than a little excited by the prospect."

"Excited?"

Berma chuckled. "Yes, why not? At the time, I imagined myself becoming ... well... godlike, I suppose. Immortal."

"Well, aren't you? Immortal, I mean."

"No. We are not like those you have encountered before. Though I am far stronger and faster than I was as a human, and my life span is now more akin to that of the elves. I will continue to age, and in the fullness of time I will die, just as any other mortal. The Vrykol were hated as much for their immortality as anything else. It provokes too much jealousy to be allowed."

"It sounds to me as if you were given a gift."

Berma shrugged. "In a way, yes, though it is not without cost. I no longer feel human. I lack fear or desire."

Linis raised an eyebrow. "And you see that as a bad thing?"

"Yes indeed. Fear and desire are part of what makes life worth living. As destructive as they can be, they are also wondrous. The fear of something new, like the rush you feel when you ride a horse at full gallop for the first time. Then there is the desire for a woman; to feel the softness of her flesh pressed to yours. These, along with countless other delights, are what I am no longer able to experience."

"So you are without any emotion at all?"

"No, not entirely. But they are dulled. They lack the fire that they once possessed."

The tragedy of this was clear. Linis could not envision life without passion—the nuanced shades of simple pleasures.

"Do not pity us," Berma added. "We have been given a higher purpose, and one day we will be granted heaven as our reward. Unlike those created by Saraf, our spirits have not been totally and irreversibly changed. Enough of who we were remains within us to bind our spirits together once our bodies cease to function."

Linis still wasn't entirely sure that he trusted the creature. There was no lie in his eyes; but then again, how could one tell when a Vrykol was lying? One thing was certainly true—knowing that they were not immortal was somehow reassuring.

There were many other questions he would have liked to ask. Did they need to eat or sleep? Could they do so, even if it wasn't needed? What would they do once their task was completed? It would certainly be difficult for them to find a place in the world that would be willing to accept them.

On all of these matters, he held his tongue. It was best not to risk becoming over-familiar. Should they prove to be false, he would not be taken off-guard.

As soon as it was fully dark, the three Vrykol rose in unison and started off at a startling pace. Linis was fascinated by their speed through the forest. He knew they possessed keen eyesight, but seeing well in the dark was not enough on its own. One had to understand the make-up of the wild in order to choose the best path. This was a skill that normally took years to learn. He wondered wryly if they had perhaps been monks with a monastery set deep in the woods before being changed.

Just as he was able to see the lights from the farmhouse peeking through the trees, he felt the presence of the lone Vrykol there at the edge of his abilities. The three with him surely sensed it as well, but did not slow their pace.

Though Linis did not share the same sort of bond with Dina that he would with a full-blooded elf, he could nevertheless feel that she was inside the house. This filled him with both anxiety and relief.

"We will ready your mount while you fetch the elf woman," Berma said.

"I'll need two horses," Linis told him.

The enemy Vrykol had not yet moved. This brought a frown to Linis's face. If he could sense the creature, surely it could sense them as well?

As they drew close, he heard the laughter and chatter of the evening meal.

"Wait for me by the porch," he instructed the other three. "I don't want you frightening people." They did not look inhuman... at least, not to human eyes. Even so, a trio of strangers bursting in uninvited would be sure to cause a bit of a panic at minimum.

"Be swift," replied Berma, before heading toward the barn with his companions.

In spite of his urgency, the scent of fresh bread and roasted pork was making Linis's mouth water. Forcing this aside, he ran to the dining room. Dina was there with several of the farm hands, eating and talking. Her eyes lit up the moment he entered and she leaped up from her seat, toppling the chair over in her urgency to greet him.

"Thank the Creator!" she cried, throwing her arms around his neck. Before Linis could speak, she crushed her lips to his.

He let the kiss linger, then wrapped his arms around her, losing himself for a brief moment in the warmth of her body. It was only with great effort that he released his hold and took a small step back. "I need to speak with you privately," he told her.

The other guests were all shouting out greetings, but Linis only waved briefly to them in return while hustling Dina from the room. Her expression, by now, was one of deep confusion.

"A dozen Vrykol are in position nearby," he whispered. "I am here to take you and Kaylia to safety. We cannot tarry."

Confusion was instantly replaced by fear. "Where is Jayden?"

The waiting Vrykol had now moved beyond his senses, a jolting reminder that time was running out. "I'll explain about him later. For now, we must hurry. They are coming."

Dina stiffened. "Kaylia is in her room. I'll go get the horses ready."

"It's already being taken care of."

Without another word, and with Dina right on his heels, he ran upstairs to Kaylia's room. She was looking much the same as ever: a testament to the quality of care Dina and the elf healer had been giving her.

"Gather her some clothes," Dina said. "I'll get her dressed.

Linis obeyed without hesitation, quickly rummaging through the dresser and grabbing a few pairs of trousers and some shirts. By the time he was done, Dina already had a loose-fitting pair of pants on Kaylia. For now, her nightgown could serve in place of a shirt.

Lifting Kaylia into his arms, Linis hurried downstairs. The others were gathered, confusion on all of their faces.

"Where are you taking Lady Stedding?" asked one of the older hands.

Linis did not waste time trying to explain. "You should go home," he ordered, not even pausing on his way to the door. "Bad people are coming. It is not safe for you here."

The Vrykol were waiting outside with two saddled horses. Dina froze at the sight of them, clearly recognizing that there was something not quite right about the newcomers.

"You know these ... men?" she asked, a wary look in her eyes.

"They are here to help," he assured her. "You have to trust me."

Thus far, he could not sense any enemy approaching, though that could change in an instant. From where their scout had been positioned, given their enormous speed, they had the ability to be on them in seconds.

Most of the house guests had followed them outside. "You can't just make off with her," protested the hand who had spoken earlier. "Not without telling us what's going on."

"I've already told you," Linis snapped back at him. "Evil men are coming. Men who will kill you without a thought. So unless you want to grab a sword and fight them, go home. Now!"

The fierce look in his eyes and the steel in his voice were enough to jerk them into doing his bidding. These men were sturdy and loyal to the Stedding family, but they were not warriors. And even if they had been, the opponents they would face were way beyond the skill of normal men. He was saving their lives.

After placing Kaylia in the saddle, he climbed up behind her. Dina mounted the second horse.

"Do not stop for anything," said Berma.

Linis nodded, then spurred his horse forward. That they were away before their enemies had mounted an attack was both a relief and somewhat troubling. What were the beasts waiting for?

Glancing across at Dina, he saw that she was looking understandably nervous. It had been years since she had faced this sort of danger; he'd hoped she would never have to face it again. As for himself, he could not deny feeling a slight sense of exhilaration. Had the lives of those he loved not been at stake, he might have actually enjoyed it.

He pushed his mount as fast as he could while still maintaining a firm hold on Kaylia. The few people they passed along the way regarded them with a fair degree of alarm. The sight of an unconscious Lady Stedding astride a galloping horse, not to mention the sight of three people running behind them who were easily able to keep up with their mounts, was sufficient to leave most onlookers openmouthed in astonishment. Village folk did not take well to out-of-the-ordinary happenings, and this would be very difficult to explain. A problem not of particular concern to him at the moment.

It was just as the outskirts of town became visible that Linis realized why the Vrykol had not yet attacked. Their foes had decided to wait for them in the main square, completely blocking their way through to the docks. This meant driving straight through them.

Berma and the other two moved ahead, swords drawn. Linis mentally prepared himself to join them in the fray. At this time of night, there would be only a handful of townsfolk about, mostly stragglers from the tavern, so at least the fight would not likely endanger innocent bystanders.

He quickly reined in his mount. "You take Kaylia," he called over to Dina.

Berma heard him and halted as well. "No," he said, turning to look back. "You cannot fight. You must lead them to safety. We will see you through."

"There are too many of them," Linis protested.

"Our goal is not victory. We can hold them long enough to see you safely away."

Linis wanted to argue. The thought of allowing anyone—even these creatures—to sacrifice their lives for him felt wrong.

Sensing his thoughts, Berma smiled and added, "How else are we to prove that we are not monsters? This is what we were sent here to do."

It was hard for Linis to deny the logic of the Vrykol's argument, or the fact that Kaylia and Dina needed him to stay alive. "Thank you," he said. "I was wrong about you."

Berma nodded, then turned to his comrades. "May Ayliazarah guide our blades."

The three of them burst into a dead run, their unnatural speed quickly carrying them far ahead. Linis and Dina urged their mounts on in their wake.

The street lamps along the main avenue were lit, though most of the windows were dark. As he had hoped, the streets were empty.

Twelve Vrykol were strung out across the main square, waiting for them. They arrived just in time to see Berma, Tylar, and Chase charge into the center of the enemy, the ferocity of their attack rapidly opening a significant gap in the line. Linis had witnessed Lee Starfinder in combat. The half-man had studied under the finest sword masters in the world, and his divine blood had given him strength and speed beyond normal men. Until this moment, Linis had thought he would never see anything to compare. That belief was now shattered.

Berma moved left, lashing out with a flurry of deadly strikes that took the heads of two foes in the very first few moments of battle. Tylar and Chase split to the right, both swinging their blades in narrow arcs, not slaying any of their opponents, but forcing the gap ever wider. This was the moment. Linis spurred his mount toward the opening, Dina keeping close behind him.

As they rode into the breach, two Vrykol broke away from the right and ran toward them. Seeing the danger, Berma raced over. Still at a full run, he thrust his shoulder into the midsection of the leading enemy, sending him crashing backward into the second one close behind. For a few seconds, the way ahead was clear.

Though he had managed to prevent the assault on Linis and Dina, Berma had left himself dangerously exposed. Glancing briefly behind, Linis saw two blades being plunged into Berma's back. He felt an almost overwhelming urge to help him, even though he knew that he couldn't. With Dina now alongside him, he drove his mount on without looking back again.

The ringing of steel on steel followed them, its intensity easily heard over the clatter of hoofbeats. Even upon reaching the market where the main docks were located, he could still hear the fray continuing.

Maybell and Penelope were waiting for them, both wringing their hands in agitation.

"Is the boat ready?" Linis called, pulling up his horse a few yards away.

Maybell pointed to the lone craft tied to the end of the main dock.

Dina hurried over to help Linis as he slid from the saddle and pulled Kaylia into his arms. The sisters ran toward them. He was about to shout for them to stay where they were when he saw Penelope's hand shoot forward. A thin stream of fire leaped from her fingertips, passing mere inches from his head.

One of the enemy Vrykol had managed to break away from the battle and was rushing in from the edge of the market. The fire slammed into its chest, instantly engulfing its entire body. Even so, it still managed to stagger on for a few more steps before finally collapsing.

All at once, the swords fell silent, which could only mean that Berma, Tylar, and Chase had been slain. Linis ran to the boat, carefully laying Kaylia at the bow.

Two more Vrykol appeared, one badly wounded, his left arm dangling precariously from a thin strip of flesh. Maybell and Penelope dealt with the threat by creating a wall of fire that first barred the creatures' way, then encircled them completely.

"There is no time," shouted Linis.

But the sisters were not finished. They closed the ring until the Vrykol, in a desperate gambit, tried to make it through before they were totally roasted. They failed, and their charred corpses fell forward with swords still in hand.

Once everyone was in the boat, Linis untied the rope and shoved hard. It took only a few minutes for him to row across, all the time keeping his eyes sharply on the departing shore. No more Vrykol appeared. Dina helped to steer the craft, while Penelope and Maybell stayed beside their mother, holding her hand. The sisters had elected to release the few boats tied at the dock and set them adrift rather than sink them. The owners might be inconvenienced and angry, but at least this way, they could recover their vessels downstream.

The small jetty on the far bank was empty aside from a single ferry that was at present unmanned. Linis gathered some wood and used the boat's mooring rope to start constructing a makeshift stretcher to carry Kaylia. It would be grueling transporting her to begin with, but he hoped they would be able to procure a wagon the following day.

"So the Vrykol were not lying," Maybell remarked to Linis as he worked. "They really were sent by Ayliazarah to help us."

"So it seems," he replied.

"Now that we're away," Dina chipped in, "would someone mind explaining to me exactly what just happened?"

Linis smiled. Dina had acted without hesitation, and with the courage he had expected of her. "Forgive me. I had hoped our reunion would be a bit less..."

"Dangerous?" she completed for him. "Or perhaps *confusing* was the word you were looking for. Insane, even?"

"It's our fault, Aunt Dina," said Maybell. "Those creatures were after us."

"Then you will be the ones to tell me all about it," she said. "That is, right after you give me a proper greeting." She threw her arms around the sisters in turn. "You were little girls when I last saw you. And now ... look at you both."

They talked for a short time, each sister telling a part of their journey. Linis kept mostly quiet while finishing his work. It would take even the Vrykol two days to reach the crossing to the south and then make it back to the road. He hoped by then to have covered enough distance to mask their trail. With luck, the three Vrykol who'd made it to the docks were the last to survive. But he had never been one to rely on luck. And even if they had all been destroyed, there might well be more awaiting them on the road ahead.

With Kaylia safely secured on the stretcher, they continued walking until about three hours before dawn, then found a small clearing a few yards off the road to rest. Maybell gave Dina a spare blanket she had in her belongings while Linis placed Kaylia carefully down near to the fire. The sisters immediately sat on either side of her.

"I've never seen her so helpless," said Maybell, tears threatening to fall.

"She'll be fine," Penelope assured her, though her tone was unconvincing. "As soon as Jayden finds Father, he'll make her well again."

Linis drew a long breath, uncomfortably aware that the time had come when he had to tell them of what he had seen. Retrieving the book, he turned to the page that bore the image of their brother.

"So, are you finally going to show us what you've been hiding?" asked Maybell.

Linis nodded. He handed her the book and lowered his eyes. "This was made during the first Great War."

After only a few seconds, Maybell stiffened. "That's not possible!" she cried.

"Let me see," said Penelope, leaning across.

Maybell showed her the image, pointing to the caption as she did so.

"*This* is the big secret?" Penelope scoffed. "That's nonsense. A coincidence. It has to be."

"I can see no other explanation," Linis sighed. "What else could threaten to break the bond between your mother and father?"

"No, it can't be true," Penelope insisted. "That would mean our brother has traveled to the past. Not even the gods can do that... can they?"

"Did Sayia believe it?" asked Maybell, clearly shaken.

Linis nodded gravely. "She did indeed. Very much so."

Dina crossed over to look at the drawing. "I must admit it looks just like him," she said in a half-whisper. Noticing the second page marker, she turned to the image of Jayden in combat.

"That's the battle of Maiden Pass," Linis told her. "Does Jayden's opponent look familiar to you?"

"It's Gewey," Dina gasped, covering her mouth. She shook her head. "No. He would never fight his own son."

Maybell's tears fell, while Penelope could only look in stunned silence.

"I have studied the Great War extensively," Linis said. "I do not recall ever coming across Jayden's name. Though details about the Battle of Maiden Pass are few and vague."

"What should we do?" Dina asked him, unable to tear her eyes away from the drawing.

"There is nothing we can do," he answered flatly. "This has already happened. We can only influence what happens next."

Maybell's anguish turned to sudden rage. She sprang to her feet, glaring at Linis. "You had no right to keep this from us."

"I gave Sayia my word. She feared that you would chase after them."

"Of course, I would have."

"And left your mother vulnerable?"

She opened her mouth but said nothing, simply standing there with fists clenched, the *flow* racing through her.

"He's right," said Penelope in a soothing tone, even though her own anger was vividly displayed in her expression. "We could not have abandoned Mother."

"But Jayden... he..."

Penelope stood and placed her hands on her sister's arm. "Jayden is strong. Far stronger than even he can know. We *will* see him again. If he did somehow find his way there, he'll find a way home again."

"How do you know that?" demanded Maybell. "What if we never see him again? What if that really is Father in the picture? They might both be lost."

"I think Mother would be dead if that were true. And Father would never hurt Jayden. We have to trust in that."

Her sister's words seemed to go far in calming Maybell. Gradually, she released her hold on the *flow*.

"I am truly sorry for keeping this from you," said Linis. "I felt I had no choice."

Maybell kneeled beside her mother, gently brushing the hair from her cheek and then kissing her brow. When she spoke, her voice was quiet, yet full of intensity.

"I don't care about your promises, Linis. Or your honor. You had no right to keep this from us. And if she dies, it will mean that we are alone." She paused to look him directly in the eye. "You say that what has happened is over and done, as if the past cannot be changed. But you can't know that. You made a decision that you had no right to make. So did Sayia. If it turns out you made the wrong choice, I will never forgive either of you."

Though Linis wanted to respond, he could think of nothing to say that would make things any better. He wandered off a short distance, yet again wondering if he had made the right decision. His reason told him that the past was the past, and that Jayden had always been depicted within the pages of this book. But was that really true? Had his sisters known sooner, could they have helped him? Or would destiny have ensured that something else intervened to prevent them from doing so?

Dina's voice broke into these thoughts. "There is nothing more you can do. Don't punish yourself. You did what you believed to be right at the time. What's important now is that we focus on keeping Kaylia safe."

Her understanding tone and kind eyes went far to quell his doubts and guilt. "I almost forgot to do something," he said, forcing a smile.

"You mean telling me how much you missed me?" She took his hand and led him to their bedroll. "I noticed."

"So long as you know, I mean it." He lay down and pulled her close, basking in the warmth of her body against his.

"Maybell will be all right," she told him in a whisper. "Jayden and Gewey will come home safely, too. You'll see."

Dina had always been able to say exactly what he needed to hear. This time, however, her words sounded hollow. There was a feeling growing inside him. He knew Maybell well enough to understand that she'd been speaking from sorrow and anger. She would come to realize that he had acted with the best of intentions. But Jayden...

It *was* Gewey in the picture, fighting his own son. There was no doubt in his mind about that. And no one could hope to stand against Darshan.

If he had fought Jayden, there could only have been one outcome.

CHAPTER 17

Jayden waited beside a small brook, a guard standing on either side of him. The surrounding forest was thick with undergrowth, and the dense canopy blocked out much of the sunlight. Only a skilled woodsman could approach without being heard. A short distance away, the elf gathering was embroiled in a heated discussion over what should be his fate.

He could recall his mother mentioning the name Theopolou, though only once. He had apparently been her uncle and had died fighting the evil of the Reborn King. Whether this was the same elf, he had no way of knowing, though it seemed unlikely. Then again, just about everything he'd experienced since jumping into the vortex he would have deemed as being somewhere between unlikely and inconceivable. Mostly inconceivable.

Theopolou emerged from the gathering a few minutes later, a bright smile on his face. "You are clearly not telling us everything, Jayden. Nevertheless, as things are, they can find no cause to hinder you. I told them about the courage you showed."

On hearing this, the two guards immediately withdrew without further prompting.

"Thank you," he said.

"What will you do now?"

"I really don't know."

He had to find a way to make his father remember. But to get near him seemed impossible. He'd considered telling the elves the truth, but they would probably think him mad... or a liar. From the best he could tell, they were somewhere south of the Old Santismal Road. Elf lands were far to the west. Not that going there would accomplish anything. He had to face a hard truth: he was without a plan, without resources, and seemingly without any hope of saving his mother.

"You're welcome to join us," Theopolou suggested. "We'll be gathering a few days' march from here for a fresh assault on the Bull's forces. Perhaps someone will recognize you along the way."

"I'm no warrior," he replied.

Theopolou laughed. "You certainly possess the courage of one. But you need not fight. Your skills with healing would be a tremendous asset."

"Are you sure I'm welcome?"

When he'd first arrived at the camp, much suspicion and animosity had been leveled against him. Most believed him to be a deserter, and only Theopolou's objections had kept his head on his shoulders.

"No one will move to harm you," he assured. "I have told them how you healed my wounds. Even those who would not want you among us can see the value of your skills. You have my word."

The camp of roughly two hundred tents was scattered loosely throughout an area of tall grass, a far cry from the orderly rows Jayden had imagined a military camp to be like. Warriors were sitting around small fires, tending their weapons and talking casually. A few cast him disgusted glances, and no one offered a single friendly word. Deserters were not well-loved. Though he had certainly proven his courage, this did not go far to changing attitudes.

Theopolou showed him to a tent and provided him with a fresh set of clothes, plus a few other odds and ends.

"I'll need to get you a weapon," he said, detaching a dagger from his belt and handing it over. "This will have to do until I can find a proper sword."

The elves he had known typically carried long knives. Although Linis owned a sword, Jayden was well aware that he too preferred smaller blades.

"He won't be needing any weapons," a voice said.

Standing in the entrance was a tall young woman with jet-black hair and dark eyes. Her features were angular and almost delicate, though her posture was one of strength and confidence. Clad in a worn set of light tan leathers, she had a bow strapped across her back.

Theopolou turned to face her. "Gia. I thought we agreed that you would stay out of this."

"*You* agreed," she retorted. "*I* did not. The deserter is to come with me."

"I'm not a deserter," Jayden insisted.

"So you say." Her gaze remained fixed on Theopolou. "Do not interfere. Lord Nambis has made his decision. This newcomer's presence will cause unrest, and that is something we most surely do not need before battle. Better that he come with me."

"Your brother would never allow this," Theopolou snapped.

"My brother isn't here." Her tone was hard and even. If her intention was to anger Theopolou, she had clearly succeeded.

"Do not think you can defy his wishes," he told her. "Just because he fights in the east, that does not make you head of your family."

"I am of age. I can do as I please."

"And does Lord Nambis condone this?"

"He insists on it."

Theopolou let out a low growl. "We shall see about that." He stormed from the tent, giving her a furious look as he passed.

Gia turned her attention at once to Jayden. "Can you fight?"

Stunned by the scene, he took a moment to reply. "Yes."

"I have heard that you possess healing talents. This is true?"

"Yes, but I've only just discovered them. I'd never tried to heal anyone before Theopolou."

"And how do you know this? Did you not tell us that you have no memory?"

When Jayden did not answer immediately, she waved a dismissive hand. "It matters not. You are not the first elf to lose heart. Since the Bull of the West appeared, many have fled." Her eyes narrowed as she locked them onto his. "But be warned. Should you do so again, you will not live long enough to stand judgment. That I promise."

Her words were chilling. Anxious to change the subject, Jayden asked, "Where are we going?"

"On a mission to save our people," she told him. "We go to find the Eldest. There's a weapon that only he knows how to find, one that can lay low the armies of the Bull."

"Where do we find him?"

"The Spirit Hills."

Felsafell, Jayden thought. He had heard the stories of the First Born many times. They said he was the oldest living being in the world. According to his father, Felsafell had been granted mortality as a reward for his service during the war with the Reborn King. This had confused Jayden. He had never quite understood why the chance to die would be measured as a reward.

"Why are you taking me if you think I'm lying?" he asked.

"For that, you can thank Theopolou. He has told us how powerful you are with the *flow*. He claims you are even stronger than I. That is why his protests will fall on deaf ears. Only those strong in the *flow* have any hope of finding the Eldest."

Jayden did not want to leave. He needed to stay near his father. But without allies, he could not hope to accomplish anything. Complicating matters even further, the only possible allies he might be able to recruit were the mortal enemy of the very person he had come to find. With each passing moment, it was feeling more and more as if the odds against him were insurmountable.

"I must ask," said Gia. "Why did you save Theopolou?"

Jayden furrowed his brow. "Because he was hurt. If I hadn't stopped to help, he'd be dead."

"We do not risk many lives to save one."

"I only risked my own life," he pointed out. What the hell was wrong with these people? "Do you really leave your wounded behind?"

"It was not always so," she answered, a touch of sorrow seeping into her voice.

Then, as if sensing trickery, her tone quickly became skeptical. "Enough of this. You will not deceive me as you have Theopolou. I do not believe you cannot remember. Though I must admit, there is something different about you."

Despite her sharpness, Jayden was not deterred. Having detected a brief glimpse of her less abrasive side, he pressed the subject. "Can't you at least pretend I'm telling the truth for now? Why do you leave your own kin behind? I want to know."

She regarded him for a long moment, then gave a sigh. "Very well. Our numbers have dwindled, and our forces are now in a constant state of retreat. We cannot afford the luxury of sentimentality. Though every life lost is a tragedy, every elf life saved keeps us that much farther from extinction. The

Bull has vowed to wipe us from the face of the world. And as it stands, he is succeeding."

This was a history Jayden had never heard before. The elves had been defeated; that much was common knowledge. But they had never been on the verge of extinction. And his father—the Bull of the West. Why had his name never come up? Had everything changed? What if, by him coming back, his mother was never born? But then, if that were so, would he himself not simply vanish?

The questions were making his head ache. None of it made any sense. At least, nothing that he could wrap his mind around.

Just then, the tent flap opened and Theopolou returned. Positioning himself directly in front of Gia, he threw up his hands. "You are truly maddening. You imagine you can just stroll into the Spirit Hills and the Eldest will simply hand over the weapon? This has been attempted several times already. Three of our kin never returned."

"Why don't you tell my brother?" she mocked. "Though seeing as how I am leaving right away, I doubt you could reach him in time."

He turned to Jayden. "You should know that Gia is not being truthful. You are not compelled to go with her. You can remain here if you choose."

"No. If I can help, I'll go."

It had occurred to him that perhaps Felsafell would have the answers he needed. If there was anyone who could help him understand what was going on and point him in the right direction, surely it would be the First Born.

"I take it Lord Nambis forbade you to come with us," Gia said.

Theopolou's face turned crimson. "You know full well he did." Removing the sword from his belt, he handed it to Jayden. "Regardless of what Gia says, you might need this."

She merely shrugged. "If you think bringing a sword along when seeking the Eldest is wise, suit yourself."

"Should you not be preparing?" snapped Theopolou.

"I *am* prepared," she told him, still maintaining a level tone. "But I will go if my presence is unwanted." Turning to Jayden, she added, "We leave at sunset. Be ready."

The moment she had exited the tent, Theopolou let out a yell of frustration.

"Don't worry," Jayden said. "I won't let anything happen to her."

The elf plopped down on a bedroll and ran his fingers through his hair. "You have no idea the trouble she has caused me. I swore to her brother that I would keep her alive. And thus far, she has done all she can to make that as difficult as possible for me. I have never known anyone as stubborn... or as determined to get themselves killed."

Jayden sat down opposite him, carefully placing the sword across his lap. It was similar to the one Linis had given him, though more ornate. The sheath was made from polished black leather that had been engraved with the image of an elf woman holding a silver orb aloft. The handle was wrapped in a soft material that Jayden did not recognize, and the pommel capped with a large emerald.

"I could go alone," he suggested. "Maybe Lord Nambis would—"

"Lord Nambis is even more stubborn than Gia. Once he has made up his mind, there is nothing more to say."

"Why wouldn't he let you come?"

"He intends for me to accompany those traveling to contact the elves from the steppes."

Jayden recalled that the elves from the steppes had refused to aid their kin in the Great War. He considered telling Theopolou that it was useless, but could not find a way to do so without revealing the truth—a truth that he knew would not be believed.

"Can't you just refuse?" he said.

Theopolou cocked his head. "You cannot be serious. You must have really lost your memory if you imagine I could do such a thing without ending up before the council of elders and finding my neck stretched out beneath an axe soon after."

"I just have a feeling that going to the steppes will be a waste of time."

He eyed Jayden curiously. "It's comments like those that tell people you have not been honest with them. Perhaps it is the steppes from where you flee? Am I right?"

Jayden longed to tell him the truth, but to say any more than he already had might prevent him from accompanying Gia to see Felsafell. And as he had no other plan, he felt that he must go.

"No. I'm not from the steppes," he replied. "Just know that if I could tell you more, I would."

Theopolou flicked his wrist. "Very well. Keep your secrets for now. I will find out the truth eventually, as I am sure will Gia. She could convince the Creator herself to give up the very secret of life." He pushed himself to his feet. "We should gather what you will need for your journey. The Spirit Hills are far, and there are none of our kin along the way to give you shelter."

He found Jayden a few changes of clothing and enough provisions to last several days.

Once packed, they sat in the tent together waiting for dusk, while a rather wistful Theopolou took to describing his home in great detail. The magnificence of his family manor was of particular interest to Jayden. His mother had told him of exactly such a place that once belonged to her uncle. He was now convinced that this had to be the same person. Which meant he was now speaking to his own great uncle. What were the odds of that? Then again, just about everything thus far in this bygone world had defied probability.

"You should go now," Theopolou said as soon as the daylight began to fade. "Gia is not known for her patience."

Jayden threw the pack over his shoulders and checked that the sword was secure around his waist. "I'll give this back to you when I return," he promised.

Theopolou smiled. "It is yours. Consider it a gesture of my appreciation. May it serve you well... though hopefully, the need to use it will not arise too often."

"Thank you. And don't worry about Gia. I'll take care of her for you."

Theopolou sighed. "If you can, then you will be a better elf than I."

She was already waiting for him just outside the tent. Apart from the bow slung across her back, her only weapons appeared to be a pair of short daggers. Jayden knew that in the hands of a skilled elf, daggers could be deadlier than the heaviest sword. Even though far less useful in a full-on battle, their intention was stealth. This thought made the sword hanging at his side suddenly feel heavy and awkward, and for a moment, he considered leaving it behind.

The temptation was quickly rejected. If they did happen to run into trouble along the way, he might be grateful to have it with him.

"I was beginning to think you weren't coming," Gia said.

"You really think I'm a deserter?"

"I think there's more to you than you are telling us. You speak like a human, you move like a seeker, and you have the ability of a great healer. Any elf with such powers would be well known among us. And yet no one has ever heard of you."

"Isn't it enough that I'm on your side?"

She sniffed. "That remains to be seen. Just know that I did not want you with me. It was the will of Lord Nambis. And unlike Theopolou, I will not question his decisions."

Jayden was about to respond, but Gia cut him short.

"I have no desire for conversation. Unless, of course, you wish to tell me the truth about who you really are."

"You know who I am."

"I know who you say you are. Until you speak honestly, I will continue to think of you as a deserter."

She started out at a quick pace, forcing Jayden to run to catch up.

"And I have no love for cowards," she added.

CHAPTER 18

The first two days were spent in almost complete silence. Jayden tried to strike up a conversation on several occasions, but as she had already told him, she had no desire to speak. They traveled at night to avoid human patrols that might be in the area.

He tried to picture in his mind where they might be. The maps he had studied while still a boy dreaming of leaving his farm were of some help, though not as much as he would have liked. He had concentrated mostly on the more modern maps—only glancing briefly at those drawn before the Great War. Since then, many names had changed. Entire cities had been razed, abandoned, or completely rebuilt elsewhere. Even the kingdoms were different. Some were greatly diminished, while others, either by force or agreement, had united with neighbors to create a larger, far more powerful dominion. A few, having suffered losses to the point of eventual collapse, had even disappeared to the point where there was now only a vague knowledge of them ever existing at all.

Great War indeed. It had altered the very face of the world.

The evening of the third day found them in a rocky area where, even with his skills in the wild, Jayden found himself having to step with caution. Gia, unsurprisingly, was sure-footed and nimble, easily navigating the rough terrain. Several times she raced far enough ahead for Jayden to lose sight of her, only to find her some minutes later waiting on the other side of some tree or bolder, an irritated scowl on her face.

"You must move faster." These were the first words she had spoken in some time. "Why do you not use the *flow*? Or was Theopolou mistaken, and your presence here is just a useless annoyance?"

Sayia had explained to him that, in time, using the *flow* would become second nature. However, at present it was still far from that. Nonetheless, he began to concentrate. To his great relief—and with a touch of surprise—this time, it came to him rather quickly. Soon the aches and pains of hard travel were washed away.

Gia's mouth momentarily curved into a smile, though it vanished as quickly as it appeared. "Much better," she remarked. "Now perhaps we can get there before the war is over."

In an instant, she turned and started out. This time, Jayden was able to keep pace. In fact, he was actually starting to enjoy himself. It wasn't the sensation of added strength that he found to be the most pleasing, more the freedom with which he was able to move and experience his surroundings. A memory of the way Linis would smile when they were tracking a deer flashed through his head. It was a look of pure joy. Though unaware of it at the time, he was now sure that the elf had been using the *flow*.

As dawn broke, the ground was beginning to level. Gia found an area of dense shrubs that would serve to conceal them from passers-by. They removed their packs and squatted on the ground.

"We have been fortunate so far," she said. "But from here on, we must be wary."

That she had spoken at all was in itself a touch surprising to Jayden. "What do you mean?" he asked.

"Humans are fearful that we plan to march south. Of course, we have no intention of doing so. At least, not for now. But they have increased their watch. The Bull has sent five thousand men to the garrison north of a human village called Vine Run."

Jayden was familiar with the place, even though he had never been there. Twice a year, for as long as he could remember, their home had received cases of wine from Vine Run. His father would be quite excited when they arrived and always threw a big party. His mother, who appeared equally excited, and father would dance all night, laughing and drinking until the sky turned orange from the coming of dawn. The wine was always very good. Despite this, he had often wondered why a simple case of wine, however tasty, would warrant celebration.

"Do you think the humans would go into the Spirit Hills?" he asked.

"Not likely. Their fear of what dwells there is enough to keep them out. Once there, we should be safe. At least from the soldiers."

"How about you? Do *you* fear the Spirit Hills?"

She frowned at him. "I spoke only because you needed to know what lies ahead. Now that you do, kindly keep your mouth closed and your questions to yourself."

Her sharp response hit a nerve. "I accept that you don't want to speak to me," Jayden retorted. "That's your choice. But that doesn't mean you get to tell me when I can speak. Is that clear?"

He could feel his pulse quicken. He'd had enough from her. "There's a lot you don't know," he continued. "If I told you my real reason for being at the battle and who I really am, you could neither understand nor handle the truth. So think of me whatever you want. I really don't give a damn."

As each word slipped out, he could hear a voice in the back of his mind telling him to remain quiet. It went unheeded. Youthful impulsiveness was overpowering his reason.

"At least you admit that you've been lying," she said, her eyes boring into him. "But I already knew that much, anyway. So tell me, what is it that you fear I cannot handle? I suspect that you may be a half-man. Perhaps I am right. Even though I have never heard of a god mating with my kind, I suppose it is possible."

That she had come so close to the mark left him speechless and ashen-faced. *Your mouth and your temper are your greatest enemies.* That's what his mother would say. And she was right.

It took several seconds for him to regain his composure. In an effort to conceal his anxiety, he curled his lip and gave a mocking snort. "A half-man? Is that the best you can think of? If that were the case, why wouldn't I have left when I had the chance? Try again."

"Half-man or no, until you are willing to tell me the truth, I do not wish to hear your voice."

"Like I said, you wouldn't believe me."

She gave a scornful laugh. "I don't believe you now."

Jayden thought on this. Perhaps he should tell her the truth. Why not? What could she do? Even if she thought him insane, it was still better than her taking him for a deserter and a coward.

Just as he opened his mouth to begin, the whistle of an arrow smothered his words. The missile thudded into the ground midway between himself and Gia. They leaped to their feet, blades flying to their hands. Off to their right, they could hear the rustle of boots on leaves.

Another arrow penetrated the shrubs, this striking Gia in the left thigh. She let out a stifled cry and dropped to one knee, clutching at the shaft. Blood instantly began soaking her leg.

"It sounds like I got one," called a voice. "Come on, lads."

Jayden stepped forward to emerge from their hiding place. He saw four men in light leather armor charging toward them, each wielding a long blade. On spotting him, they let out a chorus of hoots and roars. He squared his stance, the *flow* now entering him easily. From behind, he heard a sharp snap—Gia breaking off the arrow.

"Stay there," he barked.

"I can still fight," she insisted.

The men were only about twenty yards away when she limped into view. All four immediately veered toward her, clearly intent on engaging with the wounded foe first. Jayden could feel the *flow* running through Gia as well. She was undoubtedly strong, but compared to someone like Sayia or his sisters, she was a mere novice. Of course, in everything but raw power, so was he.

In an effort to protect Gia, with a savage cry of intent, he rushed headlong at the enemy. This unexpected aggression took the quartet completely by surprise. For a moment, their advance came almost to a standstill. Gia was in no condition to follow him, but that was the point. In her present state, and with only a pair of short knives with which to defend herself, four experienced swordsmen would be more than enough to overwhelm her.

On reaching the nearest soldier, Jayden ducked low under the man's thrust and brought his own blade sharply up. Though the strike missed by a hair's breadth, in forcing his opponent to jerk sharply away, it had the effect of sending him stumbling heavily into the side of his nearest comrade. The other two, unaffected by this, pressed on toward Gia, lashing out at her in a furious barrage.

Jayden thrust his sword at the first man's mid-section, but he twisted just enough for his armor to take most of the damage. A rapid glance back told him that Gia had been able to parry the first onslaught, suffering only a minor cut to her right arm in the process. He knew that this glance had left him exposed, but the *flow* gave him the speed he needed to recover as dual blades bore down on him.

With three rapid pivots, Jayden avoided their combined attacks and then loosed a devastating strike that severed the closest foe's arm at the elbow. Shrieks of agony pierced the air as blood spurted from the stump in time with the man's racing heartbeat. The sight of this, rather than deterring his companion, seemed to enrage him. For a short time, Jayden found himself being forced back several paces while blocking strike after strike.

Had things been on an equal footing, it was clear that the human was the superior warrior. But things were not equal. The *flow* was now raging through Jayden's spirit like the wildest of storms. With an effort that had every ounce of his strength behind it, he brought his weapon sweeping down in a long arc. The enemy steel offered up in defense simply shattered asunder beneath the might of the blow. A savage grin formed as his blade continued on with its downward path, slicing his foe cleanly apart from shoulder to stomach.

There was no time to dwell on his victory, however. Though Gia had managed to wound one of her opponents, she was losing ground and had suffered several more deep cuts, all of which were bleeding freely. Jayden moved to position himself behind the uninjured soldier, but he spotted him coming and turned his attention, thrusting his weapon out to keep him at bay.

Realizing that the odds were now even, the man facing Gia suddenly lost heart. After a short burst of half-hearted strikes, he spun on his heels and began to run. The wounded soldier, on seeing his companion flee, quickly decided it was in his best interests to do the same thing. But Gia was not about to allow them to escape. Quickly ducking back into their hiding place amongst the shrubs, she emerged with her bow. The men had barely made it fifty yards when the thwack of a bowstring heralded the end to one of their lives. A second arrow pierced the remaining soldier's right leg, sending him crashing to the ground.

Jayden grinned. "Nice shot."

The man with the severed arm was still lying on the forest turf, futilely trying to wrap his injury and stem the flow of blood. Jayden ended his suffering with a blade through the heart. Farther away, the soldier with an arrow protruding from his leg was scrambling around in a desperate attempt to regain his proper footing. A final shot from Gia's bow ended all thoughts of this.

As if to punctuate the end of the battle, she then fell to her knees, the bow slipping from her grasp. Jayden rushed to her side. Her wounds were numerous, though the worst by far was from the arrow to her thigh. The broken shaft still jutted from her ruined flesh, and blood was flowing freely.

"Help me up," she said. "There might be more of them about."

"You can't walk," he protested. "I need to heal you."

She shook her head. "You will do no such thing. Just get the arrow out of me. That is all I require from you."

"You can't be serious. How far do you think you can go like this?"

"I have medicine," she said, wincing. "I will not have you open me up."

"What the hell are you talking about?"

"I don't trust you, and I will not leave myself vulnerable. So either pull out the arrow or leave me behind."

Jayden had heard that healing with the *flow* could enable two people to read one another's thoughts. He had not experienced this with Theopolou. Nevertheless, the determined look in Gia's eyes told him that she would not be swayed.

"Have it your way," he said. "But at least let me treat your wounds."

"There's a salve in my pack. Bring it to me."

He hurried over to where their belongings lay, returning a moment later. Gia rummaged around for a moment and retrieved a small round metal box and several bandages. As she opened the lid of the box, the air was filled with a sweet aroma Jayden recognized. It was made from the viridin root. His mother always kept some handy.

Gia tore the rip in her pants wide enough to reveal the arrowhead. "Hurry. Pull it out."

"It needs to be cleaned first."

"There's no time. Just do as I say."

This was madness. Even with the salve, if she did not receive proper treatment, her wounds would likely become infected. Jayden didn't need to be an elf healer to know that.

With a grunt of displeasure, he wrapped his fingers around the shaft. "Are you ready?"

The instant she nodded, he pulled it free in one quick tug.

Gia let out an agonized cry as a fresh stream of blood spewed forth. Still moaning but determined not to let the pain defeat her, she scooped out a liberal amount of the salve and slathered it over the open wound. Seeing her hands trembling, Jayden reached for a bandage and quickly wrapped it tight for her. With this done, Gia dropped the box and pounded her fists into the ground, teeth clenched tightly while battling to contain her cries.

Without waiting for permission, Jayden picked up the salve and began applying it to the worst of her other injuries. He knew that, if not stitched, several of the deeper cuts would leave massive scars. Not that Gia would care about such a thing; he felt sure of that.

To his relief, as her pain subsided, she allowed him to continue cleaning and binding her wounds.

"You'll need to change and clean them as soon as possible," he told her once he was finished. "And I don't care what you say, you need a proper healer, or you won't make it."

"I *will* make it," she contended. "But not if more humans come. We're only two days from the Spirit Hills, and we need to move now."

Given her condition, Jayden guessed it would take them much longer than that. Gia would be unable to travel with any semblance of speed. Even now, she was struggling to stand. Barely suppressing a groan of frustration, he helped her to her feet.

"So Theopolou was right. You *are* determined to die."

"Mind what you say," she shot back. "That we fought together does not give you license to mock me."

Ignoring this remark, Jayden gathered up Gia's belongings. What was already an uncomfortable journey had now been made much worse. If she died, he would have to explain it to Theopolou. The mere thought of this filled him with apprehension. He needed to convince Gia to allow him to heal her, which meant telling her the truth about himself was now out of the question. He had to think of a believable story, something to at least gain a portion of her trust.

Though if she were as stubborn as she seemed, she very well might choose death.

CHAPTER 19

As expected, the journey took longer than Gia had stated. But to her credit, she endured her pain without complaint. And once confident they were not being pursued, she took the time to clean and redress her injuries.

After two days, Jayden was amazed that she was able to keep going. *Perhaps she is using the* flow *to self-heal*, he mused. He knew it was possible. Not that he could sense any difference. If anything, her use of the *flow* was weaker than before. Yet as they drew closer to the Spirit Hills, he was beginning to believe this must be what was happening. Though she was limping terribly, the bandages were not nearly as blood-stained as they had been.

They had run across more humans on one occasion, but without incident—simple townsfolk out gathering wild nuts and berries.

"The men we fought were the Bull's elite trackers," she told him on the day before they were due to arrive. "It's rumored that some among their number are half-men, though those we encountered most certainly were not. Even so, they are still vicious fighters and hate our kind with particularly strong vigor."

Jayden noticed that beads of sweat were forming on her brow, and also that her complexion was much paler than before. He decided not to say anything about this for the time being, instead remarking, "I'm surprised we haven't been pursued. Their bodies have surely been found by now."

"We will be, but not for a few days yet. Trackers aren't a part of the regular army, so those men won't be quickly missed. From what we know of them, they work independently of the garrison."

After a meager meal that used up most of their remaining dried fruits and the water in their skins, they moved on. At this point, the ground was still relatively flat, though the density of the trees forced them to make numerous twists and turns along the way.

Each hour they walked saw Gia's condition worsen. Jayden realized that her wounds, as he had feared, must have become infected. Her use of the *flow* had clearly reduced any further bleeding, but it had not allowed her body to truly heal. Given that she would not permit him to do anything about it, he could only hope that Felsafell would be able to help her—assuming they could find him in time.

When they did eventually reach the road that ran alongside the edge of the Spirit Hills, it was only a few hours before dawn. They waited here for a short time until sure there was no one else about before crossing over.

Once setting foot on the other side, everything instantly changed. It was as if the air had suddenly thickened, and their breathing became labored. The trees appeared gnarled and ancient; the forest floor was uneven and fraught with leaf-covered holes and hidden roots that seemed to have been deliberately set there to trap or trip them. There were no obvious trails, not even a deer path. With each step they took, the way ahead became ever more dense, as if the forest were intentionally closing in on itself to deny them access. Only the gradient of the hills offered little resistance. At this point they were no more than gentle slopes, though Jayden was sure that these too would become far more demanding in due course.

After three hours of laborious progress, with the sky beginning to glow with the dim light of dawn, he doubted that they had covered even a mile into the interior. Gia's condition had deteriorated further, as well. By now, she was struggling desperately just to place one foot in front of the other.

"You have to let me try to heal you," he said finally.

She halted to lean heavily against a pine. "I will be fine once we arrive. Healing comes slowly without rest."

"For you, it's impossible," he retorted. "You just aren't strong enough. The *flow* in you is weak and getting weaker by the minute. It could be days yet before we find him. You won't make it that long. If you're worried about revealing anything, let me tell you that when I healed Theopolou, we saw nothing of each other's mind. Not a thing. So please, stop being so damned stubborn."

He stepped toward her, but she moved away, anger flashing in her eyes.

"If you touch me, I will gut you," she warned, her hand gripping the handle of her dagger.

Jayden backed off. "Fine. Die for no reason, if that's what you want. At least I can tell Theopolou I *tried* to save you."

Gia gave no reply. With her unyielding expression still in place, she turned on wobbling legs and trudged on, hands reaching out to each tree she passed for much needed support.

Keeping a good distance back, Jayden followed. If she collapsed, he could then try to heal her. But this raised other questions. Would that be too late? How close to death could someone be before they were beyond aid? There was no way for him to know. Although severely wounded and with little chance of survival without treatment, Theopolou had not actually been on the point of death when he healed him.

As expected, by the time the sun was fully up, the hills had steepened dramatically. With each one taller than the last, they tried to thread their way between them whenever possible, though thick brambles or large piles of jagged rocks often prevented this. Jayden began to get a strange feeling that they were being watched. He listened carefully, but could not hear a thing aside from the twitting of birds and the rustle of the wind in the treetops. The air carried the musty scent of rotting foliage and wet moss, even when they crested a rise. Why anyone would want to live in such an appalling place was beyond his understanding.

I suppose if you're a hermit wanting solitude, this would definitely help to keep people out, he thought.

By now, they would have normally halted for the day. But Gia pressed on—albeit at a snail's pace. Her hair was limp from perspiration and her hands trembled badly. Jayden was on the verge of simply tackling her to the ground and holding her there while doing his best to heal her. This was insane. Why would anyone willingly choose death when help was available?

This question was still floating around in his mind when, just as they were about to ascend yet another tall slope, he heard a voice call out from behind.

"A strange sight indeed it is."

They spun, hands on their weapons. The sudden movement caused Gia to stagger and drop to one knee.

Standing beside a pile of loose rocks was an old man dressed in stained and tattered animal skins. His ashen hair and long beard were tangled and matted, and the deep lines of countless years were carved into his face. In one hand he held a gnarled tree branch—apparently a walking stick. Yet despite his aged appearance, his eyes twinkled bright blue as they looked directly at Jayden. His expression was one of intense curiosity.

"Eldest," whispered Gia. These were the only words she spoke before crumbling completely to the ground.

Jayden rushed to her side, ignoring the newcomer. He placed a hand on her brow. As expected, she was burning with fever.

"A strong one to have come so far," remarked Felsafell. "Oh, yes. Strong. Yet rash."

"Can you help her?" Jayden asked.

"A healer I am not. Keep her alive, I can for now. Until you make your choice."

"Speak sense. Can you help her or not?"

Felsafell approached with long, sure strides that belied his withered frame. Reaching into a small pouch hanging from his belt, he retrieved a tiny yellow mushroom. "Give her this. But do not heal her otherwise. Oh, no. Not yet. Not until you've had time to think. Time to choose."

The stories about Felsafell and his wisdom had not prepared Jayden for the odd little man standing over him. But if he was as wise as they said, he thought it best to obey.

Gently opening Gia's mouth, he dropped the mushroom to the back of her throat. After a few coughs and jerks, she swallowed it whole. He then tried to brush the hair from her sweat-soaked brow, but she moaned and shifted her head away. It seemed as if, even in this state, she was determined to resist contact with him.

"If you please," said Felsafell, gesturing for him to move aside. "The way is long, and we must not tarry."

Jayden looked on in slack-jawed astonishment as the old hermit hefted Gia onto his shoulder as easily as if he were picking up a small child.

"An uncomfortable way to travel," he said. "But mind she won't, I think."

With that, he bounded up the hill at astonishing speed. Jayden followed as best as he could, though soon found himself falling farther behind with every step. He tried to run, but the terrain would not allow for anything other than short sprints, just enough to keep him from losing sight of the *man*... or whatever he was.

They continued in this way for several hours. Even using the *flow*, Jayden could feel his legs tiring. At the same time, his sense of being watched grew stronger. Now deep into the interior of the Spirit Hills, the landscape here was much different from the outskirts. Tiny streams snaked their way between the slopes, their beds glistening with multi-colored pebbles. Though the trees still looked quite old, they were not nearly as menacing. Sunlight poured in through the canopy, peppering the turf with pinpricks of light, like stars on a green and brown sky.

Jayden noticed that although Felsafell moved at great speed, Gia's body jostled only very slightly, even when they were passing over the roughest of ground. He knew the old hermit's physical form was just a deception; the First Born was reputed to be able to change shape completely. One story his mother had told him said that his true appearance was almost elf-like, with ebony skin, silver hair, and standing nearly seven feet tall.

It was well into the afternoon before they slowed their pace. Felsafell then allowed Jayden to catch up and walk beside him. How much ground they had covered was unclear, though the burning in his muscles suggested they had come far.

"Almost there," Felsafell told him. "Oh, yes. Soon we will arrive."

Virtually as he spoke, Jayden spotted a thin line of smoke climbing above the treetops. Soon the air was filled with the tantalizing aroma of roasting meat and bread. His stomach rumbled with hunger.

"Empty bellies and tired legs must wait until the sun has gone to bed," Felsafell told him. "But my table will be filled once questions are answered."

"Good," said Jayden. "I have many."

The old man gave him a lopsided smile. "Oh, no. Not *your* questions. Mine."

A narrow trail led to a tiny house with a thatched roof and a broad porch stretching all along the front. On this, several chairs had been scattered haphazardly about. To Jayden's eyes, the house itself was ramshackle, to say the least. With its off-square corners and poorly fitted walls, it resembled a shelter thrown together in haste by someone not particularly skilled in the craft of building. Even the door, barely hanging in place on rusting hinges, looked badly out of sorts.

Felsafell stepped inside, with Jayden close behind. To the left, he saw an iron stove and a hearth, along with several rickety cabinets and counters. More to the center were some low-backed chairs and a round table, its top piled high with dishes and utensils in need of cleaning. On the opposite side were a pair of beds, a dresser, and several wooden chests. As for the décor, it was non-existent. Not a single picture nor keepsake of any kind had been hung on the walls. Only a bow and a quiver of arrows was propped up near the front door.

After setting Gia on one of the beds, Felsafell removed her pack and weapons, then laid her down and covered her with a blanket. This done, he walked over to the stove, where a pot was steaming, and took a long sniff. In the hearth was meat that Jayden guessed to be venison roasting on a spit. Felsafell poked this with his finger and smiled.

"Almost ready it is. Good thing my kin are watchful. Otherwise, an empty stomach would make your visit unpleasant."

Jayden cocked his head. "Your kin?"

"It matters not," he said, waving a dismissive hand.

With the same energy he had shown when traversing the hills, he quickly gathered up the dishes from the table and carried them to the door.

"Be at ease," he said. "I will not be long. Then talk we must."

He exited the house, leaving Jayden to place his belongings in the corner alongside Gia's. With some of the color returning, she looked quite a bit better than she had before. He could also see that she had stopped perspiring. He felt her brow and breathed a sigh of relief. The fever had gone down considerably. Of course, this might be just a temporary reprieve. Felsafell had plainly stated that he was not able to heal her.

The old hermit returned after only a short time, humming merrily and bearing clean dishes. After placing these in one of the cabinets, he crossed over to Gia and regarded her for several minutes.

"She will not last the night," he eventually said. "A sad thing when the young perish. Oh, yes. Time is the enemy of mortal dreams." He looked over at Jayden. "But for you, time is both friend and foe. That is what they tell me. Oh, yes. Mother's grace is laid upon you. And yet you are absent from her sight. A mystery. One I fear I cannot solve. Perhaps you can help these tired eyes see more clearly?"

"If you really are Felsafell, it is I who needs *your* help," Jayden told him.

"Help? I cannot help. You can save her. But at a price."

"I wasn't talking about Gia. I need your help to save my parents."

Felsafell looked into his eyes, then turned toward the door. "I hear my kin. Their words are peculiar. But you... even more so. Come. Let us take our ease. Even the strong must rest tired legs."

Jayden went with him to the porch, where Felsafell plopped down into one of the chairs. Jayden sat opposite. Yes, his legs were tired. But the need for urgency was growing.

"A child of gods you are indeed," Felsafell said. Reaching inside his shirt, he produced a short wooden pipe and a small portion of tobacco. After lighting the pipe and puffing several times, a tiny smile grew from the corners of his mouth. "So seldom do I have company. And yours is unexpected. I've only food to share. These pleasures I have are but a few."

"Please," pressed Jayden. "I need you to listen."

The old hermit raised a bushy eyebrow. "Why? I have nothing to say that you would hear. You, however... how is it you live? Your time is here, and yet it has not come. That is what they tell me. My kin fear you. And fear is all but unknown to them. They shun your presence."

"If I tell you why, will you help me?"

Felsafell chuckled, the pipe still gripped between his teeth. "Like the rest, you come seeking my aid. Yet I am not who you think me to be. I have no power. Only age."

"Yes or no," snapped Jayden.

He shrugged. "Tell me your tale. I will do what I can."

By now, Jayden was beginning to doubt the wisdom of coming. Here he was, hoping to find answers, and the oldest living being in the world seemed to know nothing. Nevertheless, having come this far, he had to press on. As quickly and clearly as possible, he recounted where he was from and how he'd come to be here. "My father has no memory of anything," he concluded. "I need to find a way to make him remember."

Felsafell's countenance darkened. "These are things I should not know. I now see why my kin fear you. Oh, yes. You do not belong. And you, if speak true, the Bull has come to upend creation."

"Can you help me?"

"Think I must on what you have said."

Felsafell stood and started for the porch steps. "My kin, I will consult. For now, eat and rest. I will return."

Jayden sprang up. "What about Gia?"

"The elf is lost, unless you choose her. But be warned: saving her will bind your fate. Your path will be fixed. That much my kin can see. More than that... I cannot say."

Leaving a dumbfounded Jayden standing on the porch, Felsafell moved rapidly away from and vanished down the front path.

Saving her will bind your fate.

These ominous words rang out in his mind like the ghostly howling of wolves in the deep of winter, chilling him to the core. For several minutes, he remained motionless while speculating on their exact meaning.

Still with no clear picture, he went back inside to check on Gia. Though her fever was still low, the color that had returned was now draining away once again. The tiny beads of sweat had also reappeared. Was the mushroom's effect wearing off? He had no idea how long it would last. He scolded himself silently for not having asked.

He reached down to touch her wound, but withdrew his hand before making contact. Maybe a bite to eat first? Then he could decide what to do.

A search of the cabinets produced a knife suitable for carving off some meat. Inside the pot, he found a stew of potatoes and wild onions. After filling a plate and bowl, he sat at the table and stared at the food for several minutes. His stomach was empty, but he had no desire to eat. His eyes kept drifting over to Gia. What was he waiting for? He knew he should go over and help her. It was only Felsafell's words holding him back. Would his path really be fixed? He had never believed in fate. But now...

A loud gasp from Gia broke into his thoughts. The next moment she was thrashing her head about violently, crying out in garbled words. Jayden sprang from his seat and rushed to the bed. Without thinking, he placed his hands on her shoulders, drawing in every bit of the *flow* that he could manage. In response, Gia reached up to push him away. Her strength was alarming.

No!

The single word ripped through Jayden's mind repeatedly as the *flow* penetrated Gia's spirit. She was pleading for him to stop. But it was too late. The bond had already been formed. Only now did he understand why she had resisted so powerfully. A vast flow of unfamiliar images assaulted his mind through their connection. So fast did they come, his head was swimming, much like when he had drunk too much wine.

"Afisul Si Damon."

He wasn't sure if he had actually spoken the words or merely thought them.

Gia's eyes popped open, and she released her hold, her body going limp. It was only then Jayden noticed that all her wounds were healed. Completely. It was as if they had never been there.

"Why?" Her voice was barely a whisper. Tears began streaming down her cheeks.

Unable to answer, Jayden backed away, torrents of emotion crashing over him and threatening to bring him to his knees. He staggered over to the table and leaned down on his elbows.

"I told you no," Gia protested in a barely audible voice. "You had no right..."

"I... I didn't intend..."

Sliding onto a chair, he laid his head on the table. The bond was overpowering his senses. He had experienced something similar with his sisters, only this was a thousand times more intense. Moreover, he could feel that she was within his mind. No... not only his mind. His very soul. He was open to her in a way he was completely unable to fully grasp.

Gia was attempting to sit up, but was still too weak. "You can't be," she muttered. "No. No. I refuse to believe it. This cannot be true."

At that moment, the door opened and Felsafell stepped inside. A look of consternation quickly formed. "Wise words you do not heed, I see," he remarked.

Hurrying over to a chest at the foot of the empty bed, he plucked out a tiny blue bottle. He then sat beside Gia. "You must be calm. Drink and forget. Rest. Troubles will be waiting for you. No need to seek them now."

Gia glared at him, her jaw set tight. "You told him to do this?"

Felsafell smiled warmly and held out the bottle. "Fate is fate. Like you, I am its servant, not its master. You tried to escape its hold and failed. There is nothing to be done. But do not fret. Drink and sleep for now. Strength you will need, come morning. This will see you through."

After taking a lengthy look at the bottle, she gave a resigned sigh and drank its contents. Within seconds, her eyes were closed and her breathing long and steady.

"She will sleep until dawn," Felsafell said. "Then you must leave."

Jayden was still dizzy. Even when Gia was asleep, he could feel her mind touching his own. What had he done? And how? He felt a hand touch his shoulder.

"Come with me," the old hermit said. "A journey you must take. But first there is much to say."

CHAPTER 20

Lord Zarin, the Bull of the West, stared down at the coin: just one small copper disk lying upon a huge map stretched out across the table. It elicited feelings within him that were hard to fathom... a combination of guilt, doubt, and sorrow. But why? The coin was clearly a forgery. Perhaps it was more to do with the young elf who had possessed it. Was it something he had said? Something about the way he looked at him, as if they had met before?

The sword the boy had carried was of excellent craftsmanship, a touch heavier than most elf blades, but perfectly balanced. He had decided to keep it for himself. His own sword, having hewn through the armor and steel of countless foes, was chipped and in dire need of repair.

Picking up a wine bottle from the arm of his chair, he took a long drink. It failed to satisfy him. He needed something stronger.

"Brandy," he barked over to the young captain standing beside the tent's exit.

The captain gave a salute and quickly ducked out.

Zarin finished the wine anyway, then tossed the bottle aside. He always found getting drunk to be a challenge. It took many times the amount of brandy for him than for other men. As for wine... it was impossible. His belly would burst before he felt its effects.

The escape of the prisoners had gone as planned. All of them were able-bodied, so in the eyes of their elf brothers, they were worth rescuing. Though savages who left their wounded behind, he knew they could not pass up such an easy opportunity to reclaim men still capable of fighting. That was why he had ordered the prisoners to be hanged so far away from the main camp. And the enemy had been foolish enough to take the bait.

Unable to count on the skills of his men, Zarin had personally tracked the fleeing prisoners to their secret camp. Even though his abilities in this respect were second to none, many times he had wished his own trackers possessed the talents of the renowned elf seekers. The seekers, of course, were well aware of their great superiority over their human counterparts. It was this arrogance as much as anything else that had led to their downfall. In fact, the same failing was true with nearly all elves. That was why they would soon be eradicated. Humans had feared them long enough. Even so, their strength and capabilities were still worth admiration. Most had been worthy foes, and brave too. As with the elves, desertion was now rare among his own men, though such had not been the case before his arrival from...

He creased his brow for a moment, struggling to remember. But it was pointless. Whatever had happened to make him forget his past, it was no longer important. He was Lord Zarin now—the Bull of the West. The most feared human alive. And once the war was won, he would carve out a kingdom of his own, one that would rival that of the Ancient King of Angrääl.

The tent flap opened, and the captain returned, a bottle of brandy in each hand. "Lord Ergona has asked if he may have a word," he said, while placing the bottles on the table.

Zarin sighed heavily. "Send him in."

The captain exited once again. A few seconds later, a tall, lean man with long dark curls and thin, delicate features entered. He was dressed in an extravagant blue satin robe rather than the plain wool or cotton garb typical for a military camp. Zarin didn't exactly dislike Lord Ergona, it was more a grudging tolerance. The man was arrogant and self-involved, as were most nobles. This was a trait that Zarin despised. But Ergona was also a particularly good military strategist—despite the fact that he was personally worse than useless with a blade.

"What can I do for you?" Zarin asked, foregoing any preamble.

Ergona bowed formally. "I have heard that you plan for our forces to retreat to the north, my lord."

"You have heard correctly. Am I to assume that you disagree with my decision?"

"I would not presume. Though I will admit that I do not understand your reasoning. We have the elves on the run. One more year at best and they will be utterly defeated. Why pull back now?"

"I have no intention of this war lasting for another year," Zarin told him.

He uncorked the brandy and turned up the bottle. After several gulps, he offered it over to Ergona, who looked around the tent as if expecting there to be a glass somewhere. Finding none, he smiled and held up his hand.

Zarin scowled. "You think I have some sort of disease?"

Ergona shook his head and quickly accepted the bottle. "Not at all. Forgive me. I sometimes forget myself."

"You'll be back in your manor soon enough. Then you can drink from any glass you want."

"I must admit, I do miss civilized ways," he sighed, after taking a tiny sip. "I never thought my study of tactics would be of any practical use. Had it been different, I would have spent more time in the wild with my brothers. They are more equipped to be soldiers than I."

"Don't sell yourself short," Zarin told him. "You may not be the toughest of men, but you have led your soldiers to... how many victories?"

"Fifteen," he responded, head held high. "Only *your* victories are more numerous."

"That is because you serve under me, Lord Ergona. Your victories *are* mine." He enjoyed reminding the nobles that, although he was of unknown heritage, they were under his command. They lived and died according to the will of the Bull. In reality, not even the kings and queens held more power.

"You are correct, as always, my lord."

"Is there anything else?"

"Only if you would like to tell me why we retreat."

Zarin looked at him, stone-faced. "Do you feel I am required to share this?"

He rapidly held up his palms. "No, not at all, my lord. It is just that my captains are inquiring, and I would have liked to have a reply other than ignorance to offer them."

As was often the case, Zarin felt a burning desire to bring him down a notch, to drive home the uncomfortable truth that a high noble must fear a man of low birth. But he was well aware that he might still be in need of Ergona after the war was over. The kingdoms would be out to put him down. Even the mighty Bull of the West required allies.

"The elves think we muster to fight them near the coast west of Baltria," he began. "I have sent ships to patrol the area to encourage that belief. As we speak, they are gathering a hundred miles north of where they *think* we will be."

"I admit, I too believed that west of Baltria was our destination. So your deception was certainly effective, my lord. But if not there, then where?"

"The bulk of the elves are on their way here from the Eastland. The remaining elves are two weeks' march to the west near the Tarvansia Peninsula. I've ordered the whole of our forces to join us in the north. The elves will believe we are reinforcing our position for a major assault on their lands."

"But will that not leave the kingdoms along the Abyss undefended?"

"Yes. But the enemy's strength in that area is nowhere close to being enough to threaten the major strongholds. To do that, they would need to gather their entire force. And I intend to ensure that this is exactly what they do."

Realization dawned on Ergona's face. "I see. You hope to lure them into a trap."

"And with all of them in one place, we can end this once and for all."

Ergona's smile went from one of courtesy to genuine cheer. "That is excellent news indeed."

"You see? I'll have you home and sleeping in your own bed before the harvest."

He took another drink. This time, when he offered the bottle to Ergona, the man did not hesitate. "Now, if there is nothing else."

"No, my lord. That is all." With a parting bow, he exited the tent.

Zarin returned his attention to the map in front of him. Using the tip of his finger, he pushed aside the coin covering the location where he planned to crush the elf armies forever. Maiden Pass. It would be in that narrow area of stony ground that the world would begin anew.

Eliminating the elves would be just the start. The name of Lord Zarin, the Bull of the West, would ring through the ages as the man who brought peace to the entire human world.

CHAPTER 21

Felsafell led Jayden to a small clearing by the bank of a narrow stream half a mile from the cabin. The air was crisp and chilled further by a stiff breeze. Fireflies darted just above the surface of the water—a sight Jayden would have found pleasing to watch had his head not been filled with so much confusion.

Felsafell kneeled by the water and rinsed his hands. "Bonded with her, did you?"

"I didn't mean to."

He smiled over his shoulder. "No? An accident, you say? How unfortunate. Elf bonding is not to be taken lightly. Oh, no."

"Can I undo it?"

He splashed water over his face. "Only one love have I had. That love is precious to me. Why would you wish to discard yours?"

"I don't love her."

"Are you sure? I know little of elf ways as they are today. But bonds are not given lest the heart and spirit are willing. But you are no elf. This is true, yes?"

"I told you what I am."

The old hermit stood and strolled over to a patch of soft grass where sat down cross-legged. He waited until Jayden had joined him before speaking any further.

"You told me much. Left old Felsafell with many questions. An odd thing—I had forgotten the thrill of curiosity. But a man out of his own time... that has my old brain wandering. My kin tell me not to ask too much. And wise they are to say it. Not even the undying should know their own destiny. So it is *your* dilemma we shall speak of most."

He held out a finger and a firefly landed on the tip, its green light pulsing slowly for a moment before taking off again. "The wonders of the world are endless indeed. Yes?"

Jayden sighed inwardly. Clearly, the hermit could not—or possibly would not—help with the bond he now shared with Gia. That being so, he pressed on to the reason he had come.

"How can I make my father remember?"

"Death is the only remedy," Felsafell replied. "His or yours. No power can stop him. No army can halt his march. By your hand, he must end. You alone can do this."

Jayden's back shot up straight. "That's madness! I can't kill my own father."

The old man laughed. "This is true. Oh, yes, it is. And yet you must do so to set things to rights. This is what my kin has said. And believe them, I do."

"But if I kill him, my mother will die," he protested. The thought that he would be trapped in this bygone world occurred.

"Will she? Are you sure? She was not dead before you came to this place."

"I don't know how this works," he admitted. "I don't know if I'm changing the past or just fulfilling it. But what I do know for sure is that the bond between my parents is different. She will certainly die if it's broken."

Felsafell held up his hand and wagged his finger. "Ah, yes. The unanswerable question. One not even I dare try to answer. All I can tell you is what I know... and that is not much. Perhaps that your mother lives is the key. Perhaps not. Who but the Creator can know for certain?"

Jayden could not believe what he was hearing. This couldn't be the answer. To kill his father? *And* his mother?

"If this was meant to be, all is well," the old man added. "But if not, you must ask yourself this: Will you sacrifice the elves? Even *I* fear for them. The Bull is relentless. Oh, yes. A god's passion with human fears. The end it could spell for elfkind. He will kill them all."

It was giving Jayden a headache just thinking about the possibilities. In his time, none of this had happened. He had never enjoyed studying history and was certainly no scholar, but that didn't matter; everyone knew the outcome of the first Great War. Even the split that happened toward the end was common knowledge. Did this mean that he had killed his father? No. He refused to believe it.

"Even if I wanted to kill him, I wouldn't be able to," he pointed out. "I can't even get close to where he is."

"A master of battle, I am not. You must find your own way. The Creator guides us all to the proper place and time. Though time, it would seem, holds a new meaning. When what's yet to come is also long ago. Yes?" Felsafell laughed at his own words.

Jayden's anger boiled. "You think this is funny?"

"Of course I do. How could I not? But still your rage, and forgive my amusement. Long have I lived. To find something new is a joy for old souls. And perhaps I *can* help you. Oh, yes. A weapon you need to fight with. Your bonded mate seeks me out for this purpose. Yes?"

"She is not my mate," he retorted. "And yes. She tells me you have a weapon that can help them."

Felsafell scratched his beard absently. "I have no mighty weapon. Oh, no. Never have I had a need for such a thing. But there is a place far from here. There you will find what she desires. Beneath the Maker's Temple is where it can be found. Put there by heavenly gardeners in ages past, when even I was young and foolish."

"The Maker's Temple? Do you mean the Chamber of the Maker?"

He shrugged. "Names change. The new ones rarely reach my ears. So I cannot say. To the west you must go, and with haste. For the day is coming, and coming soon. Armies of elf and human will soon join in battle. Should you fail, it will mean the end. Though the end to *what* remains a riddle."

Jayden considered what he'd heard. The heavenly gardeners were the gods, he presumed. Or were they? He had heard stories that, long ago before humans arrived, elves had once ruled the world. It could be a reference to *them*. The Maker's Temple was the real question. If it was another name for the Chamber of the Maker, they should be able to find this desperately needed weapon without too much difficulty. If it was not the same place, then perhaps Gia would have some knowledge of where the Maker's Temple might be.

Gia. Thinking her name caused him to feel their bond keenly. She was still in a deep sleep. For a moment, he could see strange images in his mind of people he had never met. Dreams; he was seeing her dreams. A wave of guilty embarrassment came over him. He had no right to invade her private thoughts. Was she aware of it? And could she do the same to him? The obvious answer was disconcerting. How did people live this way? Without privacy? There had to be a way to prevent it.

Felsafell rose with a quick hop. "I see your mind is occupied. And mine is drifting north. Overdue I am. My love awaits. She will be cross if I do not come."

Jayden jumped up beside him. "You're leaving?"

"Of course. I have no place in these affairs. My love awaits, and I must heed my heart's call ... old as it may be. There's nothing more I can do for you. The path you've chosen is yours to tread, not mine. But not alone, you venture forth. You may refuse to call her mate or wife. But she is with you now, and you with her." A sly grin crept up. "Perhaps that is why you came? To find the other half of your whole. It would warm my old soul to think this is true. A story of love to rival the most ancient of tales."

Having said this, he spun on his heels and, in a single leap, crossed the brook.

Jayden started after him, but the old man was already out of sight. He stood there for several minutes, simply staring into the night, not knowing what to do next. He had come here for help and for answers. Yet not even the oldest and wisest being in the world could show him a way out of his predicament. On top of that, there was the problem he faced with Gia. Even if he were successful in saving his parents, what would happen then? He and Gia were bonded, and his returning home might kill them both.

While making his way back to the cabin, he caught brief glimpses into her mind. Dreams of wandering alone and afraid in the forest, like a child in the dark for the first time without her mother. He had a sudden urge to be with her, to protect her and let her know she was not alone.

"What the hell is wrong with you?" he muttered. He barely knew her. There was also the small point that she thought him to be scum.

Of course, now that they were bonded, she would know the truth. The question was, how would she react to this? Not well, was his guess.

Inside the cabin, after finding a bottle of sweet wine, he finally got around to eating the food he had prepared earlier. It was cold, but he didn't care. Once finished, he removed both the pot from the stove and the venison from the spit. No point in wasting good food. By morning it would be burned, and Gia was sure to be hungry.

For the rest of the night, Jayden sat at the table staring at her, wondering what the next day would bring. For short periods, he was able to ignore their bond, pushing it to the back of his mind. Then another dream would bring it back to the fore. Though by rights he should have felt exhausted, anxiety was keeping him fully awake.

Time passed slowly. When the first light of dawn finally filtered in through the window, he was almost trembling in anticipation of what was to come. She would wake soon. The accusations and recriminations would then begin. And they would be brutal. Worse, she would be justified in her anger.

"I am not angry."

He looked over to see that she was sitting up in bed. Her face was expressionless.

"I knew this could happen," she said. "I should not have blamed you."

"What do you mean, you *knew* this could happen?"

Gia lowered her eyes. "I felt my spirit drawn to yours the moment we met. That was why I did not want you to heal me. I knew that if you did, it would bond us."

"So why didn't you tell me?"

"Would that have stopped you?"

Jayden thought for a moment, replaying the events in his mind. "No. I couldn't have let you die. Not when I could prevent it."

"I know. And because of my foolishness, our choices have become infinitely more difficult. I should have killed you."

Her words struck him deeply, far more so than he would have expected.

"I am sorry if that is hurtful," she added, though without any trace of regret in her tone. "But now I have discovered who and what you are, and why you have come here, I cannot believe otherwise."

"And now that you have, what will you do?"

"I don't know. My reason tells me that it cannot be true. It defies all sanity and logic. And yet, I know that it is."

"Is there a way to break the bond?"

"Yes. But it is dangerous. And should we succeed, it would leave us both empty and broken. I have seen it happen before."

Flashes of images entered Jayden's mind. Sullen-eyed elves without the spirit to so much as eat or drink. Dead in all but body. He shook his head, eyes shut tight.

"Don't do that," he growled.

"I'm sorry, but it's beyond my control. I am young and do not have the experience to govern what I show you. Nor can I prevent your thoughts from invading mine."

"I don't understand. I thought bonded mates had to love one another. We don't even like each other. Hell, from what I've seen, you hate me."

She shook her head. "I don't hate you. I fear you. What you are is an abomination to my people. The power you can wield is terrifying. It should never be. As for love... I have no way to know what drives the heart of a being born of both elf and god. But I can already feel myself changing. We have always known that bonds formed instinctively cannot be fought. Our spirits know the truth of our hearts. In time, I *will* love you. I will not be able to stop myself. I was meant to love you. And you me."

"How did you know this so quickly?"

She allowed herself a fragile smile. "Women are usually more sensitive to these things. I felt the pull outside the tent, even before I saw you. Did your mother not experience the same with your father?"

She had been viewing his memories. This time it did not bother him quite so much. "I don't know how it happened, exactly. Only that it was not their choice in the beginning."

"And do they love one another?"

"Yes. More than any two people I've met."

"So it will be with us."

Jayden could see tears welling in her eyes. "I…I'm sorry," he said.

"As am I."

"We have a year, right? Until then, we're not fully bonded

"Yes. One year to complete the bond. And if you decline to do so, not being full-blooded, you will likely live. Whereas I will surely die."

The thought of this happening sent a cold knot to the pit of his stomach. "There has to be something we can do."

"There is only one thing to do now. We must kill your father."

Jayden shot from his chair. "No! I won't do it. I can make him remember. I'm sure of it."

Her tears were still falling, yet no sobs came forth. "You cannot lie to me. You knew what must be done before you left Felsafell."

"But my mother…she –"

"She will follow him in death," she said, cutting him short. "And through your sacrifice, the elves will endure. This is the choice you have already made. I can feel it. I can feel the pain inside you. And when it is done, I will suffer with you."

She slipped out of bed and crossed over to him. "The Creator has brought us to this place. I must believe this is Her will. You came to save your family, but instead you will save my people from annihilation. That is why you are here. And why I will be by your side. No one should have to face such horror alone." She touched his hand.

Jayden's tears were now falling as well. The sensation of her flesh was like nothing he had ever experienced. He knew so much about her without a word being spoken. She was a woman of deep conviction, unfathomable passion, and unbreakable courage. She believed the words she had spoken.

And she would stand by him through whatever challenges they may face.

How can I kill my own father?

The unspoken words drifted between them effortlessly.

"I can see him in your heart," she said, a compassionate smile forming. "This is what he would tell you to do. As would Kaylia, your mother."

Choking back the tears, Jayden sat down again and wiped his face on his sleeve. "If you can feel what I feel, then you will know I haven't yet given up hope of saving them."

Gia took a seat at the table opposite him. "Your hope is my own. Even were we not bonded, I would never wish such a thing as this on you, or anyone else. You have my word: if there is a way, I will help you find it."

They sat in silence for several minutes, a flood of emotion continuously passing between them. What he had previously thought of as a burden was gradually becoming a comfort. He knew there were only two likely outcomes. For all his strange words, Felsafell was quite clear on this particular point. Either his father would die, or he would.

"There is one problem," he said. "My father is a god. How do you kill a god? And even if I do find a way, how do I get close enough to do it?"

"I don't know," she replied. "But I think Felsafell told you of a weapon. Is that right?"

Jayden had half-expected her to know the conversation he'd had with the old hermit word for word. That she did not was surprising. Perhaps he could think it to her?

"I can sense your emotions far better," she explained. "Words are difficult, at least for now."

He could not stop himself from laughing at his own ignorance. "This is going to take some time for me to figure out, I suppose."

He then went on to recount what Felsafell had told him.

"I know the Chamber of the Maker," she said, once he was finished. "But nothing lies beneath it. As far as anyone knows, it has no lower levels."

"It's all I can think of."

She steepled her fingers below the bridge of her nose and thought for a time. "It will take many weeks to get there. And if we're wrong, it might be too late to search elsewhere."

"I don't see another choice."

She drew a long breath. "Then it is decided. And may the Creator guide us."

"It's funny," remarked Jayden, as much to himself as to Gia. "My mother often spoke of the Creator. She said that our lives are our own, and the choices we make are made freely. The Creator doesn't bind us to Her, yet she is always there to show us the way to our destiny."

"Your mother is wise."

"I never really believed her. I always thought it was just her way of making sense of a confusing world. But now...I think she was right."

They decided to leave at first light of the next day. They spent the remaining hours going over their route. The lands between the Spirit Hills and the Chamber of the Maker were crowded with human cities, towns, and countless small settlements. Getting there unseen would test their skills to the full.

Jayden was amazed at the transformation Gia had undergone. Where before she had been unwilling to offer him even the smallest courtesy, she was now pleasant, considerate, and even playful at times. By sundown he had almost forgotten how she had behaved when first meeting her. And their bond...it was amazing how quickly he was growing accustomed to someone else being inside his mind. He found himself wondering how his feelings for her would grow. He did not love her. And yet she was a part of him, their spirits inseparable. Had it been this way in the beginning with his mother and father? Something told him that it probably had.

That night, after a hearty meal, he lay in bed staring up at the ceiling. Gia was in the next bed, already in a deep slumber. He could feel that her dreams were untroubled, and this pleased him. No, he did not love her. And she did not love him. But there was no denying that something inside him was changing. He could hear her voice in his mind as clearly as the moment she had actually spoken.

Our spirits know the truth of our hearts.

Felsafell had been right. His path was now fixed, and Gia would walk it with him. For good or ill, they would see this through together. To the end.

BOOK CLUB QUESTIONS

1. Who is your favorite character? Why? And what about them make them enjoyable to read about? Has your favorite character changed since the last book?

2. How well does the author follow the formula of the hero's journey while making the story unique in its own right? Has the journey held true from book to book?

3. How well developed do you feel the character arcs are? And how do you think they develop throughout the book and series?

4. Do you feel Jayden will be the savior he is prophesied to be or will he succumb to the temptations of power?

ABOUT THE AUTHORS

Brian D. Anderson was born in 1971 and grew up in the small town of Spanish Fort, AL. He attended Fairhope High, then later Springhill College, where his love for fantasy grew into a lifelong obsession. His hobbies include chess, history, and spending time with his son.

Jonathan Anderson was born in March 2003. His creative spirit became evident by the age of three when he told his first original story. In 2010, he came up with the concept for The Godling Chronicles. It grew into an exciting collaboration between father and son. Jonathan enjoys sports, chess, music, games, and, of course, telling stories.

Discover more at
4HorsemenPublications.com

10% off using HORSEMEN10